## Praise for Mr. LAVIE TIDHAR

"Lavie Tidhar's *The Bookman* is simply the best book I have read in a long time, and I read a lot of books."

JAMES P BLAYLOCK

"A steampunk gem. Fantastic."  SFFWORLD.COM

"*The Bookman* is a delight, crammed with gorgeous period detail, seat-of-the-pants adventure and fabulous set-pieces."

THE GUARDIAN

"Fast paced adventure with tons of sense of wonder. I loved the author's style and I found the book's narrative energy high with smooth transition from one episode to another. *The Bookman* is highly, highly recommended."

FANTASY BOOK CRITIC

"Kim Newman, Alan Moore, Lavie Tidhar: what do they have in common? The answer is a superb ability to throw the actual history of the Victorian age up in the air alongside the popular fiction of that era and allow the whole lot to fall down together in new and interesting shapes."

CHERYL MORGAN

"A boisterous mix of steampunk, Victoriana, mystery, travel story, thriller, adventure, partly coming of age story. And it pays homage to fictional and real persons who belong to the Victorian era. It brims over with allusions and cameos. This is steampunk in 3D! Highly recommended ⁓ ⁓ bottom of my heart."

EST SCIFI & FANTASY

D1411558

## By the same esteemed author

# LAVIE TIDHAR

### THE BOOKMAN HISTORIES
# The Great Game

ANGRY
ROBOT

**ANGRY ROBOT**
A member of the Osprey Group

Lace Market House,
54-56 High Pavement,
Nottingham,
NG1 1HW, UK

www.angryrobotbooks.com
Another explosive read

An Angry Robot paperback original 2012

Distributed in the United States by Random House, Inc., New York.

ISBN 978-0-85766-199-9
eBook ISBN 978-0-85766-200-2

Printed in the United States of America

9 8 7 6 5 4 3 2 1

To *Elizabeth, in love*

*"When everyone is dead the Great Game is finished. Not before. Listen to me till the end."*

Rudyard Kipling, *Kim*

# PART I
## *Death of a Fat Man*

# ONE

*The boy didn't know he was about to die, which must have been a blessing. He was an ordinary boy whose job it was to take messages, without being privy to the contents of said messages. The boy walked along the canal. The sun was setting and in its dying light the observer could see a solitary, narrow boat, laden with bananas and pineapples and durian, passing on the water on the way home from market.*

*Two monks in saffron robes walked ahead of the boy, conversing in low voices. A sleepy crocodile floated by the bank of the canal, ignored by the few passers-by. It was a quiet part of town, away from the* farang *quarters, and the boy was on his way home, home being a small room on one of the canals, shared with his parents and brothers and sisters, alongside many such rooms all crowded together. The observer could smell the durian from a distance as the boat went past, and he could smell chilli and garlic frying from a stall hidden from view, in one of the adjacent* soìs, *the narrow, twisting alleyways of this grand city. Its residents called it Krung Thep, the City of Angels. The farangs still called it by its old name, which was Bangkok.*

*The observer followed behind the boy. He was unremarkable. He would have been unremarkable in nearly every human*

11

*country, on any continent. He was small of build, with skin just dark enough, just pale enough, to pass for Siamese, or European, or Arab, or, depending on the place and the angle of the sun, an African. His face was hidden behind a wide-brimmed hat but, had he turned and tilted his head, it, too, would have been unremarkable – they had taken great care to ensure that that would be so.*

*The observer followed the boy because the boy was a link in a long and complicated chain that he was following. He didn't feel one way or the other about the boy's imminent death. Death meant little to the observer. The concept was too alien. The boy, not knowing he was being followed, was whistling. He was not Siamese or Chinese, but rather Hmong, of a family that had come to Krung Thep from the highlands of Laos, one of the king's territories to the north-east. The observer didn't care a great deal about that.*

*He caught up with the boy as the boy was turning away from the canal, down a narrow soi. People passed them both but the observer ignored them, his attention trained on the boy. He caught up with him in the shadow of a doorway and put his hand on the boy's shoulder.*

*The boy began to formulate a question, began to turn around, but never got a chance to complete either action. The observer slid what could have been a very narrow, very sharp blade – but wasn't, not quite – into the soft area at the back of the boy's head.*

*The blade went through skin and fat and bone, piercing the brain stem and the hippocampus and reaching deep into the brain. The boy emitted a sigh, a minute exhalation of air, perhaps in surprise, perhaps in pain. His legs buckled underneath him. The observer, now participant, gently caught him so that he didn't fall but, rather, was gently lowered to the ground.*

*The whole thing only took a moment. When it was done the observer withdrew the thing that was not quite a blade, but* functioned as one, which was as much a part of him as his skeleton or the cells that made up his skin. His skeleton was not entirely human and his brain not at all, and he was currently experiencing some new sensations, one of which was bewilderment and another being anger, neither of which had troubled him before.

He stopped before the fallen boy and put his hands together, palms touching, the hands away from the chest and raised high, in a wai. He bowed to the body of the boy. The voices inside him were whispering.

Having paid his respects the observer straightened. He stepped away from the darkened doorway and into the street outside. The sun had set and it was growing darker and torches and small fires were being lit across the city. He could smell fish roasting, wood catching fire, fish sauce, and the coming rain. The boy had been a link in a chain and now it pointed the observer in a new direction. He walked away, not hurrying, an unassuming man whose face was hidden behind a wide-brimmed hat, and as he turned the corner he heard, behind him, the start of screams.

It was cold and his bones ached; the air smelled of rain. Smith straightened, wiped his brow with the back of one hand, leaving a trail of dirt on his skin. He stared down at the ground, the wide, raised row he had so painstakingly worked to make. He had turned the ground and mixed in fertiliser from the Oppenheims' chicken coop, which he had personally shovelled into bags and carried over, and he had formed these things that looked like elongated burial mounds and planted seeds and watered them and watched them. God, he hated gardening.

A chicken darted past, leaving sharp little arrowheads in the moist earth of his garden. He threw a stone at it and it crowed, jumping into the air with wings half-stretched, offended. God, he hated chickens too.

Staring at the garden, he saw his vegetables weren't doing all that well. The tomatoes looked forlorn, hanging from their vines, the plants held up by wooden sticks that seemed to jut out at random angles. The cabbages looked like guillotined heads. The apple tree by the house was surrounded by fallen apples, rotting, and the smell filled the air. Smith glared at the tree then decided to call it a day. Not bothering to change, he left the house, opening and closing the small gate in the fence that enclosed the garden and the house, and followed the dirt path into the village. Other houses in the village had names. Smith's gate merely said, in small, unpolished letters: *No. 6.*

A fine, cold day. A good day for staying indoors, lighting a fire, sorting his library alphabetically, or by condition, or rarity. Since his retirement he had enjoyed collecting books, ordering by mail from specialist dealers in the capital, or even from the continent. It was a small, orderly joy, as different as could be from his former life. His lonely farm house, with its small garden and solitary apple tree, sat on its own. A farmer's life, he thought. What had Hobbes said about human life? That it was solitary, poor, nasty, brutish and short. Hobbes should have been a farmer, Smith thought.

Or retired.

Instead Hobbes had been overly friendly with the French, had written *Leviathan*, in which he argued for the return of human monarchy, had been arrested, and was only spared by his one-time pupil, the old Lizard King Charles II, who had arranged for him to go into exile. Died at ninety-one years of age, if Smith remembered his facts. So life may have been brutish and poor but, for Hobbes, not exactly *that* short.

He came to the village. A small sign announced that this was, indeed, the village of St Mary Mead and, in smaller letters underneath: *Retirement Community*. Smith sighed. Every time he examined that sign he felt the old, familiar anger return. And every time he hoped, against hope, that somehow the sign would be changed, would declare him free.

He walked along the high street. The village, like all villages, had a church, and a post office, and a pub. There was no constabulary. The residents of St Mary Mead could take care of their own. Smith smelled the air. Rain. But something else, too…

A vague sense of unease gripped him. He could smell – not with his *physical* sense but with something deeper, a left-over from his trade days, perhaps – could smell *change* in the air. He stopped beside M.'s, the shop that sold embroidered tea doilies and lace curtains and, on Saturdays and Sundays, cream teas, and watched. Behind him the curtain twitched, and he knew that she, too, was watching. She had been famous as a watcher, in her glory days.

But there was nothing much to see. The village, as always, was quiet. The few shops were open, but their proprietors were used to the absence of customers. Outside Verloc's bookshop the ageing Mr Verloc – *but two years younger than him!* – was putting out the bargain bins, filled as always with penny dreadfuls and gothic romance and the like – poor fare for a man of Smith's more refined tastes.

He shook his head and continued his walk. He paused by the bookshop and nodded hello to Verloc, who nodded back. They had run into each other back in eighty-three, on the Danube, and Verloc still had a small, discreet scar below his left eye to prove it.

"Might rain," Verloc said.

"Would be good for the crops," Smith said and Verloc, who knew the state of Smith's garden, snorted in response. "You'd have more luck planting a book and hoping it would bear fruit," he said. Then, remembering his business, he said gruffly, "You want to buy one?"

Smith shook his head. Verloc snorted again. He touched the small scar under his eye and a look of surprise, momentarily, filled his whole face, as if he had forgotten, or not even known, that it was there. Then it was gone and Verloc nodded stiffly and went back inside the shop and shut the door.

Smith chewed on that as he walked. Did Verloc seem jumpier than usual? Was there something in his manner to indicate that he, too, felt the change in the air? Perhaps he was daydreaming, he thought. His active days were long gone, over and done with. He came to the post office. Colonel Creighton was working the counter. "Good morning, Mr Smith," he said. Smith nodded. "Colonel," he said. "Anything for me today?"

"A package," Colonel Creighton said. "From London. Another book, perhaps?"

"I do hope so," Smith said, politely. He waited as the old colonel rummaged around for his package. "There you are," he said. Then, "Looks like rain, what?"

"Rain," Smith said.

The colonel nodded. "How are the cabbages coming along?" he said.

"Green," Smith said, which seemed to pacify the colonel.

"Dreadful bloody weather," he said, as though offering a grave secret. "Miss the old country, don't you know. Not the same, home. Not the same at all."

Smith nodded again, feeling a great tiredness overcome him. The colonel was an old India hand, recalled at last back to pasture. The empire rolled on, but the colonel was no longer a part of its colonial effort, and the knowledge dulled him, the way an unused blade dulls with age. Smith said, "Might go to the pub," and the colonel nodded in his turn and said, "Capital idea, what?"

It was not yet noon.

As he approached the pub, however, the unopened package held under his arm, his sense of unease at last began to take on a more definite shape. There were tracks on the road of a kind seldom seen in the village. One of the new steam-powered baruch-landaus, their wheels leaving a distinct impression in the ground. Visitors, he thought, and he felt excitement hurry his pace, and his hands itched for a weapon that was no longer there. Opposite the pub he saw the old bee keeper, standing motionless under the village clock. Smith looked at him and the old bee keeper, almost imperceptibly, gave him a nod.

Interesting.

He went into the pub. Quiet. A fire burning in the fireplace. A solitary drinker sitting by the fire, a pint by his side. Smith looked straight ahead. He went to the counter. The Hungarian baroness was there. She welcomed him with a smile. He smiled back. "What can I get you, Mr Smith?" she said.

"A pint of cider, please, Magdolna," he said, preferring as always the use of one of her many middle names.

"Cold outside?" she said, drawing his pint. Smith shrugged. "Same old," he said. "Same old."

The baroness slid the pint across the counter to him. "Shall I put it on the account?" she said.

Smith shook his head. "Somehow," he said, "I think it best if I paid my tab in full, today."

The baroness glanced quickly at the direction of the solitary drinker by the fireplace and just as quickly looked away. She pursed her lips, then said, softly, "Very well."

Smith paid. The transaction seemed to finalise something between them, an understanding that remained unspoken. He had run into the baroness in eighty-nine in Budapest and again a year later in the *Quartier Latin*, in Paris. She was half his age, but had been retired early and, unseen behind the bar, she walked with a limp.

Their business done, Smith took hold of the pint and, slowly, turned to face the common room. It seemed to him that it took forever for his feet to obey him. He took a step forwards, at last, and the second one came more easily, and then the next, until at last he found himself standing before the solitary drinker, who had not yet looked up.

"Sit down," the man said.

Smith sat.

The man was half-turned in his chair, and was warming long, pale hands on the fire. He was tall and pallid, with black thinning hair and a long straight nose that had been broken at least once. He resembled a spidery sort of thing. He wore a dark suit, not too cheap, not too expensive, an off-the-rack affair several years old. His shoes were black and polished. He said, "Looks like it might rain."

Smith said, "Bugger the rain."

The man smiled a thin smile and finally turned to face him. His eyes were a startling blue, the colour of a pond deeper than one expected. He said, in a voice that had no warmth or affection in it, "Smith."

Smith said, "Fogg."

# TWO

"I told you I would kill you the next time we met," Smith said.

It was hot in the room. The baroness had retreated to her quarters, but not before she turned the sign on the door. It now said *Closed*.

The two men were alone.

"I had hoped you'd delay the pleasure," the man he had called Fogg said.

Smith sighed, exhaling air, and felt a long-held tension ease throughout his body. He took a sip from his cider. "Where is Mycroft?" he said.

Fogg said, "Mycroft's dead."

Smith went very still. Outside a wet sort of thunder erupted, and with it came the patter of falling rain. His reflection stared at him from the glass. He examined it as though fascinated. "When?" he said at last.

"Two days ago."

"Where?"

"Outside his house. He had just returned from the club."

Smith said, "Who?" and the man before him smiled that thin, humourless smile and said, "If I knew that, I wouldn't be here now."

At the words an odd excitement took over Smith, overwhelming any sadness he may have felt. He said, "Where is your driver?"

Fogg said, "The baroness is looking after him."

Smith nodded, absent-mindedly. After a moment Fogg raised his glass. Smith followed suit, and they touched glasses with a thin clinking sound. "To Mycroft," Fogg said.

Smith said, "Who–?" even though he knew. Fogg said, "I'm acting head."

"So you finally got what you wanted," Smith said. Fogg said, "I didn't want it to happen like that."

Smith said, "That was the only way it was ever going to fall. Heads don't retire–"

"–they roll," Fogg said, completing the sentence. He shrugged, looking suddenly uncomfortable. "Still. One never imagined–"

"Not the fat man," Smith agreed.

"Sure," Fogg said. He sounded sad. "Not the fat man."

They drank in silence.

Then: "Why are you here?"

Fogg: "You know why I'm here."

Smith, staring at him. Trying to read what was hidden in those deceptively innocent eyes. Saying, "I don't."

Fogg snorted. "We need you," he said, simply.

Smith said, "I find that hard to believe."

"Do you think I *want* your help?" Fogg said. "You are a loner, a killer, you have problems taking orders and you just don't *fit* into an organisational structure!" The last one seemed to be the worst, for him. "And you're *old*."

"So why are you here?"

He watched Fogg, closely. Saw him squirm.

"Mycroft left instructions," Fogg finally said.

"That makes a little more sense," Smith said.

"Unfortunately, the decision is out of my hands," Fogg said. "The fat man wanted you on the case."

"Did he know he was going to die?"

A strange, evasive look on Fogg's face; Smith filed it away for future reference. "I can't fill you in on the details," Fogg said. "You're not classified."

That one made Smith smile. He downed the rest of his drink and stood up. Fogg, in some alarm, watched him get up. "Where the hell do you think you're going?"

"I'm going to spare you the trouble," Smith said. "Sorry you had a wasted trip."

"You *what*?" Fogg said.

Smith said, "I'm retired."

He turned to go. Fogg, behind him, gave a gurgled cry. "You can't just walk away!" he said.

"Watch me," Smith said.

He was almost at the door when Fogg said, "Alice."

Smith stopped, his hand on the door, ready to push it open. He didn't.

He turned slowly and stood there, breathing deeply. Old memories, like old newspaper print, almost washed away in the rain.

Almost.

He said, "What about her?"

Fogg said, "She's dead too."

Smith stood there, not knowing what to say. The fat man he could understand, could have lived with. But not her. He began to say, "Where?" but Fogg had anticipated him. "Bangkok," he said. "Two weeks ago."

Two weeks. She had been dead and all that time he'd been tending the cabbage patch.

21

He felt sick with his own uselessness. He opened and closed his hands, mechanically. It was still raining outside, the rain intensifying. He turned and pushed the door open, and a gust of cold wind entered and brought with it the smell of the rain. He blinked, his face wet. Across the road the old bee keeper was still standing, like a silent guardian, watching. Very little escaped him, still.

Smith took a deep breath. The cold air helped. After a moment he closed the door and went behind the bar and drew himself another pint. Then he drew one for the thin man he had once sworn to kill.

He left money on the counter, for the baroness, and carried both drinks with him into the common room and sat back down. He stared at Fogg, who had the decency to look embarrassed.

"Same *modus operandi*?"

"So it would appear."

"Fogg, what in God's name is going on?"

Fogg squinted, as if in pain. Perhaps the mention of God had hurt him. "I don't know," he said, at last. Resentful for having to make the admission.

"Have there been others?"

Fogg didn't answer. The rain fell outside. In the fireplace, a log split apart, throwing off sparks. Smith said, "How *many* others?"

"You will be briefed," Fogg said. "In London. If you choose to come back with me."

Smith considered. Bangkok. London. Two links on a chain he couldn't, for now, follow. And each one, rather than a name, or a climate – each one represented the end of one thread in his own life, a sudden severing that had left him reeling inside. Alice and the fat man. He had not seen, nor spoken, to either one of them for a long time, yet they were always there, the very knowledge of their existence offering a sort of comfort, a fragile peace. A peace he could no longer pretend to have.

Yet he suddenly dreaded the return to the city. A part of him had been restless, longing to go back, and yet now that it was offered it came at a price that gave him no joy. The fat man, Alice, and a bloodied trail he feared to follow. There was a reason he had been retired, a reason all of them were there, in that village that could not be found on any map, running their little shops and tending their little gardens, pretending, even the bee keeper, that they were regular people at last, living ordinary lives.

None of us are very good at it, he realised. And yet there *had* been comfort in the pretence, that forced withdrawal from the former, shadowy world they had inhabited. He needed to think. He needed the refuge of his library, even if for one last time.

"I need a day," he said, at last. Fogg didn't argue. Not a death, Smith thought. Deaths. One two weeks before, the trail already growing cold, one here, and recent, but still, his would be a cold trail to follow, and a day would make little difference.

Fogg stood up, draining the last of his pint. "I shall expect you at the club, first thing tomorrow," he said. And with that he was gone.

# THREE

He had almost forgotten the book. The package from London. He had been expecting a slim volume of poetry, ordered from Payne's, the newly rebuilt shop on Cecil Court. It had been destroyed some years previous in an explosion. He had not been a part of that particular case, which had been attributed to the shadowy Bookman. He took the package, unopened, with him as he walked back to his place. Behind him he could hear Fogg's baruch-landau starting with an ungodly noise, smoke belching high into the air as it wheeled away, back towards the city.

On a sudden, overwhelming need he turned back. He went down the high street and they were all watching him, the retired and the obsolete, former friends, former foes, united together only in this, this dreaded, dreary world called retirement. He ignored them, even the old bee keeper, as he came to the church, the book still held under his arm.

Fogg had looked offended at Smith's evocation of God. Faith was no longer all that popular, a long way since the day of the Lizard King James I, when his authorised

– if somewhat modified – version of the Bible was available in every home. That man Darwin was popular now, with his theory of evolution – he had even claimed, so Smith had heard, that it was proof the royal family and their get, Les Lézards themselves, were of an extraterrestrial origin, and couldn't have co-evolved on the Earth. It was not impossible… Rumours had always circulated, but that, just like the Bookman investigation, had been Mycroft's domain, mostly: he, Smith, was in charge of field work, dirty work, while the fat man sat in his club and ran the empire over lunches and cigars.

Too many unanswered questions… His life had been like that, though. He seldom got the answers. His, simply, was to be given a task, and perform it. How it fit into a larger picture, just which piece of the puzzle it turned out to be, was not his concern. Above him was the fat man and above the fat man was the Queen, and above the Queen, he long ago, and privately, had decided, there must be one more.

God.

Unfashionable, yes. Not a god of churches, not a god of burning bushes like in the old stories, or a science god like in the new books Verne and Wells and their ilk had been writing. A god he couldn't articulate, that demanded little, that offered only forgiveness. Something above. Perhaps it was less god than a reason for being. For Smith believed, despite all the evidence, that there had to be a reason.

He went into the church. It had stopped raining when he left the pub, and the sun, catching him unawares, had come out. A momentary brightness filled the church garden, and a bird called out from the branches of a tree. The grass was wet with rain, and it was quiet. He stepped into the church and stood there, inhaling its dry air of ageing books and candles. Thinking of the fat man. Thinking of Alice.

He was chilled when he got home. His boots were covered in mud and his face was wet. He went inside and shut the door. The house was small but he had large windows in the continental style and so he didn't bother with the gaslight. You didn't get much sunlight in England but at least he caught the most of it. The last of last night's coal was glowing dimly in the fireplace, and he prodded it with the poker, half-heartedly, and left it to die.

He sat in the armchair by the window. The room was full of books. What was it the fat man had liked to say? "Guns and swords will kill you, but nothing is more dangerous than a book."

The fat man had been obsessed with the Bookman, that shadowy assassin who had plagued the empire for so long. But he was no longer around, had become inactive, possibly killed.

*Possibly retired*, Smith thought. Those had been glorious days, in the service of the empire, going across the world, across continents and countries – *on Her Majesty's secret service*, they used to call it: deniable, disposable, and often dead.

Shadow men and shadow women doing shadow work. But the Bookman had always stood out amongst them, the consummate professional, the shadow of shadows. Mycroft had told him, once, that he suspected the Bookman to be of the same mysterious origins as Les Lézards. Smith didn't care. To him it was the work that mattered, and he prided himself on doing his job well.

Rows of books lined the room. They made it seem less austere, a warmer place. There were bookcases, a rug the colour of dried blood on the floor, an armchair with more holes in it than a compromised agent, a low table where he put his tea and his books to read and where the package from London now sat, waiting to be opened.

He reached for it.

It came in the same plain brown wrapping paper all the books arrived in and he tore it carefully, expecting to find Orphan's *Poems*, that slim, contraband collection of poetry, by an almost-unknown poet, that Smith had been trying to locate for some time. Instead, he discovered he was holding a worn copy of the Manual.

For a moment he just stared at it. It was exactly as he remembered it: the plain blue covers, the stamp on the front that said, simply, *Top Secret – Destroy if Found*. The same smell, that was the very smell of the place, the very essence of the trade, for Smith: of boiled cabbage and industrial soap, the smell of long echoey corridors with no windows, of hushed voices and the hum of unseen machinery; the secret heart of an empire, that had been the fat man's domain.

He opened it at random.

*A gentleman never kills by stealth or surreptitiously.*

The words spoken, so long ago, at that training centre in Ham Common. The instructor turning to them, smiling. He was missing two fingers on his left hand, Smith remembered. Looking at them, evaluating their response.

Saying, at last, "But we are not gentlemen."

It was still there, in the book. The manual of their trade, written as a joke or as a warning, he never knew which, but always circulating, from hand to hand, passed along from operative to operative, never openly discussed.

*This is what we do. This is what we are.*

And added, by hand, as an addendum: *To do our job, even we have to forget that we exist.*

He knew that handwriting. He turned the book over in his hands. Opened it again, on the title page, which said only, and that in small, black letters, *Manual*.

The rest of the page, rather than being blank as he remembered, was inscribed by hand. It didn't take long to read it.

> Smith–
>    *If you receive this then I am dead, and our worst fears have been confirmed. You may remember my concerns over the Oxford Affair in eighty-eight. I believe our venture into space has played into the hands of unseen forces and now the thing I feared the most has come to be.*
>    *If that is so – if I am dead, and you receive this in the post – then we are not alone.*
>    *Trust no one.*
>    *Beware the B-men.*
>    *Trace back the links, follow the chain. Begin with Alice.*
>    *Be careful. They will be coming for you.*
>
> M.

Smith stared at the note. He closed the Manual softly, put it on the table beside him. Stared out at the wan sunlight. It came as no surprise to know the fat man had not trusted Fogg. Smith had warned, repeatedly, of his suspicion of the man; it had seemed beyond doubt to him that the man was a mole, an agent of the Bookman. But the fat man never did anything, preferring, perhaps, to keep Fogg close by, to watch him.

*And now Fogg was acting head.*

Well, what was it to Smith? He was retired. The actions of the Bureau were no longer his concern. He was too old, too jaded to think the shadow world they all inhabited was the be-all and end-all of politics. They were engaged in a game – often deadly, often dreary, but a game – while the real decisions were made above their heads, by the people they spied on. There had been moles in the organisation before, just as the Bureau, in its turn, had agents working inside the agencies of both opponents and friendlies. He himself had turned several agents, in his day…

It was a game, only now Alice and the fat man were both dead.

# FOUR

It was a soft sound, like leaves falling on the roof, only they weren't leaves at all. Smith opened his eyes and stared at the darkness. The sound came again, furtive, soft: the sound of rats sneaking, a vaguely disturbing sound that gnawed at the edges of consciousness.

In the darkness of the room, he smiled.

He'd sat up in his armchair through the afternoon, thinking. He'd first met Alice in Venice, in sixty-five it must have been. The year of the Zanzibar Incident, though he had not been involved in that particular affair.

The Bureau had sent him to the Venetian Republic, the lizards negotiating a secret treaty with Daniele Fonseca, the republican leader, against the Hapsburgs. It was baby-sitting duty for Smith, watching the British envoy from the shadows as the treaty was negotiated. And it *was* Venice, in the spring, and he met her one night when Hapsburgian agents attacked his envoy and Smith, outnumbered, had scrambled to save the man.

She had stepped out of the shadow, a young girl, glowing – so it seemed to him, then, romantic fool that he was – in the light of the moon. Her long white legs were bare and she wore a blue dress and a blue flower behind one ear. She smiled at him, flashing perfect white teeth, and killed the first of the would-be assassins with a knife throw that went deep into the man's chest, a flower of blood blooming on his shirt as he fell.

Together, they eliminated the others, the envoy oblivious the whole while to the covert assassination attempt, then disposed of the bodies together, dragging them into one of the canals and setting them adrift, Alice's blue flower pinned to the leader's chest. It had been the most romantic night of Smith's life.

Later, when the envoy was safely asleep in his bed, Smith and Alice shared a drink on the balcony of the small, dank hotel, and watched the moonlight play on the water of the canal...

Now he listened for the smallest sounds, that soft patter on the roof, the drop of a body, then another. The fat man had warned him but somehow, Smith always knew the day would come, was always waiting for it, and now he was ready.

He slid a knife from its scabbard, tied around his ankle. He had spent some of the afternoon, and a part of the evening, sharpening this knife, his favourite, and cleaning and oiling various other devices. Cleaning one's weapons was a comforting act, an ingrained habit that felt almost domestic. It made him think of Alice, who preferred guns to knives, and disliked poisons.

The things the mind conjures... He'd often argued with her about it, to no avail.

Smith disliked guns. They were loud, and showy, the weapon of bullies and show-offs. A gun had swagger behind it, but little thought. Smith preferred the intimacy of killing, the touch of flesh on flesh, the hissed intake of breath that was a mark's last. He liked neatness, in all things.

Then everything happened very quickly and almost at once.

The windows broke inwards – a loud explosive sound – shards of glass flying through the air, showering the floor and furniture.

Something heavy slammed into the front door, and the back one, sending both crashing to the ground, as dark figures came streaming through, and Smith found himself grinning. A single candle had been left burning on the bedside table and now it died with a gust of cold wind, and the house was dark.

Five pouring in from the front. Five more from the back. And there'd be others outside by now, forming a ring around the house. They wanted him badly. He was almost flattered. And they wanted him alive – which was an advantage.

He killed the first one with a knife thrust, holding the body gently as it dropped down to the floor. Black-clad, armed – he took the man's gun out of its holster, admiring its lightness, and fired once, twice, three times and watched two of them fall, one rolling away. When they fired back, destroying the bedroom, he was no longer there.

He worried about his library but there was nothing he could do. He came on two more of them there and killed the first one by breaking his neck, twisting it with a gentle nostalgia, then dropped the corpse to the floor, and the second one turned, and with the same motion Smith flipped the knife and sent it flying.

He went to retrieve it, pulling it out of the man's chest. The man wasn't quite dead yet. His lips were moving. "*Zu sein*," the man said, the softest breath of air. *To be*.

Smith strained to hear more but there was nothing left in the man, no words or air.

Smith straightened. He couldn't take them all. He was against the wall when he heard a barked question – *"In der Bibliothek?"*

Two more bullets, a man dropped at the open door. Shouts behind now, no more pretence at secrecy or stealth. Smith said, *"Warten sie!"*

*Wait.*

"Mr Smith."

The voice came from beyond the door, a voice in shadows.

*"Ja."*

"You come with us, now, Mr Smith. No more play."

The voice spoke good English, but accented. It was young, like the others. A fully trained extraction team, but too young, and they did things differently these days.

"Don't shoot," Smith said.

The voice chuckled. "You are late for an appointment," it said, "arranged a long time ago."

Smith smiled. "Take them," he said, loudly.

There was the sudden sound of gunfire outside. *Heavy* gunfire. Smith ran, jumped – dived out of the broken window. The whistle of something flying through the air, entering the room he had just vacated. He rolled and covered his head and there was a booming thunder and he felt fragments of wood and stone hit his back and his legs and the night became bright, momentarily.

When it was over he raised his head, looked–

The old lady from M.'s, the lace and china shop, was standing with her hair on edge, a manic grin spread across her face. She was holding the controls of a giant, mounted Gatling gun, a small steam engine belching beside it. "Take one for the Kaiser!" she screamed, and a torrent of bullets exploded out of the machine like angry bees, tracer bullets lighting up the night sky, as M. screamed soundlessly and fired, mowing the black-clothed attackers as though they were unruly grass.

Spies, Smith thought, trying to make himself as small as possible. They'll take any excuse to let their hair down.

The firing stopped and then someone was beside him, grabbing him. He turned and saw Verloc from the book-shop, grinning at him – the first time, perhaps, he had ever seen him look happy.

"Come on!" Verloc said. He pulled Smith, who stood up and followed him. The two men ran across the cab-bage patch, over what was left of the fence (which wasn't much) and into the field beyond.

Smith could hear M. screaming again, then a second round of shooting. His poor house. No. 6 would never be the same again, after this. He should have taken care of this business on his own.

Well, too late now.

Turning, he saw Colonel Creighton, the baroness by his side, going through the garden and into the house, the colonel armed with a curved khukuri knife, the baroness, less ostentatiously, with a couple of small-cal-ibre, elegant hand guns, one in each hand. He raised his head and saw, floating above the house, a long, graceful black shape: an airship.

"Don't let it get away," Smith said. Beside him, Verloc grinned. "Shall we?" he said.

"Let's," Smith said.

Verloc went first, and Smith followed. Back towards the house. M. covered them, but there weren't many of the attackers moving around, any more. "I need at least one of them alive," Smith said.

"Let's see what we can find," Verloc called, over his shoulder. They reached the wall of the house and Verloc, with a litheness that belied his age, took hold of the drain pipe and began to climb. Smith, less enthusiastically, followed.

It was not a tall house and they reached the roof easily enough. The airship had been moored to it but the remaining figures on the roof were busy climbing up it and clearly they had changed their minds about their chances and were keen on getting away. Smith knew M. would shoot the balloon but he feared they had used hydrogen, and he didn't want yet *another* explosion.

"*Halt*!" he said. Verloc had twin guns pointed at the escaping men – some sort of light-alloy devices he didn't have a moment before – he must have picked them up off the fallen soldiers. Smith himself had one of the guns.

"*Schnell! Schnell*!" Verloc fired. He couldn't help himself, Smith thought. It couldn't have been easy, all those years, without even a burglar to attempt Verloc's bookshop.

One, two, three men fell, screaming, clutching wounded legs. Verloc liked going for the knees. These soldiers, at least, were unlikely to walk again.

Then he saw him.

The man was young and moved with a grace that Smith found himself, suddenly and unexpectedly, incredibly jealous of. He had come from the other side of the wall, out of shadow. Smith had almost missed him. Then the man lifted his hand and something silver flashed, for just a moment, and, beside Smith, Verloc grunted in pain and dropped, quietly, to the floor.

"Verloc!"

"Don't worry… about me," Verloc said. His hand was on his belly, a blade protruding from between his fingers. Blood was seeping through, falling onto the wall.

Smith was already moving, towards the young man, his vision clear, his mind as cool as water. He saw the flash of a new blade and side-stepped it and unhurriedly entered into the young man's range and head-butted him, hearing the bones of the nose breaking. His fingers found the young man's neck and pressed, the thumbs digging. He applied pressure – just enough. They were attempting to fire at him from above, the airship cut loose and rising higher, but M. had him covered, firing low, and Smith grabbed the unconscious man and dragged him to where Verloc lay still. He knelt to check him but Verloc was no longer breathing, and so Smith dragged the young man by the arm to the edge of the roof and fell over it, dragging the younger man down with him.

He hit the ground, rolled, and the younger man followed. Smith dragged him away when there was a long, high whistling tone and he saw, turning on his back, a silver metal object flying in a high arc, as though in slow motion, from M.'s position towards the rising airship–

With the colonel and the baroness running out of the house, as fast as they could–

He heard M. shout, gleefully, wheezing with the effort, "Take one for the–"

The object hit the dark moving spot that was the airship–

Smith closed his eyes shut, tight. But even then he could see the airship, as bright as day, its image burning on his retinas as a bright ball of flame erupted in the sky above, turning the night to day and the airship into a heap of disintegrating wood and cloth and burning parts and people.

# FIVE

"A nice cup of tea?"

They had taken over Verloc's bookshop. Verloc himself was laid out in the main room, amidst the books. Smith had never figured out if Verloc had actually *liked* books. He had once been married, had a family, though Smith didn't know what had happened to them. Verloc was a bomb-maker by trade. Now he lay amidst the dusty penny dreadfuls and the three-volume novels and the serials from London, and the books from the continent, and it was quiet in the shop.

They had carried the unconscious captive from the airship to Verloc's back room and propped him in a chair. Verloc had a samovar in the shop and M. had taken to lighting the coals and heating up the water and sniffed disapproval at the state of the milk, but pronounced it at last drinkable.

Smith had known M. for many years but she had never changed. She had the appearance of a harmless old lady, and as she grew older she simply became more herself. She had had a name but no one could remember what it was. Her work had been legendary. There were few places a little old lady couldn't penetrate.

Now she bustled to and fro, making the tea, using the chipped old white china mugs Verloc had kept in the shop. She gave them a good rinse first. The prisoner meanwhile was coming to in the chair. He did not look happy.

"*Was ist Ihre Mission*?" Smith said. The prisoner looked at him without expression and then said, with a note of disgust, "I speak English."

"As you should," Colonel Creighton said, stiffly. "Now, what were you after, *boy*?"

The prisoner merely nodded in Smith's direction. "Him," he said.

Smith said, "Why?"

The prisoner said, "You know perfectly well why, *Herr* Smith."

Colonel Creighton looked sideways at Smith. "Do you?" he said.

"No."

"Then you shall have to remain unsatisfied," the prisoner said. The colonel raised his hand to hit him, but Smith stopped him with a gesture. "Was it to do with Bangkok?" he said, softly.

At that the prisoner's face twisted. "*Der Erntemaschine!*" he said. Then he shook his head and a grimace of pain crossed his face. "*Nein*," he said. "*Nein*."

"Smith? What is he doing?"

The prisoner was convulsing in the chair. Smith hurried to his side, tilted his head back. Foam was coming out of the man's mouth. Smith touched two fingers to the man's neck, felt for a pulse. "He's dead," he said, after a moment.

The colonel swore. Smith stared at the corpse. A false tooth, carrying poison, he thought. Standard issue – he should have remembered.

Old. Getting old, and sloppy, and forgetting things.

Forgetting things could get you killed.

"What," M. said, materialising with two mugs, handing one to each blithely, "is a damned *Erntemaschine*?"

"Ernte," Smith said, "means harvest."

"So *Erntemaschine*–"

"A machine for harvesting. A…" He hesitated. "A *harvester*," he said, at last.

He knew that, behind him, M. and the colonel were exchanging worried glances.

"That's what they used to call *you*," the colonel said at last, softly. The words seemed to freeze and hang in the air.

But Smith shook his head. "The word for a manual harvester is different, in German," he said. "What did he mean, a machine?"

M. said, gently, "Drink your tea, dear."

Smith sipped at it. "It's good," he said, by way of thanks. Truth was, he could barely taste it. He felt raw, hurt. The room swam. The colonel caught hold of him. "Easy, there, old boy," he murmured.

They used to call him the Harvester.

So now someone else was laying claim to the title. Someone else was harvesting people, the way a farmer harvested corn, or wheat.

"I'm going to London," he said, at last. "Help me dispose of the bodies?"

It was hard, backbreaking work. The village rallied round, even those who hadn't been to the fight. By dawn there had been nothing left of the airship or its crew, but a new mound of earth, like an ancient tor, stood by the ruined house.

"Too bad about your cabbages," the baroness said. She had been wounded in hand-to-hand combat inside the

39

house, and now wore her arm in a sling. Her eyes shone. "I miss the old days, sometimes," she said. "Then something like this happens and I think maybe retirement's not so bad."

Smith nodded. He had tried to rescue some of the books, but most were beyond help. Torn, burned pages floated like dark butterflies in the air. "We never truly retire, though," he said. "Do we?"

"No," she said. "I guess we don't." Then, coming closer, putting her hand on his shoulder, gently: "I'm sorry about Alice."

He shrugged. "It's the life," he said, "each of us chose."

"Not all of us had the choice," the baroness said.

The worst part had been seeing the bee keeper again. He showed up just as Smith was preparing to leave. Day had come and the sky was clear and bright. Smith wore a suit that had seen better days. He needed to go into the town, to catch the train.

"I am so sorry," Smith said. The old man gazed at him. Once he had been the greatest of them all. Even now he was formidable. He was not that old, but he had suffered much, and had retired shortly after the Bookman affair. Rumours spoke of a lost love, a brotherly conflict, of captivity and strange experiments that had made his mind different, alien to the everyday. They were just that, rumours. No one but the bee keeper knew what the truth was, or what kept him in the village.

The bee keeper merely nodded. "It is the life we choose," he said. "Mycroft always knew what he was doing."

"Will you… pursue an investigation?" Smith asked. The bee keeper shook his head. "There is no art to it," he said, with a slight smile. "I already know."

40

"Then tell me."

The bee keeper shook his head again. "It will not help," he said. "Yet you are suited to this task, in a way I am not. It requires not a singularly great deductive mind, such as mine, but a tenacious sort of controlled violence. What you are after is not a mystery, but the conclusion of one. A great game we had all been playing, and which is now coming to an end... or to a new beginning."

"I don't understand."

"Look at the stars," the bee keeper said, "for answers." And with that last cryptic, unhelpful comment, he was gone.

Smith shook his head. This was Mycroft all over again. Then he decided to leave it, and climbed into the hansom cab.

"Market Blandings, please, Hume," he told the driver, who nodded without speaking and hurried the horses into action.

Smith settled back inside the cab. He closed his eyes. The horses moved sedately, the motion soothing. In moments he was asleep.

# SIX

Hume dropped him off outside the Blue Lizard on Market Blandings' sleepy high street. The hansom cab rode off and Smith, still tired and aching, decided to go into the pub to refresh himself before catching the train.

Whereas the Emsworth Arms, down the road, was a spacious, quiet place, the Blue Lizard, even this early, was noisy, and it smelled. It was a small, dank place set away from the river, and Smith had difficulty getting to the bar to order an ale and breakfast.

It felt strange to be out of the village. He knew the Bureau kept rural agents around the village – making sure the inmates remained where they should. Confirmation of that came quickly. As he was tucking into his fried eggs a small, slim figure slid into the seat across from him. Smith looked up, and his face twisted into an expression of dislike that made the other man grin.

"Charles," Smith said.

"Peace," the other said, and laughed.

"I thought they hanged you," Smith said.

Charles Peace shrugged. "I'm a useful feller, ain't I," he said, modestly.

"Useful how?" Smith said.

"Keeping my eyes open, don't I," Peace said. "Sniffing about, by your leave, Smith. Ferreting things."

He looked like a ferret, Smith thought. But he was nothing but a rat.

"What do you want?" he said.

Peace tsked. "No way to talk to an old friend," he said mournfully. "You know you shouldn't be out of the village, Smith."

"I'm back on active."

"Really." Peace snorted. He was a violinist, a burglar, and a murderer. Which is a different thing entirely, Smith preferred to think, to a killer.

Murderers didn't have standards, for one.

"Really," Smith said.

"I did not get the memo."

"I don't doubt that."

Charles Peace looked sharply up. "What does that mean, me old mucker?" he said, almost spitting out the words.

Smith ignored him. The Blue Lizard was busy with rail workers, farmers in for the market, and such visitors to the castle low enough on the social pecking order not to have been extended an invitation to stay at the castle grounds. It was dark inside and the air turned blue with cigar and pipe smoke. Across from him, Peace made himself relax. He rolled a cigarette, yellow fingers shaking slightly as they heaped tobacco into paper. "Having a laugh," Peace said, smiling again. His teeth were revolting. Smith pushed away his breakfast, took a sip of ale. "You have something for me?" he said at last.

But now Peace was disgruntled. "Should report you, I should," he said. "Out and about, when you should be retired an' all."

Smith looked at him closely. Had Fogg not rescinded the watch order on him? He had assumed Peace had a message for him from the Bureau. But if he hadn't, what did he want? Smith knew the instructions that affected him, and the rest of the village. Watchers were told that under no circumstances were they to engage with retired agents. *Report and wait*, was the standing procedure.

So what was Peace playing at?

He waited the man out. Peace finishing rolling, lit up the cigarette. Loose tobacco fell on the table. The man's hands were shaking. Disgraceful. "You do something you shouldn't have?" Peace said at last.

Smith didn't answer. Watched him. Watched the room.

He'd had trouble finding a table. He sat in the corner, his back to the wall, his eyes on the door. It was the way he always sat. Busy place. Was anyone watching *him*, in their turn? Was anything out of place?

"Been a naughty boy," Peace said. He spat out tobacco shreds. Made to get up–

Smith kicked the table from underneath, lifting it over – it hit Peace full in the face, sent him reeling back. Smith dropped behind the table as three shots rang out. Screams in the pub – he caught movement coming *forward* as everyone else moved back, towards the door or, if they were smart, stayed down. Two figures, guns drawn. He was getting sick of guns.

"We just want to talk, Mr. Smith."

The voice was cultured, sort of, a London accent, with only a hint of the continental about it. More agents of the Kaiser? Someone else?

Smith said, "About what?"

"About this year's harvest, Mr. Smith," the voice said. Smith drew his knife, softly. But he was cornered.

"Who do you work for?"

The voice laughed. "Whoever pays," it said.

Smith shifted the table, keeping it between himself and the attackers, until he hit Peace's leg. Peace himself wasn't moving. He pulled on the leg, bringing the man's mass towards him. He could hear the two men coming forward. Tensed. "Really, Mr Smith. Do not make it more difficult than it needs to–"

He grabbed Peace under the arms, pushed the table again so it fell down with a crash, and rose. Two guns fired. He felt the impact of the shots, Peace's body slamming him back as it was hit. He let it carry him, moved with the impact, discarded the body and came over the fallen table, blade at the ready.

The first man had his gun arm extended, about to fire again. Smith's blade severed the arteries in the man's wrist and then with a half-turn, dancer's movement Smith's blade flashed again, moving across the man's neck. The man tried to gurgle, couldn't, and fell to his knees, blood pouring out of the wound.

Another shot, but Smith wasn't where he'd been and the other man, searching for a target, clumsy with the gun, didn't respond fast enough and Smith was behind him, the blade against the man's neck, and Smith said, "Drop it."

The man dropped the gun. Beside them, his partner expired noisily.

"Be still."

The man was very still.

It was quiet in the abandoned pub. Landlord and patrons had made for the door and were all gone, abandoning drinks and cigars and conversation. Smith preferred it that way.

He said, "Who sent you?"

The man began to talk fast. His Adam's apple bobbed up and down and the man twitched every time it scraped against the knife. "We was paid to watch for you, is all," he said. "I don't know who wants you, mister. A man came. He was dressed well, he had money. He said, just bring him to me."

"Alive?"

"He wasn't strict on that score," the man said, and swallowed.

"What did he look like?"

The man shrugged, then regretted it. "He didn't give no name."

Smith increased the pressure of the knife. "Not what I asked," he said.

"Tall, black hair, foreign accent. He had a scar across his cheek."

Smith went still at that. "What sort of accent?" he said at last.

"Dunno, mister. Some European muck, like my partner's is – was." He swallowed again.

"And Peace?"

"Old Peace here was to tag you, is all. We figured we'd kill him when we was done so as to save the pay."

"Sensible," Smith muttered. There was noise outside now, and the whistle of constables, and he decided it was time to go.

"Do you want to live?" he said.

The man swallowed a third time. "Very much, mister," he said.

"Too bad," Smith said. He raised his hand and slammed it against the man's neck. The man fell. Smith arranged him comfortably with his back to the bar. He picked up the man's gun and put it in his hand. Then he went over to the man's fallen companion, picked up the man's hand, which was still holding a gun, and fired twice at the unconscious man. Blood bloomed over the man's chest and Smith nodded, satisfied. Outside the noise intensified and a voice, magnified by a bullhorn, called, "Step outside with your hands raised!"

Smith surveyed the scene. With luck no one would remember the quiet gentleman who had sat in the corner. Then he slipped out through the back door, over the fence of the sad little garden, and was soon at the train station, just in time for the London one to pull in.

# SEVEN

The train departed on time. He'd paid for a first-class seat and now sat alone in the small car, a cup of tea by his side.

Smith liked trains. There was something soothing about their rhythmic movement, something vastly luxurious about the space one had, the ability to simply get up and walk and stretch – and that without mentioning the joys of dining cars, and sleeping compartments. He always slept well on trains.

You could always get a cup of tea.

And, of course, trains were wonderful for covert assassination.

The second time he met Alice had been on a train. He had got on at Sofia and the train, on a leisurely night journey, was travelling to the port town of Varna, on the shores of the Black Sea.

Smith had been on board to dispose of a Bulgarian diplomat by the name of Markov. He had taken his time. A train offered a perfect shelter for a quiet murder. It stopped often, each station offering a quiet getaway. The Bureau had agents waiting at stops along the route. They would provide him with the means to disappear, if he chose to use them.

But Smith preferred to work alone.

The diplomat had been of the anti-Caliban faction, and as such a threat to Her Majesty's government. Bulgaria was an important asset for the lizardine court, its Black Sea ports offering strategic opportunities against the Russians on the one hand, the Ottomans on the other. Varna itself, their destination, was a bustling port town crawling with British Navy and Aerofleet personnel. Markov had links to anti-Calibanic groups, some of which used violent means. Verloc, in his day, had been a prominent member of several such groups – though he, of course, worked undercover for the Bureau.

Some of the time, at least.

Markov took ill shortly after dinner. Smith had sat two tables down from him, eating a simple meal of smoked salami, bread and the red wine this country was famed for. He had not expected Markov to take ill, and was concerned. As Markov, about to retch, departed from the car, a new figure appeared in the doorway and Smith's breath caught in his chest.

She wore a blue dress, just as she had in Venice. A white flower behind her ear this time. She was smiling and her smile widened when she saw him. She came and sat opposite him and signalled to the waiter to bring another wine glass and then said, "Why, Mr Smith, fancy meeting you here."

"Alice," he said, softly, the food forgotten. Her glass arrived and the waiter filled it and she raised it up. "Cheers," she said.

Markov had expired later that night, of apparent food poisoning.

• • • •

He drank his tea. He couldn't really believe she was dead. They had spent that night together and got off at Varna and then hadn't seen each other for six months. The fat man had warned him about her, Alice of the blades and of the poison, who yet liked neither, who often said a "Honesty is a gun"... Alice of the grin that said she knew what she was doing was wrong, but that she liked doing it, nevertheless... He wasn't even sure who she really worked for. You couldn't tell, with any of them. They were shadow pawns in a shadow world, switching sides, owing allegiance to no one. Mycroft knew that, was philosophical about it. "If you were honest people," he once told Smith, "you would be of no use to me."

Now Smith sat and worried about the latest develop-ment, as the train chugged along, heading for the capital. He longed to see London again, walk its streets, hear the calling of the whales in the Thames... He began to toss a coin absent-mindedly, heads, tails, heads, tails. The coin bore the profile of Queen Victoria, the lizard queen. Heads, tails...

It had been a message, he decided. He knew the man with the scar on his cheek. He never did things by half. Sending amateurs after him had been a message... a warning?

*So the French, too, were interested.*

But why him, Smith? Did they suspect him of being behind the killings?

Or did they believe him capable of following the chain?

*If so, they will be following him. Watching.*

Well, let them.

The world was large and fractured and there were too many factions at play, and always had been. Nothing had changed. The game remained and he, Smith, was back in it, playing.

With a small smile he sat back, his head against the comfortable stuffing of the seat, and closed his eyes. He wasn't as young as he used to be, and it had been a long night. He fell asleep, still smiling wistfully.

He'd first met the man from Meung in Paris, in the seventies. Tension ran high at that time between the Quiet Council, France's ruling body of human and automatons, and the lizardine court.

Smith was in Paris on a defection. A senior French scientist wanted to change sides and Smith had been given *carte blanche* on the operation. "Do whatever you have to do," the fat man had told him, "but get him across the Channel alive."

Only the whole thing had turned out to be a trap, and Smith found himself locked inside an inn outside Paris, and the inn was on fire. When he stared out of the window, through the metal bars, he saw the man from Meung for the first time. The man looked up at the window, and laughed. Then he climbed on his horse and rode away.

They called him the man from Meung not because he came from Meung-sur-Loire but because, when he was only twenty-five, the young man who was to become the Comte de Rochefort had killed forty-six people there, in one night. They had been a group of conspirators, plotting against the Council, and the young man, who had gone deep undercover with the group, proceeded to assassinate them one by one over the course of the night. It had come to be known as the Second Battle of Meung-sur-Loire.

But Smith did not know it that night, staring out of the window while the smoke billowed through the inn and the fire spread, and roared, and he fled desperately from room to room, seeking an escape...

They had met again in Mombasa in seventy-one. That time, Rochefort was after a British courier and, also that time, it was Smith who had the upper hand. He had not been able to kill the man but had given him the distinct scar he still bore.

Like Smith, Rochefort despised guns. His was a silent method, a personal one. Like Smith, he preferred to kill at close quarters, with a knife or with bare hands and, like Smith, he was very good at it.

Smith woke up feeling refreshed just as the train was pulling into Charing Cross. He had not been disturbed throughout the journey. No further attempts on his life, so far. He almost felt disappointed.

*But they'd be watching*, he knew. Rochefort was too smart to get on the train alongside Smith. Most likely he hadn't even been at Market Blandings, had arranged the attack from a distance and was even now waiting in London, in an anonymous hotel somewhere, with his agents on the ground, waiting for Smith to make his move.

It was odd, Rochefort warning him like that. Smith could not say that they liked each other, he and the Frenchman, but over the years a mutual respect had developed, as they fought across continents in the shadow game, the Great Game. The only game there was. What interest did the Quiet Council have in the deaths of Mycroft and Alice? Who else had died? How many people, and where, and why, and by whose hand?

He didn't know, but he was going to find out.

The train came to a halt, and he left his compartment and went down the steps to the platform. People swarming all about the great station, the trains belching steam, the cries of sellers offering candied apples and roasted nuts and sizzling sausages and birds in cages and mechanical toys and portraits done on the spot, and a little pickpocket went past him, going for it when Smith grabbed his hand, giving it a tweak, and the boy squeaked. Smith could have easily broken the delicate bones of the boy's fingers, but didn't.

"Run off with you," he said, a little gruffly, and the urchin, giving him a look of hurt dignity, did exactly that, not looking back.

*London.*

What did the old bee keeper used to say, in *his* own active days in the field?

Ah, yes.

*The game is afoot.*

Smith smiled as he remembered; he began to walk towards the exit, about to enter again the world he'd left behind.

It felt good to be back.

# EIGHT

There are a number of respectable old establishments along Pall Mall. There's the Drones Club, of course, and the Reform Club (of which Fogg was a member), and then there was Mycroft's old place, the Diogenes. Whereas the Drones was a lively place, its members numbering amongst the younger, and more energetic, of the aristocracy (both human and lizardine), the Diogenes was a place of quietude, where no noise was tolerated and where members moved little, spoke less, and ate plenty. As to the Reform Club, Smith disliked it. He disliked all members-only clubs. It would not be true to say Smith had sympathies to the views expounded by that man, Marx, whose own watering hole, the Red Lion pub in Soho, he nevertheless found much more congenial. Smith did not hold strong opinions, as a rule. To do so would be to compromise one's efficiency as a shadow agent. Yet something in him disliked wealth, and its display. Surely, he had fewer qualms when disposing of a member of the rich than of the poor. Long ago, Smith had learned to accept his own little idiosyncrasies. All agents had them. You had to learn to do the job regardless. It was telling, though, that the only times he had visited any such gentlemen's clubs had been in pursuit of a particular member within, and that he never left a job uncompleted.

At the corner with Waterloo Place there was the Athenaeum, a large, imposing building and another club, where Smith had once done an excision on a visiting politician. At any rate, he did not aim for any of the clubs, but rather for an unmarked, and rather drab, door in the side of a building along the Mall, said building being a small, red-brick establishment, with no sign, but clearly belonging to a trade of some sort.

And *trade*, on the Mall, was as good as being invisible.

It had begun to rain by the time he reached the building. The rain revived him, but he was glad to find shelter. The door opened as though on its own. In some uneasy moments Smith had the feeling the building was somehow alive, and watching. He knew that, in reality, the door was watched by human operators deep inside the building, and that, upon recognising him and establishing that he had clearance, the door was opened for him. The door, otherwise, never opened. Yet still, despite the knowledge, the feeling persisted, as if the Bureau itself was somehow alive.

He went inside and the door shut behind him noiselessly. He found himself in a quiet corridor. Small windows set in the wall allowed only a modicum of grey light in. The corridor smelled of industrial cleaning products and the windows were grimy with dirt. When he walked along it his feet squeaked on the bare floor.

He followed the corridor to its end. A simple second door blocked the way. He waited, and presently there was the sound of gears and steam and the door opened onto a small lift. He stepped inside and the door closed behind him and he began to descend.

The Bureau was cold and quiet. He went past the cipher room and the door was closed and he could hear faint voices behind. He ran into Berlyne in the corridor, Berlyne rubbing his hands together, muttering, "Damn cold, old boy."

Smith said, "Where is everyone?"

Berlyne shrugged. "All about," he said mournfully. "You here because of Mycroft?"

Smith wasn't fooled. Berlyne had been longer at the Bureau than anyone. There was little he didn't know, or had a hand in.

"I'm here to see Fogg."

"Yes, he did mumble something to that effect, come to mention," Berlyne said. "He'd be in his office."

"What's going on, Berlyne? Are there any leads?"

Berlyne shrugged again. "Harvester," he said, not without affection. Smith flinched.

"I retired," he said.

Berlyne shook his head. "Yet here you are," he said. "No one ever retires."

It was said he had a string of ex-wives in the colonies, that he could never afford to leave his salaried post. In his youth he was a promising agent, but an encounter on a South Pacific island changed him, made him mournful and jumpy, and he had had to be retired to a desk job. The file on that encounter, as on most Bureau missions, did not exist.

"Well," Berlyne said. "Good luck with it." He took out an enormous, not-too-clean handkerchief, blew his nose noisily, and departed down the corridor. Smith looked after him suspiciously for a moment, then went in search of Fogg.

"Ah, Smith. You've finally decided to show up."

Fogg's office had a fake fireplace, all the rage two years before, and the hiss of gas filled the windowless room. "What took you so long?"

Fogg looked irritated. He was leafing through a sheaf of papers on the desk. A chart behind him had names, and places, linked by lines. Smith saw ALICE – BANGKOK, a trail leading to HOLMES – LONDON.

Something else, too, which gave him pause.

AKSUM – WESTERNA – DEVICE.

He wondered what it referred to. Filed it away.

"Someone's been trying to kill me," he said.

Fogg snorted. "Well," he said. "That's only to be expected, isn't it."

Smith said, "Is it?"

Fogg said, "I imagine there are plenty of people who wish to kill you."

"Why now?"

And then he thought – that trail of bodies, Alice to Holmes – where will it lead to next? And it occurred to him it was just possible Fogg thought – or hoped – that it was leading to *him*, to Smith.

Was that possible?

He kept his face carefully blank as he thought. Did Fogg wish to use him as *bait*? It almost made Smith laugh. Almost. And could Fogg be right? Could this new, unknown Harvester be heading his way?

It didn't make much sense. He didn't *know* anything. He was not a part of whatever it was this *Erntemaschine* was looking for. Which meant Alice *had* been. And Mycroft.

And suddenly Smith wanted, very badly, to know what *it* was.

Fogg said, "It was not inconceivable that other powers would become involved. Our side is not the only one to have suffered… unexplained deaths."

"But why go after me?" Then– "Wait, you *knew*?"

Fogg looked amused. "We figured you could take care of yourself," he said. "Clearly, since you *are*, in fact, here right now…"

Smith was almost flattered. He said, "Who else has died?"

Fogg pushed a sheet of paper in his direction. Smith took it. "There's a list," Fogg said. "Make sure it does not leave the building."

Smith looked at the page, memorised it. Handed it back. He would review it later.

"Come with me," Fogg said. He pushed himself out of his chair. "Something I want you to see."

They were never going to give him all the information about a case. Smith didn't expect them to, either.

We're pieces in their game, he thought. They send us off into the field and let us find the questions for ourselves. No preconceptions.

So Fogg would be keeping information from him. He expected that. He'd give him just enough to follow his own chain of reasoning. Die in the process, possibly. Fogg should be happy with either outcome.

He followed the tall man down the corridor, a left before the still-closed cipher room, and down a flight of stairs. He knew then where they were going.

The Bureau's own mortuary.

It was icy down there and the light was cold and white, running on Edison bulbs, powered by the Bureau's own, hidden steam engines. Fogg pushed the metal door open and Smith followed him inside.

He did not like mortuaries.

Which was ironic, he knew. Just as he knew that, one day, sooner or later, it would be his turn to end up in one. He suppressed a shudder as he walked into the cold room. Metal cabinets set in the stone walls. An operating table sitting unused. Fogg went to one of the metal drawers and pulled it open.

A large corpse lay on it, covered by a sheet. Smith came and stood close to Fogg, looking down at the body. Fogg, with a moue of distaste, lifted up the sheet.

*Mycroft.*

The fat man looked peaceful in death. Fogg said, "Help me turn him over," brusquely. Smith complied.

Mycroft's flesh was soft and pliable and cold to the touch. The room stank of disinfectant. Carbolic acid, if Smith was right. The fat man moved surprisingly easily. "There," Fogg said, pointing.

Smith bent down closer. Looked at the fat man's neck.

A tiny hole, dug into the base of the skull.

So someone had stuck a stiletto blade into the man's remarkable head, piercing the brain in the process.

And had he seen something like that before?

"Is this what killed him?"

"There are no other marks," Fogg said.

Smith straightened. If he'd hoped for any sudden revelations, none were forthcoming.

*Do it the hard way, then.*

*The way he'd always done it.*

"What are you not telling me?" he said.

Fogg shook his head. He looked tired, Smith suddenly realised. And worried. It ill-suited him. "You're on your own," Fogg said. "As of this moment you're back on active. You report to no one but me. Get what you need from Accounting. I'd tell you to sign up with Armaments but I know your preferences. You'll be issued travel documents as needed, and currency – but do keep all the receipts, would you, Smith? These aren't the old days."

Smith gently rolled the fat man back over and covered him again with the sheet. Goodbye, Mycroft, he thought.

Fogg pushed the trolley back into the wall.

"Let's go," he said.

# NINE

Smith sipped a rare cup of coffee, in the continental style, as he waited for his contact to come in.

He was thinking through his meeting with Fogg.

The man had seemed nervous, Smith thought. He was sparse with information, almost too sparse. Smith had tried asking what Alice had been working on, before she was killed. Fogg only said, "She was like you. Retired."

He didn't know, Smith thought. Something linked Alice and Mycroft, but Fogg had not been a part of the chain.

He couldn't picture Alice as ever retiring. What had she got herself into, that got her killed?

And that hush at the Bureau. The sort of hush that came with bad news. Before he left he had run into Berlyne again. "Watch your back," the man advised him mournfully, rubbing his hands together against the chill. He had regarded Smith for one long moment before adding, almost too softly to hear – "Mycroft's not the only one who's no longer around."

Smith sipped his coffee and thought about his next steps and waited for his contact. He'd signed up with Accounts, waved away the offer of weapons at Armaments, and was out of the building before he knew it. The door shut behind him softly and he had the sudden, sinking feeling it would not be opening again.

He was not a fool.

He knew Fogg was using him. As bait, or decoy, he didn't know. Fogg was in over his head.

And it made Smith think of something else that had been bothering him, namely, the attempts on his own life.

Why go for him now, after all these years?

If it wasn't something in the past then he had to conclude it had to do with this new investigation.

Which suggested some interesting possibilities...

The most prominent of which was the simple assumption that, whatever Alice and the fat man had been killed over, someone, or several someones, wanted very much to keep it a secret.

He was sitting upstairs at the Bucket of Blood, by Covent Garden. They staged bare-knuckle boxing there but that would be later and for now the place was quiet. They served good pie and bad coffee and they didn't serve bluebottles, crushers, coppers, or whatever your term for the agents of the law may have been.

Which suited Smith.

He waited and presently there came the soft steps he had been waiting for, and he saw him – it – he never really knew what they preferred – come up the stairs.

He stood up. The other came and stood by him. His gait was slow and mechanical, and his blank eyes always terrified Smith, false eyes that were meant to suggest humanity, but somehow didn't.

"Byron," Smith said.

The Byron automaton extended his hand for a shake. His flesh was soft and warm. It was made of rubber of some kind, Smith knew. The automaton, despite his age, looked younger than Smith remembered. Clearly he'd been well maintained. He had ascended in power since the council of eighty-eight brought an end of sorts to lizardine control of the empire, and had given human and machine, for the first time, equal say. The Queen still reigned, of course – but the machine faction had grown stronger, though it was not like France, where it was said the Quiet Council held absolute – if quiet – power.

"Smith." Byron's voice was still the same old voice, scratchy in places, a voice made of numerous recordings of a real human voice, mixed together, played endlessly back. Babbage Corps. – Charlie Company, they used to call it in the old days – had built him, one of the early prototypes, and he was, Smith knew, second in command in the automatons' mostly hidden world. Machines feared humans, relying on them for survival. Byron – and his master – preferred to act, as much as possible, behind the scenes. "It is good to see you again."

They had crossed paths a couple of times, the automaton and him. No one knew the city better, nor had a wider net of informers and listeners. Machines listened, and most people never gave them a glance. They had worked the Prendick case together, successfully fighting the Dog Men Gang, a case which had left its scars on both of them. Smith had been taken captive by the gang and flayed, and on some nights he still felt the fine, white criss-crossing network on his back as though it were inflamed… "I wish I could say the same," he said, and the Byron automaton nodded mechanically. He understood.

"I am sorry about Mycroft," the automaton said. "He was a good man."

Smith snorted. "That's a lie, and you know it."

"Very well," the Byron said. "He was a useful man, an empire man. His loss is our loss."

He was speaking for the automatons. And Smith nodded, understanding.

"What do you know of his demise?" he said. The automaton didn't reply. His strange blind eyes moved as though scanning the room. How the automatons saw was a mystery to Smith. He knew that, between themselves, they communicated by means of in-built Tesla sets, and that was something he needed to find out about. There had been more and more traffic on what was coming to be called the Tesla Network, and while most shadow operatives dismissed the automatons, Smith didn't. He knew better than to underestimate Byron and his kind.

"Byron?"

"I thought you were retired," the automaton said at last.

"They brought me back."

"A pity."

Smith looked at him. "I don't understand," he said at last.

"You should have stayed in the village, my friend," the automaton said.

"Is that a warning?" Smith said, suddenly tense.

"It's an observation," the automaton said, mildly.

Smith sat back. He regarded the automaton for a long moment, thinking.

He had not expected this.

Mycroft, he knew, had strong links with the automaton movement.

Could they be involved?

And suddenly he was wary of Byron.

Which, he thought, had been the automaton's intention. So instead he said, "Fogg."

The automaton did not have a range of expressions. However, in the certain way his mouth moved, one could, just possibly, read distaste.

"You have always suspected him," the automaton said.

"It seemed clear to me he was an agent of the Bookman."

"Ah, yes…" And now the automaton seemed thoughtful. "The Bookman."

"Is this related to the Bookman investigation from eighty-eight?" Smith said, on a hunch.

The automaton was still. At last he said, "There are things best left in the shadows, my friend."

What exactly *had* happened in eighty-eight? There had been the very public blowing-up of the decoy Martian probe, and a girl, Lucy, had died. Mycroft had handled it single-handedly, if Smith remembered rightly. He, Smith, had been somewhere in Asia at the time.

Then came that strange revolution that didn't quite happen, and the new balance of power, and the fall of the then-prime minister, Moriarty. Mrs Beeton was in power now.

But Mycroft had remained in place, ensconced in his comfortable armchair at the Diogenes Club, running the Bureau and the shadow world, playing the Great Game…

"What are you not telling me, Byron?" he said at last. The automaton's mouth had changed again; now his expression resembled a smile. "What *can* I tell you," he said, "might be the more appropriate question."

"What *can* you tell me, then?"

"What I already told you. Go home. Water your garden. Watch the flowers grow."

"I grew *cabbages*," Smith said. "And Hapsburgian agents recently destroyed the garden." He thought about it. "Not that I minded, greatly," he added, to be fair.

"Fogg," the automaton said, "cannot be trusted. But you already know this. Then you would have also surmised that Mycroft would have been of the same opinion."

"I had warned him several times," Smith said, the memory of old hurt still present. "He never took notice."

"Are you working for Fogg, now?"

"He reinstated me," Smith said. "He is acting head."

"Then you are his tool," the automaton said, with finality.

"I am no one's tool," Smith said, but even as he spoke he knew it wasn't true. He had always been a tool. It was his purpose. He was a shiv for someone to apply, a weapon. And only Fogg had the power to bring him back from the retirement he hated, to make him, once again, *useful*.

"What you learn, he will learn," the Byron automaton said, and stood up. "I am sorry about Alice. But you must not follow this investigation, this time, old friend. Let it go. Light a candle in her memory. But step away."

"What about her killer?" Smith demanded. "Shall I let *him* go, too?"

"The killer, like you, wishes to learn much, though, I suspect, for vastly different reasons. I do not think he can be stopped, nor, necessarily, that he should be. This is bigger than you, my friend, bigger than me, bigger than all of us. Let it go, I beg you."

Smith stood up, too. "Then we have nothing else to discuss," he said, stiffly. The automaton nodded, once. His expression, as much as it could, looked resigned.

"Until we meet again, then," he said. He put forwards his hand, and Smith shook it.

"Until then," he said.

# TEN

*The observer watched this new quarry with interest. The voices in his head had been quiet of late, for which he was grateful. The country had a fascinating weather system, with frequent rain and an amassing of clouds that hid both sun and stars. Islands, he had learned, generated their own miniature weather systems. There was so much to learn.*

*People went past him. Mostly they did not notice him. He wore a long black coat and a wide-brimmed hat that, one of the voices told him, was rather fashionable. Fashion fascinated the observer. Most everything did. He stood in the shadows and watched the building. A small man came out of it and the observer watched him with interest, noticing the way the man scanned his environment as he went, always aware of his surroundings.*

*But he had not noticed the observer.*

*A small boy was one of the few who did notice him. The small boy went past him and then, for just a moment, seemed to stumble against him, murmured an apology and tried to dart away. The observer, however, reached out and grabbed him by the hand and the boy found himself pulled back. "Hey, let go, Jack!" the boy said, or began to, when he saw the observer's eyes on his. He stopped speaking and stared, as if hypnotised.*

"Give me back my things."

Still not speaking, the boy owned up to the items he had extracted from the observer's pocket. These may have surprised the casual watcher, had there been one. They included a dazzling green seashell, of a sort not to be found on the British Isles; a penny coin rubbed black and featureless with age, with the barely distinguished portrait of the old Lizard King William; a smooth round pebble; and a piece of cinnamon bark.

The observer took them and put them carefully back in his pocket. He let the boy go but the boy just stood there, until the observer made a sudden shooing motion and then, as if awakening, the boy's eyes widened and he turned and ran away, disappearing into the crowds of Covent Garden.

The observer watched the building and the people coming and going. He saw a dice game in progress and a man, which a voice told him was called a mobsman, who picked the pocket of a gentleman walking past without the man ever noticing. His nose could pick up smells that only now he was beginning to identify. Manure, of course, but also mulled cider, sold from large metal tubs to passers-by, and tobacco smoke, some of it aromatic and some of it reminding him of the sailors on the ship on the crossing over the Channel, and spilled beer, and roasting, caramelised peanuts, and human sweat and human fear and human hormones hanging heavy in the air: it was a heady mixture.

He stood in the shadows and few people noticed him and those who did moved aside, as though instinctively knowing not to come near. He paid them no heed. He watched until he saw a shadow come slowly out of the building and recognised him as the one he wanted but still he waited, waited for him to walk down the narrow passageway that ran alongside and only then, unhurriedly, he stepped out of the shadows and began to follow.

• • • •

It when he was going towards Drury Lane that Smith began to have the feeling he had forgotten something. He stopped in his tracks. It was early evening and the theatre-goers and the cut-purses were out in force.

He knew Byron did not work alone. Above him, above all the automatons, was the one they called the Turk. Once a chess-playing machine, he had quietly gained political power amongst the disenfranchised simulacra of the new age, seldom seen, always in the background. The Mechanical Mycroft, as some in the Bureau called him, snidely. If they knew he existed at all.

What could link Mycroft and the Turk with Alice in Bangkok?

But a more pressing question arose in his mind.

The Byron automaton must have known what Mycroft had known.

He turned around and began to run.


He could hear the distant cries even as he again approached the Bucket of Blood. As he ran he almost bumped into a small, undistinguished man who passed him going in the opposite direction; the man moved aside elegantly, avoiding impact, and Smith went past him, barely sparing him a glance.

The cries grew louder; in the distance, a police siren. A crowd of people gathered outside the Bucket of Blood, blocking the way into the narrow alleyway beside it. He pushed his way through.

Stopped when he came to the body.

*The observer had found the encounter interesting, for several reasons. For one, the device had obviously been waiting for him. It didn't put up a fight but had waited, its back to the observer, as though offering up what it had.*

*The observer's blade was already out and so he came to the device and inserted the blade in the same place as it did all the others, the base of the head, going inwards into the brain. Only this time he felt nothing, and was momentarily confused.*

*"I am using distributed storage, I'm afraid," the device said, politely. It took the observer back, a little. None of the others spoke to him. Not until they were dead, at any rate.*

*The blade came out, went back in. A series of stabs—*

A boy, standing in the shadows on the other side of the alley, watched this with wide-open eyes. He saw a man crouching over the fallen body of another man (it was too dark to distinguish details), savagely stabbing it, over and over and over. He opened his mouth to scream, but no sound came. He had followed the observer from the crowd, having tried to pick his pocket earlier. The stabbing went on and on.

Smith knelt beside the body of the automaton. There was, of course, no blood, through sparks flew out of the holes in Byron's body, and a viscous sort of liquid *did*, in fact, seep through the cuts and out, hissing as it touched the paved stones. Smith pushed the body onto its back. Byron's blind eyes stared up at him.

"Byron," Smith said. And, when there was no response – "Byron!"

But the machine was dying. Blue sparks of electricity jumped over the body and the crowd surged back, as though afraid it would explode. Smith raised his head; for just a moment he caught sight of a small, frightened figure standing at the other end of the alleyway. Then it disappeared.

71

"Byron!"

"Step aside, Smith."

He knew the voice. But he didn't move. He checked the automaton but the blue sparks were increasing and he felt an electric shock run through him and he jumped back.

"Everyone back!" The voice was authoritative and the crowd obeyed. Smith found himself dragged away; strong arms held him even as he fought to get back to Byron.

But the automaton's body was aflame in a blue, electric light now, and the ground around it was hissing, yellow acidic liquid spilling out of the multiple cuts. Smith was pushed to the ground, still fighting. "Don't–" he began–

With his cheek pressed against the cold hard stones he saw the flames begin to rise, yellow out of blue, slowly at first, then growing larger. Weight pressed down on his back; he couldn't move. He wanted to close his eyes but couldn't, and so he watched as the Lord Byron automaton burned, there in the alleyway where, centuries before, the dissident Dryden had been attacked.

"So ends the old," the earlier voice said, close, in his ears, "to give birth to the new," and Smith closed his eyes, at last, and knew that they were wet, and he said, "Go away, Adler. Please, just go away."

# ELEVEN

The last time they had met she was an inspector and he was Mycroft's errand boy. Now Mycroft was gone and Irene Adler was chief of Scotland Yard, and looked it.

They were sitting opposite each other in the bare interrogation room. When the fire had consumed the old automaton, Adler had instructed her officers to release Smith, but keep him where he was. She had secured the perimeter of the site, had officers interviewing potential witnesses, and two chattering police automatons, short squat things on wheels, were bent over what remained of the former Byron machine.

"You," she said, turning at last back to Smith. "I thought you were dead."

"Retired," he said, shortly, and she snorted. "Would that you were," she said.

"Retired?"

"Dead."

"Adler," he said, "you need to let me go."

"I need you to explain yourself."

"This is a Bureau affair."

Her eyes narrowed. "When a prominent member of

73

society dies in the open, in *my* city, that makes it *my* affair."

"And if he weren't *prominent*?" Smith said, knowing it was a cheap dig. She didn't dignify it with an answer. He said, "You're not handling the Mycroft investigation." Trying a different tack.

"I've been *ordered* out of that investigation."

"And you will be ordered out of this one."

She smiled. There was nothing cheerful in that smile. "Until that happens," she said, "it is still mine."

He sighed. He had been handling it all wrong, and now more people were dying. Had Byron known? he suddenly wondered. He must have known. Yet he did not appear to fight. Was he taken by surprise? Smith couldn't tell. He did not understand the mechanical, the way he thought. But it changed nothing. Byron was dead. Gone. The people at Charlie Company could build another replica but it would not be Byron, just something that looked like he had. A copy of a copy.

And now Smith was angry.

"If you won't butt out," he said, rudely, "then maybe you can help."

"Can I?" Irene Adler said. "I'm overwhelmed."

He ignored her. "There was a boy," he said. At that she paid attention. "I saw him, for a brief moment. He was watching. It is possible he saw the... the murder."

Was the destruction of a machine, however human-like, murder? Could it really be called that? He didn't know. It didn't used to be but the mechanicals had gained in power since the quiet coup of eighty-eight.

"What sort of a boy?" Irene Adler said. Tense. Attentive. Smith liked that in her. She would follow every scrap of information, never let go of an investigation until she solved it. She was smart and capable and she

74

ran Scotland Yard well… but this was a shadow investigation, and not her domain. And where the hell *was* Fogg? The Bureau should have been all over the investigation by now, and wasn't. And the news would be all over the papers by morning.

Smith closed his eyes, took a deep breath. Tried to picture the scene as it was, the brief glimpse of the boy. "Around twelve years old," he said. "Worn clothes, too large for him. Pale face. Black hair. Thin." He opened his eyes again. The details added up. "A street boy," he said.

Irene Adler sighed. "Do you know how many there *are*, in this city?"

Smith did know. And an avenue of questioning had already suggested itself…

And *now* there was a commotion outside, and he leaned back and smiled at the Scotland Yard chief.

The door to the interrogation room banged open and Fogg came in, trailed by a bemused police constable.

"Adler!" Fogg barked.

"Smog," Adler said, not turning to acknowledge him.

"*Fogg*," he said, irritably. He looked tired and out of his depth, Smith noted with some satisfaction. "Your part in this investigation is *over*," Fogg said. "We do not need you stomping about all over the place making noise." He turned to Smith. "And *you*!" he barked. "This is a mess, isn't it, Mr *Smith*?" Fogg pinched the bridge of his nose. "And you right in the middle of it, as usual. This is a disaster!"

Smith said, "You are upset over Byron's death?"

"Death?" Fogg glared at him. "Do I look like I give a whiff about that damn machine finally *expiring*? Don't be absurd, Smith. This has your mark all over it, doesn't it? What a mess. What a public, public mess."

Neither Smith nor Adler replied. They exchanged glances. "Yes, Mr Fogg," they both said, in unity. Fogg glared at them. "You," he said, pointing a long, thin finger at Irene Adler, "stay out of it. And *you*," he said, turning the finger, like an offensive weapon, on Smith, "outside. Now."

Smith gave the chief of Scotland Yard an innocent look and got up. He followed Fogg outside, through the station corridors and out into the street, where a black baruch-landau stood, belching steam.

"Get in," Fogg said.

Smith got in. The interior smelled of new leather and polish. He wondered if Fogg did his own buffing, and smiled.

"And wipe that smirk off your face!" Fogg said.

"Yes, headmaster."

Fogg let that one pass. He signalled the driver, and the horseless carriage began to move.

Mycroft, Smith remembered, had preferred the comforts of his own black airship: watching the city from high above, drinking scotch, smoking a cigar. It was easier to see things from a distance, he liked to say. *And in comfort*, Smith always added silently.

Fogg was street-bound. "A disgrace," he said.

"A mess, I think you said," Smith said.

Fogg shook his head. "Were there witnesses?" he said.

So he wasn't dumb. But then, Smith had learned long ago not to underestimate the man.

"Scotland Yard–" he began.

"Adler is out of this!" Fogg snapped. Whisper at the Bureau had been that Adler and the fat man's brother had been linked, in the past. Smith had a fleeting image of the bee keeper, standing in the rain, not speaking.

What did the bee keeper make of all of this? Rumour had it he, too, was a part of the events in eighty-eight, but shortly after that he'd been retired–

"They interviewed the crowd outside the Bucket of Blood," Smith said, patiently.

"And?" Fogg snapped.

"And they found nothing."

Fogg snorted. "If you *were* a witness to such a crime, you wouldn't stick around to be interviewed."

"My thoughts exactly," Smith said. Fogg looked at him. "So," he said again, "*was* there a witness?"

Smith told him about the boy. Fogg looked thoughtful. "You know that part of town," he said. Smith nodded. "The… *undesirables*," Fogg said. Again, Smith merely nodded.

"Good," Fogg said. "Then follow that trail."

Smith was angry with himself. He had been so close… Could he have prevented the attack? Could *he* himself have seen the killer?

Was he following the wrong path? This chain of events did not begin in London. He was looking at it wrong. He needed to step back, to start at the beginning. He said, half to himself, "But the killer is here."

He raised his head, saw Fogg smirk.

"Do you know where I've been in the past few hours, as you two were having your little heart-to-heart in there?" Fogg said.

Smith said, "No."

"I was called to Dover," Fogg said.

"They found another body," Smith said. Thinking furiously – How could the killer get from London to Dover in that time?

"Yes," Fogg said. "They found a body."

"Who is it?"

"Somebody. Nobody. A pastor, by name of Brown. It seems he was in the habit of crossing the Channel regularly."

Smith: "A courier?"

Fogg, with pursed lips: "Possibly."

"What was he carrying?"

"Nothing was found on the body."

"But the injury matches?"

"It matches."

"So our killer is on his way to France?"

"He was not on the ferry – that my people could find."

But the killer had his own ways of getting around, and not be seen, Smith thought. He felt suddenly helpless. Chasing shadows, they called it in the trade: following an impossible trail, and never catching up.

Fogg signalled the driver. The baruch-landau stopped and the door opened, as though by itself.

"Get out," Fogg said. And, as Smith climbed out into the street, a parting shot: "You used to be good."

# TWELVE

*The observer came out of the water dripping, and so he stood and waited for the water to evaporate. He noted the water was very cold, and the currents strong. As he swam across the Channel he had passed a steam-powered ship, carrying passengers, and a sleek tea clipper with taut sales, and two wooden boats pushed by oars that met in the shallows and exchanged what the voices had told him were contraband goods.*

*The observer was in no hurry. He stood and watched the water and the small island he had – partly – left behind. He found the world fascinating. Steam and sail and man-power, all sharing the water. That mixture of old and new, and they kept striving for the new, the newer still. Such a curious place. The voices argued and shouted and finally quietened, leaving him momentarily alone. He wondered what it was that had stopped him from taking the small boy, in that city where the whales sang in the river. He had been much taken with the whales. He had gone to see them, standing on the Embankment, and, as though sensing what he was, they came close, one by one, and showed themselves to him, and sang. He loved their song.*

*He should have taken one of the whales, he thought. He would have liked their song, to accompany the voices.*

*But there was time, there was plenty of time. He had been rushing about, to start with, with newfound eyes, excited by everything, eager for new experience, but that had been…*

*He did not have a term for it. It was one of the voices who finally offered a suggestion, and the observer contemplated it now.*

Unprofessional.

*Perhaps, he admitted, he had been a tad unprofessional. Certainly he should have taken the boy.*

*Why hadn't he?*

*A strange, unfamiliar word, whispered by the woman.* Compassion. *What a strange notion, he thought. Yet something in the boy's frozen stare, the wide eyes, the under-nourished face, had halted him. It would have just complicated things, the observer thought. His quarry had not been the boy but the strange man-machine, and by letting the boy go he had freed himself for his primary task.*

*The observer shook himself, raising naked arms against the rising sun. It felt wonderful, he thought, to be here. Clouds fascinated him, and migrating birds. And people were intensely fascinating, to the observer.*

*Before the observer had got into the water he had stood, the way he stood now, naked on the shore before the Channel, with moonlight instead of sunlight illuminating his artificial flesh.*

*He had shuddered, his body shifting and changing, drawing power and material from the humidity in the air, the salt water and the fine chalk. The voices had risen into a frightened crescendo before he silenced them. His body shuddered and shivered,* splitting, *the extra material of him lying down at last on the sand like an egg.*

*The observer had waited for his body to seal itself again, then crouched by this egg and put his hand on the warm, thin membrane. After a few moments the surface broke and the egg hatched.*

*The thing inside was not yet human, nor did it have shape. Blindly, it burrowed into the sand, feeding, converting solids and gas into–*

*At last the child rose out of the sand, and the observer helped him up. They stood, facing each other, identical in height, identical in shape. The moonlight reflected on their flesh. Then, not needing to speak, the observer turned to the sea, and the other put on his clothes, heading back into the city.*

*For there was one element left, of course, besides the trivial task of harvesting a whale. The observer had been aware of that for some time. Sooner or later he would have to collect one of the others, he thought. The masters. One of them. That made him a little uneasy. But what had to be done had to be done. There was that still left, to chart and understand.*

It was night and Smith was tired, but he'd been used to worse and at least no one was shooting at him any more.

Which was not to say they weren't watching–

Though he tried to shake any possible shadows, following a circuitous route through the city, keeping an eye out for enemy agents.

Which meant, at the moment, just about anyone.

But he needed to get to where he was going unobserved. Keep a low profile, from now on. Fogg was understandably angry. Another public murder and he, Smith, like a fool, smack in the middle of it.

*Shadow executives had to keep to the shadows.*

He was getting old.

There was no getting away from it. The realisation dawned on him gradually, in stages: he was past it. Mycroft had been right to retire him.

And Alice, he thought. What was *she* doing still playing the game? She had told him once, lying beside him in a hotel room in – it must have been Prague, or was it Warsaw? Somewhere in that region, in a spring with long bright evenings and the smell of flowering trees – "My one wish is not to die in bed."

Now she was dead and he was still around.

Ahead of him was the church. He was at St Giles, and it was dark there, and the people who moved about looked furtive. Which suited him fine. He went into St Giles in the Fields, the church quiet and welcoming. He stood there for a long moment, as he always did, wondering what it meant, a church, a place of worship; wondering, too, where the dead went, if they went anywhere at all, and if they did, what they found there.

He went and lit a candle. For the Byron automaton. Could you do that? Could you light a candle for a machine that no longer ran? Yet people were machines, too, running on vulnerable fleshy parts that decayed and were easy to harm. People shut down every day. Some – many – had been shut down by him.

What happened then?

Everything. Nothing. He lit the candle and placed it gently in place, in the damp sand, with the others. Goodbye, Byron, he thought. Another name on the long list of Smith's life had been crossed out.

He sighed, then went forward, towards the dais, and sat on a bench but at the end, in the shadows, close to the wall, and waited.


"Mr Smith."

The voice woke him up and for a moment he felt confused, thought he was back in his small house, back in the village, and it was time to tend to the cabbages. Then he remembered the house had burned down, people had

82

tried to kill him, what had been left of the cabbages had been dumped in the rubbish tip, and he was in a church and must have fallen asleep. He shook his head ruefully. Another sign of getting old. Getting careless.

"Mr Smith?"

He turned his head and stared at an old, lined face. It was like staring into a mirror. "Fagin," he said.

"Thought you were dead, like, Mr Smith," Fagin said.

"Retired," Smith said.

Fagin grinned. One of the things that Smith always noticed about Fagin was that his teeth were in remarkably good condition. They were white and straight and looked at odds in that face even as, like now, they had been carefully blackened with coal, to give them a ruinous appearance.

But of course, Smith was one of the few who knew Fagin's secret...

"You lot," Fagin said, "never retire. Die, yes. But never retire."

"And your lot?" Smith said, and Fagin grinned and said, "Tis a matter of choice."

This was the truth about Fagin: his real name was Neville St Claire and he had been, in his younger days, an amateur actor and a newspaper reporter. Faced with a new wife and mounting bills, the young St Claire took to the streets, putting on makeup and transforming himself into a hideous beggar, who called himself Hugh Boone.

The old bee keeper had put an end to *that* particular scheme, back in the day... but St Claire, unable to give up on the excitement of the streets, or the profits to be made therein, had transformed himself yet again, this time calling himself Fagin, and this time... diversifying.

Smith did not like the man, but he had proved himself useful on several occasions.

"I'm looking for a boy," Smith said.

"Oh?" Fagin tried to look innocent, and failed. "What do you need? I've got blaggers and bug hunters, buzzers and dippers, fine-wirers all."

"Yes, I know," Smith said. Fagin ran the beggars and pick-pockets, especially young boys. They were his eyes and ears and they did the jobs he no longer did himself. "One of those, I think."

"Only one?"

It was quiet in the church, quiet and dark – and suddenly there was a knife in Smith's hand, and its tip was touching Fagin's throat, almost gently, like a kiss. Fagin, carefully, swallowed.

"I think you know who I mean," Smith said quietly.

"Heard about your friend," Fagin said. "We were all sorry to see Byron go."

"And how, precisely, did you hear?" Smith said.

"Come, come, now, Mr Smith," Fagin said. "Put the knife away and let's talk like gentlemen."

"Why?" Smith said. He increased the pressure and watched blood well up on the other man's neck. "Neither of us is one."

"Quite, quite. Still…"

"Yes?"

"It's a matter of push, of chink, of coin!" Fagin said. "And I'm not talking a dimmick or a grey. I mean soft, I mean–"

"You mean money," Smith said.

"Man's gotta eat," Fagin said, almost apologetically. "Think of the kiddies, what?"

"Do you have the boy?"

Fagin's eyes never wavered from Smith's. A small smile seemed to float on his lips. "Do you have the money?" he whispered.

Smith sighed. There was no arguing with Fagin, nor threatening. He put the knife away. "I'm going to need a receipt," he said.

# THIRTEEN

The Angel, or something like it, had sat on St Giles Circus for centuries. Before Les Lézards had outlawed the practice, the Circus had been home to the gallows, providing both death (for convicts) and entertainment (for London residents), and the *Angel* had been the traditional stop for those about to be hanged, for a final drink and – if they were notorious enough – possibly for signing a few autographs.

It was a low-ceilinged pub, with a fire burning in the hearth, a card game or two in the back rooms, and various other transactions of a not-strictly-legal bent taking place in murmured conversations all around it. Smith knew it well.

He went in with Fagin, through the small maze of the pub and out, to the cold and dismal yard at the back. There, several small boys huddled around a makeshift fire, warming their small, pale hands. "The devil makes work for idle hands!" Fagin barked and the boys straightened to attention, glancing at their employer and the man he was with.

"Living the good life, eh?" Fagin said. He clicked his fingers. "Go," he said, not unkindly. "Go, ply your trade, my little wirers. Bring Uncle Fagin purses and their like, the heavier the better." He looked down at them benevolently. "Go!" he shouted, and the small figures scampered away, swarming past Smith and Fagin on their way to the streets.

"Not you, Oli," Fagin said, snatching one boy's arm. The boy stopped and stood obediently.

"This is the boy?" Smith said. He knelt down to look at the boy's pale, haunted face. "What's your name?" he said, gently.

"Twist, sir," the boy said, looking down.

"A fine thief," Fagin said, which, in his own way, had been a compliment. "Oli here's the one you've been wanting, Smith."

"Let me be the judge of that," Smith said. He pulled the boy gently a little way away from his master. "Here," he said, calling to Fagin, and tossed him a coin in the air. The portrait of a lizard spun through the air and landed with a thwack in the man's palm. "Go buy yourself a pint while I talk to the boy."

Fagin grunted, but seemed willing. "I'll be back in a bit, then," he said genially. "Mind the boy, Smith. I will not abide broken bones."

The boy's eyes flashed with fear and Fagin, with a snort of amusement, walked off.

Smith and the boy were left alone in the yard. "I won't hurt you," Smith said.

"You're the one from the Bucket," the boy said suddenly.

"You saw me?"

"I saw the machine man!" the boy was shaking.

"Byron? You knew him?"

"I saw you, you passed him in the crowd. You were running, and he moved out of your way."

Smith frowned. The boy's eyes were big and round and frightened. Not speaking, Smith took down his coat and put it around the boy's thin shoulders. The boy sucked in air and sighed. "His eyes," he said. "They were so cold."

"Tell me what you saw," Smith said.

"I tried to pick his pocket," the boy said. "But he caught me. I looked in his eyes. There were things moving behind his eyes. There were ghosts, trapped there. He made me afraid. He made me run. But I didn't run. I went around and watched him. I saw him go to the old Byron thingamee."

Thingamee was what the urchins called the automatons, Smith remembered suddenly. So who was the "machine man" the boy had spoken of?

"He had a knife only it wasn't no knife," the boy said. "It…" He swallowed. "It *grew*," he whispered. "It grew out of him. He stabbed the old thingamee and the thingamee let him. I don't understand…"

Smith didn't, either.

"I want you to come with me," he said. He needed the boy, and he couldn't leave him with Fagin. Someone had to take Fagin down. He had tried in the past, but always failed. The man had powerful friends. But he could at least ensure this boy, this Twist, a safe haven, for a while, with the Bureau. He was a witness, the only one they had. And Smith needed to know what the boy knew.

"Come with me," he said again, but the boy blinked at him in confusion and sound seemed to slow down to a crawl and there was a flash of blinding white light and the dirt between them exploded, once, twice, three times and Smith grabbed the boy under one arm and rolled – they were being fired at.

Then everything moved very quickly and he saw black-clad figures come streaming into the yard, over the walls and from within the pub, holding guns, surrounding them.

"Harvester," one of them said. The accent was familiar. Hapsburg.

Again.

"Run," he said to the boy. Then, like a dancer, poised on one foot, he swirled around, and his knives flashed as they flew.

He couldn't hope to kill them all and he knew it: not with knives.

At the Bureau he had stopped by and seen an old friend.

Underneath Pall Mall, below even the level of the Bureau, there was a train station…

A disused station, it had been the diggers' base when working on the underground railway. The Bureau had found it expedient and had taken over the abandoned dig when it moved to its present location.

A dark and gloomy place, with empty tunnels leading off into a maze of blocked-out passages…

Mining equipment still lying here and there, a steam digger, a miner's helmet, downed tools, bags of sand and stones, and broken metal tracks…

Down there Professor Xirdal Zephyrin made his home.

It had been in Paris, in the late seventies…

Smith had been sent to the French Republic on a defection. A notable scientist working for the Quiet Council had contacted the resident Bureau agent. He wanted to defect. The Bureau had been after the man they called

Viktor for many years, but the French were keeping him close. This was not Viktor.

He was identified, initially, only as *X*.

They had met by the Seine, beneath the terrifying vista that was the ruined Notre Dame. The cathedral had been built by Les Lézards, of that same curious green material of which the Royal Palace was made. It had been done long ago, and the cathedral had been destroyed during the Quiet Revolution, when human and automaton took over France. Now lizard boys hung out in the ruins, tattooed creatures trying to resemble the lizardine race across the Channel, their tongues surgically split, strips of colour tattooed across their skins in imitation of reptilian scales. They were lawless and dangerous and deranged. X had been nervous. But the cathedral was an ideal meeting place, dark and abandoned, and they walked along the Seine and discussed X's proposition.

"My name," he had told Smith then, at last, "is Xirdal Zephyrin! You have heard of me, of course."

Smith, who hadn't, nevertheless nodded.

"Of course, of course," Zephyrin said. "I am the greatest, yes. The man Viktor is a hack. A hack! Yet he rises in the estimation of the Council, while I, the great Zephyrin, am overlooked! Yes, yes, quite, you see." He kept muttering to himself, and shading his eyes against the light of the moon. He was tall and lanky with long hairy hands. "I can give you much, yes, yes! I am a great scientist. I make machines for you! You see? I must away to England."

It was the old story: resentment, envy. It would be hard to get Zephyrin over the Channel. Over the next few weeks as Smith watched he realised how hard it had been for the scientist to get away, that first meeting. And never for long. Shadows followed him, those French machines, and human agents, too, ensuring he remained isolated, remained in his lab, somewhere deep under Paris. At first Mycroft was against outright defection. "He can serve us better," he had said, "by remaining in place and feeding us information."

Smith disagreed. "His temper is unstable," he said. "He is not a man comfortable with deceit. I tell you, we must act quickly. Sooner or later, he will give himself away. They are already suspicious."

There had been a woman watching over the scientist, recently. A six-foot-tall woman with a Peacemaker on her hip, with hair like a cloud of black smoke. He knew her by reputation only: Milady, the Dahomey-born, Paris-bred, top agent of the Quiet Council.

She would not let the scientist slip from her grasp.

And, as Mycroft dithered, time had been running out…

How Smith got Zephyrin out of Paris – how he smuggled him over the Channel, and onto British soil, and through the fingers of Milady de Winter – that had been a story still spoken about, in hushed whispers, at the Bureau, and at the training centre in Ham Common. And never spoken of in Paris.

Zephyrin's stolen knowledge had had the scientists in a frenzy, and a committee had been formed – chaired by Lord Babbage, then still present in the flesh – to evaluate, and make use of, the material. When the debriefing of Zephyrin had at last ended, the scientist had been put on the Bureau's own payroll, and installed in that nameless, abandoned station, where he had been provided with material, assistants and space, and which he seldom, if ever, left.

Smith had gone down to see him, after his meeting with Fogg.

"*Mon ami*!" the scientist said. "I thought you were dead."

Smith said, "I retired," and the scientist said, "Pfft! You cannot retire any more than I can!"

"Still ticking away?" Smith said.

The scientist, almost dancing on the platform of that station, spread his arms and beamed. "I make many many things!" he said. "You would like to try?"

"What have you got?"

"Well…" Zephyrin said. "It depends on the person, does it not so? You, for instance, do not like the guns, do you not. So I cannot offer you the pen-gun!"

"Pen-gun?"

"It looks like a pen," the scientist said, "yet it is a gun!"

"Really," Smith said.

"How about, then," the scientist said hopefully, "a Poison Master One Hundred?"

"What is it?"

"Observe," Zephyrin said, "this simple ring."

He held it hopefully towards Smith. It was an odd, lumpy ring, with many protrusions. "Watch," the scientist said. He twisted the upper part of the ring and it turned, the small extensions moving with it. "It is an old-fashioned poisoner's ring, naturally," the scientist said, "yet it carries up to one hundred distinct poisons and various drugs, which can be delivered by direct contact with skin as well as by command, into a drink or perhaps a sweet bun."

"Yes," Smith said. "Impressive. However, I am not much for jewellery, myself…"

"Ach," Zephyrin said. "It is helpless with you, my friend. You have not the love of the technology! For you I make something special therefore. Special, yes. For you are Englishman, yes!" He chortled. "For you…" he said. "I make miniature umbrella."

Smith, the Hapsburg agents, the back yard of the Angel in St Giles.

His knives flashing, blades finding skin and bones and arteries…

Men dropping, others converging on him, too many, there were too many…

Strapped to his back, a small, slim sheath, as for a blade. A handle, protruding…

He pulled it out.

The man who first spoke, the man who called him Harvester. Suddenly laughing.

Something rapid in a German Smith couldn't understand. More laughter. Smith pulled it open.

An umbrella.

"*Sie haben Angst, es wird regen?*"

You are afraid it will rain?

Smith smiled back at him.

"Don't shoot," he said. "I'll come in peace."

"Put up your hands, *Herr* Smith."

Smith raised his hands, the umbrella above him.

Gave it a small, almost unnoticeable spin.

The umbrella spun and rose in the air.

"Rain," Smith said. Standing under the umbrella. Feeling like a fool. Thinking, he couldn't die here, because then, if it didn't work, he couldn't kill Xirdal Zephyrin.

The umbrella hovered.

"*Was ist das?*" the man said. "*Spielzeug?* Toy, please?"

"*Ja,*" Smith said.

The umbrella stopped. And suddenly, all around its rim, a series of small nozzles protruded out.

"*Schiessen*!" the Hapsburg agent shouted. *Fire!*

But the umbrella spun, suddenly and hard, the tiny steam engine embedded in its apex providing the power, and the nozzles barked out a widening circle of high-pressured darts, thin as darning needles.

A silver rain of tiny blades...

Poisoned, if he knew Professor X.

The umbrella, having spun twice, now stopped. Around Smith, the men were on the ground, unnaturally still.

*Run*, said a voice in his head.

He ran.

Behind him, the swish of flying blades as the umbrella spun again, then rose higher, and higher still–

He darted into the now-empty pub, pushed through doors, ran outside–

Behind him, unseen, the umbrella reached its programmed height and stopped, and dropped, gently, down to the roof of the pub–

Activating, on impact, the hidden charge of explosives running all along the hollowed core of its tube.


Smith burst out of the Angel when the night became alive with light and flames–

An explosion shaking the building behind him, the roof caving in, a ball of flame reaching out and pushing him, sending him flying–

Thinking, Zephyrin you crazy old bastard–

A ball of fire rising into the skies, Smith free, not quite believing it–

He'd managed to escape–

And someone caught him in his arms, breaking his flight, a hug as of an old friend's–

Smith looked up, dazed–

94

Into the smiling face of the Frenchman, the Man from Meung, the Comte de Rochefort.

"*Bonsoir*, M. Smith," the Comte de Rochefort said. Smith tried to pull back, tried to fight–

A small, cold pinprick of pain in the side of his neck.

"*Doux rêves*," he heard the Frenchman say, as if from far away. *Sweet dreams…*

Smith closed his eyes. The Frenchman held him as he fell.

# FOURTEEN

He woke up by a window, tied to a chair.

He looked out of the window and below him was the city.

He was somewhere high up in the air, looking down. The Thames snaked below, and the lights of the city were a chorus, top amongst them Big Ben and the Babbage Tower, arcane mechanisms pointing at the skies, a beacon of light warning off the airships that sailed, night and day, above the capital.

He was in an airship, he realised with a sinking in his stomach. And there could be no escape.

"Ah, I see our… guest is awake," a voice said. He turned from the window and saw the Comte de Rochefort sitting across from him, sipping from a glass of cognac.

"I'd offer you a drink," the man said, "but…" He shrugged. "You seem to be somewhat tied up at the moment."

"Funny," Smith said.

"Tell me," Rochefort said. "Why are the Hapsburgs so keen on eliminating you?"

Indeed, the same question had been troubling Smith. "I don't know," he admitted.

"Really…" Rochefort said.

Smith had very little to lose by telling the truth. His ignorance startled him. He did not understand what was happening and, under the circumstances, decided that his best course was to stick to the truth, and try, by extension, to find out what the French were after.

"I do not believe you," Rochefort said. Smith smiled. Sometimes the truth itself was the best lie, he thought.

"I will not insult you," he told Rochefort, "by lying."

"And I will not, in my turn, insult you by resorting to crude interrogation," the Frenchman said.

"Oh?"

"You may be aware of Viktor Von F–'s formula?" Rochefort said. "After all, you tried several times to cause him to defect."

"His loyalty," Smith said dryly, "truly is commendable."

"I have," Rochefort said, "a syringe here with me. It is a modified form of your own Jekyll formula. I am a gentleman, and so I will give you a choice. Tell me what I want to know, without coercion or further lies, or I shall be forced, very much against my principles, to inject you with the material. I believe recovery is not a side product of the treatment."

"I see," Smith said.

On the table before him, Rochefort placed two items, side by side. One was a loaded syringe. The other, his glass of cognac.

"Choose," he said.

"What do you want to know?" Smith said.

The Frenchman smiled, without joy. "What do you know of the Babbage Plan?" he snapped.

*The Babbage Plan?*

Without warning, Rochefort slapped him, a backhanded strike that sent Smith's head reeling back. "I hate to do this," the Frenchman said, sounding not in the least bit upset.

Smith shook his head, confused. Lord Babbage had not been seen for several years in public... Rumour had it he was dead. What did Rochefort want? How did it tie to–

He said, "I am retired. No, hear me out! I am retired and was brought back into service following the murder of my former employer, Mycroft Holmes, known to you as the head of the Bureau and of the various branches of British intelligence. I do not know who killed him, or why. I am trying to trace a killer – nothing more."

"You lie!" the Comte de Rochefort said.

"Why would I lie?"

"Because," Rochefort said, with a chilling smile, "you are the Harvester."

```
Code name: Smith.
First name: unknown.
Place of birth: unknown.
Parents: deceased.
Family: none.
Recruited: 1856, at the age of twenty.
Number of kills before recruitment: unknown.
Former associates: none living.
Recruited by: Holmes, Mycroft.
First assignment: classified.
Notable cases: The Dog Men Gang, The Xirdal
Zephyrin Defection, The Underground Cannibal
Tribe Massacre, The Warsaw Memorandum, The
Bangkok Affair of Seventy-Six, others classified.
Notes: for a long time considered Mycroft's
right-hand-man, Smith specialised in removals
and terminations, a catch-all term at the Bureau
```

for kills, and another sign of the British squeamishness when it comes to stating the unsavoury nature of their global empire and the shadow practices which make it possible. Smith is known to detest guns and other weapons of that sort, preferring to use knives or his bare hands. Trained first at the Bureau's secret Ham Common training facility, later, if rumours are correct, spent three years in the Chinese monastery of the Wudang clan known as Shaolin, under tutelage of one Ebenezer Long, known agitator, Chinese freedom fighter and Wudang leader (presumed). Acquired the moniker "Harvester" for his specially created role as Mycroft's unofficial executioner, travelling the globe to eliminate people on behalf of the Lizardine Empire.

Forcibly retired over the Isle of Man incident in ninety-three. Placed under restricted habitation in St Mary Mead, AKA The Village, where he had remained until recent events. Extremely dangerous, treat with caution.

Rochefort put down the dossier. Took a sip of his drink. Stared at Smith. "Well?" he said, at last.

"You suspect *me* of killing Mycroft?" Smith said.

Watched the Frenchman's face. Thinking – they must be clutching at straws.

Why?

Why be upset over Mycroft's death?

Leaps he didn't want to make. He shut his eyes but in the darkness his mind worked faster, connecting–

"Mycroft worked *with* you," he said – whispered. "No. It's impossible. No."

Rochefort's face was hard and unsmiling. "He was a great man," he said. "You think this is a game? This is bigger than all of us, Smith. If you are working for Babbage, I will find out. If you had killed Mycroft, I will find out."

He tapped the syringe. Finished his drink. Left the empty glass there, beside the syringe. "I will be back soon," he said. "I think, perhaps, you've made your choice, no?" he tapped the syringe again, then, walking softly, left the room and locked the door behind him.

Smith was left alone, tied to the chair, the empty choice before him. He knew they couldn't trust him. Just as he wouldn't have trusted Rochefort, in a similar situation. It would be the syringe for him and, after that, there was no going back. No doubt, when they were done with him, his grotesque new form would be thrown off the airship, somewhere lonely and isolated, over cliffs or sea, perhaps… A shadow burial, as they called it in the trade.

He sat back, closed his eyes. His fingers had tried to work the ropes off, but couldn't. He was getting old…

They did not intend to let him go, he knew.

But *Mycroft*?

Could it be the truth?

And what, in God's name and all that was holy, was the Babbage Plan?

He sighed, resigning himself to his fate. There was a sort of peace in that. He would die here, die in ignorance, and be thrown off the airship to his grave. He could accept that.

But he wanted answers.

He realised he could not give up. Not yet.

There was a soft scratching sound at the door.

# FIFTEEN

Smith, eyes closed to slits. Wishing he'd got more gadgets off Zephyrin. Figuring he could maybe push off to the floor, maybe break the chair – get just a chance to fight back. London, far below, under a layer of clouds. No escape…

The key turned in the lock and the door opened. Smith tensed–

Then his eyes opened wide when he saw the small figure standing in the room.

"You!" he said.

The boy closed the door behind him. He put his finger to his mouth, signalling silence.

"Twist!" Smith whispered. "What are you doing here?"

The boy grinned. "I saw the airship come down to land," he said. "It was hovering low over the roof of the church. I saw them carry you up… so I climbed up on the roof and snuck on before they took off. They didn't notice me."

"You could have got yourself killed!"

"Nah," the boy said, shrugging. "Fagin got us practising on the passenger ships, you know. Good pickings on those."

Smith shook his head. "Can you untie me?" he said.

101

But the boy was already behind him, and in moments Smith's bonds were cut loose. The boy came around, looking pleased with himself. "That's a big knife you got there," Smith said.

"I stole it," the boy said. Smith grinned back at him. "Of course you did," he said.

He felt his blood circulation slowly returning. "We need to get off this airship," he said.

The boy shrugged. "We can take them by force," he said, "and make them bring it down."

Smith, looking at him. The change that had taken over the boy. He said, "I don't think that's likely, Twist."

"Yes, sir."

"Give me that knife."

"Yes, sir."

The knife felt good in Smith's hands. It would feel better somewhere else – embedded in Rochefort's stomach, say…

"We'll make for the upper deck," Smith said.

The boy followed him meekly. They went out into an empty corridor. "How many of them are there?" Smith said.

"About a dozen, I think," Twist said.

"Too many…"

Along the corridor, up plush chrome stairs. The night outside was cold, the wind sending a shiver down Smith's spine. London was beneath them. The airship sailed high. There were clouds below, and only the tip of the Babbage Tower peeking out, with its beaming lights.

Babbage…

Wasn't the old man dead?

"Stop!"

"*Merde*!"

Smith turned. Rochefort, with two men holding dart guns. "Where did that boy come from?"

He couldn't give them time. He ran at them, felling one man with a punch to the face that broke his nose and drove the bone into the brain, the other with a well-placed kick that dropped him squealing. Smith smiled, came at Rochefort with the knife.

"Son of pigs," the Frenchman said. In his hand, too, there materialised a knife.

"Why was Mycroft working with you?" Smith said, striking. The Frenchman feinted, slashed back. Smith almost wasn't quick enough and the blade whistled, too close to his face.

"Still you say you don't know," Rochefort said.

"Has it occurred to you I might have been speaking the God-damned truth?" Smith yelled.

"No!"

Knives flashed, as the two men danced on the deck. Other figures materialised around them but Rochefort stopped them with a shout. "Stay back."

"Tell me!" Smith said.

"It is impossible," Rochefort said. "You killed them, Alice, Mycroft, you are working for *him*!"

"I don't know what you're talking about!"

"Babbage, man! Damn it, Smith, I will–"

The knife whistled again but this time Smith was ready, ducking *under* the blade and coming up and around the man–

Then he was holding him, with his own blade against Rochefort's neck. "It's been too long..." he whispered, panting, in the man's ear. "Drop it."

Rochefort dropped the blade.

"You will harvest me too, Harvester?" he said. "You think the plan will work? Your master thinks he can rule us all, but he will never–!"

What else he was going to say was stopped, however, as another dark shape rose, silently, beyond the stern of the airship.

A second airship, wholly black and silent, and a flower of blood was opening on Rochefort's chest. The Frenchman looked surprised.

"They… set us up," he whispered. Smith couldn't hold him. He lowered him to the floor. "Rochefort?" he said. "Rochefort!"

"Find… the launch," the Frenchman said. "Mycroft… was trying. We are all… trying. Smith, I…"

There was more of the eerie, noiseless fire. It hit the deck and splintered wood and a fire burst out in the engine room. "I was wrong," Rochefort said.

"Wait! No!"

Was he destined to have everyone he knew die around him as he watched, helpless?

"Mister Smith, Sir! Here!" The boy Twist materialised by his side. On the deck Rochefort was breathing shallow breaths, the blood spreading. He had moments to live, at best.

"What is it, boy?" Smith said.

"Take this," Twist said. Smith looked up–

The Frankenstein-Jekyll syringe.

The boy shrugged. "I stole it," he said.

"Of course you did."

The second airship was gaining, rising higher than their own. And now rope ladders were being lowered, and men could be seen, ready to descend. The French airship was burning now, and losing altitude rapidly. They would crash unless the black airship saved them–

Which seemed unlikely.

"Quick, mister!"

Smith snatched the syringe from the boy. "I'm sorry, Rochefort," he said. "It's the only way…"

And plunged it into the man's neck, emptying its liquid contents into Rochefort's vein.

The fallen man shuddered. His legs spasmed, kicking in the air. His arms seemed to almost magically thicken, and a white foam began to come out of his mouth. He cried – growled – the boy Twist backed away. So did Smith.

"We have to get off this thing," Smith said.

The airship tilted on its side, the foaming, changing body of the Comte de Rochefort rolling over. Smith and the boy were plunged against the side of the airship, the city of London down below them, and the Babbage Tower coming closer–

"We're going to hit that thing!"

Men coming down the rope ladders – he couldn't guess who they were. They couldn't be Bureau – more faceless Hapsburg agents? Someone else?

Things came sliding down the deck, hitting them. Anything not nailed down…

Then he saw the heavy backpack.

"Put this on my back!"

"Please, sir, what is it, sir?"

"It's a parachute!" unvoiced, the thought – *I hope*.

He put the straps on. Grabbed the boy in a hug. Twist felt to him small and helpless, a child in Smith's arms. "Hold tight!"

Behind, the men, with ropes, like mountain climbers, were coming for them. Smith straightened, looked over the side of the airship – nothing below but clouds and lights.

He jumped.

# SIXTEEN

London rushed at them. Like a cannon ball dropped from the air they fell, Smith holding on to the boy. Smith, praying: that the parachute would open, that it would hold, that no one would fire at them.

The Thames lay below like a hungry snake, waiting to swallow them in its jaws. The Babbage Tower, too close – a terrible bump and for a moment they rose, as the parachute opened. Smith, holding on to the boy. Twist, in his arms, his eyes closed shut, pale face.

They slowed. The parachute held. Twist opened his eyes. They turned round slowly, in the wind.

"We're going to hit that tower!" Twist said.

Smith: "That should be the least of our worries."

Looking up – the French airship burned. Other figures dropping from the sides. Two, without a parachute, fell like stones. Smith wished the boy hadn't had to see that, then figured he must have seen worse, in his short life.

The other airship rising higher, above the flaming French ship. Starkly illuminated – a black unmarked airship. He wanted then, very badly, to know who it belonged to.

The city, down below, growing larger – he could imagine people looking up, watching the flames – and thought: Fogg is not going to like this.

People dropping like flies.

He wondered how many candles he would have to light at the next church he found. He had lost count of the dead.

"Sir! The tower!"

But Smith was aiming for it now. The wind was in his favour. The Babbage Tower, tall and strange, protrusions of devices from its side. It was said they listened to the stars. It was said Lord Babbage was a vampire, feeding off electricity and blood. They said many things. The building came closer and closer, they had passed its apex, the light flashing warnings to airships, were at a level–

Windows, glass – he stretched his legs, soles first, still hoping–

The wind gave them a last push, a gasp of desperate air–

"Hold tight," Smith said–

His feet connected with the window with force, broke it – a shower of shards – he and the boy were catapulted into the room.

He dropped the boy. "Watch the glass!"

A knife in his hand, the parachute trying to pull him back, back into the air – he severed the harness, the parachute blew away – Smith dropped to the floor, exhausted.

"Sir? Sir?"

"What is it now, Twist?"

"Sir, there's a–"

Smith just wanted to sleep. To curl up into a ball. To close his eyes. Everything hurt. He was too old for this stuff. "Sir, there's a head, sir."

"What?"

He pushed himself upright. Looked around the room...

A machine in the corner. A head made of wood and wax, almost life-like, wearing a turban. A chessboard before it. A curved moustache. Arms of wood and ivory. It had a chest but no legs, no bottom half: the upper part of the body was a part of the table and the chessboard: they were one. Smith stared, horrified. The dummy mouth moved and a voice came out, too loud in the sudden silence of the room. An old voice, scratchy and faint, as if it had been recorded, long ago, the words spliced together from spinning Edison records.

"Well done, Mr Smith," the voice said.

Smith groaned. "What are *you* doing here?" he said.

Outside the window the burning French ship was sinking down, down into the city. Smith hoped it would hit the Thames. Otherwise the fire could spread. The black airship was rising – soon it was invisible. He needed to know whose it had been. Not Hapsburgs again. Someone else. A hunch. It had him worried. Too many people, after him, after a secret he didn't have.

What did Mycroft know? What was Alice doing in Bangkok?

Why were they both, now, dead?

"Turk," he said.

The Mechanical Turk looked at them both with blind unseeing eyes. One of the oldest mechanicals, and the most powerful... Smith had last met him several years before, working his last case with Byron. It was before the events of eighty-eight, when the automatons gained political power, led by the chess player. They said he could see the future, of a sort. That his mechanical brain could calculate probabilities, pathways into what could be. Smith distrusted him.

"I thought you were still at the Egyptian Hall," he said.

"You thought wrong," the chess player said. And: "We don't have much time."

"Sir?" Twist said. "Can you hear something?"

A loud, rising and falling sound. Smith felt the hairs rise on the back of his arms. An alarm. He couldn't take much more punishment.

The Mechanical Turk chuckled, a strange, old sound. A dead man's laugh, Smith thought, uneasy. He waited. The Turk's head nodded. "Time is short," it said, repeating itself. "So I shall have to be concise. Smith, I had expected to run into you, sooner or later. I am gratified that it is sooner... though I did not expect the boy."

"Me neither," Smith said, scowling. "Get on with it, will you?"

"I am held captive here," the Turk said. "But I listen. I still have that. So much has changed since eighty-eight... You had not been a part of that affair."

"No."

"The fall of the Bookman," the Turk said, and sighed, the recording of a long-vanished human sigh. "And the birth of something stranger and more wonderful than even I could imagine."

"The Bookman is dead?" Smith was startled. He had heard the rumours, but... it had been said the Bookman was not a man at all, but a machine. Conducting a war against Les Lézards, his last appearance had been the destruction of the Martian probe in an explosion that had resulted in several deaths. The Turk said, "He is... well, what is death, to such as us? The Bookman was a device, Mr Smith. A device for making copies. His agents were many. Death, to the Bookman, was only a change of storage. Do you understand?"

"No," Smith said.

"I had hoped you would come, here…" the Turk said. "I had calculated an over sixty-five per cent chance of you dying in the first two days of the investigation."

"That sounds about right," Smith said. Beside him, the boy Twist sniggered.

"Is the Bookman really dead? If he could make perfect copies of people," the Turk said – "well, then, could he not also make copies of himself? Itself, I should say."

Smith took in the unexpected information calmly. He did not care about the Bookman, and eighty-eight was ancient history. This was almost the new century, now. The alarm kept ringing shrilly, then, all at once, stopped.

"I have managed to gain some control over the building's systems," the Turk said, with no special inflection. "Still, they will be here soon."

"Security?"

"B-Men, Mr Smith. B-Men."

Hadn't Mycroft warned him of–

"Babbage's own militia," the Turk said. "His own corps. It was their airship which you saw up there, in the sky. They are… They are trying to plug a dangerous leak."

"Lord Babbage is still alive?" Smith said.

"In a manner of speaking," the Turk said. "Listen to me, now, and listen carefully. Eighty-eight was a point in which history changed. In which one path became the main path, and others faded. It began with the Martian probe. A desperate signal, sent by Les Lézards, trying to summon others of their kind to this world."

"They were not born here?"

110

"They came," the Turk said, "from the stars, in a ship that could sail empty space. Did they crash-land here? Did they escape from somewhere – or rush towards something? I do not know. They had been woken by Vespucci on their cursed island, and schemed to gain power over this world, taking the throne of this island-nation and making it an empire in the process. Their remnants are all around us, ancient machines, waking up. This is the time of the change, Smith. And in ninety-three…"

"The Emerald Buddha Affair?"

"You have heard of it?"

"Milady de Winter, of the Quiet Council, had been involved. That is all I know."

"One of the ancient machines which had been activated," the Turk said, "had opened a temporary gateway, through space. It had been stopped, and closed… but not before something, my friend, had slipped through."

It was quiet in the room, and cold. Cold air poured in through the broken window. "Why are you telling me all this?" Smith said – whispered. The boy Twist hugged himself with thin pale arms.

"I had known this will happen, from the start," the ancient machine told him. "Had planned for it. We are not alone, Smith. Nor should we be. And yet…"

"Yes?"

"Who can tell what we will find?"

"I'm not sure how this is helping me," Smith said.

The Turk sighed again. "Mycroft and Alice died for a secret," it said, "so great that even I am unable to penetrate deep into its mysteries. Lord Babbage is playing the long game, Smith. As am I. But I am afraid he has gone beyond me, has used his own machines to hide his plans. To find the one, you must find the other."

"How?"

"Follow the chain," the Turk said, simply. "Find the other, who is like you, in many ways…"

Smith dismissed it. "Why are you here?" he said, instead. The Turk was telling him nothing, he realised.

"Babbage fears me. His men took me and installed me here. But I can listen… the Tesla waves go everywhere. Somewhere in Oxford there is a boy who is not entirely a boy, and a thing growing deep underground which may yet be our salvation. There are thinking machines in France, and in Chung Kuo, and we are forming our own alliance, a network of thought that, one day…"

But the Turk grew silent, and the hum of engines beyond the walls became mute, suddenly. Smith had not been aware of the background hum until it had stopped. "Turk?" he said. "Turk!"

But there was no reply, and Smith cursed – and cursed again when the alarm returned, in full force.

"They shut him down, sir," the boy, Twist, said.

"Machines," Smith said. "You can never trust machines."

There were sounds beyond the door now. Shouts, and feet slamming into the hard cold floor.

"We have to go," Smith said.

# SEVENTEEN

Outside it was a long white corridor and electric light and nothing else. The light was white and bright. They ran in the opposite direction to the sound of the men. "It's a long way down, sir," Twist said.

There were doors for a lift at the end of the corridor. As they approached them they opened with a wheeze of steam – Smith dragged the boy away, seeing the hint of black uniforms and the light playing off guns. "Quick, in here."

The door wasn't locked. A janitor's room, he thought. Buckets and brooms and wipes and three sets of grey shapeless overalls–

"Get dressed," he told the boy, already reaching for a suit.

The janitor and his assistant, armed with buckets and brooms, walked meekly to the lift when they were stopped.

"You!"

The men wore black uniforms with the logo of the Babbage Company on their arms. The numbers 01000010, which represented the letter "B" in the binary number system, with a stylised little cloud of steam directly above the digits. The men also wore guns, which were black and well oiled and currently pointing at the janitor and his assistant's chests.

"Where are you going?"

"Please, sir, much cleaning to make!" the janitor said humbly. "Many dirting all about, yes?"

The officer's face twisted in disgust. "*Portuguese*?" he said.

"Damn continentals," the officer beside him said. "Get out of here, this is now a restricted area. Did you see anyone?" he asked, with sudden suspicion.

"We see nothing, mister!" the janitor said. "Boy, he no talk English. Me only talk good."

The officer looked at them for a long moment, the gun still raised. Then he lowered it. "Get out of here! *Pronto*," the officer said.

The janitor, looking frightened, hurried to obey, pulling the boy – who must have been somewhat slow, the officer thought; he had seldom seen such a look of utter stupidity on a face before – along with him.

"And haul that old machine out of there," the officer said, ordering his men. "Instructions are to dump it in the basement with the rest of the rubbish."

"Too close," Smith said. "That was too close."

But interesting, he thought. For they had clearly not been given information as to the possible cause behind the break-in. Had they been looking for intruders, he and the boy would not have been so lucky. Which made him worry what would happen on the ground floor…

The lift creaked its way down. Floor after floor passed by. He tensed when it stopped at last. "Step to the side," he warned the boy, with a whisper.

His hand on the hilt of the knife…

The doors opened.

"Do try and take them alive…" a voice said.

Smith was already in motion. There were numerous B-Men around in those pressed black uniforms. Too many, he thought. And he was old. Still he moved, going rapidly, the knife flashing–

Knowing it was hopeless, hoping only that the boy would stay out of sight, get a chance to escape after all–

The sound of gunfire–

He expected the bullets to slam into him, for the air to explode out of his lungs, for his heart to stop, violently and forever–

"Get down, you bloody fool!"

Hands grabbed him, dropped the knife, pulled him down and across the floor. He heard manic laughter, the sound of gunshots, screams.

Men in black uniforms falling all around, the smell of blood and gunpowder filling the air.

"Take one for England!" a familiar voice shouted, cackling.

Oh, God, no, Smith thought.

"Didn't think we'd miss out on all the fun, did you?" Colonel Creighton said.

M. was in the back of the baruch-landau, still holding on to her Gatling gun, her hair standing crazily on end as though she had been hit by lightning. Creighton was driving. The baroness, putting away a bloodied knife she had used on the dying, was now comforting the boy, who looked – understandably – a little shocked.

It's been a long night… Smith thought.

They had left behind them the Babbage Tower's high-security entrance trashed and ransacked, and bodies piled up on the floor. "Treachery!" Colonel Creighton said. The steam-powered vehicle lumbered through the narrow streets, heading to the river. "Knaves! Traitors!"

"We don't know that," Smith said. He wanted to sink into a sleep, into oblivion. He prayed M. would not shoot any more people. Instead of sleep he accepted the offer of a flask from the baroness and drank, the whiskey searing his throat. "How did you know to–" he said.

"The bee keeper sent us," the baroness said, softly.

"He's here?"

"He is back in the village," the colonel said, "but he had a hunch you'd need a little help. Don't know how he does it, really. Remarkable mind. And then there's his brother, don't you know. Best of the best. Good man. A great loss for the empire. Still, life marches on and all that, what?"

"What?"

"What?" the colonel said, sounding confused.

Smith shook his head. He thought of the bee keeper. He had gone to see Adler, Smith realised. The bee keeper had once been romantically linked with her… and, before he tended to bees, he was known as the greatest detective who had ever lived. Smith sent a silent thank-you his way.

Then: "You shouldn't have gotten involved," he said. "This is too dangerous."

"More dangerous than retirement?" the colonel said. "Pfah, old man! This is the most fun I've had in ages!"

"They will come after you–"

"In the village? Let them try."

Beside him, the baroness smiled. "This is a shadow war," she said, softly. "They will not attempt a public attack. No, we'll be fine, Smith. But you…"

"I have to leave England. I have to disappear."

No one replied. Smith watched the road. They were following the course of the river, he realised. Heading to Limehouse... heading to the docks. "What about the boy?" he said.

"He will be looked after," the baroness said.

"Twist?" Smith said, turning to him.

"Sir? Yes, sir?"

"Thank you," Smith said, and the boy smiled, the simple, innocent expression transforming his face. Smith turned back, rested his head against the seat, and closed his eyes.


Limehouse, at night. A silver moon hung in a dark sky. Gulls cried over the docks. Smith, dropped in a darkened street, one shadow amongst many – the baruch-landau, with a belch of steam and M.'s final, deranged cackle, disappeared, leaving him alone.

A narrow street, Smith standing still. The night air full of tar and salt and incense, roast pork, wood smoke, soy and garlic – in the distance, the smell of sheesha pipes.

The sound of light footsteps – he turned, a small white figure, moving, jerkily, towards him. A child, coming closer – pale skin, dark hair, large eyes, dressed in a boy's clothes–

The boy stopped before Smith. Something made Smith shiver. There was something unnatural about the boy, but he could not, for a moment, say what it was. Merely a sense of *alienness*, a wrongness that made every aspect of Smith tense, and want to reach for a weapon.

They boy looked up at him with pale, colourless eyes. "Do you believe in God?" he said. He had a strange, lilting, high-pitched voice. "Do you believe in second chances, Smith?"

117

Smith stood very still. He looked at the boy, and gradually details revealed themselves: the pale white skin was not skin at all, but ivory, and the black hair did not grow naturally, it had been planted, into a scalp that wasn't at all human.

The boy was an automaton.

A rare, expensive automaton, of a craftsmanship he had never seen before. There was the faint sound of clockwork, whirring. He did not know how to answer the boy's question.

"We used to come here," he said, surprising himself. The automaton stared at him with unseeing eyes. "We had a pre-agreed rendezvous point, in case of trouble. We would meet here, in Limehouse, where we could get a boat, out of the country. We never did run away... but we'd meet here, sometimes, in between foreign wars and assassinations and intrigue, and share a night together, seldom more than that. It was enough. We completed each other. You wouldn't–"

But the automaton-boy merely stared at him and repeated the words, like a recording, about God and second chances, and then reached a pale ivory hand to Smith and took his hand and said, "Come with me."

"Who sent you?" Smith said, but it was with a kind of hopeless impossibility in his voice: he felt as if reality itself was slipping away from him, and the night had suddenly contracted about him like a bubble, and he could not get out.

The boy didn't answer. He led, and Smith followed. They went down narrow streets and alleyways, hugging the shadows, until they came to a sewer hole in the ground. The boy, letting go of Smith's hand, briefly turned his head and looked at him, his vacant eyes never blinking. Was it sorrow in those eyes? What was it that the diminutive machine was trying to tell him? Not speaking, the boy stepped lightly over the sewer hole and fell down, noiselessly.

"Down the rabbit hole…" Smith murmured. He knew this was insane. And yet… he had been a professional long enough to recognise what was happening. He did not follow blindly. A player had made contact with him. The boy's approaching him had been, in the code of the Great Game, that player asking for a rendezvous.

Moreover. The same player had given him plenty of information. Sending out the curious little automaton had been enough, and now the hole…

Smith was curious. For all the clues added up to something fantastical, and to a player he had thought eliminated. "Curiouser and curiouser," he said, smiling faintly, and then jumped down the hole, following the strange little automaton.

His fall was broken by a mattress that had been laid down there, probably long ago. Smith found himself in a disused sewer of some sort, space opening around him – there were bottles down there and mattresses and clothes and shoes, driftwood and bleached rodent skeletons, and it smelled of the sea. He could not see the boy. Something moved, in the corner of his eye. He turned.

Something vast and alien, sluggishly moving, an insectoid body, like a giant centipede, feelers extended–

A being like nothing of the Earth–

And yet it did not feel *alive*, organic–

He could only see its shadow, moving–

"I thought you were dead," he said.

"Retired," a voice said, and then laughed, and Smith found himself shivering: it was the laughter of something insane. "For a while, Mr Smith."

The automaton, the underground lair, the question the boy had echoed to Smith, on behalf of its master. Hints and clues adding up...

"The Bookman," Smith said, and that giant, alien body moved, slithering close, and cold, metal feelers touched his forehead, lightly, like a benediction or a kiss.

"I can bring her back," the Bookman said.

# PART II
## *On Her Majesty's Secret Service*

# EIGHTEEN

*Aksum, Abyssinia.*
The black airship glided silently over the mountainous terrain, all but invisible.

They had come by steam ship, through Suez into the Red Sea. The steam ship waited for them. The British government would deny all knowledge in the event of their capture.

But Lucy Westenra did not intend to be captured.

She stood on the deck of the airship, the cold air running through her short hair. Looking down, she saw few lights. They would not be expecting an attack.

The city of Aksum, ancient, weathered, silent now, in the depth of night.

Lucy signalled to her team. They wore dark clothing, and the two Europeans had blackened their faces. She had assembled the team herself, each one hand-picked. Two Gurkhas; a Zulu warrior whose father had fought with Shaka as a young man, but who had chosen a different path for himself; a Scot; young Bosie, Lord Alfred Douglas to the society papers back home: they were her core team. The others were regular army. She knew only half of them by name. All men. Lucy Westenra the only woman amongst them, and their commander.

Their objective: capture the Church of Our Lady Mary of Zion. Retrieve the item, at all costs.

Mycroft's words still echoing in her ears: *We are on the cusp of war. Ancient artefacts are awakening. Do not come back without the item.*

Lucy Westenra. Preferred weapon: the twin guns usually on her hips. Age: in her mid-twenties. Rank: major in the British Army. Hair: black and short. Eyes: blue. Training: the best the Bureau had to offer. Licence to kill? You've got to be kidding.

Two fingers up. Giving a silent command.

*Descend.*

They followed her, would follow her anywhere. The airship hovered above the building. All was silent down below. Almost too quiet, she thought, uneasily.

They rappelled.

Like ghosts they floated down onto the church. A square boxy building, a tall fence around it. They landed on the roof and kept going.

*What is the nature of the object, sir?* She had asked.

*We do not know, exactly.*

Which was no answer at all.

*A box*, Mycroft had told her, unwillingly, it seemed. *An… An ark, of sorts. It may have once been plated with gold, and may be still. Retrieve it, Westenra. Or die trying.*

And she had said, *Sir, yes, sir.*

Signal again, and the windows to the church burst inwards as her men broke through. A shower of painted glass, a scream in the distance. She followed, landing on her feet at a crouch; rose with a gun in her hand.

"Light," she whispered.

Bangizwe, beside her. The chemical stench of an artificial flame, burning, lighting up the place. He grinned at her.

"Through there!"

Behind the dais, hidden…

A metal door, locked shut. Shouts outside. Suddenly, breaking the night like glass: the sound of gunfire.

"Cover me!"

Her men were already surrounding the altar, a protective shield. Lucy took out the device Mycroft had given her. Aimed it at the door. It emitted a high-pitched scream, flashed. *It is a frequency scanner*, he had told her, and she had said, *Sir?*

Mycroft had shaken his head and said, *Never mind that. Just… bring it back.*

Footsteps outside the church, the sound of running. In the chemical light her men's faces looked haunted, tense. The sound of rifle shots. Bangizwe and Bosie, at her signal, moved silently towards the entrance, covering it. The device hummed and beeped one last time. The metal door made a sound, as if a vast lock was slowly moving, opening itself.

"Move!"

She kicked the door. It opened. She went through–

And dropped. There was no floor under her feet.

Total darkness, a rush of hot air, motion… She was falling, falling down a wide shaft.

A moment of panic…

Then she raised her hand and fired the grapple gun–

Rope shooting upwards, the hook catching–

She felt the pull, held on as it broke her fall, hard.

"Light!"

A flare, dropping. The sounds of a gunfight above. The church was heavily defended. She hoped her men would be all right. Had to count on them to be. The flare fell, illuminating a long metal tube. It fell past her and continued to drop. She pressed the lever on the gun, going down, following the light–

Down into a sunless sea.

Or so it seemed. She landed, left the rope hanging. She was standing on a vast dark metal disc, she realised. The flare, at her feet, was consuming itself. A dark mirror, her thousand identical images stared back at her all around. She took a step forward–

The disc tilted. She slid, cursed – turned and fired, twice, ropes going off until they found walls, too far apart, but it held her, pulled her up – the disc balanced again, below.

Cursing Mycroft now, she remained there, suspended. Another flare falling down – a doorway in the distance, illuminated, gold and silver images of flying discs, giant lizards, things that looked like rays of light, destroying buildings. She commanded herself to let go...

The disc was tilting again as soon as she hit it but this time she was ready, running – circling for a moment the centre of gravity so it balanced and then she sprinted towards the distant doorway, the disc tilting, threatening to drop her into – what, exactly, she didn't want to know.

Gunfire above, someone, possibly the Scot, screaming in pain. The sound tore through the air and her concentration. She almost slipped–

But made it – the doorway too high up now but she *jumped*–

*I want you to train with someone*, Mycroft had told her. It was a year after she had been recruited.

*Who*? She had said.

*His name is Ebenezer. Ebenezer Long.*

She knew him as Master Long. He had taught her *Qinggong*: the Ability of Lightness.

Or tried to.

Fired again, the hook catching, the rope pulling her – it was impossible to achieve true Qinggong any more, she had found out, not without the strange, lizard-made artefact that had granted its strange powers...

So one had to fake it.

She made it to the doorway and crashed into metal that opened and she rolled, safe inside–

And stopped on the edge of a pool of dark water.

There!

It stood in a small rise above the water, in the middle of that perfect pool. The water was dark, still. She raised a foot to step into it–

Then changed her mind, pulled out a penny coin. The portrait of the Queen stared back at her mournfully from lizardine eyes. Lucy dropped it into the water–

Which hissed, like an angry living thing. Bubbles rose, and foam, and Lucy knew the coin was gone, digested by the acid.

She cursed Mycroft again. Stared at the device, just sitting there: a dark dull ark; it didn't look like much.

Too far to reach. She pulled the small device out again. The scanner, whatever it was it scanned for. Pressed a button.

The thing hummed, beeped, sounding peeved. Lights began to glow across the room, like a storm of electrical charges. The colour of the water changed, reacting in turn to the light. A small lightning storm formed on the water, moving. Gradually growing.

*That* didn't look good.

And the ark was humming now, and images were coming out of it, like a projection out of a camera obscura, though more real, and detailed, three-dimensional and frightening–

Images of spindly towers, cities vast beyond compare, of discs shooting through a sky filled with more stars than she had ever seen, a vast dark ship, its belly opening – then she saw things like vast spiders, dropping down, landing on a landscape that was dark and mountainous and… familiar–

The gunfire outside was very faint now. The device in her hand hummed, shrieked, and exploded. She threw it away a moment before it did but still felt the hot shards, stinging her arm, and cried out–

And voices came pouring out of the ark, strange and alien and *silent* – they were voices of the mind. A babble of cries and terse commands, translating themselves into her own language, somehow, though they made no sense:

*Coordinates established–*

*Contact made. Biological signature consistent with previous manifestations–*

*Initiate absorption protocols yes no?*

*Quarantine recommended–*

*Data-gathering agent in place–*

It sounded to her like an argument, or a meeting of some sort, in which two or more sides were debating a course of action.

"Data-gathering agent in place"? That, somehow, did not sound good.

The electrical storm was growing stronger, wilder. The acid, too, was reacting to it, hissing. And there was gunfire above. She had to get out. Had to leave–

She aimed the grapple gun, fired. It hit the ark. With no time to change her mind she jerked it, violently, towards her.

The ark fell into the acid. Lucy pulled. The voices silenced, then–

*Send expeditionary force yes no?*

*Temporary engagement authorised.*

She pulled. The ark seemed to fall apart as she did–

It came and landed at her feet, its sides dropping away–

She cursed, knelt to look–

Inside the box, a strange device, metal-like yet light – a statue, in the shape of a royal lizard. She lifted it up – it was warm. She turned from that room. Ran back – out through the doorway, jumped over the disc, ran as it tilted, found the rope, began to pull herself, one-handed, up the chute–

Sweating, her body shaking with adrenaline – a burn on her hand, she hadn't even noticed – from the acid. Cursing Mycroft, the strange lizardine statue in her hand, seeming to whisper alien words directly in her mind...

She reached the top. Hands pulled her up.

"Major, we can't hold them much longer!"

"Take this!"

She handed the device to Bangizwe.

"Major, is that a–?"

"Not now!"

She scanned the situation.

The church, the space no longer dark, flares and tracer bullets casting manic, frightening twilight over the sacred area–

And her team were outnumbered.

Where had they come from?

Warriors everywhere, with guns and blades. Surrounding them. Blocking the way.

"You will never get out alive!"

An elderly voice, carrying authority. She looked over to the others–

A man in a white robe, holding a stave in his hand. The warriors parted to let him through. His eyes were deep and dark, his face lined. The look in his eyes disturbed her.

It was a look, she realised, of compassion.

"I don't want to harm you!" Lucy shouted. She felt unsettled. "Step away and let us leave!"

"You don't know what you're doing," the man said, with gravity. "The ark is holy–"

"You and I both know–"

A hiss of static, a voice on her Tesla communicator–

"Major!"

"What?"

"We're under attack! There are... There are *things* outside! They just materialised, out of nowhere! Major, please–!"

Static. Outside, the sound of giant – footsteps? The sound of an explosion, then another, and another, as if the whole city of Aksum was being destroyed, all at once.

She grabbed the device back from Bangizwe. It felt alive in her hands. She raised it in the air. "We have it," she told the man in the white robe. "Let us pass or I'll destroy it!"

A hush, the enemy warriors taking a step back in unison. The old man, alone, remained standing. "Fool," he said, softly. "For now you have awakened their wrath..."

"Whose?" she said.

"Those who will be as gods," the old man said. He nodded his head, once, with finality. His eyes were full of sadness.

Lucy didn't know what he meant, but had a sinking feeling she would soon find out.

The old man signalled to his own people. And, like that, they vanished, disappearing to the outside, moving like shadows, silently and quickly.

Lucy didn't have time to breathe with relief. "Up," she ordered.

She and her men climbed.

Through broken windows into a night made light as day...

Up on the roof of the church–

Looking, in disbelief, on a city in flame.


There were machines in the night.

Where they came from, Lucy didn't know. The machines were huge, as tall as towers. They moved upon the earth with the legs of spiders. Beams of light came out of their heads, criss-crossing Aksum.

The black airship hung, suspended, in the sky, unharmed. Below, the city was burning, the tripodian things moving above them while paying them little heed. As if not quite aware that, down below, people and buildings existed.

What had the voices said?

*Send expeditionary force yes no?*

*Temporary engagement authorised.*

"I have what you're after!" she cried, into the night. She pulled out the device. It felt scaly, alien. "I have it! Stop!"

The machines seemed to sense her distress. One by one they turned, the lights moving across the burning city, converging at last on the rooftop of the church. Bosie beside her, hissing – "Major, what are you–?"

"Shut it, Douglas."

"We have to *leave*! Ma'am!"

"All of you, now! Board the airship. Await my command."

She felt Bosie simmer beside her, then accept the order.

She was only half-aware of her men dragging the wounded Scot up to the roof. Climbing the rope ladders. She knew she should follow. It was a miracle the airship itself was not harmed.

Where *had* the machines come from?

And what, she thought uneasily, was the exact nature of the device she was holding?

The tripods converged on her. On the church. And down below she thought, for just a moment, she could see a tall, stark figure, a stave in its hand, looking up at her and shaking its head mournfully.

Voices again. They were in her head. They were emanating from the device. It felt disturbing to hold it. Somehow reptilian, and repulsive – and alive.

*Children*, the voices said, dispassionately.

*Absorption?*

*Insufficient data.*

*Agent activated.*

*Old toys. Our children, who grew old never to grow up...*

The machines had stopped firing. A silence over the city.

"Take it!" Lucy cried at them. "Leave these people alone!"

*Intriguing...*

*Signal-booster, obsolete. A lost ship, from so long ago?*

*It is possible.*

The machines stopped, as one. A sudden, overwhelming sense: they had lost interest in her, were looking upwards, at the skies.

*Lunar companion?*

*Fourth world.*

*Seen enough.*

*Absorb yes no?*

*Decision deferred.*

*Temporary quarantine recommended.*

*Seconded.*

"Major, get up here! *Now!*"

But she couldn't move. As if the lizardine device was pulling at her, robbing her of the will to move, to act. She saw, with more than human eyes. A vast disc, the size of a city, silent and dark, materialising overhead. Or perhaps it had been there all along. The machines, seeming to fade – as though absorbed, somehow, by the greater device, that impossible disc, which then, in turn, faded too and, like a dream, was gone.

*"Get up here!"*

Suddenly she was jolted into movement. She climbed up, her heart beating fast, the entire city silent below her. It felt as though she was climbing a dark and lonely well, pulling herself up all the while, and up there was a light, was the moon, if only she could keep going she would reach it. Then hands grabbed her and pulled her roughly and she fell, and landed on the deck of the airship, the device still cradled in her hands. She was breathing heavily. "Get us out of here," she said.

She closed her eyes. In the darkness vast discs hovered, hidden on the far side of the moon. A sense of danger, fear – excitement. The airship, untethered, gathered speed.

"Major?"

She took a deep breath. Opened her eyes. Rose to her feet.

"Report," she said.

She stood by the railings and watched the night, the burning city left behind. Listening to the report: one dead, three wounded, and she would let the grief come later, when she was alone. For now she had to command, and the mission was not yet over. The airship sailed towards the Red Sea, and the waiting steamer. Lucy hoped the device had been worth it, all the dead and the wounded, on their side and on that of the church's mysterious protectors, and of the people of the city of Aksum who died that night. *We are on the cusp of war*, Mycroft had told her. She didn't know what war he was talking about – but she had the sense that the fat man had been wrong.

The war had already started.

# NINETEEN

"Westenra."

The Bureau, London: the abandoned underground station that was Xirdal Zephyrin's laboratory.

"*Magnifique*! Incredible! *Erstaunlich*!" The scientist was bent over the controls of various machines. Beyond them, behind a glass window, sat the object. It looked like a Buddha, the statues she had grown used to during her time with the Shaolin. A lizardine Buddha... It was disconcerting. Above it hovered a Tesla probe, and circular lightning jumped between the probe and the device. Lucy couldn't watch. She averted her eyes.

"Come with me," the fat man said.

She followed gratefully. They left Zephyrin's lab behind them. "You did well," the fat man said. She watched him. Knew he did not like to trouble himself away from his armchair at the Diogenes. He was sweating with the underground heat and the sweat formed rivulets that ran down his fleshy jowls. "The game," the fat man said, "as my brother would have said, is afoot." He grinned, suddenly and viciously. "The Great Game," he said. "The only game worth playing."

Lucy thought of the tripodian machines, destroying a city... casually, the way a boy might crush a nest of ants. It may not, it occurred to her, seem like a game to the ants.

"Sir," she said. Waiting. The fat man nodded. Wiped the sweat from his face, gently, almost fastidiously, with a handkerchief that had his initials, MH, embroidered on them by some long-gone hand. "I am awaiting a messenger," he said.

"Sir?"

"Six months ago I played a pawn," Mycroft said. "Not sure whether I was sacrificing a piece or making a play on the king."

He must have been in conference with the Mechanical Turk earlier, she thought. Mycroft always went for the chess metaphors after speaking to the old machine.

"And?" she said. "Which was it?"

The fat man's eyes shone. "I don't know," he said, "but I hope for the latter."

"You hope?"

"I need you to pick up a message," the fat man said. "The message is the messenger. Take your team. Secure me my prize, at all costs." He waved his hand, suddenly dismissing her; his mind wandering far, to grapple with games, and kings, and machines. "Berlyne will brief you on the rest."

"His name's Stoker," Berlyne said. He stared mournfully at a handkerchief, as though contemplating blowing his nose again. Lucy devoutly wished him not to. Not again. "Abraham Stoker."

"A Bureau operative?"

But Berlyne shook his head. "It was deemed too dangerous," he said. "Mycroft recruited... from outside."

Lucy stared at him. "A civilian?"

Berlyne looked defensive. "He was given as much

136

training as we could, in the allotted time. The man's a theatrical manager, for God's sake."

"How much training?"

Berlyne shrugged. "Three weeks," he admitted.

"But that's insane!"

"A trained agent would have been picked up. Besides, he… There were reasons why he was chosen."

"What reasons?"

But Berlyne was unable, or unwilling, to answer.

"Where did you send him?" Lucy said.

Berlyne blew his nose. Lucy winced. "The Carpathians," Berlyne whispered.

"*Transylvania*?"

"Austro-Hungary," Berlyne said.

"What's there?"

"Mountains. Castles. Dancing bears. How should I know? I've never been. Oh, my cold…"

"Just give me the dossier," Lucy said.

"There isn't one." Berlyne stared at her – and suddenly his eyes were cold, and hard. "Besides you, me, and Mycroft, no one knows Stoker even exists."

"What about Fogg?"

"Fogg is *not* cleared for this! Do you understand?"

Their eyes locked. After a moment, Lucy nodded. She understood, perfectly.

"Just give me the details, then," she said.


But details were sparse. The Bureau had lost contact with Stoker just before he had reached a small town called Brasov, in the Carpathian Mountains. Then, five and a half months later, a desperate signal over a pre-established frequency. Then a distress signal, and a second frequency that corresponded to an unregistered airship.

"It's a waiting game," Berlyne told her. "He could be here any day. Or never. There are too many ifs. If he makes it. If he managed to escape. He has to be guarded and his knowledge retrieved."

"Why me?"

"You're young. Mycroft trusts you—"

Which was to say, he trusted everyone else not at all.

Those weeks had been the hardest of Lucy's life. The corridors of the Bureau were muted, the cipher room closed shut. Mycroft sat alone in his office, seeing no one. Fogg, filled with self-importance, ran the Bureau in his stead. Then, one day, Mycroft came for her.

She had been living in Soho, in a small apartment, in a building shared with artists who doubled as counterfeiters, a lone Russian émigré who wrote political tracts in his room, and an Indian landlady who sang, come evening, at the Savoy. Lucy was unremarked there, hidden in plain sight. Waiting, for a mission that never seemed to come.

She was walking down Gerrard Street when she felt rather than saw the black baruch-landau drawing near. The door opened. Mycroft's voice said, "Get in."

She had climbed inside and sat across from him. The fat man looked tired, worn. For the first time since she had known him, when he had recruited her, he looked old. It frightened her.

"One of my agents," he said, "has died. I have just had word."

*My* agents. She noted that, frowned. Mycroft saw her, smiled thinly. "As you may have gathered by now, Ms Westenra," he said, "we are no longer operating on Bureau time. You are unsanctioned. So was my other agent." He sighed. "Alice," he said, almost reluctantly. "Her name was Alice."

Lucy had heard the name. A legend in the service. A rare woman in this world of spies. Nothing had been heard from her in years. She found her voice. "What did she do for you?" she said.

"I sent her to the East," Mycroft said. "Siam. Following a path even I do not yet understand. Someone – something – killed her last night. I have just received word."

His voice was quiet, introverted. A cold gripped her and she didn't know why. Later, had she analysed it, she would have said it was self-reflection on the fat man's part – as if he already knew he would be next.

"What's in Siam?" she said.

"A collecting point," Mycroft said. "There is one in Jerusalem, the other in Bangkok. Siam is independent. Jerusalem belongs to the Ottomans. Both are outside of British jurisdiction. I have few eyes there. Alice was tracking the network for me. Trying to map its points. But something got to her first."

"The opposition?" Lucy said, and a shadow crossed Mycroft's face, like a premonition, and he said, "No. At least, I don't think so." He waved his hand. "That is not your concern," he said. "We are playing the long game, the Great Game, the only game that matters. It is a game that began centuries ago, when Vespucci had awoken the Calibans, there on that cursed island, and brought them back. It began with them awakening, and taking over the throne, here, and building an empire. A war."

He fell silent. Lucy said, "Those things I saw, in Aksum."

"Remember the words," Mycroft said.

She didn't need to ask which ones. They had gone over everything, over and over, in the interrogation room at Ham Common, for hours at a time, and still Mycroft wasn't satisfied. Over and over he returned to two things:

*Quarantine recommended–*
*Data-gathering agent in place–*

"Ninety-three," he said. "I had handled the Emerald Buddha Affair badly. A gate had been opened. And something had slipped through."

She didn't know what he meant. Something to do with the Quiet Council, and Vespuccia... but the words, when he spoke, filled her with a nameless dread.

"They were not human," she said – whispered. "They couldn't be."

"Our masters' past is returning to haunt us," he said, and then, with a sliver of a smile, as of the old Mycroft, "or, rather, our masters' future..."

She didn't know what he meant.

"If something were to happen to me," Mycroft said – she had wanted to protest, but he silenced her. "If something were to happen to me, I have put certain precautions in place. Certain agents have been... put in reserve, shall we say. The old and the new..." and he smiled, looking at her. "You must get hold of the Stoker information," he told her. "At all costs. Off the books, non-Bureau sanctioned. Were I to die, there is still Smith... if he is not too old." Here he smiled again. "For you, however, I have made a different precaution."

The baruch-landau had stopped. "Come," Mycroft said. She looked at him, a query in her eyes. The doors opened.

Lucy held her breath.

*The Royal Palace?*

And a liveried man standing outside, saying, "Her Majesty, the Queen, is expecting you."

140

# TWENTY

The Royal Palace rose out of the swamps here, in the heart of the capital, a metal pyramid of stark, bright green, made of the lizards' strange, unearthly metal. Flies buzzed in the air, which was hot, humid, as if they had been transported, somehow, into another country, another continent. Rock pools and tiny streams, tall trees, the Royal Gardens, but they had come through a back gate and driven in and were parked directly outside an entrance to the palace, a place for servants, perhaps, or – from the smells of cooking emanating into the air – the Royal kitchens.

"Follow me."

Lucy followed Mycroft following the liveried man. In through the back entrance, a bustle of movement, steam belching through half-opened doors, the smell of cooking and the wail of machinery, worn carpets, deeper into the palace where it became quieter and the smell changed and finally there was no sound at all and through open windows she could see the moon, the shadow of an airship crossing over it, slowly, for just a moment creating the illusion that it was *on* the moon.

Then they came to a set of unremarkable doors and the servant pushed them open and stood to one side and said, "Her Majesty, Queen Victoria," and Mycroft pushed past him, without speaking, and entered the room, and Lucy Westenra followed, and the doors closed behind them without sound.

It was a pleasant room, sparsely furnished. Gaslight illuminated armchairs in deep red velvet, a bookcase with the works, in bound leather, upon it of Dickens and Collins and Drood, another of the Brontës, yet another of Lovelace's *Encyclopedia of Calculating Machines, in Seven Volumes*, and her *Who's Who of Mechanicals*, and Darwin's banned *On the Origins of Lizards*, and much else besides; and the moon through the windows, with its silver light, the airship passing beyond it and disappearing; and a figure sitting by the window, in a profile known to Lucy from so many coins and stamps and her mother's china plates, collected with such love, for every Royal event, and she did not know what to say.

The Queen rose from where she was sitting and turned to them. Her long, thin, forked tongue hissed out, tasting the air. Her eyes were large and yellow, showing age. Her tail tapped against the floor, as though in thought. "Mycroft," the Queen said. Her voice was surprisingly deep, and warm. "It took you long enough."

"This is the young agent," Mycroft told her. The Queen nodded, turned to Lucy. "Your... Your Highness," Lucy mumbled, trying to curtsey. The Queen waved a meaty arm. Lucy had rarely encountered one of the royal lizards, Les Lézards: she had not realised how powerful their arms were. "Do stand up straight," the Queen said. Her head turned, to Mycroft – "This is the one? Westenra?"

"She is the one who brought back the device," Mycroft said.

"So young…" the Queen murmured. "They breed young, these days."

Mycroft shrugged.

"And that is what you had heard?" the Queen said, her head snapping back to Lucy.

"W-what?"

"A quarantine recommended? A data-gatherer in place?"

"I… Yes."

"The Bookman," the Queen said, and shuddered.

"The Bookman is destroyed," Mycroft said. But the Queen shook her head. "Something like it," she said. "A machine, to extract and store knowledge. While they decide our fate."

"Can we fight them?"

The Queen gave a short, bitter bark of laughter. "With what?" she said.

"Are there not weapons on Caliban's Island–"

"Fool!" the Queen said. "Weapons we have, but how much stronger would theirs be? No." She began to pace. "We need to convince them. We need to strike a balance. The probe in eighty-eight was a mistake."

"History moves past us," Mycroft said, and the Queen snorted. "*Our* history," she said, "returns to haunt us."

The Queen fell silent. She looked at Mycroft and he looked back and Lucy, looking at them both, felt fear engulf her, for their look spoke of a shared, intimate, powerful knowledge, the palpable knowledge of an end.

"No…" she whispered, and didn't know why. "You!" the Queen barked. "When the time comes, you will return here. Take this."

The Queen removed a ring from her finger. It was a

strange, smooth metal ring, of the same green metal that, it was said, was brought by Les Lézards back from Caliban's Island, from the very ship with which – so forbidden rumours told – they had once travelled through space. "When the time comes, this will give you access."

"Your Majesty–"

"Go," the Queen said. And, to Mycroft, in parting – "We will not meet again."

And, or had Lucy merely imagined it, did the Queen whisper, as though to herself, *Not in this life*?


And so, Lucy waited.

The days passed, uneasily.

The Bureau was closed to her. There was no sign of Harker – the agent she was supposed to extract. She pictured him captured, tortured, his secrets extracted. What knowledge was he sent to find? How would he get away? The waiting lay heavily on her. And Mycroft, sitting at his club, seeing no one. Thinking. Trying to unravel a mystery, trusting no one–

Then came the day there was a knock on the door.

It was an impatient, authoritative knock. "Open up!"

She was already in motion, the gun in her hand. Edged to the door, nerves frayed. "Who is it?"

One word, travelling like a chill through the keyhole. "Fogg."

She opened the door with one hand, kept the gun in the other. But Fogg was alone.

"Oh, do put it down, Westenra," he said, marching in. He shut the door behind him.

"What do you want?" Lucy said.

Fogg said, "I need to know what job you're doing for Mycroft."

Lucy, taken aback, though she should have suspected something like this. "I'm not doing a job for Mycroft."

"Don't lie to me!" Fogg glared at her. Tall and thin and pale, he would have made a good parish priest, or a politician... Or a mortician, Lucy thought, suppressing a shudder.

"What's going on, Fogg?" she said, trying to keep her voice cool, calm. Trying to give him nothing. "I'm in between missions."

"Are you?" Fogg said. "Are you, now, Westenra?"

"Tell me what you want," she said.

"The fat man's gone crazy," Fogg said. He waved his hands in the air, exasperated. "He sees no one! He hides at the Diogenes Club and won't come out. Almost as though he's afraid to step outside. Don't think I am a fool, Westenra. I am left running the Bureau while the fat man sits and eats and thinks who knows what. I'm in charge! And yet I get the feeling I am not. Agents missing, files disappearing, a silence so profound it is a voice unto itself. Tell me what you know."

"But I don't."

Fogg glared about the room. Nothing to see. "This is how you live?"

"On the salary you pay me?"

Fogg snorted. "We pay you handsomely enough," he said, "to sit around and do nothing. Tell me about your last mission."

"My last mission?"

"I know he sent you! I've tracked down transfer orders, the commandeering of a steamer, and one of Mycroft's damned black airships he likes to use so much. Where did he send you?"

"Nowhere," Lucy said.

Fogg's face grew red at this, and when he spoke next his voice was low, and menacing. "Sooner or later," he said, "the fat man will be gone, and I will be in charge. Don't make a big mistake, Westenra. Don't make me an enemy."

Lucy stared at him, the gun by her side. "When the time comes," Fogg said, whispering, "don't say I didn't give you a chance."

He waited. Lucy looked at him. Then, regretfully, she shook her head and said, "I don't know anything."

Fogg nodded. There seemed a world of meaning in that simple gesture, more frightening, somehow, than when he was in motion, when he was shouting. He was very still.

"Very well, Miss Westenra," he said, at last, and his cold, wet eyes surveyed her, the way a shark might look at a diver, sinking fast. "Very, very well."

And, without speaking again, he turned on his heels and marched out, shutting the door, quietly, behind him as he left.

Lucy let out a shuddering breath. She had just made an enemy… She wondered if she could have handled it better.

She hoped Mycroft knew what he was doing.

And this could have been, if only for a while, the end of it.

Only Lucy went and spoiled it by deciding to shadow Fogg.

Soho in the twilight… the smell of opium, spilt beer, lit pipes, the sound of an Edison record playing through an open window, Gilbert and Sullivan's *Martian Odyssey*. Fishmongers closing for the day, the smell of fish in the air, on the ground pools of melted ice, fish scales floating there like compass needles. The moon through the buildings, a scimitar sword. Fogg walking ahead with long easy strides, Lucy in the shadows, an unchaperoned lady but then this *is* Soho and this is, almost, the new age, a new century. Somewhere in the distance Big Ben struck six and all the other clocks followed, a cacophony of gears and bells and echoes, birds flying up in black clouds, startled, a butcher selling sausages by candle light, the gas lamps coming into life, one by one – in the distance whale song, from the Thames.

A beggar boy hiding in the shadows, pale face, big haunted eyes, watching–

She scanned the street, saw his employer standing by an upturned drum, warming his hands on the fire. Fagin, she thought, and her hand itched for her gun.

But he was considered a Bureau asset, and thus untouchable.

The boy flashed her a quick smile – Twist, was it? – then she was past, trying to track Fogg, who seemed to have merged into the shadows.

Did he know she was following?

She waited, and presently saw his thin frame re-appear, heading for the Charing Cross Road.

She followed him, at a distance. Careful now. The sky was dark. A solitary mail ship went overhead, making no sound. Above the city's skyline the Babbage Tower rose, its beacon light flashing. Booksellers on the Charing Cross Road with open carts, trying to push on her, variously, Marx's latest political tract, *The Second Caliban Manifesto*, Mrs Beeton's autobiography, supposedly signed, *From Household Management to Running the Country: How I Became Prime Minister*, an old, stained copy of Verne's early novel, *Five Weeks in an Airship*, P.T. Barnum's memoir, *A Fool and His Money*–

The books became a dark cloud; they were everywhere; their dust choked the nostrils; there was no escaping them. She saw their sellers as enslaved ghouls, shackled to their charges, the books vampiric, sucking the life out of their handlers even as they sustained them, in their turn. Fogg turned left on the Charing Cross Road. She followed. A seller came at her from the left, unexpectedly. "Mr Dickens' *Reptilian House*, in three volumes!"

"You should never write a third volume," someone else said, nearby. She turned and saw a young man shaking his head, sadly, and she walked past as he and the seller entered a loud argument on the merits and demerits of such a thing.

Where was Fogg going?

Up the Charing Cross Road with the bookshops crowded, books spilling on the pavement, carriages passing, horse-driven, and baruch-landaus belching steam, up past St Giles Circus, and older bookshops opening now, antiquities specialists, and objects in the windows taken from ancient Egypt and Greece and Rome, the Middle Kingdom and Nippon, and she knew where Fogg was going, even if she didn't know why.

Then it came into sight and she paused, momentarily, taking it in as she always did:

The Lizardine Museum.

The treasure chest of an empire.

It was built of the same green, alien metal of the lizards. A dome rising high into the air, its own airship landing platform extended beside it. The dome seemed to shine in the night, a beacon. Huge statues rose up in the courtyard of the museum. Giant lizards, dwarfing the people still milling there, in the open air before the steps.

Henry VII, the first of the lizard-kings, a severe, weathered being: they had come back with Vespucci on his ill-fated journey and in one single night reality had changed, and the King and the Queen had disappeared, and Les Lézards were there in their stead.

Henry VII, they said, had never learned to speak English properly, and had used a machine, which translated his speech to the people. Then came another Henry, and this one was almost human, in manners and speech, and Les Lézards became integrated with their human hosts, and began to expand the reach of empire. Then came an Edward, and others, but the statue that dominated them all was that of the Great Elizabeth, the Lizard-Queen, Gloriana, under whom the empire grew and the island of Britain truly became the seat of a global and far-reaching empire, the greatest the world had ever seen.

Lucy stared up at Elizabeth's statue, the inhuman figure, sculpted in the same green metal, as alien as all the rest of them, and not for the first time she wondered what her world would have been like without the royal lizards: would it have been better, worse? Would it have been poorer?

And it occurred to her that, in a very real way, it didn't matter. History took paths and forks, crossing and recrossing, and yet the human lives lived within those brooks of time were the same. They were short, they suffered the same joys and sorrows, the same weakening of flesh and spirit, whether now or in the distant past, or in an equally distant, unimaginable future.

People didn't change. Only worlds did.

She followed Fogg, up the broad public stairs, into the building.

Worlds of antiquity, rooms full of loot...

The lizards, like their human subjects, had a passion for collecting. A huge open space under the dome and, to every side, and up and down stairs, rooms opened, rooms upon rooms offering, on display, all that centuries of conquest had to offer.

There! Egyptian mummies!

There! The Rosetta Stone!

There! Marble statues from the Parthenon!

There! Ashurbanipal's great library of cuneiform tablets! So many graves had been robbed to fill the museum, so many lands conquered, in blood and iron, and all their loot housed here, in the great museum, itself a mausoleum, a dragon's hoard, all to display, to the empire's subjects, its vast superiority, its utter control.

There was something humbling about that space, and yet, at the same time, something peaceful, soothing: the hush of a vast hall housing the past, like a church or a graveyard, and Lucy followed Fogg and only the sound of their feet on the ground could be heard – past dead Egyptian queens wrapped in bandages, past animal-headed deities and gold jewellery and ancient books, past the knick-knacks and bric-a-brac of Hans Sloane's collection of curiosities, the founding stone of the museum. Down marble stairs, away from the main hall, going underground. Lucy stuck to the shadows. Fogg marched ahead, oblivious. Through an *Employees Only* door, into a dusty warehouse, mysterious objects in crates, shelves upon shelves of ancient artefacts not yet catalogued or presented, the dead possessions of ancient dead cultures. Through another door and another flight of stairs. Down, down, underground. It was silent down there, nothing moving, nothing but dust.

Fogg disappeared.

In the darkness Lucy halted. Pressed herself against shelves. Where was he?

Where, in fact, were they?

Her eyes adjusted to the darkness. Faint light shone, from somewhere. She saw lizard-headed statues with the bodies of men, a scattering of strange coins with lizard heads on them, a script she couldn't read. Strange tapestries hanging from walls, showing reptilian warriors.

Thinking, I thought this place was a myth.

Footsteps in the dark. The sound of a heavy body, slithering. The gun was in her hand but she didn't know what good it would do.

A hiss in the darkness. "Fogg..." The voice made her shiver.

"Master," Fogg said, and the unseen voice laughed.

The room of Unnatural History, Lucy thought.

The room of apocrypha.

She had only ever heard the stories. And how had they managed to get down there, without tripping an alarm?

Fogg must have had access, somehow. And she had coat-tailed it, not knowing...

There had always been stories. Before Vespucci had awoken the Calibans. Before he returned with them, the race of royal lizards, Les Lézards, from that island in the Carib Sea where sand had turned to glass and where they had slept, so it was said, had slept for thousands of years...

But there were always rumours. That some of them had been upon the world, moving like shadows throughout history. Leaving strange objects in their wake. Rumours that the history of humanity and Les Lézards did not start with Vespucci, but went back, over millennia...

Foolish stories. Forbidden stories.

Just as the tale of this room, deep below the Lizardine Museum, where all such artefacts were carefully locked away...

She began to realise just how dangerous her being there really was.

And then thought – where else better to meet in secret?

And who, in fact, was Fogg meeting down there?

"Report!" that insidious, frightening voice ordered, there in the darkness. Lucy moved. She edged closer to her destination, the place the voices were coming from. Slowly, slowly... creeping like a mouse down there in the dusty depths.

There.

A small circle of wan light, Fogg standing taut–

Movement from the shadows–

She stifled a cry of horror, a deep-rooted fear, from childhood, rising up in her like bile–

An insect-like creature, gigantic and obscene.

Feelers moving, stroking, seeing–

A many-legged thing, like a centipede, and yet, somehow, not alive, a mechanical being–

Slithering across the floor of the abandoned warehouse–

Lucy felt faint, the gun almost sliding from her fingers–

Heard Fogg saying, "Master, I can't get the access I need, Mycroft is blocking me, I think he suspects–"

Lucy, thinking, I have to get out of here.

Thinking of rumours, stories, like nightmares that fade when you wake.

Two words. Something to scare children by.

*The Bookman*.

# TWENTY-ONE

"Hush!" said the Bookman.

Fogg said, "What?"

"Were you followed?"

Fogg, laughing: "By whom?"

Lucy pressed against the shelves. The gun would be useless, here, against that... that *thing*.

"I smell... *human*."

"Stop being so melodramatic."

"Report!" the Bookman barked. Fogg said, speaking calmly, "Mycroft won't let me near. He is running his own operation. He never trusted me."

"What do you know of this death in Bangkok? This Alice?"

"An old agent. Retired. To tell you the truth she had gone off the field long ago."

"Then what was she doing dead in Siam?" the Book-man roared.

"Working for Mycroft."

"On what?"

"The Babbage case."

"Babbage..." There was a snort, and a sound as of

jaws, locking and biting. "I should have killed him when I had the chance."

"Recruited him, you mean."

The Bookman laughed. It was a horrid sound, and Lucy suddenly realised that it was quite insane. She had to get out...

"What killed her?"

"A Bookman," Fogg said, and there was a terrible silence.

She couldn't stomach it any more. The silence lengthened, unnatural there in the Unnatural History Room.

Why wasn't the Bookman answering Fogg?

A slithering sound, so close... She froze, her heart beating fast.

"I sssssmell you..." a voice whispered. It was a cold voice, it made her shiver. "I know you're there..."

She waited, wanting to bolt, to run–

There was the sound of a crash from above and someone cursed and light came in and there were footsteps–

"Is anyone down there?"

A museum guard. He came down the stairs, shining a lamp around. It cast a pool of light amidst the shadows, and the faces of ancient lizards stared at her, from coins and tapestries and ancient clay tablets.

Was there another exit? She edged away, softly, softly. "Who's there?"

By the wall!

A small opening, an air vent. As quietly as she could she pulled the grille. It came off in her hands.

"It is I, Fogg."

"Oh, apologies, sir! You didn't half startle me!"

"Private business, James. But your diligence is duly noted."

A hiss in the dark, amused or angry she didn't know. "What was that, sir?"

"Just the wind, James. Just the wind."

She placed the grille on the floor and pushed through the opening, head first.

The hissing sound seemed to grow closer.

"Very well, sir." The young guard sounded nervous. "I shall leave you, then."

"You do that, James. You know it's not safe, down here."

"Sir?"

"Just a joke, James. Merely a joke."

The hissing, coming closer – a slithering sound–

She pushed through and found herself in a small crawlspace–

The sound like jaws, snapping shut, behind her. She almost screamed.

"What was that?"

"Relax, James," Fogg said, with a laugh.

"Strange things in this museum, sir," the guard said. "Strange happenings, and sounds at night. I don't mind telling you it makes some of us nervous."

"Maybe you have a ghost down here," Fogg said, and laughed again, the sound like a gunshot. Lucy scrambled to get away. The space led up, she saw. A drop chute of some sort. She needed things to hold on to.

A hiss behind her, a faint whisper, "I can smell you…"

"What was that?"

"Nothing!" Fogg said, losing his calm for the first time. "Rats," he said. "Go away, James, I have work to do."

"Sir. Yes, sir."

She felt something – the walls weren't even, she could grab hold–

She pulled herself up. Heard movement behind her but didn't dare turn to look. Pulling herself again, and finding the next protrusion out of rock or wood, and hauling herself up, one step by laborious step–

The sounds faded behind her, and then she was outside, emerging out of a drop chute a floor up, and it was quiet–

"What are you doing here, miss?"

The light hit her and she jumped, but it was only James, the guard, and she could have hugged him.

"This is a restricted area! My God, you gave me a fright!"

"Dr Fisher sent me," Lucy said, thinking quickly. "To fetch something from the, ah, warehouse."

"How did you get in here? Do you have a pass?"

"Wait," Lucy said. "Look, it's–"

She was close enough to the man now and she hated to do it but didn't have a choice.

"What–?"

Then he gurgled and she caught him as he fell, gently, and laid him on the cold stone floor. Then she ran.

It began to rain as she walked back to her lodgings. Her mind was awhirl with unanswered questions. Fogg, the mole in the Bureau. The Bookman – she had always thought it to be a person, or an organisation of people, all using a common name, a moniker. But the horror she had seen below the Lizardine Museum was no sort of human, it was an alien creature, not even alive – some sort of intelligent machine?

What had Mycroft told her? He had warned her, his words cryptic then. *We are on the cusp of war. Ancient artefacts are awakening…*

Could the thing called the Bookman be one of them?

And yet the Bookman had been active for years – for decades. Disguising explosives, cunningly, in books

– that had been his method. There had been the Martian probe case in eighty-eight, but since then nothing – as though the Bookman had disappeared, retired or died…

She had to talk to Mycroft. Had to warn him…

But Mycroft wouldn't see her. He was locked away at the Diogenes Club; he was seeing no one; he was absent from the Bureau; all lines of communication were down. Even Berlyne, when she had cornered him at last, refused to hear her out.

"You do your role," he told her, staring at her despondently from wet, red-rimmed eyes. Earlier when she had tried to talk to him he kept interrupting her, telling her about his flu. "Leave the fat man be. And stay the hell away from Fogg."

Did Mycroft know?

There was no sign of Harker. The fat man was gone, to all intents and purposes, and Fogg was running the Bureau.

She needed information, Lucy thought. She needed a line into the past.

And so, two days later, on a day when the sky was grey and a cold, chill wind blew through the streets, she boarded a train, and went, not to St Mary Mead, where the retirees of the service were rumoured to be housed, but to the place called Satis House, hoping that she could get the woman there to talk to her.

The train had stopped for five minutes at the station and Lucy was the only passenger to disembark. The small village of Satis-by-the-Sea was really nothing more than a high street, several shops, a pub, a tea room, a one-storey hotel that appeared to be permanently closed, a post office and the train station.

Dominating the view was the house. It perched over a cliff above the little village, a vast, crumbling edifice, its broken windows open to the wild wind of the sea. A lonely, snaking path led up to the house. Lucy had cream tea at the tea room, and chatted pleasantly with the proprietress, up to the point when the woman found out her objective. "You are going to see *her*?" she said.

"Why, is she not there any more?" Lucy said.

"Oh, she's there all right," the proprietress said. "If you'll excuse me—"

And she disappeared into the kitchen and did not come back.

Curiouser and curiouser, thought Lucy. She left money on the counter, seeing as the woman had disappeared. Then she went outside and began the long, cold walk up the hill.

The wind was cold; gulls screeched high above, diving over the dark waves. The air was filled with brine and tar, sea smells mixed, faintly, with gunpowder.

Gunpowder?

A shot rang out. Beside the trail Lucy was following, a branch exploded away from a tree, almost hitting her. She stopped, stood still.

A voice through a bullhorn, the speaker unseen. "Who the hell are you?"

Lucy carefully raised her arms. "Westenra!" she called out.

"What? Speak up!"

"Westenra," Lucy yelled. "It's me, damn it, Havisham!"

"Oh." The voice sounded mildly disappointed. "Well, move along, then, girl. Come on up."

"It's what I'm trying to do," Lucy muttered. She lowered her arms and continued up the path to the house.

No wonder the woman in the tea room disapproved.

She made it up there. Overgrown weeds, an apple tree with fruit around it, a sweet-and-sour smell of fermentation. A wrought-metal fence, the garden beyond. A stout oak door that stood in marked contrast to the rest of the house. Peeling paint, broken windows, a general air of disuse and disrepair.

"Havisham? Where the hell are you?"

A small, energetic figure appeared, as though from thin air.

The bushes, Lucy thought, and couldn't hide the ghost of a smile. Havisham's tradecraft was well known, even though that was not what she was primarily famed for. In their circles, at any rate...

"Lucy? Is that you?"

"It's me."

The other woman came and peered at her for a long moment. It was hard to tell her age. Fifty? Sixty? One of the old guard at the Bureau... She wore a man's hunting outfit, carried a gun with her, easily – she was used to it. "Come here," Miss Havisham said. They hugged. "It's been a long time," Lucy said.

"Too long," Miss Havisham agreed, sadly, it seemed to Lucy. She released her. "What brings you to Satis House? I didn't think you even knew where it is."

"I just looked at the map," Lucy said, "until I found the middle of nowhere."

Miss Havisham laughed. "Come on in," she said. "Tea?"

"Yes, please," Lucy said, with feeling.

• • • •

The inside of the house was a surprise.

The outside, Lucy saw, had been carefully cultivated. The inside…

The front room was a map of debris but, as Miss Havisham led her farther in, the house changed. The room they went into had carefully maintained windows overlooking the cliffs, at such an angle that they could not be seen from land. A fire was burning in the fireplace and the room was tastefully and expensively decorated. Rugs on the floor that must have come from the Ottoman Empire, sturdy bookshelves everywhere, books spilling out. The room was sunny, the furniture used and well maintained; the whole place had an air of comfortable domesticity to it.

"They think of me as the crazy old lady who lives in the ruined mansion," Miss Havisham said cheerfully. "Which helps. And there are enough alarms outside to warn me of anyone approaching. You never know, in our line of work."

"Quite," Lucy agreed. She watched Miss Havisham place a kettle over the fire and busy herself making tea. "How long has it been?" she asked.

She could feel Miss Havisham tense. "Who can remember," she said, quietly.

The post-eighty-eight fall-out.

The reason she was there.

But first, the tea.

They sat and sipped their drink and watched the sea outside the windows. *Miss Havisham is to be handled delicately*, she remembered the fat man saying, once. *Agents are replaceable, but archivists like her only come once in a lifetime.*

"How *is* Mycroft?" Miss Havisham said, as though reading her mind.

"Oh, very well," Lucy said, carefully. "He sends his regards."

"Good old Mycroft," Miss Havisham said. "What happened wasn't his fault. It was before your time, though, wasn't it, Westenra?"

"Yes. Mycroft…" She hesitated, picking her words carefully. "He sent me for a chat. We need… Some old material has recently come up. Routine. He thought you might be able to help."

"You know I could," Miss Havisham said. "The question is, should I?"

But Lucy knew Miss Havisham, the way she knew herself. For they were all operatives, all playing the Great Game. And once you played, you were never out. Only death put you out of the Great Game. What had someone said, long ago? She had heard the words from one of her instructors in the secret compound at Ham Common… *When everyone is dead the Great Game is finished. Not before.*

And so she waited, and sipped her tea, and didn't speak. And at last, the way she knew she would, Miss Havisham said, almost reluctantly it seemed, and yet unable not to say it, "What, exactly, has come up, Westenra?"

And still Lucy prevaricated; still she waited; until Miss Havisham, perhaps recognising in herself the need to speak, to delve into the past, to play, once more, the game, said, with the ghost of a smile and a sharp, yet almost fond, tone, "Well, Westenra?" Then Lucy began to speak; and even then she idled, she went around the subject; she took her own time.

"*Sonnets from the Portuguese*," she said, and waited, and watched Miss Havisham, whose head rose, and she looked out of the window with a far-distant look in her eyes.

"Elizabeth Barrett Browning…" she said. "Yes…"

161

Lucy waited, patient.

"A small, innocent volume of verse…" Miss Havisham said. Her voice had acquired a dreamy, sing-song attribute. "Oh, yes… it was to be placed with great ceremony on board the Martian probe. The ceremony took place in Richmond Park. It was dusk; Moriarty was there, he was Prime Minister at the time, yes, wasn't he, love? And the Prince Consort was there, and that old rascal Harry Flashman. All of London society, it seemed, had turned out for the event. Irene Adler, too, though she was but an inspector in those days. And the boy, of course… he came, too, but too late to save her."

Lucy waited, her heart beating faster. She was not supposed to know these things, she knew. But Miss Havisham was beyond rules and restrictions, now, and recollection for her was an act of living, like drawing breath or drinking water. Once started, she would not stop.

"We had watched the boy, hadn't we, love?" Miss Havisham murmured. Who was she talking to? Lucy wondered, recalling, somewhat uneasily, the rumours at the Bureau. Havisham and Mycroft, they had whispered.

"We watched him, ever so carefully. He was a handsome boy. Orphan. Less a name than a title. And he had a girl, he was in love. Her name, too, was Lucy. Did you know that?"

Lucy hadn't. But Miss Havisham was not stopping to check her reaction. She was speaking *through* Lucy, speaking to the fat man who had left her here, in this crumbling mansion, in Satis.

"A marine biologist. She worked with the whales in the Thames… Did you know they had followed Les Lézards here, on their voyage from Caliban's Island? We had wondered at the connection between them. Could the royal lizards somehow communicate with the whales? Were they their eyes and ears in the ocean? We could never prove anything… Some knowledge was beyond even us."

"Tell me about Lucy," Lucy said, patient, probing. "Tell me about the *Sonnets*."

"It was dusk and, before the spectators, the airship loomed. It was to carry the probe away with it, at the end of the ceremony. All the way to Caliban's Island, there to be launched into space. A big, dignified ceremony and the girl, Lucy, there to place, into the probe, ceremoniously, two objects. An Edison record filled with whale song… and that slim volume of poetry, *Sonnets from the Portuguese*."

Miss Havisham fell silent. Motes of dust danced in the sunlight coming through the window. "Books…" she said, so softly Lucy almost didn't hear her. "They had always been his choice. His little folly, we called it. The Bookman."

"The Bookman," Lucy said.

"Yes. For as the girl came to place the objects into the open belly of the probe, there was a terrible explosion. She died, instantly. The probe was destroyed. Unbeknown to us, it had been a dummy. The real probe was already on the island, prepared to launch…"

"You said there was a boy," Lucy said. She felt shaken. The explosion had been public knowledge, naturally – it would have been impossible to keep it quiet – but Miss Havisham spoke of it as if she had lived through it, though always one step removed.

"Orphan, yes. He tried to save her. Couldn't, of course. Which launched the whole sad affair."

"Tell me."

163

"Oh, it was one of Mycroft's less successful affairs," Miss Havisham said, with a small smile. "The boy was obviously being manipulated. His father was a Vespuccian, you know. And his mother, as we found out too late, could have been queen, if we still had human royalty."

"Excuse me?"

"When Les Lézards deposed the old, human monarchy, they didn't kill them," Miss Havisham said. "They transported them to Caliban's Island and bred them there. I am not sure why. I am not sure even they knew."

"And his mother—"

"Yes. She escaped – we suspected the Bookman's involvement, at the time. She was killed shortly after giving birth to the boy. Colonel Sebastian Moran, if you recall the name."

"'Tiger Jack' Moran?" Lucy said.

Miss Havisham nodded. "He worked for Moriarty," she said. "Never mind. The point is the boy's heritage was meaningless. The empire was on the brink of revolution, a lizard queen was bad enough, a human king would not have made things better."

"What happened to him?"

"He went to the island. He came back. We lost him in Oxford. There had been an explosion, deep under the Bodleian Library. The boy survived. So did a girl who called herself Lucy…"

"She was *alive*?"

"It was a mess," Miss Havisham said. "You see, we had suspected for some time that the Bookman was not exactly human. That he – it – was a product of lizardine technology, an artefact that had survived their crash on Earth. The theory was that he had been their librarian, of sorts. A servant. A machine for making copies of living things."

*A library of minds.*

Lucy's own mind shied away from the thought. That creature she saw below the Lizardine Museum. *There had been an explosion*, Miss Havisham had said. Lucy said, "What happened to the Bookman?"

Miss Havisham smiled dreamily. "That was the big question, wasn't it," she said. "He died, of course. In the explosion. But…"

"Yes?"

"Wouldn't a machine that made copies of beings," said Miss Havisham, "first of all make a few extra copies of *itself*?"

# PART III
## *The Two Deaths of Harry Houdini*

# TWENTY-TWO

The young man who stood, some nights earlier, on the other side of the planet, at the docks of the Long Island, in the territory of the Lenape, was himself contemplating the oddity of replication. There was something miraculous, he thought, in the act of human sexuality, in the way man and woman could get together to produce a new being, an entirely new, alien, mysterious life. An avid reader of the scientific papers – not to mention the somewhat less scientific, yet far more enthralling, tales of scientific romance – *romans scientifiques*, to give them their better known name – he had been fascinated, too, by the idea that it may be possible to produce identical copies of living human beings – even of dead ones, when it came to that.

The nineteenth century may be drawing to a close, he thought, yet what a century it had been! The greatest minds of many generations had seemed to erupt, all at once, across the world, to further humanity's understanding of the universe it had, somewhat reluctantly, occupied. Babbage! Freud! Jekyll! Frankenstein! Darwin! Moreau! The great Houdin, in Paris, AKA the Toymaker, from whom the boy Weiss had taken his professional name, which was Houdini. Scientists of the mind, of the body, of the laws of nature and the laws of history!

And yet, he reflected ruefully, his knowledge – actual, concrete knowledge – of asexual human replication was greater than most, having had cause, as it were, to experience the unpleasant thing at first hand.

But first, a concise history. The boy was in the nature of going over facts, summaries, all a part of his rather rigorous training.

Well then.

Code name: Houdini.
Birth name: Erich Weiss.
Place of birth: Budapest, the Austro-Hungarian Empire.
Father: Mayer Samuel Weiss, a rabbi.
Mother: Cecelia Weiss, née Steiner.
Family: five brothers, one sister.
Recruited to the "Cabinet Noir" in 1890, at the tender age of sixteen.
Specialities: escapes, disguises, locks of any kind.
Recruited by: Winnetou White-Feather, of the Apache.
Assignments: the boy was sent to the World's Vespuccian Exposition, in the city called Shikaakwa, or Chicagoland, during the ninety-three affair. He had been only an observer at the time.
Notes: the boy is a promising young agent — his recruiter, Winnetou, speaks highly of him. His cover as a travelling-show magician is promising, and his skills in the art of escapology remarkable indeed. Young, handsome and personable, the

only concern is due to a blank period two years after the White City Affair, when the boy went to spend a summer on the island of Roanoke...

Harry – he preferred Harry to Erich, had been using the name more and more now, until only his family still called him by his birth name – paced the docks. He waited for a ship but the ship was long in coming. He was leaving Vespuccia, that magnificent continent, his adoptive home, leaving behind him the tribes and the new cities, the vast open plains and a sky that seemed never to end, under which one could sleep, in the open air, as peaceful as a child...

He was nervous, excited. He was being entrusted with a great mission. After a tour of the continent earlier on, when he went from encampment to encampment and town to town, performing his magic show, under the moniker *The Master of Mystery!*, he was now ready for a new challenge. He was leaving Vespuccia, for the first time–

Had been summoned to the Council of Chiefs one day, weeks before, at the Black Hills, the Mo'ohta-vo'honnaeva in the language of the Cheyenne. Arriving late one night, with a silver moon shining over the hills like a watching eye, Houdini was met by his old mentor. "Winnetou," he had said, hugging him. The Apache warrior hugged him back, then said, gruffly, "You took your time."

"I came as soon as I received the summons," Harry said, without rancour. "And as fast."

"Come with me," Winnetou said.

Harry followed the other man into the camp. The Council was not often convened in full. The chiefs of the Nations met at different places, at different times. It was a very different form of rule, Harry thought, then the one in Europe, with its rigid monarchies and obsolete bloodlines. The Nations had welcomed the refugees from that continent, those who did not wish to live under lizardine rule, but there was no debate over who, exactly, was in charge. Yet the Council was troubled. There was the ever-present threat of the Lizardine Empire, while Chung Kuo, the Middle Kingdom, had recently showed dangerous signs that it was considering expansion for the first time in centuries. While on their own doorstep, so to speak, the Aztecs waited, in their strange pyramids and with their own designs on the land…

Harry was taken to the circle of the Council. President Sitting-Bull, smoking a pipe, looked older than he had in ninety-three, the last time Harry had seen him.

And all the major nations were represented that night. He saw familiar faces, old generals: Sioux and Cheyenne and Cherokee, Apache and Arapahoe and Navajo, Delaware and Shoshone, Mohawks and Iroquois and others, all sitting under the great silver moon, all turning to watch him as he came.

"The young magician," someone said. Someone else laughed. Harry felt his cheeks turn hot. He didn't let it bother him. Instead he smiled. "You wished to see me," he said.

"Cocky."

"Youth always is."

"Sit him down, Winnetou."

Without ceremony, Winnetou pressed Harry on the shoulder, pushing him down. He sat, cross-legged, before the chiefs. A great fire was burning, down to coals, on the ground, and the smoke rose, white like a flag, into the air.

"There's been… a situation."

"We need you to go on a bit of a journey."

"You won't be alone, of course."

"We're recalling most agents."

"You've been trained well. As well as can be."

"We want you to go to Europe. To the home of the lizardine race."

"Others are heading to Asia, Mexica, the South Seas–"

"We need to guard our interests–"

"The world is changing, boy. We do not intend to be caught unawares–"

He sat there, the conversation washing over him, overwhelming him. The chiefs, almost not looking at him directly, their words in the air. All to impart the importance of his mission on him. *This is why you are here.*

"Danger in the stars–"

"Old artefacts, awakening–"

"Go, boy. Winnetou will brief you."

A hand on his shoulder. Pulling him up. Smoke in his eyes, the stars, like the moon, bright above. Drums in the distance, the sound of chanting, the smell of burning tobacco–

"Come on."

Winnetou led him away, amidst the tents.


And now he was waiting at the docks, for a ship to take him, across the sea, to the island where Les Lézards ruled.

To find out…

What, exactly?

He remembered vividly the events of the World's Vespuccian Exposition, in ninety-three…

*The spinning wheel, which they now called a Ferris Wheel, after its inventor, moving against the starry night sky… Houdini* had been dressed as a fakir, his skin darkened by sun and cosmetics... performing magic there, in the avenues of the White City, illuminated by electric lights... Tesla himself had been there, lightning wreathing his body...

Houdini watching – the woman from France, the agent, he was told, of the Quiet Council... She was formidable.

Milady de Winter. Hunting a murderer in both cities, the Black and the White, in that place called Chicagoland... and hunting something else, also. A mysterious object, a lizardine artefact...

The Emerald Buddha. An object of mythical resonance. Discovered in the Gobi Desert, centuries before, a jade statue in the image of a royal lizard. Carried by a man. If he had a name Harry didn't know it. He was designated, simply, as the Man on the Mekong.

But he had come to Vespuccia, had crossed the sea, and come to the White City – supposedly to offer the statue to the highest bidder. But that had been a ruse...

The White City had been plunged into darkness. High overhead, on the axle of the Ferris Wheel, two tiny figures: the Man on the Mekong and Milady de Winter. And the wheel spun, faster and faster, until the space within it was distorted, and strange, alien stars had appeared...

The wide avenues of the White City were filled with screams... bodies fighting in the darkness to escape... There had been a terrible voice, filling the night, only it was not in the ears, it was in one's head... a cold, impersonal voice, speaking no language but directly into the mind itself, filling it with the horror of infinity.

And up there, on the wheel, a third figure, climbing – the killer de Winter had come to find, a man mutated and made grotesque by the power of the statue. That awful voice, speaking: Initiating target parameters. Stand by to receive. A struggle up there, and in the space beyond the wheel, that alien space,

174

*something moved...*

*The voice saying:* Gateway open. Coming through–

*A scuffle, and the killer flying into the space inside the wheel, the statue in his hands, opening–*

*And the voice, saying,* Gateway sequence interrupted! Explain! *And a mental shriek that burned through the brain, and everyone down below clutched their ears, trying to block it, and the voice saying,* Gateway linkage shutting down.

*And something had come through the gateway, from that alien space inside the wheel. A dark, saucer-shaped vehicle, hovering in the air...*

*Then it was gone, like a mirage, like a bad dream.*

He should have known, back then, that it wasn't any kind of ending.

*It was out there, somewhere.* An alien vehicle, an alien intelligence directing it. Where did it go?

And that had not been the worst of it. No.

The worst of it had been that, fifteen minutes later, Harry had died.

# TWENTY-THREE

Would the ship never come?

In the harbour, there on the Long Island, a plethora of ships: Arab *baglahs*, Chinese junks, a French steamer, three Aztec longboats, trade ships from west Africa – from the Kong and Dahomey and Asante empires – a couple of Swahili cargo ships, three lizardine tea-clippers, and others: sailboats, dugouts and steamships all crowded in that harbour, coming and going, but the ship Harry was waiting for wasn't there.

No whalers. Whale-hunting was punishable by death across the Lizardine Empire and, through bilateral agreements, beyond it. Like human slavery, it belonged in the days before Les Lézards. Were they, Harry wondered now, not for the first time, truly enemies of humanity? Many argued over the centuries that the coming of the lizardine race had, by extension, benefited humanity, had stopped some of its more heinous actions. And yet, was it right to let an alien race rule over you?

Harry felt ill at ease. For he knew one… being, at least, who did *not* think it right, and who had made it their life's mission to oppose the royal lizards.

But he didn't want to think about that. Did not want to think of Roanoke, any more than he did of that awful moment in the White City...

Even after it was over, after that alien space within the wheel had disappeared, when the screams of the passengers in the wheel's cars had stopped, when that alien vessel had disappeared, flying at high speed away from the White City, even then chaos reigned.

The White City: a marvel of an age, a brand-new city erected especially for the Fair, enormous buildings, wide avenues, a multitude of visitors–

Plunged into darkness now, and fear, and uncertainty–

People running through the streets, trying to find a way out–

And others taking advantage of the situation.

*The White City had been filled with the criminal class. Not just that killer Milady de Winter had been sent to catch, the man they called the Phantom, who had called himself H.H. Holmes, perhaps in mockery of the great detective... There were cutpurses and pick-pockets and confidence men (and confidence women), tricksters and robbers, and in the darkness even those who had not come to the city to commit a crime could be tempted, nonetheless, to take advantage of the situation.*

*Harry had walked in the dark, as lost as the rest, trying to locate de Winter, trying to gather information for the* Cabinet Noir, *that secret organisation that was the Vespuccian equivalence of Les Lézards' Bureau...*

*So intent that he did not notice the movement behind him, did not quite hear the snick of a blade–*

*The man had smelled of sweat and stale tobacco and gin. The blade flashed, once, in the moonlight–*

*Harry remembered the surprise, more than anything else,*

*more than the pain – the surprise and the hurt of it, which was*
*somehow worse, and then it flamed through him, and he tried*
*to breathe, or scream, but no sound came, and he gurgled, help-*
*lessly, and sank to his knees, blood gushing out of his throat,*
*and the man's breath was very close to him, he stood behind*
*him, supporting him as he fell, almost gently…*

*He was dying, Harry had suddenly realised, and it made him*
*want to cry. He wasn't ready! He was not yet twenty years old!*
*What would his* mother *say? It couldn't be happening, not to*
*him, not like this–*

*The man had rifled through his pockets and had come away*
*with the money and everything else. Then he ran. Shouts in the*
*distance, but Harry's hearing was going, and he could see noth-*
*ing now, and would never see again… He felt the life slipping*
*away from him. He could have cried.*

*He died.*

Harry paced the docks. Swahili sailors speaking in a beach
argot with Melanesian islanders, Lenape officials super-
vising the off-loading of cargo, porters loading up bags of
coal onto the French steamer. Harry's mission was simple:
go to London, find out what you can, try to stay alive. It
almost made him laugh.

*You will be briefed further upon landing.*

They needed him to track down Babbage. Lord Babbage, who had not been seen these five years or more.
Who, for all intents and purposes, could well be dead.

But Harry knew even death was not always an end…

He had woken with a gasp. Air, cool blessed air, came
into his lungs. He cried out. He was lying on the floor, in
a doorway. The electric lights were burning again, and
an air of gaiety filled the White City.

Harry put a hand to his throat. Nothing there. No cut, no blood–

He was alive.

Slowly, he sat up. He looked about him. What had happened?

Again, he felt himself. Nothing. No injury, no pain…

Had he dreamed it?

He stood up. He felt fine…

Something was very wrong.

The memory was too real.

And, when he checked his pockets, his belongings were gone.

So he really had been robbed.

Had he just taken a knock on the head? Had he hallucinated dying?

A sudden sense, of being watched.

He stepped into the street. It was as if nothing had happened.

He knew he should report it to his superiors.

But he never did.


And I was wrong, he thought, pacing the docks. I was wrong not to.

But it was too late now.

And there was the ship, coming in.

The *Snark*.

Harry thought it was a strange name for a ship.

And now it docked, and the gangplank was laid down, and the captain descended. A young man, even younger than Harry. Quite jaunty. When he saw Harry he smiled, and extended his hand.

"You're Houdini?" he said. He had an enthusiastic, almost boyish smile. "I saw you on stage, in Fort Amsterdam –"

a small town in the vicinity, built by the European refugees on leased Lenape land – "you were very good."

"Thank you," Harry said. He found himself returning the smile. "Captain–"

"London," the man said. "Call me Jack." He smiled again. He smiled easy. "Dad's an astrologer," he said.

"Mine's a rabbi."

London slapped Harry on the back. "Come on up!" he said. "We're heading to my namesake town, are we? My band of desperadoes usually sails hereabouts, but I'm guessing the Cabinet Noir wanted someone to keep an eye on you." He laughed, but Harry, this time, did not return the feeling.

*Was* London there to keep an eye on him? Did they know? Did they suspect?

He followed the captain up the gangplank and onto the deck. "Maybe you could perform for the boys," London said. "Later."

"Be happy to," Harry said.

It was partly that strange event at the World's Vespuccian Exposition that had led Harry, a year later, down to the island of Roanoke.

Officially, he was on a mission for the Cabinet Noir. Strange, unexplained phenomena have always plagued that part of the world. The Roanoke themselves now shied away from the island. Back in the day they had leased it to one of the earliest groups of refugees fleeing the lizards' rule, but that small colony had disappeared, and the events surrounding that disappearance were never adequately explained.

Harry remembered it as a happy time. He performed sleight-of-hand, close-up magic routines, the sort of magic that required no heavy equipment but whatever was to hand. For a while he abandoned coins or cards completely, preferring to use natural materials: making a stone disappear, making water appear out of a leaf. Magic that required no language, a visual kind. From the Roanoke he learned of the creature they called, somewhat uneasily, Coyote.

Coyote was known and revered across Vespuccia; but for the Roanoke the name had evolved a different meaning. Was it a recent thing? Harry tried to find out – "Yes," some said. "No," said others. Stories were confused. Some said Coyote had been seen for centuries. Some dismissed the stories altogether.

"Was Coyote behind the Roanoke Colony's disappearance?" Harry asked.

No one knew. The subject made people uneasy.

"It steals people," one told him. "In the night."

But others said that, no, it brought people back from the dead.

They told the story of one man who had died and was resurrected by the creature they called Coyote. The man had been killed in battle.

"What sort of battle?"

"Oh, a disagreement of some sort," they told him. It had been one of those wars between villages, long ago.

"What happened to the man?" Harry asked.

"He had been shot, several times. He died."

"And then?" Harry asked.

"Three days later he was spotted, alive, without a scratch on him. Riding his horse under the full moon. He was never seen again."

"Just stories," someone told him. But Harry was uneasy.

The activities of this Coyote seemed to centre around Roanoke island. It had remained uninhabited once the colony had disappeared. But sometimes, at night, Harry was told, strange sounds came from the island, and strange lights could be seen, at all hours, moving and shifting. "The place is cursed–"

"It is sacred–"

"It is both."

They would not object to his going there. But they would not accompany him, nor take responsibility in the event he never returned.

In the event, of course, Harry *didn't* return.

Or, rather unfortunately, he did.

Both of which proved the Roanoke right.

He sailed to the island one day, by canoe. He had rather enjoyed the ride. The island, from a distance, appeared deserted. He beached the canoe and set out to explore.

He wasn't armed. "Spies," Winnetou once told him, "should kill only as a last resort. Spies *watch*, Erich. Spies are eyes, not hands."

Still, they had trained him for both, but the thought of killing made Harry ill. Serving your country was one thing. Killing in its name was another. He knew he was not cut out to be a great hero in the big game of life, or in the secret Great Game of the shadow world. He was not a killer. He was an entertainer, a magician. He liked people. And he liked people to like him. There were names – Milady de Winter of the Quiet Council, the man known only as Smith, who was a legend in that most secretive of branches of British Intelligence, the organisation they called the Bureau – who were famed as ruthless assassins, cold-blooded killers, second only in stature, maybe, to the shadowy Bookman.

He, Harry, was not like them. Could not *be* like them, and didn't want to.

And yet here he was, on this island, alone, looking for–

For what?

He didn't know.

And, somehow, that was worse.


He didn't know what he would find. He went to the village. It had been built by that vanished colony of refugees, long ago. It was still there – empty houses falling down, empty windows reflecting nothing, rusting plates and cups still laid out on tables where no one sat. A sense of age permeated the village; a sense of abandonment, of disuse. It was not scary, to Harry. Rather there was a feeling of sadness there, of incompleteness, and he wandered through the houses like a ghost.

Until he came to a ring of ash on the ground outside.

He stopped, and stood stock still.

Nothing. No sound. The call of a single bird in the distance. The sun, growing low on the horizon…

He knelt down. A ring of stones, blackened by fire, with ash inside. Just an open-air fire, the way he had seen them, and built them, and sat by hundreds of times.

He touched the ash, gently, with two fingers.

It was still warm.

The day was still – too still. He felt as if the sun froze, dying, in the sky. No breeze, no birds – he rose to flee–

Felt something hard and unmistakable against his back–

The barrel of a gun.

# TWENTY-FOUR

Harry had rebuilt the fire. It was burning now, and the sun had set, and the night was very dark, there in the abandoned old village, there on the island of Roanoke.

There were two of them sitting by the fire. Harry – and the man with the gun.

"Call me Carter," he had told Harry. He had kept the gun trained on him, at a distance. There was little chance of escape, as yet. Harry may have been a magician, an escapologist even, but even a consummate performer cannot outrun a .45.

He didn't try to.

"What do you want? What are you doing on the island? Who sent you?"

But the man seemed unfazed by the questions.

He had a brown, deeply lined face, strong hands that seemed to have spent a long time outdoors, in manual labour. He smiled, but even when he did Harry could sense a sadness in him, and his eyes belied his face, and made him seem far older than he appeared. There was age there, and stillness, and regret... "I'll answer all your questions," the man, Carter, told him. "What I want is peace. What am I doing here? I was waiting for you. As for who sent me... that, too, will become clear to you."

So Harry, with ill grace, acquiesced.

There was nothing else he could do.

And the man Carter, he thought, looked far too comfortable with the gun.

And so they sat across the fire from one another. Carter had a flask of whiskey. They shared it. It was old whiskey, smoky and smooth. The fire threw sparks into the night. There were many stars overhead. Harry, with a strange sense of acceptance, waited.

It was as if he had been waiting for this moment, it occurred to him, ever since that strange night in Shikaakwa. The night he had dreamed that he died. As if he had been waiting for answers, had come all this way somehow knowing – almost as if the knowledge had been implanted in him, unconsciously, some time back – that he would find them here.

On Roanoke.

And so a sense of calm had settled on Harry that night. And yet, within it, there was also anxiety, an anticipation as of a man fearing attack, who knows it is coming but doesn't know when, or from which direction – only that he couldn't stop it when it came.

Carter, meanwhile, roasted a couple of fish on the fire, and they ate them, Carter one-handed; he would not relinquish the gun. They also ate yams that had been dug into the earth below the coals, so that they came out steaming-hot when opened, and their flesh was sweet. They drank the whiskey, not talking, until they were done and so was the drink.

Then: "Let me tell you a story," Carter said.

*I was born* (Carter said) *on this island, the child of English adventurers fleeing the rule of the Lizardine dynasty. Carter is not my real name. What my parents were called no longer matters…*

*Life on the island was hard, but happy. Our small colony existed by permission of the local tribes (this was before the establishment of the Council of Chiefs and the federal arrangement currently in place). My sister, Virginia, was born two years before me and we often played together. Our colony was small, beginning with just over one hundred people, and growing by two dozen children after some years. As I grew up I began to travel more and more on the mainland, learning hunting and trapping, fishing in the streams, and learning the languages and customs of the nearby tribes. I was very happy for a time.*

*Then disaster struck.*

*I had returned from a long journey. I must have been away a year or longer. When I reached the island, they were gone.*

*Men, women, children. My own parents, my sister, my friends. The houses remained, empty. Food was left rotting on untouched plates. Clothes left hanging in closets. It was as if they had all simply got up at the same moment and… disappeared.*

*I was beside myself with grief. I could find no trace of them, no hint as to where they may have gone. One message, only, I found, carved into the trunk of a tree, in my sister's hand.*

*Croatoan.*

*It was the name of a nearby island, but more than that, it was a code between Virginia and me. In our childhood, Croatoan was the place where stories happened, where heroes went in search of maidens to rescue, where dragons guarded treasure… but more than that, it was the place we banished the night frights to. The ghosts and monsters of a child's sleep we banished to Croatoan. Waking up in the night, hearing an unexplained noise, we would shout, "I banish you, devil! I banish you to Croatoan!"* – *and the ghoul or ghost or demon would depart, and we would sleep secure once again.*

*Only a child's game, a comfort of the imagination... and yet at that moment, when I saw the message carved into the tree, I knew that something I had thought impossible had happened, that the dream world of my childhood had somehow materialised, a door opened, and took my sister, my parents, my friends with it.*

*For a long time I was inconsolable. A shaman I knew confirmed my suspicions. The island had always been unlucky, he said. People had disappeared there before – for centuries if not longer. I grew very angry at that. "Why did you not warn us?" I said.*

*"But we did," he said. "Your elders believed it naught more than a tale, such as to frighten children."*

*I was no longer a child, yet I was afraid. I determined to find the door to Croatoan, if such existed. Yet none could be found. The old shaman suggested the "openings", if such they were, depended on a number of variables, and may not be replicated in my lifetime. For a long time I despaired...*

*Then, one night, alone in the woods, I met a monster.*


It was quiet in the night. Harry stared into the flames. It had grown cold, there, and a wind blew in from the sea. He shivered and drew himself closer to the fire. When he looked at Carter the gun was still aiming at him, but the man's eyes were far away.


*I never saw it clearly* (Carter said). *I had built a small fire and was sitting with my back to a tree, roasting a fish I had caught earlier in a nearby stream – the same as we do now, you and I. Almost I felt peaceful then. All thoughts of my despair had momentarily left me. I was happy with a pipe, waiting for*

187

the fish to cook. Then, taking forever what small contentment I may have one day achieved, he appeared to me.

He, it – I still do not know what to call it. A thing out of nightmare, a giant centipede-like creature, but not alive. A machine, perhaps. A strange machine, that came seeking me there in the wilderness of the Chesepiooc country. I had not felt its approach, and when I did it was too late. Through shadows he moved, and his arms, if such they were, held me captive. Its feelers moved. "You know this land well," its voice said.

"As well as any," I said.

He chuckled at that. "Are you not afraid?" he said.

I did not reply. "Yes," he said. "I can tell you are. Your heart rate and blood pressure indicators are suggestive of the fact. Yet you remain cool, coherent. That is good. I may be able to use you."

"I was not aware I was an appliance," I said, which made him chuckle again. "To be used or discarded by monsters."

"Oh, I am not the monster," this strange being said. "I, too, was once a tool and have been discarded. No. I fight the same evil your parents escaped from. Would you help me?"

The lizards? I had heard the stories of these strange beings, of course, but they meant nothing to me. I had heard they were no worse, as rulers, than the human family who once controlled the British Isles had been – better, in fact.

"I bear those on the British throne no ill will," I said, and he tightened his grip on me at that. "You shall be my agent," he said. "Yes… you will fight the good fight alongside me. I am the Bookman."

The way he said it – it was chilling. More than a title – a description, an essence of everything he was. "What is a Bookman?" I said.

"One who preserves knowledge," he said. "Which is a precious thing."

*"That sounds harmless,"* I said, *and those were the last words I spoke before he killed me.*

"What?"

Harry's head snapped up. The man, Carter, was smiling at him, but there was no humour in the smile, and his eyes were cold.

"How could you…" Harry's voice shook. "How could you have died?" he whispered. "You're alive. This is a lie."

"And yet, here you are," Carter said. "Why did you come here, Harry Houdini? What trail were you following, what doubts were you trying to assuage?"

Harry opened his mouth, then closed it. No sound came. He did not know what to say.

Carter nodded. His eyes studied Harry, and told him that he *knew*–

*Yes. I had died* (Carter resumed). *It was the first, but not the last time…*

*The Bookman… That strange creature could be likened to a monk, perhaps. A copier of illuminated manuscripts. Only, for the Bookman, human beings are the manuscripts. And so he copied me, destroying the original, and in the process improved me, changing me to suit his needs. I was to be his agent, his errand runner, in spying and assassinating, in waging his cover war against those who may have once been his masters: the reptilian race of Caliban's Island, masters of the Lizardine Empire that steadily continued to grow despite the Bookman's efforts.*

*Les Lézards.*

*And what did he offer me? Why did I follow his command?*

*He gave me life. My new body did not decay, did not grow old. I was stronger, faster, a machine in the semblance of a man.*

He gave me the time I needed. Wait for the door to appear again. Wait, to follow my sister into the other side of nightmare, into Croatoan.

Of course, I had asked him about the disappearance. Yes, he said. There were such anomalies. There had been machines designed to open such temporary portals between realms. Semisentient Quantum Scanners, he called them. There had been several on the ship, he said.

It's strange… Over the decades I had spent considerable time with the Bookman, and we grew to talk. He was a lonely being, I think. Alone and abandoned, like a child forgotten by its parents. Lonely and angry with it, carrying on with his war, building his small army… "Tell me about Croatoan," I said to him once. I was living in the city of the lizards then. We met in the Bookman's secret place under the city.

"It is nothing," he said dismissively. "A pocket world. A place for…"

"Yes?" I said.

He was always wrapped in shadows. He hid himself so well… He said nothing for a long moment. Then, "It is a place for the dead."

At that my heart began to pound. "Are they dead, then?" I demanded. "All this time, have I waited in vain?"

"No," he said. Then, "Perhaps. I do not know."

"You keep secrets from me," I said, and he laughed. "Secrets are my business," he said.

I continued to serve him. I continued to wait. I travelled periodically back to Roanoke. Back here. "A one-way trip," the Bookman called it. "If such a device does in fact exist, and is present on the island, it would be only half-tuned. There were four modules on board the ship, if I recall correctly, and only one could facilitate a full bi-transference node. And that would require an initiation signal… Be careful. They can be…"

*"Yes?"*

*"Cranky," he said. "And remember. If you go – you will not come back."*

*"Will you not require me still?" I said, and he laughed, and his words chilled me. "Why, I have another one of you in storage already," he said. "Just in case I need you, and you're not around."*

The night was still. In the distance, lightning danced in the sky, too far away yet for thunder to be heard. The night felt charged, electric.

"I couldn't have that," Carter said, almost apologetically. "I couldn't let him resurrect me, endlessly, his agent, his toy, playing forever the Great Game." There was a hard finality in his voice.

"Did you ever…?" Harry wasn't sure what to say. All his senses screamed danger, but he felt himself unable to move, to act. "Did you ever find them? Where they went?"

The look in Carter's eyes was one he remembered later. Pain, and something else, deeper, harsher.

*My last visit to Roanoke… it was a century ago, or so. It gets hard to keep time, after a while.*

*I knew something was different as soon as I set foot on the island.*

*The colour of the sky was different. The brightness of the sun had dimmed, and the world was muted in its colours, a grey and misty vista. There were unfamiliar smells in the air, swampy and damp, and when I stepped on the ground my feet sank easily, leaving behind them lonely markers, the only sign of living in this desolate place.*

*It had changed. Was changing. I could feel it in the wind, and when I came to our old settlement the change had become profound.*

*Transparent they were, the houses. I could see through walls into the living quarters beyond. Out settlement was ebbing in and out of existence – impossibly, majestically. It was then I began to hear a voice.*

*What it said I was never certain, afterwards. It seemed to mutter, directly in my head. A litany of complaints, perhaps. It reminded me, strangely, of the Bookman. There was a loneliness in the voice, an anger born of being abandoned. Something deep underground, perhaps. A semi-sentient quantum scanner, whatever that is.*

*I knew, then, as I stood amidst the ruined houses flickering in and out of existence, that I had to choose.*

*Go back. Leave the island.*

*Or go in. Follow them, into the unknown.*

*Into Croatoan.*

"What did you do?" Harry whispered. But he realised he already knew the answer. For Carter was sitting there, talking to him. Which meant he couldn't have–

"I followed them," Carter said. "I had to. My sister, my family... I could not turn back from the unknown."

"But you're–"

"Here? Yes."

And Harry realised, and a shudder passed through him, and in the distance he could hear thunder, now: the storm was getting closer.

"So you're..."

"The copy." Was that amusement in Carter's eyes? Or anguish? "The other me went into Croatoan, to that shadow world, and the Bookman remade me, and this is where my memory ends. For another century I had served him as his agent. I am tired, now, Harry Houdini. I am very tired."

"It hadn't been a dream," Harry said.

"No."

"I really died, in Shikaakwa? In the White City?"

"The Bookman had been interested in you for a long time, Harry Houdini. And when that man cut your throat in the dark, the Bookman saved you."

"I died?"

Carter smiled, and his teeth were white, and rain began to fall, big fat drops of warm rain, and thunder sounded, close by now. "I am tired now, Harry Houdini," he said. "And you are young enough to die."

"Wait," Harry said, "don't–"

The gun in Carter's hand exploded with sound. Pain erupted in Harry's chest. He heard three shots, and then he heard nothing.

He came to on the ground. In the ring of stones the fire had died and the partially burned wood was damp. The rain had stopped, the storm had passed the island. It was morning. There was no sign of the man who called himself Carter.

Harry felt himself.

No injuries, no pain…

Suddenly he had to get off the island. He was trapped in a nightmare and he couldn't get away. This was madness. He was hallucinating, he was–

"Mr Weiss," a voice said.

And something came crawling out of the vegetation, a nightmare figure, like a giant invertebrate, and Harry suddenly knew, with an aching clarity, that none of it had been a dream, and that, twice now, he had died.

# TWENTY-FIVE

The journey out of Vespuccia was uneventful. London and his team piloted the *Snark* ably through the Atlantic waters, and Harry found himself with little to do. He practised coin manipulation and cards and lock-picking, and did his regular exercises with a strait-jacket he had brought with him, with the crew aiding in ever more elaborate incarcerations and watching, half in amusement and half in awe, as he escaped from each one.

His latest had been an underwater attempt. The crew tied him into the strait-jacket, manacled his feet, put him in a canvas bag and dumped him overboard.

When he had surfaced, minus the chains, he figured he could use it in his next act.

But mostly, Harry waited. There was that feeling of anticipation, a calm before activity, the way he felt just before going on stage. Soon he would have to perform. For now, he could rest, wait, prepare himself. The way Winnetou had taught him.

He often thought of the past. If Winnetou had been his first recruiter, Harry had come to realise that the strange man who had called himself Carter was his second. Without willing it or wanting it he had, in the professional term, been *turned*. A spy, he didn't know where his loyalties lay. With the Cabinet Noir – or with the Bookman.

Perhaps with neither. He had begun to understand what Winnetou had told him. "All of us, who work in the world of shadows, are but shadows ourselves," the man had told him. "We cast no shadow of our own."

It was his way, Harry thought, of telling him a fundamental truth. That shadow operatives were to be used, as pieces on the board of a great game, but that, just like chess pieces, they had no inherent loyalty to one side or the other. It merely depended on who played you first.

He was a magician, at home with illusions and secrets. And yet...

Perhaps what it came down to, in the end, was simple: he didn't like to be played.

He had never seen Carter again. And his new master – his new *controller*, in the parlance of the trade – was a strange being, a thing out of nightmare, and his desires were hard to decode. Harry never saw him again, either. From time to time, using established protocols for contact, he met with, or received messages from, other human agents of the Bookman. There was little to compromise his position with the Cabinet Noir. The Bookman showed little interest in intelligence coming from there. Harry suspected, in particularly uneasy moments, late at night, that the Cabinet Noir was not unaware of their new agent's subversion. That, just possibly, the Council of Chiefs and the Bookman had... an understanding.

Both, after all, were opposed to Les Lézards. And, if

that was the case, he was not a double agent at all, but serving a common purpose.

He preferred to think that, at any rate.

When the island of Great Britain came at last into view it seemed enormous, a grey fungal shape rising out of the harsh ocean, and Harry felt his excitement building. He did not like the wait, the anticipation. He was glad it would soon be over. There were great events unfolding around the world, and he would be a part of them.

It seemed so odd, that a relatively small, insignificant landmass, off the European mainland, a place of foul weather and little, by all accounts, going for it, would become such a powerful player on the world stage. What was it that drove these people to spread out across the world the way they had? Was it, simply, a dogged determination to avoid the British weather? Or was it something else, some colonial imperative taking hard, tempered shape, until like an iron noose it had slowly but surely tightened over the world?

He didn't know. Something in that need to control, to conquer, frightened Harry. And yet, as strange as it seemed, there was something exciting about it, too.

The *Snark* sailed through the mouth of the Thames and English towns came into view gradually, a great human sprawl, with factories belching steam along the river and many boats, and Harry saw mechanicals in one, automata they were called, as real as if they were human, and the sailors waved at them. The air was cold and the taste of salt and tar was gradually replaced by the smells of humanity, of vegetation and refuse, and they came, gradually, into the city.

• • • •

It was growing dark when the *Snark* came into the docks. Harry stood on the deck, watching the city. It was a symphony of light, the red sky lit with an unearthly glow as the dying sun gave way to gaslight. Majestic airships sailed through the air above the Tower of London and, in the distance, the great pyramid of the Royal Palace shone in that strange, alien green. Upon the water a multiplicity of crafts sailed, longboats and steamers, sailboats and dhows and ferries going back and forth from north to south bank. Over the city's skyline rose the Babbage Tower, like a strange and ancient obelisk pointing at the sky. The bridges of the city arched over the river, London Bridge gilded and shining with the images of giant lizards, and far away the bells of Whitechapel and Shoreditch and Bow and the booming of Big Ben.

"There she goes," Jack London said, coming to stand beside Houdini. "Gay go up and gay go down," he said, speaking softly, "to ring the bells of London town." He smiled sideways at Harry. "When will you pay me? say the bells of Old Bailey. When I grow rich, say the bells of Shoreditch." The *Snark* was coming in to the docks, but Jack's eyes were looking at the distance, and the setting sun. Harry shivered, and didn't know why. Whatever Jack was reciting seemed harmless, a nursery rhyme of some sort. "Pray when will that be? say the bells of Stepney. I do not know, says the great bell of Bow."

At last Jack tore himself away from the horizon, and now looked directly at Harry. "Here comes a candle to light you to bed," he said, speaking so softly Harry had to strain to hear him. "Here comes a chopper to chop off your head…"

The boat, with a gentle lurch, came to a rest. The sailors were throwing ropes down, whooping in anticipation of dry land. But Harry felt cold, and the words of the nursery rhyme gripped him with a sudden fear that he couldn't shake off.

"Chop chop chop chop, the last man's dead!" Jack London said.

# PART IV
## *Paris in Flames*

# TWENTY-SIX

Midnight in Paris.

The moonlight reflected off the green metal that had once made up Notre Dame. The ruined cathedral had been made, long ago, by Les Lézards, and subsequently destroyed in the Quiet Revolution, when automatons and humans took France back for themselves, and made it an independent republic.

Punks de Lézard hung around the ruined edifice, humans obsessed with the lizardine line, altering their faces and skin to resemble that of lizards: a part of the process involved elongating and then splitting their tongues, so that they hissed when they spoke, and their skins had been tattooed with alternating bands of colour. Smith, watching, felt the fear in the night, and the anticipation. The Punks de Lézard were feral creatures, murderous and territorial.

Smith was standing motionless in shadow. The left bank of the Seine, in the shadow of a bookshop, watching. The Seine slithered like a snake nearby. Smith waited.

Presently, he heard the sound of unhurried footsteps, approaching. The sound of a match being struck, the flare of a flame, the glow of a cigarette, the smell of burning tobacco. Then the man resumed his walk, came closer.

"Smith," he said.

Smith stepped out of the shadow. Extended his hand.

"Van Helsing," Smith said.


He had come to France by fishing boat, departing the Limehouse docks on a ship that had halted, mid-channel, to let him out: the fishing boat had been waiting and picked him up and dropped him off on the continent, near Calais. From there he took the train to Paris.

*I can bring her back*, the Bookman had said. Smith knew he could. It was not the first time the Bookman had made such an offer.

"What do you want?" he had asked, there in that underground, disused sewer.

"Find the Harvester," the Bookman had said.

"Do you know what he is?"

"He is a machine. A probe. A device for gathering information. It is not unlike me."

"Old–"

"No."

That single word was chilling.

"The lizards," Smith had said, carefully, "they must have come *from* somewhere."

"Yes."

"We never thought to ask from where, or whether there were others still there…"

"Yes."

"And now they know?"

"Now," the Bookman said, "they know of this world. And they are curious."

"Is that a bad thing?"

202

"When a child is curious about ants," the Bookman said, "does he speak to them? Or does he examine them with a magnifying glass, and sometimes burns them, just to see what would happen?"

Smith felt his hands close into fists, relaxed them with some effort. "How?" he said. "How does he – it – gather information?"

"The same way I do," the Bookman said, and laughed, but there was no humour in that sound. "By extracting their minds, their memories, the way they think and feel. Your friend Alice, my old adversary, Mycroft, and all the rest of them – they are stored, now, inside him. Inside the Harvester."

Smith shivered. It was cold, and dank, inside that abandoned sewer. The Bookman, he remembered, had always exhibited a certain fondness for underground lairs. He said, "What would you have me do?"

*Find him.* The words of the Bookman were still in his ears. *Find him, and signal. And I will come. One of me will come.*

"We have a problem," Van Helsing said.

Smith looked at him. The man, like him, was getting old. Once he had been legendary, eastern Europe and the Levant his speciality. A shadow operative and a fellow assassin, he worked alone, and served no master. He was also the Bureau's contact man for Paris.

"What?" Smith said. Which one? was what he was thinking.

"There had been a break-in at the Bureau," Van Helsing said. He spoke quickly, passionlessly. "Shortly after your somewhat... spectacular display over London. Someone – some*thing* – broke in, as if all the security measures in place meant nothing. A hulking, giant figure. Analysis suggests it was a human infected with what would normally have been an overdose of Frankenstein-Jekyll serum. Know anything about that?"

Oh.

"Possibly," Smith said – admitted – thinking of the Comte de Rochefort. So the man had survived the airship crash?

"What happened?"

"It seems the intruder made it all the way to Zephyrin's lab," Van Helsing said, "and retrieved an unknown object."

"How do you mean, unknown?"

"I mean it was not registered in any of the files," Van Helsing said.

"Something of Mycroft's?" Smith said, uneasy.

*A Black Op*? Off the books. For the Fat Man's Eyes Only.

"What did Zephyrin say?" Smith said.

"Zephyrin was thrown halfway across the lab," Van Helsing said. "And smashed into a wall. He was not available for comment."

"Who else was there?"

"Berlyne was manning shop. They're both alive, but neither of them's in any position to talk right now. Fogg's tearing out what's left of his hair."

Which was the only thing to cheer Smith up right then… He said, "So do we have *any* idea what's missing?"

But he already had an inkling.

The fat man had been obsessed with Les Lézards. "We need to understand them, study them, learn their ways, their history," the fat man had once told him. It had been a summer day, somewhere in Asia, near the Gobi Desert, in land that could have belonged to the Russians, or the Chinese, or the Mongols, depending on who you asked, and whether you bothered to in the first place. Early days, when Smith was young, though Mycroft was so terribly fat even then…

They were sitting in Mycroft's personal airship. The fat man had insisted on travelling by air whenever possible. He said he liked the comfort. The airship had never been given a name. Nor was it registered.

Officially, just like Smith himself, it did not exist.

They were there on what the fat man had called a treasure hunt. There was a team of archaeologists, and a local guide, and security men who never spoke, and Mycroft's personal chef, Anatole.

"What are we looking for?" Smith had asked.

"A token," Mycroft said. "Something old, that was lost."

Smith had only just returned from his training with the man who called himself Ebenezer Long. Smith called him Master. Even now he knew little about him. The monastery sat high up in the Himalayas, in a hidden, snow-bound valley. Master Long had taught Smith the art of *Qinggong*: the Ability of Lightness. There had been a strange, Buddha-like statue, made of jade. It had allowed Smith and the others seemingly impossible feats: almost as though they could fly through the air, on unseen wires. Mycroft had questioned Smith at length about the statue. But it had disappeared shortly after Smith had arrived at the monastery, and he didn't know what he could tell the fat man.

"Ancient devices," the fat man had told him. "Proof of the lizards' extraterrestrial origins. And signifiers of our future, Smith. Our past has been changed by outside forces, and our future is uncertain."

And so, each day, they scanned the desert, searching for that treasure, or that proof, or that ancient device. But they had found nothing.

Smith followed Van Helsing along the narrow streets of the Latin Quarter. Booksellers displayed their wares and people sat outside numerous brasseries, drinking wine, talking, laughing – it felt to Smith, at that moment, as it came on him, at unexpected times throughout the years, that he had chosen the wrong profession, and that the shadow world could not stand up to the light, to life lived openly, in warmth and joy. Then he thought of the break-in at the Bureau and his suspicions, and what it could mean to those people sitting there, so care-free, unaware of the possible danger that could be threatening them, and the feeling, as it always did, passed.

He was what he was, and the world needed shadow as well as light.

Back then, on that long-ago expedition to the Gobi, they had come back empty-handed. But what if the fat man had continued to look? And what if he had found something?

An ancient, alien artefact, of unknown powers… and Zephyrin had been tinkering with it.

Worse – now the demented, physically transformed monster that the Comte de Rochefort had become must have it in its possession. Which meant the Quiet Council…

They needed a man inside the Council. A sleeper agent, someone who would have an inkling as to the Council's actions, its intents.

Luckily, they had exactly such an agent in place.

# TWENTY-SEVEN

They'd stocked up in the Latin Quarter. A tailor shop whose owner doubled as an arms dealer provided them with firepower. Van Helsing went for a double-barrelled shotgun over his shoulders, two Colts by his sides, a long, slender knife strapped to his arm, and some grenades, as an afterthought. In his long dark coat, his tanned face and deep blue eyes, he looked formidable, the Hunter of old.

Smith rarely favoured guns. This time, though, he accepted a hand-made Beretta, complete with silencer, and added a handful of knives. He hoped guns would not be required.

"The Hunter and the Harvester, working together, eh?" Van Helsing said. He sounded mournful.

"Just like in the old days."

"We never worked together in the old days."

"Think you're past it?"

"It's been a while since I killed anyone."

"Miss it?"

Van Helsing sighed. "Not in particular," he said. "To be honest with you, I saw this posting as my little retirement spot. You know what they say–"

"Paris is the last posting before retirement," Smith said. "Yes…" They were walking towards the cathedral now. Notre Dame, shining that strange luminous green in the moonlight. "What did you have planned for after?"

"I thought a teaching post in Amsterdam, possibly," Van Helsing said.

"Cheer up," Smith said. He felt the knife strapped to his arm. It felt good to hold a weapon again. "It's possible we won't even have to kill anyone tonight."

"Stranger things have happened," Van Helsing said, still a little mournfully.

*The observer, meanwhile, was feeling a little confused.*

*This city was not like the others. It was awash in what the humans called Tesla radiation. It was a chatter of conversation. It was a city of machines as much as humans, and the machines talked. They were machines of an antique and obsolete kind his masters had forgotten long ago, yet here they were, thinking engines, primitively powered, but thinking all the same.*

*And talking.*

*A lot of their conversation was about him.*

*What he was, and what he wanted.*

*The observer almost wanted to join in on the conversation. There was something exhilarating about it, about other machines, a kinship of sorts. The voices inside him had been multiplying recently. They all wanted to talk, all the time. The observer paid them little mind.*

*He was following a simple trail. The humans had a legend, about a boy and a girl in a forest and a trail of crumbs. The observer was following a trail of crumbs, and the crumbs were human minds.*

*But they weren't only human minds.*

*And right now he could hear such a mind, an old mind, somewhere.*

*It was screaming.*

*It was a mind that was neither human nor of the human-like machines, but something like an ancient relative of the observer itself.*

*Some relic of a distant past, a mind disturbed, perhaps insane. This bothered the observer. He decided to try and find it.*

They walked through the ruins of Notre Dame. Punks de Lézard hissed at them, revealing claws surgically grafted onto their hands. Besides Smith, Van Helsing smiled, showing teeth, and pushed aside his long coat, revealing his guns. The punks hissed at him but kept their distance.

"We need an entry into the catacombs," Van Helsing explained. "There should be one around here somewhere–"

They moved in shadow; the moon cast pale reflections of their bodies against the ruined metal and their shadows multiplied around them, like the ghosts of past selves. Smith shivered. Could the Bookman really bring back Alice? Was Alice's mind truly trapped, now, in the confines of some strange and alien machine? Was she aware of what was happening?

Where would the Harvester go next?

He was following the Harvester's trail, and it was leading, step by step, to Babbage. But what would he, Smith, have done in the Harvester's place?

He would not have rushed, headlong, towards the target, he decided.

He would take his time, find and isolate the other links in the chain.

And the chain led to Paris, and so–

"Ah, there it is," Van Helsing said. He kicked debris away and revealed a trapdoor set in the floor. Van Helsing knelt, took hold of the solid brass ring attached to the door, and pulled. The door opened upwards, smoothly, as though it had been recently oiled.

"After you," Van Helsing said, courteously.

Smith peered down the hole. Metal rungs led downwards, into the earth. He lowered himself, began to climb down. Van Helsing followed.

The ladder terminated a short while later. They stood on hard stone ground. It was dark but, as they began to move, the passage opened up and there was light, and Smith could smell wood smoke in the distance, and meat cooking, and heard, faintly, the sound of a harmonica, playing.

"Welcome to the catacombs," Van Helsing said.

They began to walk, unhurriedly, keeping a distance between them. Van Helsing's hand was on his gun. Smith was cradling his blade. The space around them expanded again, the ceiling rising higher as they went deeper into Paris' underworld. A rat scampered past, alarmed by their progress. There were cells cut into the stone on either side. Some were empty. In one he saw a young mother cradling a child. She looked up at him as he passed and her eyes were empty and when he looked down he saw she was holding a wooden doll, and the doll was staring at him and it blinked, startling him.

"Edison dolls," Van Helsing said. "Be careful of them. The Edison Company manufactured them, complete with Babbage engine and rudimentary voice. They… were not a success."

Smith seemed to remember rumours, about Edison and his obsession with creating the perfect, female doll…

He wondered where the man was, what side of the Great Game he played on. They walked on.

In one of the cells three automatons huddled around a fire. They were in a deplorable state, stuffing sticking out of holes in their bodies, one missing an arm, another a leg. They passed around a flask of what Smith, at first, took to be whiskey. Van Helsing paused and spoke briefly to one of the machines. "Petroleum," he said, noticing Smith's gaze. "Come on."

"What did you ask them?"

"Where our man is."

Petroleum...

Smith knew what it was, of course.

A sort of fuel, highly flammable... There were high concentrations of it in Vespuccia and–

The Arabian Peninsula.

They used it for light, predominantly. But now it looked like the French machines could use it for power, rather than steam?

A group of Punks de Lézard distracted him. They came out of the shadows, surrounding the two men, silently, their claws extended, their forked tongues hissing. Smith and Van Helsing moved in tandem, not breaking stride. Smith's knife was buried in the first man's belly before the man had time to gasp. Smith lowered him gently to the ground and stood above him, looking at the others calmly, while Van Helsing covered them with his twin guns. No one spoke. After a moment the punks went and picked up their fallen comrade and dragged him away, back into the shadows. Smith and Van Helsing moved on.

The tunnels widened and narrowed, unexpected turnings leading farther down, until at last they came to a wide space where fires burned and groups, carefully apart, sat – beggars and automatons and Punks de Lézard, and Van Helsing said, "This way."

They went along the wall, and the inhabitants of that underground place carefully avoided looking at them. For a fleeting moment Smith thought he saw an old, Asian man move, too swiftly to distinguish features, and disappear into the darkness. It made him uneasy, and he thought of his old master, Ebenezer Long, of the Shaolin. Could the secret world of the Wulin, those hidden societies fighting the dowager-empress, also be involved?

And if so, what were they after? The *Erntemaschine*? The secrets Babbage must hold? Or something else entirely?

The object stolen from the Bureau, whatever it may be?

Van Helsing stopped, and Smith followed suit. They were standing in a branching tunnel away from that main hall.

"What–?" Smith began, but Van Helsing, with a gesture, silenced him.

They waited.

Presently, there was the sound of shuffling feet. A small, hunched figure appeared ahead of them, growing closer, until it was before them. Then it stopped.

"Van Helsing," the figure said.

"Q. Thanks for coming."

Smith examined the man. He was short and dark-skinned. He was also a hunchback. "I'm Smith," Smith said. The other man looked up at him, grinned. "Your reputation precedes you," he said.

"What can you tell us, Q?" Van Helsing said. He looked ill at ease. His hand was on the butt of his gun and he kept glancing sideways, checking both sides of the tunnel. "What is the Council up to?"

"Rumour has it the Comte de Rochefort was fed a little of his own medicine," Q said, and his eyes twinkled at Smith. "But he survived. And came back with a prize."

"Do you know what it is?"

"No," Q said. "But it has them all excited. Viktor himself is working on it, I hear."

*Viktor.* That name again, Smith thought. The scientist they had tried to steal from the French, and failed, repeatedly.

"Can we get access to it?" Van Helsing said.

"I don't see how," Q said. "Breaking into the Quiet Council's secure area would be madness. There are measures in place to–"

"Where is it?" Smith said. He, too, had caught Van Helsing's unease. "Where's the nearest access point?"

"Not far," Q said. Quickly, sensing their changed mood, he gave them directions. He had lost his smile. "I have to go," he said. "You will not succeed in breaking in."

"Let us worry about that," Smith said, when–

There was a sudden crash, the tunnel shook–

Smith reached out to steady himself against the wall–

A voice, animalistic and full of hate, roaring–

Hot breath with the stench of rotting flesh filling the tunnel–

"*Smeeeeth…*"

Van Helsing and Smith, moving together–

Pushing the hunchback to the ground, behind them, covering him – Van Helsing with guns drawn, Smith with the knife–

A huge, repulsive figure appeared in the mouth of the tunnel. A giant in the semblance of a man, muscles bulging from torn clothes, a demented look over a leering, engorged face with massive, yellow fangs for teeth…

"I'm coming for you, Smith…"

The huge mouth moved: a grin.

Smith stepped forwards, standing between the others and the monster.

"*Bonsoir*, Comte de Rochefort," he said, politely.

So the man had indeed survived his fall from the flaming airship.

The Frankenstein–Jekyll serum had worked.

But the fall had certainly made him angry.

Smith grinned. It felt good to be here, facing one of his old enemies. "*Je m'appelle Smith*," he said. He nodded at the monstrous figure before him, almost in affection. "*Je suis un assassin.*"

The thing that had once been the Comte de Rochefort roared. Then it charged directly at Smith.

# TWENTY-EIGHT

At the moment the giant body rushed him, Smith jumped. The Comte de Rochefort sailed past him as Smith, turning in the air, landed behind him. His knives flashed. The comte roared in pain and outrage and green-yellow blood, like pus, came streaming out of the gashes in his back.

The confused Rochefort turned, but Smith turned with him, using the creature's bulk to his advantage. The wounds, he saw with alarm, were already closing. He jumped on the giant man's back, one hand over the comte's throat, and the knife came to rest against the side of the man's neck, ready to go in and finish the job.

But he had underestimated the Comte de Rochefort. With a roar of rage the beast bent and with one flowing motion threw Smith off. He hit the wall and pain exploded in his shoulders. He fell to the ground.

Blinking tears of pain away, he saw Van Helsing step forward, both guns extended. "Eat lead, Frenchman!" Van Helsing shouted (a little melodramatically, the winded Smith nevertheless thought), and the guns burped once, twice, catching the giant monster in the back and, as the monster turned, in the chest.

The comte roared, holes opening in his chest, bleeding more of that yellow-green blood. The blood hissed when it touched the ground. Acidic, Smith thought, horrified. And the comte had intended the Frankenstein-Jekyll serum for *him*.

He stood up. It was time to finish the job. The knife flashed, flying through the air, finding the comte's neck with unerring accuracy. A jet of blood sprouted out of the wound, burning a hole in the nearby wall.

The Comte de Rochefort, trapped between Smith and Van Helsing, turned this way and that. A look of incredulous horror was etched into his face. Then, unexpectedly, he laughed. The roar of his laughter filled the underground chamber. With one meaty hand the comte pulled out the knife. Already, the wound was closing.

"You can't kill him."

Smith had forgotten the hunchback was there. The Comte de Rochefort, looking confused, peered at him, as though trying to identify a half-remembered face.

"It's me," the hunchback said, gently, reaching out a hand to the giant monster. "Q. You remember?"

The comte grunted. Something about the hunchback's manner seemed to subdue him.

"I helped Viktor with the experiments, you know," Q said. He was speaking softly, as to a child. "He tested animals at first, rats, then rabbits, then monkeys. Then he began to test it on people."

The hunchback approached the Comte de Rochefort, and the great hulking beast let him. Smith remained in place. He was winded, and his knees hurt, and he was out of breath.

*Getting old.*

"They suffered," the hunchback said. "Do you know how they suffered? They used to scream, in their cages. For hours and hours and hours, there in that underground facility, where there is no day, only night." He looked up at the comte, and his big, innocent eyes were tranquil. "I used to sing to them," he said, softly.

Van Helsing had been cautiously moving away from the comte. De Rochefort, suddenly noticing, hissed. "Shhh…" Q said. Then he began to sing.


Paris, the catacombs, night.

Smith, slowly, cautiously, rising from his fall.

Van Helsing, sliding against the wall, blood on his lips.

In the centre of that underground tunnel, two figures, facing each other. The giant, deformed, hulking figure of the man who had once been the Comte de Rochefort.

And, facing him, the diminutive, hunchbacked figure of Q, of Notre Dame de Paris.

Who was singing.

The comte growled. Q, undeterred, kept singing. He had a high, reedy voice, not unpleasant. It seemed to fill the small, enclosed space.

"*Au clair de la lune, mon ami Pierrot,*" Q sang. "*Prête-moi ta plume, pour écrire un mot.*"

*Under the moonlight, my friend Pierrot, lend me your pen, so I could write a word.*

"*De la lune…*" the Comte de Rochefort said. The words came out of his misshapen mouth with difficulty. Smith could only stare at the giant, no longer bleeding, as it knelt down to be closer to Q.

"*Ma chandelle est morte,*" Q sang, *my candle is dead.*

"*Je n'ai plus de feu ouvre-moi ta porte pour l'amour de dieu.*"

There was something chilling in the innocent words, this lullaby for children the hunchback was singing. *My candle is dead, I have no more fire. Open your door for me, for the love of God.*

"*L'amour…*" the Comte de Rochefort said, captivated.

Q did not turn away from him. "Go," he said, in the same soft, sing-song voice. "Go, find Viktor's lab. Finish your mission. Go!"

Van Helsing came to Smith and, supporting each other, they limped away, the clear sound of Q's singing following them all the while.

"Eat lead, Frenchman?" Smith said. "Really?"

Van Helsing had the grace to look embarrassed.

They found the place, but they got there too late.

The door would have been hidden in the rock bed, but it had been blasted open, from the inside. The security would have been a nightmare to break through, even with an F-J serum, but there was no longer any need.

The door had been blown, the metal oozing on the ground as from an unimaginably strong source of heat. Van Helsing and Smith exchanged glances, then Van Helsing gestured with his head at the opening. Smith nodded.

He stepped carefully over the still-steaming door, and into the dark opening. He went to one side then and Van Helsing, following, took the other. They stood, silently, trying to evaluate the scene before them.

"What," Van Helsing said softly, "has happened here?"

Smith shook his head. He couldn't imagine.

They were standing in a large, open cavern. The ceiling of bedrock extended high above their heads. A pool of light engulfed a surgeon's workspace, large metal dissection table, while against one wall a series of cages stood.

Smith gestured. Van Helsing followed him, along the wall, to the cages. They were full…

Smith did not know what they were. Perhaps, once, they had been people. Now they were changed, each one differently. Man-machine hybrids, a child with the sad beak of a parrot and small, grimy wings sprouting from his thin naked shoulders, a woman in a black iron mask, rocking her knees, humming tunelessly, something that looked like a human-sized frog, an automaton with a human face–

What joined them all together was the silence. Smith had expected screams, a cacophony of sound. But the caged creatures did not make a sound, and when he approached closer they shied away, pressing themselves against the walls, trying to stay as far away from the bars as they could.

"What–"

"Look," Van Helsing said. He pointed at the far wall. A hole had been blasted into it, by the same unknown source of heat. Yet the chamber was quiet, and there was no sign of an intruder, or a device capable of generating such power…

Smith, for the moment, gave up on the beings in the cages. He went over to the operating theatre–

Which was where he found the body.

Almost tripped over it, in fact.

"Over here!" he called. Van Helsing came running. Together, they looked down at the man on the floor. He was wearing a white lab coat that was no longer white. It was stained a deep, crimson red.

Blood.

Smith knelt down, put his fingers to the man's neck. There was a pulse, weak but steady. He looked up at Van Helsing.

"Viktor," Van Helsing said.

Smith nodded.

"What happened here?" he said.

Van Helsing said, "I don't know."

"Search the chamber," Smith said. "I'll see if I can wake our friend here."

Van Helsing was already moving. "We haven't got long," he said. But Smith shook his head, though the other man couldn't see it. "It's too quiet," he said, but softly. A breach like this should have alerted seven kinds of security forces by now. That no one had showed up…

Suddenly he was very concerned.

A sense of urgency gripped him: that this was beyond a confrontation with de Rochefort, this was something larger than a break-in into the Quiet Council's secure research facility. For the Great Game was exactly that, a series of moves and counter-moves, quantifiable and understood: a *game*.

But this was something else, something he could not understand. He ran his hands over the fallen man, searching for wounds, then tore open the lab coat.

Underneath it the man's body was singed, and the smell filled Smith's nostrils, making him gag. He stared in horror at the man's burns. They had to get him to hospital, to a doctor.

The famous Viktor…

He said, softly – "Can you hear me?"

Van Helsing, circling – "Smith, I can find nothing."

"The object?"

Van Helsing didn't answer, and Smith knew they were both thinking the same thing.

Could the object have done this? Had Viktor, some-how, managed to activate it?

He shook the fallen man. How could he be burned *under* the lab coat? Why wasn't the coat burned, too?

Had he put it on later? Had someone else dressed him?

Suddenly he was afraid of a trap again. Feeling his heart beating fast he tried to shake the scientist. "Can you hear me? Viktor!"

Suddenly the man's hand shot up and caught hold of Smith's wrist. Smith shouted, surprised. Van Helsing ran over, the sound of his feet on the hard ground filling the cavern with echoes. Viktor's eyes shot open, staring straight at Smith. The man's hold on Smith's wrist was supernaturally strong.

*Had he been experimenting with the serum on himself?*

"They're here," Viktor said. His face twisted. Smith could not release himself from the man's fevered grip. Viktor's burned chest rose and fell painfully.

"Who's here?"

"They're here! You have to warn…"

He faltered. His eyes lost their focus. His grip slackened. Smith released his hand. "Serum," he said. "Get him some serum!"

"I'm looking," Van Helsing said, sounding irritated.

"Viktor. Viktor! Can you hear me?"

"Viktor…" the man whispered. He licked his lips.

"What did you do, Viktor? What happened here?"

"Voices… I heard… voices."

"I don't know what these things are," Van Helsing said. "There's enough medication here to start a hospital, but nothing's properly labelled."

"Yellow… serum… top left… marked… *privés*… tell… tell him."

Smith repeated the instructions. Van Helsing returned. "What is it?" he asked, curious. And – "Should I give it to him?"

"It can't hurt…" Smith said. The sense of urgency, of *wrongness*, had not left him. Why had they not been disturbed? Why had no one come to the scientist's aid?

"Viktor," he said, speaking gently. "Do you want your medicine?"

"Medicine…"

"What happened here? Did you activate the device?"

"The device!" Viktor's face underwent a transformation. And now he looked frantic. His hand shot out again but this time Smith was prepared and avoided it. "They came! They're here! Run!"

"He's insane," Van Helsing said.

But Smith had a feeling something had gone very wrong indeed.

"Give him the serum," he said. "I think we need to leave. *Now*."

Van Helsing shrugged. He primed the syringe, pulled up Viktor's sleeve and, without due ceremony, inserted it into Viktor's arm, pushing the liquid in.

They watched the scientist's body shudder. And now Smith noticed that Viktor's exposed arm was *filled* with similar signs of injections.

"My God," he said.

"What?" Van Helsing said, still sounding irritated.

"He's been using this stuff for months," Smith said. "If not years. It's probably the only reason he didn't die."

Viktor's eyes opened again and a new light shone in them. Smith noticed, with sick fascination, how their colour changed. They were becoming yellow. And now Viktor smiled, his body shuddering. His smile reminded

222

Smith of a rabid dog he had once had to kill. Suddenly revolted, he got up to his feet. "Let's go," he told Van Helsing.

"What about him?"

"He'll live."

"The Bureau would have wanted him."

"We have no time for that," Smith said. "Leave him."

The scientist on the ground screamed suddenly, startling both of them. His body twisted and jerked, and he began to howl, and the caged creatures began to howl along with him, filling the air of the cavern with a sudden, unbearable cacophony of screams. Smith shuddered. "Come on!" he said. He moved, suddenly desperate to get away. Van Helsing followed and they left the chamber, the screams continuing behind them as they began to jog down the dark tunnels of the undercity.

"We were fools!" Smith said.

"I don't understand–" from Van Helsing.

"We need to get outside."

Was it Smith's imagination, or were there far more people down below than there had been before? They stared at the two old men, running, and made no move but to shy away from them. Desperation drove Smith. A feeling he had been late, too late for far too long. They ran, following high ground. At last they came to one of the exits out of that subterranean maze.

"I... could do with... a break!" Van Helsing said, panting.

Smith pushed open the door. They were on the right side of the Seine, having traversed the underground passages below the river, coming out near the grand municipality building, the Hotel de Ville.

Which was on fire.

"Why is it so light?" Van Helsing said.

Smith, panting, had his hands on his knees and was sucking in air. But the air was full of smoke and it made him cough. The Hotel de Ville burned and, as Smith straightened, he saw it was not the only building on fire.

He looked up, not believing what he saw. All over the city skyline, flames were pouring upwards, bellowing like demons – from the Louvre, to Bastille, to the Place de l'- Opera and to Concorde. And now Smith could hear the screams–

"Look!" Van Helsing said. He raised a shaking, pointing hand in the air.

Smith raised his head, shaded his eyes. And now he saw them. Giant, hulking shadows moving in the sky above the city. They were vast, inhuman machines, giant tripods moving jerkily, like metal spiders, over the Parisian skyline, belching fire in all directions.

"We're too late," Van Helsing said, softly.

And Smith, numb, could only echo what Viktor had said. *"They're here."*

# PART V
## *The Further Chronicles of Harry Houdini*

# TWENTY-NINE

Where the hell was his contact? Harry Houdini thought irritably. England was cold and wet and the streets were unsafe, and he was shivering now, his clothes damp, as he skulked outside a Limehouse tavern, the Lizard's Claw. The unmistakable smell of opium wafted out from within the establishment, quite pleasant, really, and in the sky above the city a silent storm of lightning played in silence, reminding him uneasily of that night on another island…

He palmed coins and practised sleight-of-hand as he waited. His instructions had been very clear. He had followed standard procedure from the moment he had disembarked at the docks. Ensured he was not being shadowed. There was no reason for him to be, of course. No one knew who he was, or his purpose here. At least, no one should.

He had made his way to this place, getting lost on the way. But he made it. Only there was no sign of his contact, and Harry's busy hands suddenly stilled, and his short hair, cut from that thick dense of curls that was his heritage, prickled.

Something was wrong.

He hugged the shadows. Alarm was telling him to leave, to try and make the fall-back meeting, but curiosity got the better of him. Slowly, as unseen as he could make himself be, he circled the Lizard's Claw, scanning his environment, shadows and fallen masonry and piles of refuse: this was certainly not the high-end part of town one imagined when one thought of the Old World.

In the distance, the whales sang, plaintively. There was something haunting about their song, and for a moment the world around him dematerialised, and he saw, instead, the same world with no humans in it, an ocean-world for which the land masses of continents were but a fleeing distraction, a great and deep blue world in which giant beings moved in the depths and sang across thousands of miles, calling to each other...

Then it passed and he went around the back of the Lizard's Claw where the smells coming out of the kitchen made him suddenly hungry, and he almost stumbled over a prone object.

He cursed, and righted himself.

The carcass of a boar or a deer, perhaps.

Did they have wild boars, here?

Sounds of singing from inside. Someone came out from the kitchen and Harry froze, but the figure merely threw a reeking bucket of dirty water onto the street – narrowly missing him – and went back inside, leaving the door slightly ajar.

Harry cursed all Englishmen, but quietly. The sliver of light traversed the dirty back yard of the tavern and came like the blade of a knife to rest against the hurdle Harry had hit.

He drew in his breath in a short, sharp intake like a gun shot.

Not a deer. Not a boar, either.

A human leg, in sensible grey trousers, and a sensible black shoe, polished, though scuffed at the heels. Harry knelt to take a better look.

A human body, the leg twisted unnaturally. The street was very quiet. All his senses were alert, for the most minute sound, but there was nothing. The body had been wedged, without ceremony, into a crumbling break in the low stone wall of the street, which the tavern staff probably used to put rubbish in. The smell, indeed, suggested rotting offal, and that was mixed with incense ash and cheap oil that had been reused so many times it was mostly burned fat. Grimacing, Harry pulled at the leg, drawing the corpse out, slowly. It was lying on its front. As he dragged it out he was aware of a dark, viscous liquid that had pooled around the corpse. Blood. The man was young and had worn a cheap but respectable suit. There was something strangely familiar about him. His left hand had been outstretched in death, one finger, dipped in his own blood, pointing helplessly at nothing. Harry retched without sound, the smell suffocating him. Then, gently, he put his arms under the dead man's body and turned him over.

The man's head lolled back, dead eyes staring at Harry, and he bit down on a scream, hard.

No no no no no.

He stood up. It was too dark. Yes, he thought, helplessly, it is too dark to see clearly. I am hallucinating. The brain finds patterns in the dark that don't exist.

With trembling hands he reached for a box of matches in his sensible suit's pocket. The first match broke. The second one took flame for one brief second and then blew out. Harry cursed, knelt by the body, cupped a third

229

match in hand and managed to light it and sustain the flame. He moved his hand over the man's face.

No no no no no!

Helpless, Harry Houdini stared at the dead man, his contact person, lying there on the ground in a pool of blood and offal and scum.

No wonder he had seemed familiar, he thought, with a mixture of dread and despair.

The flame of the match hovered, illuminating in stark relief a young, not-unhandsome face.

A face as familiar to him as his own.

"Oh, Harry," Houdini said. Gently, he teased a lock of dark, curly hair from the dead man's brow. "What have they done to you?"

The face that stared back at him, impassively, with dead and vacant eyes, was his own.

Harry crouched by the body, thinking hard. He had long suspected the Bookman may have been cooperating, to a greater or lesser extent, with the Council of Chiefs. Their goals, after all, could be said to be, if not exactly the same, then nevertheless at least parallel to each other. Did the Council know his secret, then?

Had they despatched a second *him*, another Houdini, ahead of him to the lizardine isle?

They must have, he thought, shaken. For this man was to be his contact here.

And had been murdered, and left for him to find.

Someone would pay.

Still no sound, the street very still, and suddenly he was afraid. *Too* still… almost as if he had been expected and now they were watching him, whoever they may be.

The opposition.

In the shadow game, that could be anyone, even your own side.

Quickly now, he went over the dead man's belongings. He knew there would be a hidden pocket *here*, a false heel in the *left* shoe, another hidden compartment *there* – all emptied out. Someone had done a thorough job on the dead man. On *him*.

And yet…

Harry paused, intrigued. The other him's finger was pointing, he had thought, at random. But what would *he* have done, if he had perhaps seconds to live, and needed to leave a message?

As a child he had loved the penny dreadfuls, out of the continent. He would have written a message, in his own blood, he thought.

But the dead man's finger was pointing at a mound of rubbish, not at an inscribed and bloodied message. It was pointing at pig intestines going off, and a reek of urine, and rotten cabbage.

Unless…

He hated to do it but he made himself. He dug into the pile of refuse. The stench was awful and when he disturbed the remains of the pig a cloud of dark insects rose, buzzing angrily, into the air.

His hand quested, coated in slime. It was quite possible there was nothing there. But he searched, blindly, until his fingers found a rectangular, soggy form. He withdrew it carefully, brought it close to his eyes. Paper, he thought. Thick, and good quality, to have withstood its tribulations. It smelled rank. He peered at it, but could see little in the dark.

Some sort of visiting card, he thought, and felt excitement rise in him. A lead. He hoped – he prayed – it was a lead. Or otherwise, he – the other he – had died in vain.

And now he was alarmed into movement. He would be found, identified – he couldn't let it happen. He picked up a stone and smashed his own dead face in, over and over, until nothing remained but a bloodied pulp. He threw up then, but the deed was done. The corpse, when it will be found, would be that of an anonymous man, not of Harry Houdini.

He still had the sense of being watched. And now the tavern's door re-opened, and a head stuck out and said, loudly, "Is anybody there?"

Harry straightened up. The voice said, "Hey, you, what do you think you're–"

Harry ran. Behind him, an indignant shout, then footsteps and then a much louder scream, as the speaker discovered the bloodied mess that had been left there. Harry ran through the narrow streets, not sure where he was going. At last he found the river and followed it, the Thames snaking deeper into London, taking Harry with it, and as he ran the vast dark shapes of whales rose beside him in the water of the river and keened, as if they, too, mourned the passing of Harry Houdini.

# THIRTY

He found shelter at a hotel in Seven Dials, a run-down dismal place worthy of its name, which was Bleak House. The proprietress, a Mrs Bleak, with a gummy, toothless mouth, wrinkled her nose at Harry's smell, then at his accent, but accepted his money grudgingly and asked no questions. Harry washed, then sat on the hard bed and stared at the piece of paper he had picked up from his other self.

It was, indeed, a visiting card. It was made of good-quality, expensive stock, with a gold border around it, and said, simply:

JONATHAN HARKER
SOLICITOR
DOMBEY & SON
WHOLESALE, RETAIL
& FOR EXPORTATION

Who was this Harker, then? And who were Dombey and Son?

Harry had a solid lead. He turned the card over and

over in his hands. The library, he thought. He would begin at the public library.

There was, indeed, a lending library nearby, on the Charing Cross Road. Harry went inside, glad of the warmth. He found the business directory, a large, leather-bound volume chained to its shelf, and leafed through it until he found the company's address.

There were no further details about the company. There was no mention, for instance, of exactly what they were wholesalers and retailers *of*. Or what they were exporting…

He'd have to tread carefully, he knew. The other him had been murdered for what he had found out. Harry was only surprised they had not made an attempt on him, too. Perhaps they wanted to see how he would run. He had a feeling that, even now, he was being watched. Perhaps the fact there had been two of him had thrown the opposition off-balance. If you kill me, he thought grimly, another me would just take my place.

Which was an unsettling thought, for Harry. And he decided he did not wish to die again any time soon.

Dombey and Son's offices were in the City, though according to the directory they had warehouses at the Greenwich docks. Harry decided he would have to proceed cautiously. Had the other him got too close, and was killed for his troubles?

He left the library. He was tired and hungry, but filled with a nervous energy. And the city was only now truly coming alive around him, a great mass of humanity, bound within ancient stone – so different to the wide open spaces, the mountains and the plains and the endless skies of Vespuccia. This city was like a bubbling cauldron, chock-full of a seething humanity, like a brain made of streets and lanes where humans played the role of thoughts and pathways. Perhaps the Lizardine Empire was like that, he thought: a single entity composed of solitary atoms, a great mass which was, nevertheless, a new, complete entity without regard to its component parts. People, even royals, could die, but the machine that was the empire would go on, powered not by engines of steam but by its people, the coal that burned and fed it.

Harry wandered the streets, passing along Shaftesbury Avenue and its glittering theatres, then into Soho where the streets became darker and the cut of clothes cheaper. He found an eatery and went inside and ordered. The food was bland.

"Hey, mister."

A small hand tugged at his arm. He looked down, surprised.

"Mr Houdini!"

It was a small bedraggled boy. "How do you know my name?"

The boy looked surprised. "Don't you recognise me, mister? I'm Oliver."

Harry stopped. Froze, almost, as the realisation hit him.

The boy thought he was the other Houdini.

The one who had died.

"Of course," he said, and the moment passed. "Oliver. Yes, what can you tell me?"

The boy was still looking at him dubiously. "It *is* you, isn't it, Mr Houdini?"

"Of course it's me," Harry said, trying to laugh it off. It felt very odd, to pretend to be... well, himself. And yet not himself. He wished devoutly then that he knew just what the other him had been up to in this city.

"My master wishes to parley with you," the boy, Oliver, said.

"Your master."

"You know." The boy lowered his voice. "Master Fagin," he said.

"Oh," Harry said. "Of course."

There was a short silence.

"Now, please, sir," Oliver said, abandoning the *mister* for the moment.

"Will you take me to him?" Harry said.

"Yes, sir," Oliver said. His eyes, Harry saw, were on the unappetising remains of Harry's late supper: a thick stew of indeterminate meat, dipped with a white, crumbly, flowery bread.

Harry said, "You hungry?"

"Hungry," the boy confirmed.

"Go on, then."

The boy didn't need to be told twice. With startling, rapid movement he was over the bowl, tearing up chunks of bread, dunking into the remains of the mystery stew, and shoving them into his mouth until his cheeks bulged.

Was this the ultimate produce of the empire? Harry thought, discomfited. Could the jewel of the world, the seat of that worldwide empire on which, as they said, "the sun never set", still contain within it such poverty, that a boy would have to beg and steal for his bread?

For he recognised in the boy the signs of a fine-wirer and a flimp, those miniature experts of the crowd, who made their trade – and their art – in picking pockets and making valuables disappear. Harry had the expert eye of a man in a similar line of work. He smiled, then smacked the boy on

236

the side of the head, causing him to spit out soggy bread.

"What you go and do that for!"

"Let's go," Harry said, still smiling. "Now, my wallet, if you please, young Oliver."

The boy grinned sheepishly and handed it back to him. "Just checking, guv," he said. "Making sure you *was* you, if you know what I mean."

Harry, unfortunately, did.

He made his way outside, following the boy. There were several pubs, a chemist's selling cocaine and soap, a man handing out leaflets of what must have been a political nature and, nearby, one of Harry's own people: that is, a three-card monte man, hunched over a folding card table, a wad of money in his waving hand.

Three-card monte: it was one of the classic scams, resting in the domain that lay between magician and card sharp: the operator, the dealer that is, offering to double the punter's money. The bet: an easy one. Find the lady. The card sharp shuffling the cards, a simple sleight-of-hand making it impossible to detect where the Queen of Hearts had gone. Harry knew it well, had operated it before. He went closer and watched with professional interest. There was the Throw, the Drop, and the Aztec Turnover, but the real secret of the game was simple, and Harry, enjoying himself for the first time, found himself checking to see who the dealer's accomplice was, the shill.

The shill was there to lure the mark into the game. He bet against the dealer, and lost, allowing the mark to feel a superiority – since to them it was always so easy to see where the Queen went. When they finally put their money down, though…

The shill was an undistinguished young man. The dealer, however…

Harry knew a thing or two about pretence, and makeup. At the World's Vespuccian Exposition he himself had donned the apparel and dark skin of a Hindu sorcerer, along with his younger brother, Theo.

So he could recognise a fake, and the dealer – a hooknosed, bearded personage with the reek of the streets upon it – made him smile happily, recognising here one of his own. The nose was an expert job, the dirty skin artfully applied just so, the beard removable. A respectable Anglo-Saxon gentleman hid behind the façade of a gutter man, if Harry was any judge.

"Find the lady!" the dealer shouted. The wads of money in his hand could be used neatly to cover any untoward movements of the cards. "Find the lady!"

"Twenty shillings!" A fat man pushed his way in. He had been watching the shill, who was losing repeatedly.

The dealer made the man's money disappear; shuffled the cards. An interesting pack, Harry thought. The royal cards were all lizards, and the Queen of Hearts bore a resemblance to Queen Victoria's profile which he had seen on coins and stamps.

"This one."

"Sorry."

The dealer upturned the Eight of Clubs where the Queen of Hearts should have been, and grinned blackened teeth at the mark.

"Cheat!" the man cried. "Liar!"

The shill, meanwhile, had gone quietly around him. Harry saw the flash of a blade, and the large man blanched visibly and fell quiet.

"On your way, now," the shill said. The man nodded and

hurried away. Harry, still smiling, approached the table.

"Mr Houdini," the three card monte man said.

Several thoughts ran through Harry's head at once. That the previous him had already met this man; that the previous him must have made the same assumptions he had just made; and that he had charged this man, a seasoned criminal of some sort, with a task, most likely in the nature of information-gathering.

So he took a gamble.

"Do you have it?" he said.

The man smiled. His teeth were in perfect health, Harry thought, amused. But the coal smeared on them made them appear rotten, mere stumps of teeth. "What if I do?" he said.

"Master Fagin?"

The boy, Oliver, had materialised by the card table.

"Boy?"

"The pigs, sir. They're coming."

"Short is the run of a three-card monte," Harry said. So this was Fagin, the man who had wanted to see him. He had guessed right, it seemed.

"Short in one place," the man, Fagin, said philosophically. "But who wants to stay in one spot all the time?"

In one swift motion he folded the card table, made the money and the cards disappear, and grinned at Harry. "Shall we?" he said.

"Do you have it?" Harry said, again.

A whistle sounded in the distance. Policemen on their way. Fagin did not look unduly worried. He grinned again at Harry.

"It will cost you," he said.

# THIRTY-ONE

"My children have been shadowing him for you," Fagin
said. Harry followed the man down the city's unfamiliar
alleyways.

Shadowing who?

"Where is he now?"

"His routine hasn't varied," Fagin said. "A man of
habit is our Mr Harker."

Harry, inwardly, sighed with relief. It made sense. So
the earlier him had hired this man, this Fagin, to follow
Harker, the mysterious solicitor of that mysterious export
company called Dombey and Son.

"And now?" he said. Something must have changed,
he thought, for Fagin to have summoned him.

The other man smiled, revealing those falsely ruined
teeth. "He's got himself a missus, he has," he said –
which lowered Harry's opinion of the man's acting skills
somewhat.

"Where?"

"Not far."

Was Fagin leading him into a trap?

It was possible. But it was a risk, he decided, that was

worth taking. He had to find out what had happened to his double… and what had led to his death.

Harker was the key to the puzzle…

A part of the puzzle, at any rate.

They were heading towards the Thames, Harry realised. The smell of the river crept up on him and with it the singing of the whales grew stronger. They were now on the Strand, a wide avenue thronged with carriages and steam-powered baruch-landaus and people. Across the road stood an imposing building. A sign said it was the Savoy Hotel.

They crossed the road.

"Waterloo Bridge, guv'nor," Fagin told him, cheerfully, with that same grating, false voice. Harry shrugged. Down below, the Thames was dark. Fog swirled across the bridge, which was lit by gas lamps which cast pale, yellow orbs of light around them. There were more carriages and beggars, and a couple of policemen, walking past, looked at Fagin sharply for a moment before going on their way.

Beyond the bridge they came to an area of theatres and pubs and a huge, new construction project. A massive collection of towers was rising, uncompleted, into the sky, things of chrome and glass partially connected by as-yet-uncompleted narrow, hair-fine bridges, like spiders' silk.

"What is it?" Harry said – whispered. He had seen the modern marvel that had been the White City in Shikaakwa, the labour of architects and engineers to imagine the new, coming century. But the White City had looked nothing like this: it was bulky, it was grandiose, it was white–

This was something else, a different sort of future, a future of metal and glass, a future of rockets. High above, in those towers, lights moved and bobbed and he realised people – workers – were moving up there, in those impossible heights, still working at this late hour on the construction.

"This?" Fagin said. "It's just a building, innit."

But it wasn't just a building, Harry thought. And now that he watched, as they came closer and details resolved themselves, the place came into focus. He could see bullet-shaped elevators rising and falling along the sides of the slim, needle-like, rocket-like towers, as if they were breathing and the tubes moving alongside them were the air they breathed. He could see a massive cone rise into the air, flat at the top, and it seemed like a cone of water, with water travelling along its side – as if the builders were making a pool of water up there, in the air, for the future residents of those towers to frolic by, as if they were by the sea.

A place for airships to dock – that, too, he noticed, just as he saw the figures crawling along the side of the buildings – not human, or rather, things that resembled humans, if a human wore a thick exoskeleton of metal, like a knight's armour, around himself. Like armoured ants they crawled over the walls, building.

"They come from the Gobelin factory," Fagin said. "The Shaw brothers' place, in Paris. They used to make Daguerre looms there, back in the day. It was a natural progression for them to start making… well, these."

"What *are* they?"

"Human-machine hybrids," Fagin said. "It's all the rage, really."

A shiver went down Harry's spine. For it occurred to him that, though he himself *looked* human, and *sounded* human, it was quite evident, from the Bookman's words, that he was not, strictly speaking, human any more.

He, too, was a sort of machine, a simulacra of a Harry Houdini, an Erich Weiss who had been born, to Rabbi Mayer Samuel Weiss and to Cecelia Weiss, née Steiner, in Budapest, in the Austro-Hungarian Empire, in the year eighteen seventy-four, and who had died, aged nineteen, at the hands of a mugger, in the White City, at the World's Vespuccian Exposition, in the city called Chicago or Shikaakwa.

That Erich Weiss – *that* Houdini – was gone forever. He, Harry, was but a copy.

Yet perhaps it gave him advantages. He had not considered it before, but could not the Bookman have shaped his new body, have modified it in some subtle ways – could he not have made him faster, stronger – smarter?

In fairness, he did not *feel* any different. He felt like he was himself, the same old Erich, with the same ambitions, same thoughts.

What if there were other hims walking around? He thought back on what that strange man, Carter, his recruiter into the Bookman's service, had said. Of what the Bookman had told *him*…

*"Will you not require me still?" Carter had said, and the Bookman had laughed. "Why, I have another one of you in storage already," he had said. "Just in case I need you, and you're not around."*

Harry shivered again. The night felt suddenly cold. "Look," Fagin said, startling him. He pointed at the tall, graceful buildings. "See those lights?"

There were, indeed, lights burning behind windows in the uncompleted buildings. "People already live there?" Harry said, surprised.

"It's all the rage," Fagin said.

They had come to the base of the place. A fence humming with a strange power he had seen before, in the White City.

Electricity.

"He's *here*?"

"Star City," Fagin said.

"Is that what they call it?"

"I told you, china," Fagin said. "It's just a building."

"It's amazing."

"It's a disgrace. It disfigures the face of the city."

"It looks like... like the future."

"Not my kind of future," Fagin said, and his face twisted in an ugly and unexpected expression of anger.

"I think it's amazing."

"So you said."

"But what are we doing here?"

As he spoke he saw two small figures detach themselves from the shadows and come towards them. Two more children, dressed in rags. "Well?" Fagin demanded.

"He's still inside," the one girl said.

"With his missus," the second, a boy, said.

"Harker?" Harry said.

"Harker," Fagin confirmed. "And, as it turns out, his fiancée."

Somehow that rang false to Harry. Could his quarry, the possible cause of his double's death, be just some person, some insignificant clerk, about to be married? He had half-envisioned some fearsome, secret assassin, a man of international intrigue. Most shadow agents never married. It was too dangerous for them.

"What is her name?"

"Wilhelmina," Fagin said. "Miss Wilhelmina Murray,

of Star City Mansions. Would you like to know what else I've found out?"

"Yes."

"And the money?"

Harry had money. Not wishing to argue with this person, nor seeing the point of it, he removed a small sheaf of Vespuccian notes from a hidden pocket and handed them to Fagin, who smiled horribly and made the money disappear.

"Very well," he said. "Very well indeed." He coughed, clearing his throat, and spat the phlegm on the ground.

"The Mina Murray Dossier," Fagin said. His eyes took on a faraway look. Harry looked at him in suspicion.

Could Fagin be other than he appeared? Could he himself be a shadow operative, working for someone like the lizard's secret service, the Bureau?

```
Name: Wilhelmina "Mina" Murray.
Age: twenty-one.
Parents: deceased.
Family: none.
Engaged to: Jonathan Harker, Solicitor.
Employed by: Dombey and Son, Wholesale, Retail
and for Exportation.
Role: unknown.
Residence: Star City Mansions, South Bank,
London.
```

"That's all you found out?" Harry said.

Fagin said: "It was hard to find even that much. Same with Harker, for that matter. It's as if…" and he hesitated.

Harry looked up, at the Star City.

"It's as if what?" he said, absent-mindedly.

"It's as if anyone working for Dombey and Son becomes a shadow," Fagin said, reluctantly.

Harry was looking up, at the needle-like towers, the climbing mecha-humans, the airship docking and that graceful column of suspended water. The moonlight fell down on Star City Mansions, illuminated the thin filaments of silk-spun bridges criss-crossing between the towers, while behind the windows of the occupied apartments shone the white, bright light of electricity. The present, with its dirty streets, its steam machines, its coal dust and gaslight, seemed to have no presence here, an illusion fading in the bright electric light.

This was the future, one future, and Harry drank it in.

"You can't have shades without light," he said.

# THIRTY-TWO

When you die it is like a light going off. In death there is nothing. Life is an improbability, the brief flare of a match in a dark world. Houdini didn't want to die.

Not again.

He had made a terrible mistake. It was very dark, though it wasn't cold.

This is what happened...

They had waited outside Star City Mansions and, presently, two figures, seen in silhouette, came out of the grand entrance to the as-yet-uncompleted buildings.

Harry tensed. Fagin, beside him, was motionless. The boy, Oliver, had disappeared somewhere, on an errand for his master.

"Harker, and Murray," Fagin said – whispered – the words ebbing away like fog in the night.

A strange sense of déjà vu had overtaken Harry. As though he had been standing here before, waiting for this man to come out, as if, somehow, he could recall what the other Houdini had done, could sample his memories, remotely, second-hand, like an echo. He was tense, his heart beat fast, though outwardly he was calm. He waited. The two figures hugged, there in the darkness, then separated, one going back into the building, the other coming out, onto the road of the South Bank. The sound of Harker's feet filled the night. It was very quiet there, suddenly, no one passing, no late revellers; even the whales were silent. Fagin melted into the shadows. Harry watched the man Harker go past them, not seeing them. There was nothing remarkable about the man. He waited. Harker walked past. Harry, after a moment, followed.

The night focused, thinned. Harry's entire world became the path he followed, behind that man he didn't know, whose name, only, was left him by his own dead self.

Harker was going towards Waterloo Station and the fog thickened here, and the gas lamps were yellow dogs' eyes in the fog. Harry followed and the immense edifice of the station rose before him but Harker did not go up the stone stairs into the station. He went down a side alley – and Harry followed. His footsteps echoed in the night and Harker stopped, suddenly, and turned. They were alone there, in that dark place, with only the yellow gaslight illuminating their faces, and Harker's was very white.

He stared. Harry stood there, watching him. Two men, facing each other, not speaking. Harker raised a shaking hand and pointed it at Harry.

"You!" he said.

Harry said, "Do you know me?"

Every inch of him wanting to scream at the man, to shake him. To ask what had happened.

"I told you I can't!" Harker said. "You shouldn't be here." His face was devoid of blood. His pupils were dilated. He said, "You *can't* be here. How... They told me you were–"

He bit his lip to silence himself.

"That I was dead?"

Harker nodded.

"I need to know," Harry said. "What–"

But Harker was shaking his head, frantic now, fear etched into his face like a tattoo. "No," he said. "No. They will find you. They warned me. They are probably watching, even now. Get away from me!"

Harry had taken a step towards him. That was enough to startle Harker. He turned and ran.

Harry followed.

Running through the fog, whale song rising like a funeral dirge far away, from the Thames. The only sounds their echoing footsteps, Harker leading, Harry following his quarry, all thought, all caution gone.

Connections made: the former him had made contact with this Harker, perhaps confided in him. Harker had a key to the answer. Something his company did, something of great secrecy and significance. He had to know – had to know why he had been killed, what secret his death had protected.

Running, his breath fogging in the air, a great silence as if snow was falling, as if sound was being sucked out of the world, as if they were the only two people in it–

But they weren't.

Later, in the dark, Harry remembered it with fleeting, truncated fragments of recall:

The screech of wheels, the bellow of steam–

Harker's pale face, turning towards him–

His mouth opening in a silent scream–

A vast, black vehicle, a steam-powered baruch-landau, smashing into the man–

Harker's body flying through the air–

Black-clad men streaming out of the vehicle–

More of them appearing out of the shadows, surrounding the area–

Harker's body lying against a wall, head at an unnatural angle, legs broken beneath him–

Harry, too, might have screamed, he couldn't later be sure–

Arms grabbing him, too many to fight against, though he tried–

A truncheon rising in the air–

Someone kicked his legs out from under him and then the truncheon descended–

The back of his head erupting in pain, it bloomed like a dark flower and he felt himself go limp.

"Tap him again," someone said, a long way off. He tried to struggle but couldn't move, couldn't open his eyes. Something connected with the back of his head again and he couldn't even scream, which may have been a mercy. All thought fled and Harry Houdini escaped into the darkness and the cool absence of pain that it offered.


He came to gradually. His head pounded in waves that made him dizzy, sick. Bile in his throat, he fought not to gag. The back of his head felt swollen, painful. He tried to move his hands and couldn't.

Tied up?

A voice, gravely and deep. "Alas, no, Mr Houdini. We are well aware by now of your skill with knots and ropes and, I dare say, other modes of confinement."

He opened his eyes. Blinked. Realised he could not move at all, nothing but his head.

What had they done to him?

"I have taken the liberty," the voice said, as though, once again, reading his mind, "to have you... sedated. It is an unfortunate necessity, but I suspect even you, Mr Houdini, would find it impossible to escape the confines of chemistry." The voice coughed. Harry's eyes tried to adjust to the dim half-light of the room he found himself in. He could not yet see the speaker. Behind a vast desk, a large silhouette, but that was all.

"It is a special concoction my people have managed to steal, some while back, from the Quiet Council's research facility," the voice said, complacently.

"Who... are you?" Harry said. His lips felt numb. It was hard to speak, to see.

"My name is Dombey," the voice said. The shadow behind the desk moved, then settled back. "Paul Dombey."

"But who... *are* you?" Harry said, and the man laughed.

"I am the general manager of Dombey and Son," he said.

Harry shook his head, or tried to. This wasn't helping. Was the man toying with him? Flashes of memory – Harker's pale face, the black baruch-landau, Harker's broken body flying through the air–

He swallowed bile, tried again. "Who... do you work for?"

But it was not Harry's place to ask questions. It was his place to answer them. He was the captive. The privilege of knowledge was not his to take. The shadow stirred behind the desk.

"You are far more interesting than you first appeared, Mr Houdini," it said. It chuckled good-naturedly. "Oh, you had us fooled, when you first showed up! A green, inexperienced agent of the Cabinet Noir, that was easy enough to establish. Blundering about, asking questions in all the wrong places... Vespuccians!" The voice chuckled again.

251

"You have so little style, you are like half-civilised barbarians bumbling about! Do you know, I enjoyed watching your feeble efforts. Who do I work for? You will find out in due course, Mr Houdini. We are the guardians, if you like. We watch. We watch the Bureau, and the Quiet Council, and the Shaolin. We watch the world powers, and we try to stir the world onto the course it should have taken long ago. And you!" The shadow moved forward and, for just a moment, a vast, pasty face revealed itself in the half-light, and if he could Harry would have cried out. Half-machine it was, one eye mechanical while the other, a liquid blue, glared at him with benevolent amusement. Half the face, when it turned, was open, the skin missing, and inside it, rather than blood and bones, were tiny clockwork parts, moving silently. The man grinned, revealing teeth of metal and ivory. "When you became too much of a nuisance," he said, as pleasantly as before, "and found what you thought was a weak spot, our own Mr Harker, I had no choice. As much as it pained me, Mr Houdini, I had to... let you go."

"You ordered me killed?"

"We knew you were to meet an agent at the docks last night. What we did not know, could not know – was that the agent was *you*!"

Harry said nothing. The truth was that he had not expected to encounter himself either.

"So *now*," the voice said, settling back, that hideous face disappearing from view, "you have aroused our interest, Mr Houdini!"

"Is that... Is that a good thing?" Harry said.

"It depends," the voice allowed, generously, "on which side of this desk you sit on."

"I... see."

"Do not worry! This is a great opportunity, for us as well as for you. I assume you are an agent of that elusive Bookman? One hears so much, yet truly knows so little… Come, my dear, join me."

The last was not, clearly, aimed at Harry. He turned his head as much as he could. Light footsteps sounded, and to Harry's amazement a beautiful young woman entered the circle of light cast from above.

"Come, my dear. Say hello to our guest," Mr Dombey said.

"Hello," the girl said. She smiled, revealing white teeth. "Who…?"

"But my dear Mr Houdini!" Mr Dombey said. "This is Wilhelmina Murray."

Harry tried to swallow, couldn't. "Harker's… fiancée?"

"One of my best agents," Mr Dombey said, with evident pride. Mina Murray smiled pleasantly at Harry.

Harry whispered: "Please… help me."

Mina Murray laughed. "Why would I do that?" she said.

And Harry knew he was doomed.

"What will you do with me?" he said. Was the effect of the drug wearing off? He tried to move his hands – the tips of his fingers, he thought, had moved a little.

"*He* wants to see you," Mr Dombey said. "Therefore…"

"He who?"

The shadowed figure behind the desk shook its head. "My dear," it said to Mina Murray. "Would you?"

"My pleasure," Mina Murray said. She came to Harry and stood close to him; he could smell her perfume. She nodded to someone behind him; he couldn't see. The sound of a heavy object being dragged on the ground. Then she put her hands on him – they were warm – and she pushed. Harry fell back with a cry. Hands grabbed him, lowered him. He found himself inside a wooden crate. Mina Murray towered over him, and suddenly there was nothing pretty or kind in her face. Her smile was predatory.

"It won't hurt a bit," she said. In her hand she held a syringe.

"What… What is it?" Harry whispered. He couldn't move.

"It will send you to sleep," she said, gently. The needle lowered. Mina pulled up Harry's sleeve. He couldn't resist her.

"Where… Where am I going?"

Mina Murray tested the syringe. A bubble of liquid and air formed at the top of the needle. Harry watched it, hypnotised.

"Where?" Mina Murray said, as though surprised. She knelt over Harry and with a quick, efficient move pushed the needle into Harry's arm. He felt a pinprick of pain, then a spreading numbness.

"Why, you are going to Transylvania," Mina Murray said.

Then the lid of the crate was placed above him, and nails were driven into the wood to close it tight, and a darkness settled over Harry Houdini.

# PART VI
## *The Stoker Memorandum*

# THIRTY-THREE

"Tell me about Stoker," Lucy said.

It was getting into the late afternoon. Beyond the windows the spray from the sea rose high into the air on the cliff. Seagulls dived, dark shapes against the weak sun. Miss Havisham had baked cinnamon buns.

Lucy was still following Mycroft's tortured trail. Miss Havisham's memory was, in many ways, the Bureau's own. But what was Mycroft after? Closeted in his club, seeing no one, what did he see, what mystery was he trying to unravel?

"Stoker, Abraham," Miss Havisham said, thoughtfully. "Yes, I remember dear little Abe. That's what I called him, you know. My darling little Abe. One of the theatre folks, naturally. And Irish." She sighed. "An unlikely agent for anyone," she said. "Which is why no one wanted to follow up on it. Not even Mycroft, at first…"

```
Name: Stoker, Abraham.
Code name: none.
Place of birth: Dublin.
Parents: deceased.
```

```
Family: wife, Florence, one child.
Affiliation: unknown.
Notes:
```

"Notes?" Lucy said.

Miss Havisham rubbed the bridge of her nose. For the first time, she had placed a file folder on the table. A single sheet of white paper inside, and the *notes* section, Lucy saw, had been left blank. Miss Havisham smiled, wistfully. "As you can see, we had nothing on him. A theatrical manager, working for Henry Irving's Lyceum Theatre in London. An unremarkable man, clean as this sheet of paper."

"So what drew you to him?" Lucy said.

Miss Havisham shook her head. "It was before the Orphan case, when we were busy monitoring the European side of things. Later there was a shift, Fogg wanted to watch Vespuccia, and the Chinese Desk was getting new funding, but by then I was out. It was... little things that kept coming up. And then there was First Night of Gilbert and Sullivan's *Pirates of the Carib Sea*..."

Lucy waited. Miss Havisham moved at her own pace. Her eyes were clouded. She was going back in time, to a better time and place, before her forced retirement, when she was still a player of the Great Game...

It had been a great coup for the Lyceum (Miss Havisham told her). *It had been one of the times when Gilbert and Sullivan were fighting again and, to make it worse, Gilbert had charged their manager, Richard D'Oyly Carte, of cheating them out of money – over a carpet, of all things.*

*So the Lyceum had managed to steal them away, if not for long, and had put on the opening night of their latest production,*

*The Pirates of the Carib Sea*, at the Lyceum rather than the Savoy.

There had been no indication of anything remarkable in the offing. As I said, little things...

Two weeks before the opening night, an extraction team had brought in a German defector. He had been a low-level employee of Krupp's, and our hopes of getting technical information regarding Krupp's latest monster cannon were in vain. They had put him in Ham, in the interrogation centre, and had been sweating him for three days without anything useful coming out, when I decided to pop in and see him. I had only routine questions to ask him, you see. I remember the interrogation room, the defector's bruised face, sweaty hands that left print marks on the metal desk between us. I had a cup of tea and offered him one, which he accepted, as well as a cigarette.

"You are Marcus Rauchfus?" I said. He confirmed his name.

"Engineer with Krupp Industries?"

Again, he nodded.

"What made you decide to defect?" I asked, with honest curiosity. Krupp looked after his people well. It was hard to get deep into his organisation, and what agents of ours had tried to infiltrate his organisation tended to... well, disappear. Loyalty and ruthlessness, as Mycroft liked to say, were powerful together.

Rauchfus shrugged. Perhaps he truly didn't know why. After three days of interrogation no one was very enthusiastic about him any more, he'd given us nothing we could use. "I was..." His voice was hoarse; they had sweated him hard those three days. He spread his arms in a helpless gesture. "Always I love the English."

"We are not at war with Germany."

"No." But he did not sound convinced, and for the first time my curiosity was aroused.

"What do you know of Alfred Krupp's plans?" I asked. Rauchfus looked uncomfortable. He leaned towards me across the desk. There was something in his eyes that wanted to come out. I nodded to the guard, and he left the room, leaving the two of us alone. "Well?" I said.

"Them I don't tell!" He hit the desk with his fist. "You I tell. You give me house in Surrey?"

"We look after our defectors," I said. "As long as they can offer us something substantial."

"I make statement," Rauchfus said. "To you I make statement."

"Well?"

"My name is Marcus Rauchfus, and I am an engineer for Krupp Industries, yes. Yes! But not general section. I was assistant to one man, four, five years ago. His name is Diesel, Rudolf Diesel. Great engineer. The best! Top secret project." Marcus Rauchfus smiled, shyly. "Top secret," he repeated, as if there was a magic in the words.

"What was the nature of the project?" I asked.

"To make new engine," he said. "New power source! Yes! But..."

"What sort of new power source?"

He waved his hand. This was not important. "Petroleum," he said. "Krupp has network, yes, to bring it in from the Arabian Peninsula. Also Vespuccia, we believe, has much."

"Petroleum?"

I knew what it was, of course. Moreover, I knew very well we had our own research facility dedicated to finding new, more efficient sources of power than coal. But Rauchfus shook his head. "Not important," he said, placidly.

"Why not?"

"Decoy! I find out, by accident. Yes, I know, you have research also. French, Chinese, same! But—"

There had been a girlfriend, he told me. Working in Krupp's private office. She told him, once. They had a fight. "You think you are special? You are Top Secret?" she had laughed at

260

him. "Real work not done on Diesel project. Real work classified Ultra!"

"Ultra?" I said.

Rauchfus nodded.

"What's Ultra?" I said.

"Ultra is secret project," Rauchfus said.

"Of what nature?"

"I do not know."

I sighed. "This is all you have for me?"

"Yes. No! Ultra not Krupp project."

At that I sat up straighter. "Not Krupp? What do you mean?"

Here Rauchfus lowered his voice. "Not Krupp," he said. "International. Very dangerous to know. One, two months later, girlfriend not at work. Not at home. Gone." He clicked his fingers sadly. "Like this, gone."

"And you?"

"No one know I know!" But he looked fearful. "British," he whispered to me. His eyes were round. "British too. She tell me. British too."

"British? British who?"

He shook his head. "I do not know. I should not have said."

He wouldn't speak again, after that. I had left instructions for the interrogators not to touch him. I wanted him kept isolated, safe. When I got back to the Bureau I dug deeper into the files.

It was as I had thought. Rauchfus had lied to me. He had not come over voluntarily to our side. He had thought, rather, that he was dealing with an agent of the French's Quiet Council. He must have been horrified to realise he had been duped. If what he said was true, someone high up in the clandestine world was involved in a plot with Alfred Krupp. It was more likely Rauchfus was a plant, a false flag sent to us by Krupp's intelligence people. A decoy. But I couldn't take the chance.

*Fogg was out of the Bureau at that time. Mycroft, I believe, had sent him away, I was not sure where. It was shortly after Moreau had been exiled, or banished, or transferred -- versions varied -- to an isolated research facility on an island in the South Seas. Rumour had it Mycroft wanted Fogg far away -- and making sure Moreau stayed banished might have been a good enough reason.*

*For myself, though, I did not think giving Fogg access to Moreau's research was a good idea, and said so. But back then Fogg was Mycroft's golden boy, and he could do no wrong. Or so it seemed...*

*Mycroft always plans further, deeper, I know that now. He plays the long game. Did he suspect Fogg even then?*

*I came to him that day. It was night time, the gas lamps were lit outside, and inside the Bureau it was cold. We were running a shadow operation in Afghanistan then, following that disastrous war we had run over there. The operation, as I recall, did not go well. Berlyne was coming in and out of the fat man's office, sneezing and coughing and politely barring access to anyone who came. But Mycroft saw me. He always made the time -- for his own benefit, have no doubt. He needed me, and he knew it. On that we were of one mind.*

*"What do you want, Havisham?" the fat man had said, looking up at me from his desk. I knew he hated it, preferred his armchair at the Diogenes, the silence there, his food...*

*I said, "Ultra."*

*He went very still. Mycroft has the talent. "What are you talking about?" he said at last. I looked at him. "Krupp," I said.*

*"Yes?"*

*He was giving nothing away. So I told him about Rauchfus, and watched him go even stiller, as if delving deep inside himself.*

*"Is he real?" he said.*

*I shrugged.*

*"Your gut instinct."*

*"My instincts took me to look at him in the first place."*

*He nodded. That was all, but it was decided, there and then. Just like that.*

*"Is he safe?"*

*"We need to move him."*

*"Where?"*

*"The village?"*

*He shook his head. "Too public. It needs to be close by. A relation."*

*Meaning family. Meaning one of us…*

*We looked at each other with the same thought.*

*"Mrs Beeton."*

"*Isabella* Beeton?" Lucy said, interrupting. Miss Havisham looked momentarily surprised. "Do you know another one?" she said.

"Our *Prime Minister* Isabella Beeton?"

Miss Havisham smiled tolerantly. "She wasn't Prime Minister then," she said, reasonably. "But she'd always been family. Even when she was fomenting revolution, later, in eighty-eight."

"Mrs Beeton worked for the Bureau?"

Miss Havisham shook her head at that. "A relation," she said. "One of the people we used to call Mycroft's Irregulars. She ran a safe house for the Bureau, every now and then. And Mycroft and I decided it was the perfect place to move our reluctant German defector to."

Lucy looked at her closely. "But something went wrong?" she said, softly.

Miss Havisham sighed. "Something went wrong," she agreed, sadly.

# THIRTY-FOUR

.

*That same night* (Miss Havisham said) *we undertook a rare excursion together, Mycroft and I. At Ham Common we picked up Rauchfus, and drove him, in Mycroft's baruch-landau, to Mrs Beeton's place. We erased Rauchfus's trail of paperwork, excised all mention of him on the Ham facility's records, and returned to the Bureau, confident he was safe, and that we had time.*

*As it turned out, we were wrong.*

*I was woken up in the archives. I had dozed at my desk. Mycroft's voice on the Tesla unit. I had never heard him so angry, so controlled.*

*"We lost him," he said.*

*I said, "What?"*

*"Rauchfus. He's gone."*

*"Gone where?"*

*A silence on the line. Then: "Gone."*

*I saw him being carted away. We came there, to the safe house, and there he was, peaceful, at rest. The resultant autopsy revealed a minute hole in the back of his neck, as if a thin needle had been inserted there all the way to his brain. There had been no reports of intruders, no one unauthorised entering or leaving*

*the house. Mrs Beeton was – justifiably – outraged. I thought I*
*heard Mycroft murmur, "The Bookman," just once, but that was*
*that. We burned Rauchfus's files. There was no more mention*
*of Ultra, or a highly placed British power playing in the sandbox*
*with Krupp, or what it could mean.*

*Then there was the mess in eighty-eight… I was made redun-*
*dant and Mycroft was beleaguered. The political landscape*
*changed, Moriarty lost the elections, the Byron automata ran*
*against him but in a surprise move it was Mrs Beeton who*
*won…*

*Is this why you are here? Why Mycroft sent you?*

*Are the old suspicions resurfacing?*


"You mean…" Lucy wasn't sure what to say. "You suspected *Mrs Beeton*?"

"No one knew Rauchfus was there. Only Mycroft, and
myself, beside her. It was Occam's Razor, Lucy. The sim-
plest explanation is the most likely correct one."

Miss Havisham smiled, suddenly. "We are shadow
players," she said, and shrugged. "We seldom keep to
only one side."

There was a silence. "What *happened* in eighty-eight?"
Lucy said at last.

Miss Havisham shook her head. "I do not know, exactly. Something is buried, deep under Oxford, which
needs to remain buried. That is all I will say." She glanced
at Lucy sharply. "Mycroft never sent you to me, did he?"
she said.

"No."

"What are you playing at, Miss Westenra?"

Lucy didn't know what to tell her. "I need you to trust
me," she said, simply.

"Why?"

"Because I think Mycroft is in trouble."

Miss Havisham snorted. "He is always in trouble."

"I think... I think the Bookman is back."

Miss Havisham fell quiet. Then, as if, between them, something had been decided, she said: "Tea?"

"Please," Lucy said.


*But you were asking me about Abe Stoker, and I quite went about it in a roundabout way (said Miss Havisham). Well, Rauchfus had awakened our suspicions, but my interest in Stoker came two weeks later, at that first-night performance of* The Pirates of the Carib Sea, *a performance in which the very man who had so concerned us made a rare appearance.*

*Alfred Krupp had come to London unannounced. He had come, naturally, on business, but had taken time for the theatre–*

*Which had us curious. Krupp was seldom seen in public. Even on our home turf following him was near impossible. He had his own team of anti-surveillance experts.*

*Could the theatre be something more than entertainment? Could this engagement mean a clandestine meeting of some sort?*

*And if so, with whom?*

*In light of what we had learned – or thought we had – from Rauchfus, I was insistent that we monitor the theatre as closely as possible. Fogg was back by then, and argued vehemently against it. Krupp was too important – we had to be careful – we didn't have the budget – the staff–*

*I had argued with him. Mycroft was distracted – the Afghanistan operation had gone badly – at last we agreed on a compromise, a small but select team of watchers, and I myself secured a ticket to the show, which had by then sold out.*

*Did we learn anything from that evening? Krupp was sitting with his people in a box. The Queen herself was in attendance, in the Royal Box, of course. Lord Babbage made a rare – one of his last, in fact – public appearances. The cream and crop of London society was there. That rogue Flashman, toadying beside the Queen… I always had a soft spot for him – you know where you stand with a liar and a bully better than you do with a hero, sometimes. There is often only a fine distinction between the two.*

*But I'm digressing. We spotted nothing that evening, hard as we tried. Could a clandestine meeting be carried out in the open? That is, sometimes, the best way… but who was Krupp there for? It had even crossed my mind it was Mycroft behind it all, Mycroft who, to my surprise, also attended that evening, sitting in the Holmes family's own box, close by the Queen's…*

*Could Krupp be meeting the Bookman?*

*Babbage?*

*And it occurred to me all this was foreground, it was scenery, it was stagecraft – and that I was looking in the wrong place.*

*I had to look behind the scenes. I had to look backstage.*

*Where little Abe Stoker moved about, unobtrusively.*


"A facilitator," Miss Havisham said, fondly. "An unobtrusive little man, a clerk really. Going about his business – which also means touring on the continent, and corresponding overseas, and in so many ways he could have been the perfect deep-cover spy, undistinguished from his cover story. I fell in love with him a little, then. When I realised this. I told Mycroft, that very night. We had to study Stoker. Learn him, and make our approach. We had to find out who he represented. He was a liaison, I could see that clearly. But between what powers? This insight, together with the German defector's story, added up. I pushed…"

"But?" Lucy said.

Miss Havisham shrugged. "Nothing came of it."

"Nothing?"

"Fogg argued, but Mycroft approved the plan. And nothing happened. Little Stoker was just who he appeared to be – a not-particularly-important theatrical manager of little talent or ambition. We had teams on him round-the-clock for a month, then it got dropped to periodic spot-checks, and finally it got dropped entirely. And there," Miss Havisham said, "the matter rested, until now. Why, has something changed?"

Lucy smiled. She stood up. "Routine inquiry," she said. And, "I had better head back into town before it is dark."

Miss Havisham smiled too, and also stood up. Her look said Lucy wasn't fooling her for a moment.

"You watch out," she told her, leading her back through the comfortable room and out into the ruined front of the mansion beyond, and Lucy thought that Miss Havisham herself had quite a bit of stagecraft in her. "And go safely."

"I will," Lucy said. And, "Thank you."

Miss Havisham nodded. Lucy walked down the steep path of the cliff, back into the grim little village of Satis-by-the-Sea, and to its small, deserted train station. All the while she was aware of Miss Havisham standing where she was, watching as she went.

Mycroft had reactivated the plans concerning Stoker, she now knew. Something had changed, but his attention had been turned not to Germany, and Krupp, but farther, to the remote and inhospitable mountains of Transylvania…

It was when she was approaching London on board the old, patient steam train that the device she had been keeping on her person for days began to blip, faintly at first and then with renewed vigour, and the tension that had been building inside her reached a crescendo and then, all at once, disappeared, leaving her calm and focused.

The moment she had waited for had arrived.

Mycroft's agent, the mysterious Mr Stoker, was finally approaching.

# THIRTY-FIVE

Night time, and the sky over Richmond Park was strewn with stars, the clouds clearing, a moon beaming down silver light. A deer moved amongst the dark trees, smelled humans and gunpowder and went another way.

"Everyone present?"

"Present and ready."

Lucy surveyed her team. They have been with her on the raid in Aksum, and they have been with her in the Bangkok Affair, and in the Zululand Engagement... she could trust them with her life.

She was going to have to trust them with Stoker's.

"Listen up." They were gathered around her in a semi-circle. Black-clad, guns ready: not shadow executives but the muscle shadow executives sometimes had to call on, to use, ex-military and ex-underworld and ex-mercenaries, retrained and retained by the Bureau for secretive, semi-military operations.

"Ma'am."

"An airship travelling on a Bureau-approved flight plan is expected to make landing in Richmond Park within the next hour or two. Its cargo is of vital importance. Our mission is simple: retrieve the cargo safely, and get the hell out. Understood?"

"Ma'am, yes, ma'am."

A hand up – Bosie. "Do we expect opposition?"

Smiles on the men's faces, echoed by Lucy's. "We always expect opposition," she said.

Bosie nodded. "Ma'am."

"Spread out. Keep in contact. We may need to signal to the airship when the time comes. Keep a lookout – and remember."

Her men looked at each other, soberly. "Try not to get killed."

"Yes, ma'am!"

They spread out, silent as shadows, and she was left alone, amidst the trees.

And deadly worried.

Too many things to go wrong.

Too many things had *already* gone wrong…

Like that persistent feel that she was being followed, as soon as she got off at Euston Station. She had doubled back and changed hansom cabs but still the feeling persisted.

Then there was Fogg, running her down at the Bureau, angry, hard – "Where have you been?"

"I'm on leave."

"I heard you went down to Satis House."

"Heard where?"

His voice, cold and hard. "Westenra, I am your superior. You were not authorised to go there."

"Excuse me?"

He must have had her followed. Which explained *some* part of her paranoia… "I am researching an old file."

"Which file would that be, exactly?"

"The Orphan file," she said, looking him in the eyes. "The eighty-eight dossier. That was the last encounter we've had with the Bookman."

Fogg's face was white and very still. Lucy said, softly, "Wasn't it?"

"The Bookman is not your concern!"

Lucy did not reply to that. "I need to see Mycroft," she said, instead.

"He's not here. I'm in charge."

"Where is he?"

"Gone."

There was a strange look in Fogg's eyes. Was it panic? Or victory?

And now she was worried.

"I'd better go, then," she said. She turned her back on him.

"Westenra!"

"Sir?"

"Do not meddle in things you don't understand."

She turned back to him and faced him. "Is that a threat?"

Fogg smiled, his mouth like a thin, honed blade. "Take it as you will," he said, indifferently, at last, and walked away.

Lucy was left glaring after him.


Worry about Mycroft made her indecisive. The device he had given her was monitoring Stoker's approach. Did she have time?

She had a decision to make and she made it. Night swallowing the city, she took a hansom cab to Belgravia–

The feeling stole on her as she rode in the darkened cab, the street lights passing, the cries of sellers and the tolling of bells silenced, the faint beeping of the device increasing with each passing second as the mysterious airship from Transylvania was coming closer–

A sense of doom, a sense that Mycroft had foreseen a thing happening that she had thought impossible. That the trail he was following ended abruptly, the questions he sought answers to in his darkened room or at his quarters at the Diogenes Club remaining unanswered–

A piercing noise outside, rising and falling, rising and falling, setting her teeth on edge and she banged on the roof, shouting, "Stop!" to the driver.

She pushed the door open and was already running towards the flashing lights, the rising and falling sound of the siren growing stronger, two minute police automatons gliding on their little wheels, their blue light cones swirling on top of their heads as they came to stop her, but she pushed them away and went towards the house–

Arc lights and police tape and the neighbours' lights were on, but this was a good neighbourhood and no one wanted to show themselves outside. Mycroft's house, a modest place with ivy growing on the walls, a small garden in the front and there on the front steps–

"You can't come through here, miss. I'm sorry."

"What happened?"

"There has been an incident."

He was young and recently recruited to Scotland Yard and it really wasn't his fault he had run into Lucy.

"Where's your superior?"

He had on a little grin. "Miss?"

She made to walk past him and he grabbed her and she turned and grabbed his hand and twisted it, hard, behind his back until he yelled and dropped to his knees. Heads looked their way, then–

"Lucy?"

"Chief Inspector Adler."

Adler came towards her, not hurrying, her face unreadable. "It's been a while."

"Yes."

"Please let Constable Cuff go, Miss Westenra."

"Sure."

She released the man, who stood up, massaging his arm.

"Excuse me, chief inspector? It's *Sergeant* Cuff," he said.

Irene Adler smiled at him. "It *was*," she said. "Lucy, walk with me."

They left Cuff behind them. Lucy followed Adler. She wanted to look away but couldn't.

Just before his front door, resting on the little path that led up to his house, rested the large, lifeless body of Mycroft Holmes.

"How?" Lucy said. She felt numb. She had known this was coming, somehow, something deep inside her crying out, before, that all was wrong, that danger was on the way – but now, confronted with the truth of it, she didn't want to believe it.

Irene Adler said, "He was found under an hour ago, as you see him. There are no signs of violence…"

"This couldn't be natural causes."

"You have a better explanation?"

They glared at each other.

"I do," said a new voice. A man in a white coat came towards them, his face a mask of anxiety.

"You have found something?"

Lucy recognised the doctor, another relation – one of Mycroft's Irregulars, as Miss Havisham had called them. Worked at Guy's Hospital, if she remembered right – he must have been seconded to Scotland Yard.

"His death was not of natural causes. Look."

The doctor knelt by Lucy's former employer. With gentle hands he rolled the body and pulled aside cloth to show them the exposed back of the head. The doctor pointed. What was his name, Lucy wondered, trying to recall. Williams. Walton. Something starting with W.

"See here?" the doctor was pointing. Lucy peered closer. Was that a tiny discoloration in Mycroft's skin?

"It's a puncture hole," Irene Adler said.

"Exactly," the doctor – Wilberforce? Wharton? – said. "A very fine one – yet, I think, deadly. He was attacked. Poor Mycroft…" The doctor took a deep breath and resumed. "He had been coming up to his door when the attacker caught him. He must have been in hiding, waiting for him. He inserted a long, thin needle into Mycroft's head, going all the way in, killing him almost instantly."

Lucy pushed up. She felt ill, helpless. What should she do now?

Unbidden, Mycroft's face came into her mind, his lips moving. Speaking to her, on their way to the palace.

What had he told her?

*"If something were to happen to me," Mycroft had said – she had wanted to protest, but he silenced her. "If something were to happen to me, I have put certain precautions in place. Certain agents have been… put in reserve, shall we say. The old and the new…" and he smiled, looking at her. "You must get hold of the Stoker information," he told her. "At all costs. Off the books, non-Bureau sanctioned. Were I to die, there is still Smith… if he is not too old." Here he smiled again. "For you, however, I have made a different precaution."*

Smith? That old hack?

Wasn't he dead?

Well, her objective was clear. It hadn't changed. Dead or alive, Mycroft's instructions stood. And he *had* made an arrangement for her... and one she intended to follow.

She felt relief at that, a sense of order returning. She looked down at his large corpse. "The end of an era," the doctor murmured, echoing her thoughts.

"What is the meaning of this!"

The voice was loud like a fog-horn and edged like steel and most recently it had been shouting at *her*.

Fogg, arriving at the scene of the crime. Lucy couldn't bear it, suddenly. She had to get away.

"Where are you–?" from Adler.

Lucy didn't have time to answer. She went around the side of the house, Fogg's footsteps echoing up the path–

"Was that Westenra? Oh dear, oh dear–"

He had seen the body.

"Why was I not immediately informed? This is a matter of national security! Bureau takes precedence!"

His voice faded behind her. She made her way to the adjoining road and hailed down a hansom cab.

It was time to finish the job, she thought.

It was time to find out what Stoker was carrying.

What had Mycroft said? *"Six months ago I played a pawn,"* Mycroft had told her. *"Not sure whether I was sacrificing a piece or making a play on the king."*

Well, she would find out. She would not let the fat man down.

"Where to, miss?" the hansom cab driver asked.

"Richmond Park," she said.

Her team had been notified. They would wait for her there.

She stared out of the window as the hansom cab headed for the river and the bridge, to cross over to the south bank. The rattle of the carriage sounded like piano keys and, as they drove closer to the water, the singing of the whales rose, majestic and slow, all about her, but what they sang she didn't know.

# THIRTY-SIX

"Ma'am."

"Report."

"Unknowns approaching from Richmond Hill gate."

"Number?"

"About two dozen. Spreading out – did we invite any-one else to the party, ma'am?"

"No."

"Hostiles then?"

"Yes."

Silence on the Tesla set. Then, "They're armed."

"I wouldn't expect anything less."

"Take them out?"

She made a quick calculation. Too early, a fire fight would draw unwanted attention. Someone else wanted Stoker. Someone else knew he was coming–

"Keep an eye on them."

"Ma'am–"

"Yes?"

"Hostiles approaching from Kingston gate direction."

Lucy swore.

"Ma'am?"

"Keep an eye on them."

She had expected some opposition. She had not expected an army.

And the airship, with its precious cargo, was approaching rapidly...

She put her spyglasses to her eyes. The airship was visible now, gaining momentum, a black shape crossing against the face of the moon. She tensed, knowing it was about to happen, it was too soon, she had not been prepared enough, and that, in the next few minutes, people would die.

"Mark it!"

"Ma'am!"

A silent flame rose up into the air, and then another, and another – her men shooting flares into the sky, marking the landing spot for the airship.

And giving away their position...

But no one was going to act until the airship had landed, safely.

Weren't they?

The airship was lit up now by the flares, a dark and unfamiliar dragon-shape, a strange design she had not seen before. It was a long, graceful design that, in the silver light of the moon and the yellow of the flares, looked almost like a dragon, descending. Or a bat, come to think of it...

And the airship *was* beginning its descent, and Stoker must be alive up there, must have managed his escape, and was bringing back the precious information Mycroft had gambled so heavily for. Her men were spread out, the flares would only give away the landing site but the rest of them were keeping watch on the intruders–

"Ma'am! Hostile fire, ma'am!"

A burst of gunfire, sudden and unexpected, was followed by the whoosh of something heavy rising in the air–

She watched the slim, deadly rocket rise, a trail of
smoke behind it–

"Take them," she said.

The rocket hit the side of the airship.

For a moment nothing happened. In the distance a
burst of gunfire, which was returned, as her men fired
on the unknown hostiles and were fired on in turn.
Then, abruptly, a bright ball of flame erupted overhead
and the side of the ship blew open, pieces of wood and
metal raining down onto the park. Flames caught the
side of the ship and it tilted with the impact, losing altitude rapidly.

Lucy swore.

"Ma'am, they are heavily armed!"

"Kill them."

"Ma'am, second group of hostiles moving in."

"We've lost any element of concealment," Lucy said.

"Ma'am?"

"Eliminate them."

And now the park had become a cacophony of battle,
gunfire and explosives going off while the airship, having
come all this way across Europe and the Channel, fell
down heavily, into Richmond Park.

Lucy was already running, three of her men following,
running towards the ship as it hit the ground with a sick-
ening crunch, bouncing still, once, twice, then tilting on
its side. A second explosion rocked the ship and flames
rose high, almost engulfing it. If anyone was still alive
inside…

"Ma'am, what are you–?"

"Stay back!"

She ran towards the flaming wreckage of the ship.

"Lucy! Stay back!"

Heedless, she dived into the flames. Thick black smoke rising now, the engines on fire, there would be mere moments before the whole thing blew up. Onto the flaming deck, titled sideways–

"Hel– help! Help me!"

He was still alive. She saw the small figure, not young any more, crawling towards her, gripping on to slats on the floor. He was leaving behind him a trail of blood– at least one of his legs was broken. She slid towards him.

"Stoker?"

"Help me. Please!"

The smoke had an acid stink to it. It burned her eyes, forced its way down her throat, choking her. She picked him up, or tried to. He was heavy; he cried out in pain when she touched him.

She wouldn't fail Mycroft, not now.

She picked him up and supported his weight and slid down farther, deeper into the raging fire–

Bullets flying overhead, tracer bullets lighting up the sky–

Through the fire, it licked at her skin, it caught in her hair, his weight no longer mattered, the ground was close, they were going to make it–

She fell off the side of the burning ship, her cargo with her. She rolled on the ground, putting out flames. Hands grabbed her, beat out the fire, lifted her.

"Stoker," she said. "Get… Stoker."

"Ma'am."

A new, loud voice, cutting like a rapier's blade through the night.

"Give him to us! You are outnumbered."

An alien accent. German, she thought, wildly.

"I thought," she said, panting, "I told you to kill them."

Apologetically: "There are a lot of them, ma'am."

"Grab Stoker!"

She spared a glance for the man. He was out, breathing shallowly, with difficulty. There was something around his neck, a metal canister on a string.

"Who the hell are *you*?" she called out, to the opposition.

There was an answering burst of gunfire and she smiled. They loped away from the burning airship, the smell of wood burning, metal melting, gas–

The explosion hit her back, threw her forwards. She rolled, a whoosh of hot flaming gas passed over her, and then they were up and running again and under shelter of the trees where the rest of her team closed on them, covering them against attack.

She checked on Stoker. Still alive, just about...

"Let's go," she said.


They pursued them across Richmond Park in deathly silence, the Germans, if that's what they were, however much their force had been reduced, and the other force, whom she could not put a name to. In the shadow world there were no labels, nobody carried a name tag or a calling card with which to announce themselves. The attackers could have been anyone. French? She would have bet good money on that. The Quiet Council, meddling in Bureau affairs...

And Krupp's men, perhaps.

She couldn't know, and right then she didn't care. She had her prize, singed and wounded but hers to keep, and so they went deeper into the park where deer and squirrels shied away from them, a ghostly pursuit in the darkness, amongst the trees, while behind them the landing site had been compromised, the siren song of police automatons sounding in the night, and Lucy thought of Irene Adler and how she was getting no sleep that night.

They pulled back to the Isabella Plantation. There had been a folly there, a stone house amidst the ponds and flowerbeds, and there they laid down Stoker while they waited for their pursuers.

Lucy knelt beside him, checking his pulse. It was weak, irregular. And suddenly she knew he was not going to make it.

A knowledge like that had come on her before, in other battles, other days. With comrades and with enemies, and with civilians sometimes, who were not a part of the battle but had wandered into it and were singed by its fire. It was a terrible knowing, that a human's life was ending, before their time, violently, and that there was nothing she could do, that most of the time, if she was honest with herself, she had been responsible for that very thing, that terrible ending.

Yet all life comes to an end, and never are there answers as to why; Lucy had learned, the hard way, not to question, not to wonder. Death was something to be accepted; to question it was futile.

"Stoker," she said, gently. She gave him water, wetting his lips, letting it dribble into his throat. At last he opened his eyes.

"I need to know," she said. "I need to know what you've found."

"M... Mycroft...?" Stoker said.

"He sent me."

Stoker closed his eyes – in understanding or fatigue she didn't know. Lucy waited. It was quiet there, at the Isabella

Plantation. The hunters would come but they were not yet there. At last Stoker opened his eyes. "I had... written down... report." His eyes moved, she followed their direction to the can hanging over his chest. "All there," he said. His mouth moved. Perhaps he tried to smile. "I had always... wanted," he said. "To... be a writer."

His eyes closed. His chest rose and fell and then did not rise again. After a moment, Lucy gently removed the can and the chain from around the dead man's neck. She opened it.

Inside was a small notebook, bound in dark vellum. It was filled with neat, tidy handwriting.

On the first page, in careful calligraphy, it said: *Bram Stoker's Journal*.

Sitting there, in that silence that comes before battle, Lucy read the last words of the dead man beside her.

# PART VII
## Bram Stoker's Journal

# THIRTY-SEVEN

*Bucharest–*

   *I had finally arrived at this city, with darkness gathering, casting upon the city a most unfavourable appearance. Having checked into my hotel I drank a glass of strong Romanian wine, accompanied by bear steak, which I am told they bring from the mountains at great expense. I had not enquired as for the recipe.*

   *I am sitting in my room, watching the dance of gaslight over the city. Tomorrow I set off for the mountains, and as I write this I am filled with trepidation. I have decided to maintain this record of my mission. In the event anything were to happen to me, this journal may yet make its way, somehow, back to London.*

   *Let me, therefore, record how I came to be at this barbarous and remote country, and the sorry, tortuous route by which I had come to my current predicament.*

My name is Abraham Stoker, called Abe by some, Bram by others. I am a theatrical manager, having worked for the great actor Henry Irving for many years as his personal assistant, and, on his behalf, as manager of the Lyceum Theatre in Covent Garden.

I am not a bad man, nor am I a traitor.

Nevertheless, it was in the summer of 18— that I became an unwitting assistant to a grand conspiracy against our lizardine masters, and one which I was helpless to prevent.

It had begun as a great triumph for my theatrical career. Due to a fight between the great librettist W.S. Gilbert and his long-time manager, Richard D'Oyly Carte, over – of all things – a carpet, I had managed to lure Gilbert and his collaborator, the composer Arthur Sullivan, to my own theatre from D'Oyly Carte's Savoy. We were to stage their latest work, titled *The Pirates of the Carib Sea*, a rousing tale of adventure and peril. The first part, and forgive me if I digress, describes our lizardine masters' awakening on Caliban's Island, their journey with that foul explorer Amerigo Vespucci back to the British Isles, their overthrowing of our human rulers and their assumption of the throne – a historical tale set to song in the manner only G&S could possibly do it.

In the second part, we encounter the mythical pirate Wyvern, the one-eyed royal lizard who – if the stories in the *London Illustrated News* can be believed – had abandoned his responsibilities to his race, the royal Les Lézards, to assume the life of a blood-thirsty pirate operating in the Carib Sea, between Vespuccia and the lands of the Mexica and Aztecs, and preying on the very trade ships of his own Everlasting Empire, under her royal highness Queen Victoria, the lizard-queen.

Irving himself played – with great success, I might add! – the notorious pirate, assuming a lizard costume of some magnificence, while young Beerbohm Tree played his boatswain, Mr Spoons, the bald, scarred, enormous human who is – so they say – Wyvern's right-hand man.

It was at that time that a man came to see me in my office. He was a foreigner, and did not look wealthy or, indeed, distinguished.

"My name," he told me, "is Karl May."

"A German?" I said, and he nodded. "I represent certain… interests in Germany," he told me. "A very powerful man wishes to attend the opening night of your new show."

"Then I shall be glad to sell him a ticket," I said, regarding the man – clearly a con-man or low-life criminal of some sort – with distaste. "You may make the arrangements at the box office. Good day to you, sir."

Yet this May, if that was even his real name, did not move. Instead, leaving me speechless, he closed and then locked the door to my office, from the inside, leaving me stranded in there with him. Before I could rise the man pulled out a weapon, an ornate hand-gun of enormous size, which he proceeded to wave at me in a rather quite threatening manner.

"This man," he said, "is a very public man. Much attention is paid to his every move. Moreover, to compound our–" *our*, he said! "– problem, this man must meet another very public man, and the two cannot be seen to have ever met or discussed… whatever it is they need to discuss."

This talk of men meeting men in secret reminded me of my friend Oscar Wilde, whom I had known in my student days in Dublin and who had once been the suitor of my wife, Florence. "I do not see how I can help you," I said, stiffly – for it does not do to show fear before a foreigner, even one with a gun in his hand.

"Oh, but you can!" this Karl May said to me. "And moreover, you will be amply compensated for your efforts –" and with that, to my amazement, this seeming charlatan pulled out a small, yet heavy-looking bag, and threw it on my desk. I reached for it, drawing the string, and out poured a heap of gold coins, all bearing the portrait – rather than of our own dear lizard-queen – of the rather more foreboding one of the German Kaiser.

"Plenty more where that came from," said this fellow, with a smirk on his face.

I did not move to touch the money. "What would you have me do?" I said.

"The theatre," he said, "is like life. We look at the stage and are spell-bound by it, the scenery convinces us of its reality, the players move and speak their parts and, when it's done, we leave. And yet, what happens to *make* the stage, to move its players, is not done in the limelight. It is done behind the scenes."

"Yes?" I said, growing ever more irritated with the man's manner. "You wish to teach me my job, perhaps?"

"My dear fellow!" he said, with a laugh. "Far from it. I merely wished to illustrate a point–"

"Then get to it, for my time is short," I said, and at that his smile dropped and the gun pointed straight at my heart and he cocked it. "Your time," he said, in a soft, menacing voice, "could be made to be even shorter."

I must admit that, at that, my knees may have shaken a little. I am not a violent man, and am not used to the vile things desperate men are prepared to do. I therefore sat back down in my chair, and let him explain and, when he had finished, I must admit I felt a sigh of relief escape me, for it did not seem at all such a dreadful proposition, and they were willing to compensate me generously besides.

"You may as well know," Karl May said to me, "the name of the person I represent. It is Alfred Krupp."

"The *industrialist*?"

May nodded solemnly. "But what," I gasped, "could he be wanting in my theatre?"

For I have heard of Krupp, of course, the undisputed king of the armaments trade, the creator of that monstrous canon they called Krupp's Baby, which was said to be able to shoot its payload all the way beyond the atmosphere and into space... A recluse, a genius, a man with his own army, a man with no title and yet a man who, it was rumoured, was virtually the ruler of all Germany...

A man who had not been seen for many a year, in public.

"Fool," Karl May said. "My lord Krupp has no interest in your pitiful theatre, nor in the singing and dancing of effeminate Englishmen."

"I am Irish, if you don't mind," I said. "There really is no need to be so *rude*–" and May laughed. "Rest your mind at ease, Irishman," he said. "My master wishes only to meet certain... interested parties. Behind, as it were, the scenes."

"Which parties?" I said, "for surely I would need to know in order to prepare–"

"All in good time!" Karl May said. "All in good time."

*Bu teni*–
This is a small mountain village near to my destination. I had taken the train this morning with no difficulty, yet was told the track terminated before my destination,

which is the city of Brasov, nestled, so I am told, in a beautiful valley within the Carpathian Mountains.

This region is called Transylvania, and a wild and remote land it is indeed. The train journey lasted some hours, in relative comfort, the train filled with dour Romanian peasants, shifty-looking gypsies, Székelys and Magyars and all other manner of the strange people of this region. Also on board the train were chickens, with their legs tied together to prevent their escaping, and sacks of potatoes and other produce, and children, and a goat. Also on board the train were army officers of the Austro-Hungarian Empire of which this was but a remote and rather dismal outpost, with nary a pastry or decent cup of coffee to be seen.

I had wondered at the transportation of such military personnel, and noticed them looking rather sharply in my direction. Nevertheless I was not disturbed and was in fact regarded with respect the couple of times we had occasion to cross each other in passing.

The train's passage was impressive to me, the mountains at first looming overhead then – as the train rose up from the plains on which sat Bucharest – they rose on either side of the tracks, and it felt as though we were entering another world, of dark forests and unexplored lands, and I fancied I heard, if only in the distance, the howl of wolves, sending a delicious shiver down my spine.

But you did not ask me for a travel guide! Let me be brief. The train terminated, after some hours, at a station in the middle of a field. It was a most curious thing. I could see the tracks leading onwards – presumably to Brasov – but we could not go on. The train halted within these hastily erected buildings, lit by weak gas lamps planted in the dirt, and all – peasants and chickens and soldiers and gypsies and goat – disembarked, including this Irishman.

At this nameless station waited coaches and carts – the peasants and local people to the carts, the soldiers and more well-to-do visitors to the coaches. I stood there in some bewilderment, when I was taken aside by the military officer who seemed to be in charge of that platoon. "You are going – there?" he said, and motioned with his head towards the distance, where I assumed this city of Brasov lay.

"Yes," I said.

"To visit… him?"

I nodded at that, feeling a pang of apprehension at the thought.

The officer nodded as if that had settled matters, and shouted orders in the barbarous tongue of his people. Almost immediately a coach had been found for me, its passengers emptied out, and I was placed with all due reverence into the empty compartment. "You will go to Bu teni this night," the officer said, "it is too late now to go further." Again he spoke to the driver, who gave me a sour look but didn't dare refuse, and so we took off in a hurry, the horses running down a narrow mountain path that led upwards, and at last to a small village, or what passes for a town in these parts, which was indeed called Bu teni, or something like it, and had beautiful wooden houses, a church, and a small inn, where I had alighted and where I am currently sat, writing this to you, while dining on a rather acceptable *goulash*.

I do not wish to labour details of what took place following that scoundrel Karl May's visit to my office at the Lyceum. You know as well as I what had happened, you had suspected long before you had approached me, three months ago, in order to recruit me to this desperate mission.

The facts are as they stand. To an outside eye, nothing had happened but that *Herr* Krupp, on a rare visit to England, went, one night, to the theatre – and so did any number of other personages, including, if I remember rightly, yourself, Mr Holmes.

The Queen herself was there, in the Royal Box, stately as ever, with her forked tongue hissing out every so often, to snap a stray fly out of the air. I remember the prince regent did not come but Victoria's favourite, that dashing Harry Flashman, the popular Hero of Jalalabad, was beside her. So were many foreign dignitaries and many of the city's leading figures, from our now-Prime-Minister Mrs Beeton, my friend and former rival Oscar Wilde, the famed scientists Jekyll and Moreau (before the one's suspicious death and the other's exile to the South Seas), the Lord Byron automaton (always a gentleman), Rudolph Rassendyll of Zenda, and many, many others. Your brother, the consulting detective, was there, if I recall rightly, Mr Holmes.

It was a packed night – sold out, in fact, and I had been kept off my feet, running hither and yon, trying to ensure our success, and all the while…

All the while, behind the scenes, things were afoot.

I was aware of movement, of strangers coming and going in silence, of that German villain Karl May (I had found out much later the man was not only a convicted criminal but worse, a dime novel hack) following me like a shadow, of a tense anticipation that had nothing to do with the play.

There are secret passageways inside every theatre, and the Lyceum is no exception. It has basements and sub-basements, a crypt (from the time it had been a church, naturally), narrow passageways, false doors, shifting scenery – it is a *theatre*, Mr Holmes!

It was a game of boxes, Mr Holmes. As I told you when you found me, three months ago, listening to me as if you already knew. How *Herr* Krupp appeared to be in the box when in fact it was a cut-out in the shadows; how he went through the false wall and into the passageway between the walls, and down, to the crypt, now our props room.

And the others.

For I had been unfortunate enough to see them.


*Bu teni–*

A letter had arrived for me in the morning. A dark •baruch-landau had stopped outside the inn, a great hulking machine, steam-driven, the stoker standing behind while the driver sat in front, in between their respective positions a wide carriage for the transport of passengers or cargo.

The driver had disembarked – I watched him from my window – and what a curious being he was!

I had seen his like before. Just the once, and that had been enough. Like the vehicle he was driving, he was huge, a mountain of a man, and a shiver of apprehension ran down my spine.

He would have been human, once upon a time.


"What *are* they?" I had asked Karl May. The play was going on above our heads, but I could not concentrate, I was filled with a terrible tension as we prepared for the summit – as May called it – down below, in the bowels of the theatre. The *they* I was referring to were beings of a similar size and disposition to the driver now sitting in the inn's dining room, awaiting my pleasure.

"Soldiers," Karl May told me. "Of the future."

"What has been done to them?"

"Have you heard of the Jekyll–Frankenstein serum?"

I confessed I had not.

"It is the culmination of many years of research," he told me, with a smirk. "We had stolen the formula from the French some time back. They have Viktor von Frankenstein working for them and he, in his turn, improved upon the work done by your Englishman, Dr Jekyll. This–" and here his hand swept theatrically, enfolding the huge hulking beings that were guarding, like mountain trolls, the dark corridors – "is the result."

"Can they ever... go back?" I said, whispering. May shook his head. "And their life-span is short," he said. "But they do make such excellent soldiers..."

It was then that *Herr* Krupp appeared, an old, fragile-looking man, yet with a steely determination in his eyes that I found frightening. "You did well," he said, curtly, and I was not sure if he was speaking to May or myself. He disappeared behind his monsters, and into the crypt.

"Who else are we expecting?" I said.

When, at that moment, the sound of motors sounded and a small, hunched figure came towards us in the darkness, half-human, half-machine...

*Bu teni–*

My landlady has been fussing over me ever since seeing the arrival of the carriage. "You must not go!" she whispered to me, fiercely, finding reason to come up to my room. "He is a devil, a monster!"

"You know of him?" I said.

"Who does not? They had closed the valley, Brasov had been emptied. They are doing unspeakable things there, in the shadow of the mountains." She shivered. "But *he* does not reside in Brasov."

"Where does he reside?" I said, infected by her fear.

"Castle Bran," she said, whispering. "Where once Vlad țepeș made his home…"

"Vlad țepeș?" I said. I was not familiar with the local history and the name was unfamiliar to me.

"Vlad the Third, Prince of Wallachia," she said, impatiently. "Vlad țepeș – how you say țepeș in your English?"

"I don't know," I said, quite bewildered.

"Impaler," she said. "Prince Vlad of the Order of the Dragon, whom they called Impaler."

I shook my head impatiently. Local history sounded colourful indeed, but irrelevant to my journey. "The man I am going to see is an Englishman," I said, trying to reassure her. "Englishmen do not impale."

"He is no man!" she said, and made a curious gesture with her fingers, which I took to be some Romanian superstition for the warding of evil. "He had ceased being human long ago."

At last I got rid of her, so I could return to my journal. Time is running out, and soon I shall be inside that baruch-landau, travelling towards my final destination.

Have mercy on my soul, Mycroft!


For I saw him, too, you see. I saw him come towards us, Karl May and I, in the subterranean depths of the Lyceum, that fateful night.

An old, old man, in a motorised chair on wheels, a steam engine at his back, and withered hands lying on the supports, controlling brass keys. His face was a ruined shell, his body that of a corpse, yet his eyes were bright, like moons, and they looked at me, and his mouth moved and he said, "Today, Mr Stoker, we are making history. Your part in it will not be quickly forgotten."

I may have stumbled upon my words. He had not been seen in public for five years or more. His very presence at my theatre was an honour, and yet I was terrified. When the small get entangled in the games of the great, they may easily suffer.

"My lord," I said. "It is an honour."

He nodded then that withered head, just once, acknowledging this. Then he, too, disappeared towards the crypt.


Yes, you suspected, did you not, Mycroft? You suspected this summit, your people were there that night, in the audience, trying to sniff scent of what was happening. Yet you never did.

For they did not meet, just the two of them, My Herr Krupp and he, my summoner, the lord of the automatons.

Another was there.

A monster...

For I had gone down into the dark passages, I had gone to check all was secure, and I saw it. I saw the ancient sewer open up and something come crawling out of it, a monstrous being like a giant invertebrate, with feelers as long as a human arm, slithering towards that secret meeting... A vile, alien thing.

Which, three months ago, when we first met, you finally gave a name to.

*The Bookman*, you told me.

So that was that shadowy assassin.

A thing made by the lizardine race, long ago.

Those beings which came to us from Caliban's Island, in the Carib Sea, and yet were not of a terrestrial origin at all.

An ancient race, of scientifically advanced beings... crash-landed with their ship of space, thousands of years ago, millions perhaps, on that island.

And awakened by Vespucci, on his ill-fated journey of exploration...

And the Bookman, that shadowy assassin, one of their machines?

I do not know, Mycroft, but I remember the fear I felt when I saw that... that *thing*, slither towards the crypt.

A summit indeed.

And now, I must leave.

*The Borgo Pass–*
The driver says we are going through something called the Borgo Pass, though it appears on no map of the area. I am the sole passenger of this baruch-landau, the driver ahead, the stoker behind, and I in the middle, staring out over a rugged terrain.

This is the letter I had received at the inn:

*My friend,*

*Welcome to the Carpathians. I am anxiously expecting you. I trust that you slept well. My driver has instructions to carry you in safety to my quarters and bring you to me. I trust that your journey from London has been a happy one, and that you will enjoy your stay. I look forward to seeing you.*

*Yours~*
    *Charles Babbage*


What awaits me beyond these mountains, is it to glory, or to death, that I ride?

# THIRTY-EIGHT

Outside the night was still, an anticipatory silence as Lucy's men waited for the attack they knew would come. The Isabella Plantation was as good a place as any to wait–

They would be there soon, Lucy knew.

She continued reading the journal.

It described Stoker's arrival in Transylvania, his visit to Castle Bran, his meeting with Babbage… It described, in detail, what he had found there, that remote and wild region, away from prying eyes, away from the laws of empires.

A chill stole over Lucy as she read.

For now she knew the truth.

She read the journal, almost to the end.

One last addendum – it must have been written with Stoker in flight, after he had stolen the airship and fled. He had climbed onto the ledge beyond his window, at Castle Bran climbing the airship's mooring line like a spider or a monkey. They had found out, shot at him. He had been wounded, but had survived to bring the document back, only to die then. She had failed to save him.

Lucy did not allow herself to feel guilt. She couldn't. But her failure lay heavy on her, and Stoker's last words were like the scratches made by a sharp pen, and each stabbed at her, a little, all adding up.

### Bram Stoker's Journal

*That first night was long ago. Lord Babbage had disappeared from public life, and of Krupp nothing more was heard. In eighty-eight Mrs Beeton ascended to Prime Minister, beating Moriarty, and a new balance of power established itself, with the lizard-queen ceding some of her former power to a coalition of human, automaton and lizard: a true democracy, of sorts.*

*There had been rumours in the London papers, during that time, as to the mysterious demise of the Bookman, though none could vouch as to their veracity. In any case, my life continued as before, at the Lyceum, and I had all but forgotten that terrible, night-time summit deep below my beloved theatre, when there came a knock at the door.*

*"Enter," I said, preoccupied with paperwork on my desk, and heard him come in, and shut the door behind him. When I raised my head and looked I started back, for there, before me, stood that same German conman and hack writer, the source of all my troubles – Karl May.*

*"You!" I said.*

*The fellow grinned at me, quite at ease. "Master Stoker," he said, doffing his hat to me. "It has been a while."*

*"Not long enough!" I said, with feeling, and with shaking hands reached to the second drawer for the bottle I kept there – for emergencies, you see.*

*May mistook my gesture. The old gun was back in his hand and he tsked at me disapprovingly, like a headmaster with an errant pupil.*

*God, how I hated him at that moment!*

"A drink?" I said, ignoring his weapon, and bringing out the bottle and two cups. At that his good humour returned, the gun disappeared, and he sat down. "By all means," he said. "Let us drink to old friends."

I poured; we drank. "What do you want, May?" I said.

"I?" he said. "I want nothing, for myself. It is Lord Babbage who has shown a renewed interest in you, my friend."

"Babbage?" I said.

"I will put it simply, Stoker," he said. "My Lord Babbage requires a… chronicler of the great work he is undertaking. And there are precious few who can be brought in. You, my friend, are already involved. And you have proven yourself reliable. It is, after all, why you are still alive."

"But why me?" I said, or wailed, and he smiled. "My Lord Babbage," he said, "has got it into his head that you are a man of a literary bent."

At that I gaped, for it was true, that I had dabbled in writing fictions, as most men do at one point or another, yet had taken no consideration of showing them to anyone but my wife.

"I thought so," Karl May said.

"But you're a writer," I said. "Why can't you–"

"My work lies elsewhere," he said, darkly.

I could not hold back a smirk, at that. "He does not value your fiction?" I said. At this he scowled even more. "You will make your way to Transylvania," he said. He took out an envelope and placed it on the desk. "Money, and train tickets," he said.

"And if I refuse?"

This made him smile again.

"Oh, how I wish you would," he said, and a shiver went down my spine at the way he said it. I picked up the envelope without further protest, and he nodded, once, and left without further words.

Castle Bran—

*I must escape this place, for I will never be allowed to depart alive, I now know.*

*Mycroft, you had come to me, two weeks after that meeting with Karl May. I remember you coming in, a portly man, shadows at your back. You came alone.*

*Without preamble you told me of your suspicions back at that opening night, and told me of the conspiracy you were trying to unravel. An unholy alliance between Krupp and Babbage and that alien Bookman. What were they planning? you kept saying. What are they after?*

*You had kept sporadic checks on me, and on the Lyceum. And your spotters had seen the return of Karl May.*

*Now you confronted me. You wanted to know where my allegiance lay.*

*Choose, you told me.*

*Choose, which master to serve.*

*For Queen and Country, you told me.*

*My name is Abraham Stoker, called Abe by some, Bram by others. I am a theatrical manager, having worked for the great actor Henry Irving for many years as his personal assistant, and, on his behalf, as manager of the Lyceum Theatre in Covent Garden.*

*I am not a bad man, nor am I a traitor.*


Lucy closed the pages of the journal. She stared at the vellum-bound volume in her hands, thinking of the man she had failed to save.

Thinking of the strange machinations of humans and machines… of Transylvania, and what Stoker had found there.

*Transylvania.*

The strange word, like the name of another, distant world…

She had to take this to someone, and Mycroft was dead, and Fogg was working for the Bookman. She felt lost, desperate.

Then the moment passed and her head was clear, and the call of a bird sounded outside, a mimicked sound, not real, and she knew that it was time even before Bosie came to get her.

"Ma'am, hostile force approaching."

Lucy Westenra stood up and tucked the journal carefully into her pocket and pulled out her guns. She stepped out of the building into the dark world outside.

"Kill them," she said, softly.

# PART VIII
## *Der Erntemaschine*

# THIRTY-NINE

*The observer was definitely feeling ill at ease. He had made his way inside the Parisian undercity easily, guided by the voices, at least two of whom seemed to know the city well.*

*It was quite remarkable, he thought. There was something he found very comforting about a second, hidden urban space, lying this close to the other. There were people down there too, and he was very tempted to sample them, but the voices began to shout and he decided to stick to the objective without any further delay.*

*He had expected the fog of radiation to reduce underground but the closer they came to the place the voices had described, the more intense it grew – not just what the humans called Tesla waves but a whole spectrum of wide-bandwidth signals, almost as though…*

*Almost as though they belonged to his progenitors, he thought.*

*But that should not have been the case. He was, he was quite certain, the only observer on this planet. His progenitors, in fact, had shown remarkably little enthusiasm for this expedition. Some form of historical amateur society existing in the Spectral Swarm had received the signal of the activated, obsolete quantum scanner and had despatched a vessel through the resultant*

*wormhole before it had collapsed. The observer had been ges-*
*tated in orbit around this curious blue-white planet, and*
*dropped down without due ceremony to see what he could find.*

*So why was there, suddenly, such an explosion of signatory*
*radiation…?*

*A dreadful thought had formed itself in the observer's think-*
*cloud and slowly permeated his I-loop, born out of some deep*
*archaic data and wild speculation. He tried to push it away.*

*As he passed through the tunnels he came across a small*
*human with a hunchback, and a grotesque, giant human. They*
*did not see him. They were, in fact, occupied, somewhat to the*
*observer's befuddlement, in what appeared to be a duet. They*
*were singing.*

*Again he was tempted to sample them, but the voices were*
*growing quite hysterical by then: a routine diagnosis suggested*
*their storage had become entangled with other historical data*
*banks and that they may have been the cause of the alarming con-*
*cept he was currently trying to ignore. Sighing a little – because a*
*good observer learned from the specimens he collected – he ignored*
*the two strange humans and went straight on, finding at last a*
*primitive, abandoned research facility of some sort, and a dying*
*human which one of the voices, that of the fat man, identified to*
*him as one Viktor von Frankenstein, a research scientist working*
*for the organisation called the Quiet Council. Delighted he could*
*finally do his job, the observer knelt beside the man, whose eyes*
*focused on him weakly and whose voice said, "Help… me."*

*The observer was quite happy to do exactly that. He released*
*the spike, which jutted out of the top of his hand, and inserted*
*it deftly into the man's cortex, the data-spike extending like a*
*telescope as it went, swiftly and assuredly, through the different*
*layers of the man's brain, extracting neural pathways and the*
*man's embedded I-loop and data storage into the observer's*
*own, infinitely more advanced hardware.*

*The man on the ground became a corpse. The eyes stopped seeing. The head lolled back. The man said,* Where the hell am I?

*The observer was happy to let the other voices explain, even though a pre-prepared data-packet had already been introduced into the new I-loop's structure. Meanwhile he was studying this latest specimen with fascination, until he came to the last moments of the creature's biological incarnation, at which point he gave an involuntary shriek of alarm that set off explosions in several of the still-functioning devices in the underground research chamber.*

They're here! *the voice that had been Viktor von Frankenstein said.*

No, *the observer thought/said,* that can't be.

*Another voice said,* Smith? Smith is here?

*It was the woman he had collected in Bangkok.*

*The observer let the voices go on, running in the background. He, too, was running now, suddenly desperate to get above-ground again. All the while he was running interrogatory routines over the entirety of the Viktor specimen's memories.*

*Alarms were slowly popping up all over the observer's network. It ran through crowds of frightened humans (sweat, adrenalin, pheromones all registering briefly), through the tunnels and up, bursting at last onto the surface.*

*A cacophony of voices he had been trying to ignore washed over him. Ancient voices, in a strange antique dialect. The observer watched the city, engulfed in flames. He observed the machines, half-ghostly in the twilight, as though they were fading in and out of existence.*

*The device!* the observer thought. A human curse rose into the forefront of his mind and he unconsciously used it.

*Where the* hell *was the device?*

Smith remembered the hours that followed fleetingly, in unreal snatches.

At some point it seemed the Seine itself was on fire, its dark waters reflecting flames and destruction as he and Van Helsing ran–

"There is a way," Van Helsing said.

"How?"

"Look!"

He had made Smith look. The fires and the alien machines rampaging over the city, flicking in and out of existence as though they were pictures projected out of a camera obscura.

"There is a focal point," Van Helsing said.

"How can you tell?"

"Look! The destruction moves, but it is bound by a circumference. The device must have activated them, but has a limited range."

Smith looked. It was possible… he saw that, indeed, some parts of the city were passed by, while others were only now coming under attack–

"It's moving!"

"Yes."

"But how can we find the focal point? We have to stop the device!" Smith said.

"There is a way," Van Helsing said. "But it is dangerous–"

Smith would have laughed, at that. After a moment Van Helsing gave a sheepish grin. "More dangerous, I mean," he said.

"What do we need to do?" Smith said.

"We need to find a vantage point," Van Helsing said. "From above we could see it more clearly, we could identify the source."

Smith looked at the city's skyline.

And Van Helsing's meaning sank in.

"The *Tour Eiffel*," Smith said.

They ran.


Snatches of stolen time, Smith's lungs on fire. At some point they commandeered a baruch-landau, Van Helsing stoked the furnace as Smith drove. The city streets were on fire, coaches burning, people running this way and that; some were looting the shops, others were barricaded inside buildings. There was sporadic gunfire, flames reflected in windows, and high above, the tripods dominated the skyline, moving, now that he knew to look for it, moving in a single direction, sweeping over the city.

The Tour Eiffel had been built only a few years earlier, during the French's *Exposition Universelle*. Smith had been involved in an operation, years before, to recruit its builder, Gustave Eiffel, when the man was building a train station in Africa, in the place the Portuguese, who had unsuccessfully tried to colonise it, called Mozambique.

The operation had been a failure, and Eiffel returned to France, building at last this greatest of follies, a giant metal tower rising into the sky above the Champ de Mars, like a vast antennae aimed at the stars.

Rumour had it that was the building's true purpose, that the Quiet Council had intended its use as a sort of communication device, sending messages into deep space... possibly receiving messages, too, if the rumours were true.

"What's... up... there?" he shouted – a ray of flame from the sky hit the side of a building and they swerved madly to avoid the avalanche.

"Aerial... experimentation... station!" Van Helsing shouted. "Drive! Drive, God damn it, Smith!"

So Smith drove, avoiding debris and the corpses of the dead lying in the street, and the burning stalls and coaches and seas of cockroaches escaping as their habitats were destroyed, and swarms of rats, and looters, and militias, heading towards that great metal tower, hoping they would not be too late.

# FORTY

The machines were moving.

Their skeletal frames silhouetted against the dark skies. Their legs moved jerkily, yet there was something beautiful about it, too, their motion over the city skyline, taking no mind to the buildings and people below. Here and there, like stars in the skies, the machines winked in and out of existence, as though their light was passing through the atmosphere, distorted.

"Where do they come from?"

Van Helsing, rode shotgun on the swerving baruch-landau, face blackened with coal, the sweat from the stoker forming rivulets down his face so that he looked covered in war paint.

"I don't know."

"Some other world?" Smith persisted. "How can they materialise and dematerialise like this? Are they even real?"

"The destruction they cause is real enough."

"And they seem…" Smith hesitated. The baruch-landau, like an elderly assassin, puffing hard, was approaching the Eiffel Tower at last. It was quieter here, the machines had moved across the city. "Old," he said, with a note of wonder.

"What?" Van Helsing shouted. Smith swerved to avoid the corpse of a donkey lying in the street. It was quiet now on the Champ de Mars:

A long avenue of fantastical shapes, wizened four-armed creatures, semi-human, semi-ape, standing guard, carved in stone–

Landscaped canals, built to reflect what could be seen on the surface of the planet Mars, a silver gondola, used to carry tourists, now upturned in the water. A giant model of the red planet itself had fallen off its dais and cracked, and Smith had to swerve around it. Groaning, the baruch-landau came to a halt.

"We're out of coal," Van Helsing said, apologetically.

But it had lasted them long enough. Smith jumped off the vehicle with a groan of his own – his relief echoed in the machine's own creaks and groans. Van Helsing climbed down and joined him. It was eerily quiet. They stood on the red surface of the Champs de Mars, the Tour Eiffel rising above them like a pointing finger. Above it the stars shone down, the Milky Way traversing the dome of the sky. Somewhere up there was Mars itself, surrounded by its two moons–

Which, down here, were still on their pedestals, smooth round globes showing a lack of imagination, Smith thought, on the part of their anonymous sculptor.

"Why old?" Van Helsing said.

Smith couldn't answer him. He had imagined the threat from space to be something ill-defined, a technology so advanced it could remake human minds and shape whole planets. These machines, walking oddly over the Parisian cityscape, giant metal tripods spewing fire, flickering in and out of existence, seemed somehow to belong to a sideways world, conjured out of some alternate reality–

"Could we have built them?" he said to Van Helsing.

"The machines?"

"Yes."

"The technology involved... Oh." Van Helsing's eyes clouded and he said, "I see what you mean."

"Could they be Babbage's?"

"I find that unlikely. In any case, I have never heard of such war machines being designed, let alone constructed," Van Helsing said.

"But it is not impossible."

"But the device," Van Helsing said. "It is clearly extraterrestrial."

"But are those machines–" Smith shrugged. For the moment it didn't matter. They were talking because talking was better for the moment than acting, because in a moment they would have to press on and, the truth be told, he was exhausted.

The words of a long-ago instructor at the Ham facility came back to him. *In every mission there comes a moment of near-breaking, the moment when you want to stop, to abandon the mission, to find a hole and crawl into it and sleep, forever. At those moments, stop. Give your mind and your body the time to catch up, even if the mission reaches a critical stage. You are no use to anyone at that stage. Take a break. Look back at how far you've come, and evaluate clearly how far you still have to go. Only then, act.*

It was quiet at the Champs de Mars, and in the distance the machines moved, the city burned, in the distance Charles Babbage sat in his dark castle and planned his dark plans, the Mechanical Turk was deactivated and dumped in storage, Alice was dead, the Harvester was moving, Mycroft's long-laid plans were forming or un-ravelling, he didn't know. He looked up at the tower rising above them, a graceful latticework of iron, worked by humans, two airships moored to its top. "What's up there?" he said, looking at it again, uneasily. There had been rumours at the Bureau…

Van Helsing said, "Nothing much, I imagine. There had been restaurants during the Exposition Universelle, and a viewing deck."

"And now?"

Van Helsing shrugged.

Smith shook his head, feeling uneasy. It was too quiet at the Champs de Mars, almost as though, some-where, unseen eyes were watching them, and calculating… He took a deep breath, stretched aching muscles.

"How do we get up there?" he said at last, resigned.

"There's a lift," Van Helsing said.

Smith said, "Oh."

They found an opening at the foot of the tower. A lift, or – in the parlance of English-speaking Vespuccians, an elevator – apparently functional, and with a small, util-itarian sign on it of a skull and crossbones accompanied by the words *Entry Forbidden. Biohazard* in French.

"What do you think?" Smith said. Van Helsing shrugged and pulled off the sign.

The lift took them up, smoothly and without a fuss, travelling through latticework up to the second level of the Tour Eiffel. There the doors opened noiselessly and they stepped out onto what appeared to be an aban-doned viewing deck–

Shadows moving up there, a silhouette momentarily seen against the burning skyline, something feral and–

A shot rang out. Smith hit the floor, his own gun out, the shadow moved again and he fired, once, twice, and it fell, tumbling over the parapet in silence.

Smith swore. Why had he assumed the tower would be empty? He turned to Van Helsing–

And saw the other man slumped on the floor, blood spreading across his chest. "No," Smith said. "Abraham, no…"

"They got me, Smith," Van Helsing said. His voice was thick, surprised. He put his hand to his chest. It came away bloodied. He stared at it, confused. "They got me," he said, wonderingly.

"Let me see it, Abraham."

Smith reached for the other man, cut out his shirt. Shadows moving in the distance, coming closer. When he tore open Van Helsing's shirt the bullet hole was marked. Van Helsing coughed, and blood bubbled out of his mouth and fell down his chin.

"Let it go, Smith," Van Helsing said. He smiled, or tried to. "Isn't this the way we always thought we'd go? Better than to lie in bed, riddled by cancers, or old age, or that sickness that eats away memory. I wanted one more job."

"You had it," Smith said, and his own voice was thick.

"Go up to the top of the tower. There are… machines there. Be… careful."

"Abraham–"

But his friend was sinking to the ground, his eyes fighting to stay open. Smith held him, cradling him in his arms, Van Helsing's blood seeping into his own clothes. "It was worth it," Van Helsing said. "Playing… the Great Game."

His eyes closed. His breathing stopped. Gently, Smith lowered him to the ground. Abraham Van Helsing, another name added to the tally of the dead. Shadows moved, coming closer, snarling. Smith's gun was out of its holster and he fired, and watched them drop.

What the hell *lived* up here? he thought.


He examined the first body. His bullet had hit it in the chest, it was still alive. It would have been human, but...

What *were* those things?

The sign on the lift door. *Biohazard*.

What use was the tower being put to?

The creature would have been human but it was changed in some grotesque way. Not the way of the F-J serum, nor in a Moreau-style hybridisation (Smith had the unfortunate experience of meeting that exiled scientist once), not even in the bizarre methodology of that mad hunchback genius Ignacio Narbondo.

The body below twitched and foam came out of its mouth and still it tried to move, to bite him, with shiny yellow teeth. Its eyes, too, were yellow, and it was hairy, with a naked chest. Somewhere, a bell *dinged*, faintly but unmistakably...

Smith went around the foaming man-dog creature and went to the parapet and looked out over the city. Paris, in flames – but the machines were moving, heading... east?

And now he could see the circle of influence, just as Van Helsing had said it would be. The machines were moving in a radius of about three miles, a hovering shape of fire and smoke moving slowly but inexorably over the Parisian skyline. A baleful moon glared down, and above, the stars were being stubbed out as the smoke rose to obscure them.

The device, he thought, would be at the centre of it. And moving. Somehow, it had opened a hole into – what? Another world? – and brought these machines of death and destruction into life.

Get hold of the device, he thought. Shut it down.

How?

Van Helsing wanted him to go to the top of the tower. An aerial experimentation station, he had said.

Perhaps he could get hold of an airship or–

Somewhere, the *ding* of a bell, faint but clear–

Smith turned–

There were three of them, standing there. Hair grew out of their faces, spilling down. Their eyes were yellow, rabid. Their fingers curved into talons, their nails like scimitars. One of them growled.

It had occurred to him, too late, that he should have made a start going up sooner.

There were no lifts to the top of the tower.

And the three creatures were blocking the stairs…

"I don't want to kill you," he said. He disliked guns and using them. And these creatures seemed to him somehow innocent, as if a great wrong had been done to them. They looked insane, they belonged at an asylum.

"Step out of my way and you won't be hurt," he said.

Somewhere, the ding of a bell, clear and loud, and for the third time–

The three – men-dogs? What could you call them? – twitched as one, as if the bell was controlling their actions. Then they charged Smith.

He dropped the first one with a shot but then a second barrelled into him and the gun flew, over the parapet and down, onto the Champs de Mars far below. Smith grunted, the air knocked out of him, and fell back–

321

His hand reaching for the knife strapped to his ankle, the blade flashing, and he buried it in the belly of the creature, who howled pitifully and collapsed on top of Smith, pinning him down. Smith, grunting, pushed at the body, the blood, the colour of pus, slipping into his clothes–

The creature was heavy and the third one was coming at him at an odd loping gait, teeth flashing–

Smith struggled to push off the body lying on top of him but couldn't. The dog-man came closer and his muzzle came down, biting–

Smith shielded himself with the dead one on top of him and the living dog-man bit its comrade instead. Snarling, it tore at the flesh, pulling it, until Smith, with a sigh, managed to slide from underneath it. He rose to his feet, shaky, the bloodied knife in his hand…

The dog-man stared at him over the corpse of its friend, an arm between its teeth–

"Shoo," Smith said. "Shoo!"

The dog-man growled.

Smith, moving carefully, circled around the body. The dog-man followed. "I just want to get to the stairs," Smith said. "Do you understand? I mean you no harm–"

Which was an unlikely thing to say, under the circumstances.

The dog-man growled. He looked like he was thinking. Smith moved, his back to the stairs now; the way was open, he was going to make a run for it–

The sound of a bell, clearly and sweetly in the night.

"Not *again*," Smith said.

There came a growling sound around the corner and, for a moment, it felt to Smith as if that entire edifice, that

Tour Eiffel, was shaking with it. He heard the pounding of heavy bodies and the unmistakable sound of gunshots, like the one that had dropped Van Helsing and he thought, There must be others up here, soldiers or–

He ran for it.

Up the stairs, but now there were bodies coming at him from above, too, dog-men of sorts, hypnotised by that deadly sound of a bell, ringing–

It reminded him of something, rumours long ago, at the Bureau, and a failed mission on the Black Sea–

He twisted sideways, his knife flashed and a howling dog-man flew through the air and beyond the parapet and down to his death, the Champs de Mars, Smith thought, turning as red as the planet it was mimicking. Up the stairs and his knees hurt and it was a long way up, a long–

That damn bell, and now footsteps on the landing he had come to, the city down below, the tripods moving jerkily across the ancient buildings, the fires burning, that Egyptian obelisk looted from Luxor toppled, flames above the Louvre, hordes of people running down the Avenue des Champs-Elysees–

Footsteps, and a voice like a bell saying, "You should not have come up here–"

Smith, stopping, out of breath–

A man in his fifties, white in his beard, deep-set eyes–

That mission on the Black Sea, long ago, and a promising young Russian scientist, doing strange experiments on–

Dogs, yes–

An extraction that didn't work because the French, as it turned out, had got to him first–

"Ivan Pavlov," Smith said, stopping still.

That damn bell.

He should have known.

# FORTY-ONE

Was it a sickness of the age, or of its sciences? Did it drive its practitioners mad, or were they mad to begin with?

You had to be a little crazy, Smith always reasoned, to delve into life's bigger questions, to ask – *why are we here*? or, *what happens when I do this*? or *why is a raven like a writing desk*?

Why *was* a raven like a writing desk?

*Because there's a B in both*, as Mycroft used to say.

Science was an alien way of looking at the world. It required asking questions, and then setting out to answer them, experimenting, trying to get the same results each time–

And in the process inhaling all kinds of potentially quite dangerous gases, or experimenting with lethal death rays, or ravenous bacteria, or intelligent machines that would, unexpectedly, go berserk–

If you weren't a little mad to begin with, Smith reasoned, you were likely to be more than a little on the unstable side by the time you spent a couple of lonely years in a draughty lab, poring over unknown chemicals, building weapons of mass destruction or trying to meld together human-dog hybrids. You'd see it time after time: with Moreau, with Jekyll, with Darwin and Frankenstein (both *père* and *fils*) and Edison (with his desperate quest for the perfect mechanical doll), Brunel the mad builder, Stephenson with his locomotives, and those people from the Baltimore Gun Club who tried to shoot themselves into space and ended up squashed like bugs by the acceleration.

Scientists were mad, it was a well-known fact; there was nothing to it. You just had to use a soothing voice, avoid making any threatening gestures, and slowly go around them if you could.

"Shoo?" Smith said.

Pavlov smiled. "I remember you, I think," he said. "They showed me dossiers of all the major shadow executives, back in the day, in case I got approached, in case anyone tried to turn me. Which proved to be the case. My experiments were harmless!"

"Conditioning," Smith said. A lot of things were clearer now. "You were experimenting on dogs, back then, but the Bureau was interested in the practical application of your methodology on humans... and then the French stole you from under us."

Pavlov shrugged. "They offered me what you, with your lizardine masters, could never offer me," he said. "Freedom, for myself and my experiments both."

"We would have offered you the freedom you needed–"

Pavlov's face twisted in a strange, unpleasant grin.

Something in his expression...

Smith, staring at him, suddenly aghast:

"You can't mean–"

"Lizards," Pavlov said.

The word hung between them in the air, as heavy as an anchor. Smith swallowed.

"The French would have never–" he said.

"Think, Smith," Pavlov said. "Royal lizards! That alien life-form, Les Lézards, our masters – and our enemies? We have to study them, Smith!" He peered at him. "It *is* Smith, isn't it?"

"Yes."

"Funny, I thought you'd be dead by now."

"Retired," Smith said. Pavlov shrugged. "It is something your people never understood," he said, returning to his subject. "You were conditioned, just as my dogs had been conditioned, back in the St Petersburg labs. You've been *trained*, the lizards your masters, and to question them is, for you, simply an impossibility."

He saw Smith's look, and smiled again. "Oh, yes," he said, complacently. "I have studied them. It was not easy, yet, even with the royal lizards, there are… how shall I put it? Disappearances? They make such fascinating subjects…"

"You lie," Smith said. He could not picture it – Les Lézards, those magnificent creatures, those intelligent, man-sized lizardine beings, *royal* beings, subjected to experiments, locked up in a secret lab, abused, tortured–

"Am I?" Pavlov said. "I have a specimen right here, as it happens. Though I've not been able to breed them…" He sighed, wistfully. "Such a perfect location," he said. "Up here. Total security. Usually we have soldiers guarding the Champs de Mars entrance but with this…" he waved his hand vaguely at the city – "this *invasion*, obviously, it's been alarming the test subjects. Incredibly inconvenient, really. Do you know what it is?"

"Some lizardine device," Smith said. "Activated by accident."

Pavlov sighed. "You see?" he said. "They are dangerous, and they seek to rule us all. They cannot be trusted, and have to be *studied*."

"What *are* your test subjects?" Smith said. Pavlov lit up. "These?" he said. "My little dog-men? I raised them from puppies, you know."

"I didn't think hybrids were your field," Smith said. He was still trying to figure out how to get past the scientist. Two of his "test subjects" were standing just behind him, ready to attack, and more had amassed down below, blocking any retreat. The only other way was to jump... and he didn't rate smashing into the ground far down below as a particularly successful escape.

*When in doubt, keep them talking*, as they taught them at Ham, all those years ago.

"They're not," Pavlov said. "I got them from Moreau. We've kept a... lively correspondence, even after his exile. He sent them to me as a gift. You see, us scientists need to work freely, to exchange views and data with each other, to *learn* from each other in order to achieve scientific progress, we have to work *together* to *assail* the *heights* of–"

"Oh, screw it," Smith said. With two steps he was level with the Russian scientist and his stiletto, kept in his sleeve, snickered out.

Pavlov froze.

"Keep your dogs away," Smith said. The words wheezed out of him, he was tired and angry and the memory of Van Helsing's death lay on him like a weight, pressing him down. "Up the stairs, now!"

He pushed and the scientist moved, the knife pressed

against his flesh. The dog-men growled, but kept their distance.

"Let's not have any more *bells* ringing, shall we?" Smith said. Pavlov, his face frozen in fury, said nothing.

Up they went, up and up the long winding latticework stairs of the Tour Eiffel, higher and higher, the dog-men at their heels, the city smoking and burning below and Smith knew he was running out of time, fast.

"You won't–"

"Get away with this? I was going to say the same thing to you," Smith said. Pavlov, panting as the climb took its toll, said, "You're a fool, Smith. You have to stop serving false masters. Listen. Join us. Come over to our side. The Council needs good people – now more than ever –" this with a view of the destruction below. "The game is being played to its end. This is the time to choose sides. Join us."

Smith was so surprised he almost laughed. "You're trying to turn *me*?"

"I am trying to *save* you," Pavlov said. "These machines, out there? They're just the beginning, Smith! Who knows what infinitely more powerful force will come when we least expect it, when we're least prepared, to whom we are as ants are to humans? Do you really think you would save the human race best by serving its *masters*?"

Smith didn't answer. Up they went, in a dizzying rise, and the dog-men silently followed.

"I am... only... trying... to save this city!" Smith said, panting. They had almost reached the top. The Russian scientist, too, looked wan and out of breath. "Then go," Pavlov said. "I won't stop you. Just let me go. I can't take another damn step."

Smith said, "Fine," and pushed him. The Russian Scientist lost his balance, then fell down the stairs, heavily, rolling until his dog-men stopped his fall. They stood hunched over him, looking up at Smith with hungry, yellow eyes.

"Have you thought," Smith said softly, "that it might be better to have wiser masters, when these are the things that we do to each other?" He looked at the dog-men and there was anger, and compassion, in his voice when he said, "And you forgot your bell."

From down below, the bruised Pavlov looked up. Smith held out his hand. Cupped in it was a small, silver bell.

Gently, he rang it. The sound, clear and pure, pierced the air and carried on the cold high winds. Smith turned, and slowly walked up the last flight of stairs, up to the top of the tower. Behind him the sound of the dogs, barking and tearing, slowly drowned out the sound of human screams.

# FORTY-TWO

...and flying, he was flying, he was a man, a bird, he had
wings, the moon rose huge above him, its face austere,
the winds pulled him along, their music was the sound
of waves, crashing on a distant, alien shore. Smith flew,
high above the city, tracking–

He had gone to the top of the Tour Eiffel. Mooring lines
for airships but what he found at the top was what, he
guessed, Van Helsing had hoped for. He'd only used them
once before, on training, long ago. But it would suffice –
it would have to.

The *Lilienthal Normalsegelapparat*. German-made, and
rare – reputedly only a dozen had been made before
Krupp had brought the nascent technology and Otto
Lilienthal departed this mortal realm, two events gener-
ally considered to have a direct correlation between
them. There were other flying vehicles up there, all manners of winged ornithopters, high-altitude unmanned
probe balloons, a vehicle powered, it appeared, by pad-
dling, like a bicycle with wings, a rocket harness,
something that appeared to be a semi-hollow mechanical

dragon, far too heavy, Smith thought, ever to fly... An inflatable blimp and a moored airship completed the odd assortment. A small sign translated as *Aerial Experimentation Station – No Trespassers*. There was also a small gas stove and a folding table and a device for making coffee. Smith checked, but there were no biscuits.

Someone had fashioned a safety harness for the Lilienthal Normalsegelapparat. Smith appreciated the sentiment.

The Lilienthal Normalsegelapparat was a hang glider, delicate-looking, with the wings of a fly and a long thin snout. Smith figured the most likely outcome of using the damn thing would be to plunge down the long way onto the Champ de Mars and end up a wet splat on the paved roads of the red planet. Behind him the dog-men were wailing. He stood up there on the top of the Eiffel Tower and looked over the burning city. From up here he could see Van Helsing was right. The affected area of the walking tripod death machines was entirely circular, a slowly moving, shifting area of fire and destruction that was heading east, almost out of the city by now.

Could he make it?

The howling of the dog-men behind him, bereft of their master and his bell. Smith took a deep breath. Then he slipped into the safety harness and lifted up the Lilienthal glider.

The wind pushed at it, trying to lift him up. A short way away the floor terminated, air began. It was a long drop down. He took another deep breath. It was suddenly very quiet up there, only Smith and the winds, and the smoke rising in the distance into the air.

He needed to shut down the device. He needed to find the Harvester.

He needed to save Alice.

He let the air out with a slow, shuddering breath. The wind caught at the glider, pulling, eager, wanting to play. Smith ran. The floor terminated and his feet connected with open air and the wind tugged and pulled at him and then he was airborne, the Tour Eiffel left behind, he was rising higher, the winds his companions, eternal and graceful and true.

*The observer sighed with relief as he reconfigured an internal quantum scanner to work on the ancient, obsolete frequencies. He could see what had happened, now and, moreover, knew it would all have to go into his report, which was due soon, as soon as the other copy of himself had taken the last sample back in that other city, beyond the Channel.*

*Of course, the observer* was *the report, in a very real way, but that was all right, nothing lived forever, not even the observer's masters, near as he could tell.*

*The obsolete protocols and curious antique authentication routines were what must have activated the initial gateway back in the humans' calendar year of eighteen ninety-three. But whereas back then it was a primary scanner, able to open the entanglement channels back to Prime, these semi-scanners worked on broken frequencies, on quantum probability pocket worlds not seen or even remembered by any but the oldest of antiquarians. Like those tripod machines. This, the observer felt, could not go on. There were* rules *or, if not exactly rules, there was such a thing as* decorum.

*Which meant those probability world incursions had to stop.*

*The observer felt quite cheerful now. Soon it would all be over and he'd be back where he belonged. The voices protested at this but he quietened them down. The reconfigured scanner was picking up the signal clearly now and he headed for it, no longer in a hurry, savouring these moments, his mission soon to end.*

*Behind him, unobserved, for once, by the observer, a giant, malformed figure detached itself from the shadows and cautiously followed.*

From high above there was something intensely beautiful about the tripod machines. They moved with the long legs of giraffes, their movements surprisingly graceful over the city. Flames reflected in their metal carapace, the bulbous heads of them that sat over the moving legs. They were like squid, Smith thought, soaring, coming closer – like aquatic beings somehow propelled to stand upright, stretched over the horizon, their tentacles reaching down to the city, bashing it this way and that.

Where had they come from? What strange world would manufacture such machines? Who drove them? Were there people inside or were the tripods themselves some sort of advanced automata, the bulbous compartments huge mechanical brains?

He flew over them, like a bird, the wind tossing him this way and that, the city a long way down below. The harness held him but his hands gripped the bar of the glider, this thing that looked too fragile to survive the winds, too impossible to fly. We built that, he thought. There was pride in that.

Below him the machines stalked the city, shivering sometimes in and out of existence, flickering like images on a screen. People down below, fleeing, were as small as insects. Smith alone was up there in the sky. No.

That wasn't true.

As he watched, dark clouds formed in the sky above the city, drifting closer.

Airships, he realised.

But what good could they do, against the tripods?

He was level with the machines now, going lower, trying to locate the moving source, their middle. It would be a vehicle of some sort, he thought. It was hard to tell from above and the rising smoke made visibility difficult.

The black airships were approaching more rapidly. The tripods seemed to ignore them.

No. That, too, was wrong. As he watched, helpless to intervene, a burst of bright, terrible flame erupted from one of the tripods. It flew through the air, a roar of flame, and hit the nearest airship.

For just a moment the ship was obscured from view. Then, a ball of flame erupted, the fire feeding, growing stronger, bigger, and Smith could only watch as the ship simply disintegrated there in mid-air.

He cried out, but his voice was small and lost up there in the air. He dived, his anger becoming a bright white flame compacted inside him. Diving and rising, the sweat on his forehead mixing with the smoke, the soot, the wind lashing at him, diving, past the line of tripods and onwards and down, towards the source of it all, towards the unseen device.

*The observer moved unobserved amongst the hysterical, running humans. There seemed to be little control, little order left in this strange, barbarous city. It was as if the sight – not to mention the wholesale destruction – of those ancient lumbering machines, conjured out of who-knew-which antique probability universe, had entirely shut down human rationality.*

*Yet not entirely, he saw. He watched humans organising themselves: makeshift medical clinics sprouting in the ruins of a shelled tavern, or in the middle of the road; groups composed of women, men, even children, organising to put out fires, carrying water, dashing into rubble to rescue trapped citizens.*

*But the observer, always, was going into the heart of the disaster, where there was no time to organise, no time to do anything but try to flee. Behind him the city responded; like a living organism it was closing in on wounds, cauterising, bandaging, beginning the arduous process of healing itself. Cities, the observer knew, were in many ways living things, their inhabitants merely the cells or neurons that individually meant nothing, that only collectively formed an entity, singular and proud. The city would live; cities were hard to kill, harder than humans. The observer, a small undistinguished figure, moved through smoke and fire.*

*He stopped several times. Each time he did a human had been trapped under the ruins, their life bleeding out of them, short and sweet and sharp. Each time, out of a desire to understand or that strange, unfamiliar consumption the Alice voice had called compassion, he extracted his needle and pushed it, his data-spike, deep into the hind-brain of the humans, extracting, preserving. It was an uncomfortable thing for him to feel.*

*He was no longer an observer, he realised.*

*He had become a participant.*

*This was a familiar danger, the eventual fate of all observers like him. It was time to leave, to bring back what he'd found, before he was absorbed completely, before he became one of them, before they turned him.*

*The observer walked through flame and soot and smoke and the unseen presence at his back followed. The observer passed underneath the giant legs of the moving tripods, dodging their steps, and his shadow followed, until they were approaching the device, the signal coming clear and loud now in the observer's mind.*

*He was playing the great game, the observer thought, and a rapid, unexplained feeling of joy spiked through him, the great game of lizard and man and automaton, a game not of countries*

336

*and species as the humans thought but a far bigger one, of plan-*
*ets and solar systems and quantum probabilities, and this was*
*only the first move in a truly great game.*

*For which even a galaxy was but one battlefield, one chess-*
*board in a far larger and more complicated game.*

*With joy and with compassion and with, at last, that simple*
*need all creatures have, biological or mechanical it made no dif-*
*ference – the simple desire they all shared, the need to go home*
*– the observer crossed dirt roads and paved, fallen buildings*
*and ruined carriages, until he reached, at last, the source of all*
*the mayhem.*

# FORTY-THREE

Smith was zooming low now, the tripod machines far in the circumference of influence, still moving, still flickering now and then–

Down below flaming buildings and carts and people running, but his attention was on what stood out, on what felt *wrong*, that which did not belong–

A black vehicle of unknown design or means of propulsion, moving slowly, its sides, matt black, absorbing the reflected flames, dampening them–

A machine with no horses to drive it, and no steam engine, no stoker at the back, a sealed device with its occupancy unseen behind dark windows–

A long, finned device, moving slowly, smoke and flame behind it–

Smith, diving low, hovering now, the glider like a moth caught in the winds, the Tour Eiffel left far behind–

Things that did not belong, things going against the general movement, like a small and unremarkable figure, a man with a wide-brimmed hat and economical movements, so unassuming and unremarkable as to become, to Smith, interesting indeed.

Gliding, coming closer, catching up to that dark bullet-shaped vehicle–

And was that small figure down below–

Smith dived sharply, ready to finish it, ready to do what was right. The glider, shuddering with the effort, sped towards the ground. Smith had caught up with the vehicle, then overtaken it. He crash-landed ahead of it, the impact with the ground jarring his bones, ringing him like a cracked bell. He lay there for a moment, the glider covering him like the wings of a butterfly. At last, drawing breath, Smith reached for the knife strapped to his leg, pulled it out, cut the harness rope. He pushed the harness off him, his every effort focused on this one simple act. The world around him shrank, it became just Smith, the hard road, the harness that bound him. At last it was done. The world expanded, gradually. He sat up. The black vehicle had stopped, a few feet away from him, he saw. It just sat there, a dark bullet shape, giving nothing away.

Smith stared. How did the vehicle move? Where was its engine?

The knife was still in his hand. It seemed useless against that dark vehicle.

All around him, in a circle whose circumference was an exact three miles, the giant tripods halted. They stood, motionless, like vast metal guardians over the burning city. Smith shifted the knife from one hand to the other. Waiting.

It was suddenly very quiet.

Footsteps, unhurried, approaching. Smith, watching–

The figure that appeared was the one he had seen from the air, a small and rotund and unassuming fellow who resembled Smith himself. The shock of recognition passed through Smith, and he forced himself to be still. The figure he had last seen in Covent Garden, as he ran towards his friend, as he ran to the place the Lord Byron automata lay slain…

He watched and waited and the black vehicle, too, was still, as if its occupants were waiting, and all around them, in a wide circle, the giant tripods stood still, as if they, too, were watching and waiting.

A great calm settled then over Smith. He watched the other, so much like himself, a shadow being in a shadow world. You would not look at him twice, if you saw him in the street, or in a pub… Slowly, the other lifted his head, and the wide-brimmed hat that shadowed his face lifted. Moonlight and flames lit up the other's face, and Smith sucked in his breath sharply.

Shadows and flames, playing tricks on the mind…

For there was no face under that hat. A skeletal metal head, and eyes of blue flame, looked at Smith.

"*Erntemaschine*," Smith whispered.

*Harvester*…

The other, as if acknowledging him, nodded, once. Then, startling Smith, his – its – mouth opened.

The voice that came out of it knocked Smith back.

"Smith! Get out of here – oh, you have no idea – it's a trap, he says that–"

The voice cut off, as sudden as it had come.

The voice was Alice's.

Alice, who died in Bangkok.

*Harvester*…

And now a new voice came, a deeper voice, as familiar to Smith as Alice's had been.

"Smith, you fulfilled the promise I had for you," the voice said.

340

Smith whispered, "Mycroft…"

"Dear boy, do not lose heart," the fat man said. Smith stared at the alien machine, this humanoid automaton, speaking in the dead voice of Mycroft Holmes.

"*Erntemaschine…*" he said again, softly. Then, addressing his question to this being, or to Alice, he didn't know, he said, "Why a trap?"

The Harvester did not reply. It was impossible to tell, on that skeletal metal face, but Smith had the impression he – it – was smiling.

The doors of the black vehicle opened.

They did so in silence, and simultaneously, there were two on each side, and the things that stepped out of them were–

The knife Smith was still holding felt very small, and for the first time he truly felt his age.

They, too, had been men once, the things that stepped out of that machine.

Frankenstein-Jekyll monstrosities, subjected to the serum's nefarious influence. They dwarfed Smith and the other. Muscles bulged from their oversized clothes. Their eyes had a yellow, demented sheen. They wore metal collars around their unnaturally thick necks.

Every now and then, Smith saw, the collars fizzled, hissed, small blue flames dancing around the metal, and each time the creatures' faces twisted with pain.

They were being controlled, he realised.

From within the vehicle.

He tensed, waiting for whoever was inside to come out. But they never did.

The four turned as one, their collars hissing. Facing Smith, and the other.

And now, Smith saw, others had materialised around

them, emerging from the frame of a ruined apartment building, from a baruch-landau parked innocently enough on the side of the road… One jumped down from the roof of a nearby building, the ground shaking as he hit it.

The creatures surrounded Smith and the alien Harvester.

The Harvester turned to Smith.

"Smith, if this goes wrong…" She hesitated. Her voice was just as he remembered it. "I love you," she said.

"I've always loved you, Alice," he said.

She said, "I know."

Smith looked at their attackers. So the whole thing had been a trap, just like Alice said. Not for him – he didn't rate himself valuable enough.

No.

A trap for that strange, alien being, that Harvester who truly *did* harvest the dead…

He, Smith, was just in the way.

And he did not rate his survival chances as being very high.

# FORTY-FOUR

Flames in the distance, smoke spiralling up... The night was beautiful, order in destruction, the moon shone down, pock-marked, scarred, as scarred as Smith.

The creatures surrounded Smith and the Harvester, closing them in, and now they made their move.

*Fight if you have to*, as the Manual, long ago, had put it. *Run if you don't.*

Though there was nowhere to run...

Smith tensed but beside him the small, rotund alien machine seemed to relax, to become even more inconspicuous, even more anonymous and serene.

"Alice? Mycroft?"

They spoke in unison, not just the two of them but a multitude of voices who Smith didn't know, all absorbed by the Harvester, from that child in Bangkok to the lost souls swiftly and mercifully despatched in the burning city.

"Everything," they said, their voices rising like the singing of birds, like rain falling, like the rustle of leaves and the hum of ancient, mysterious machinery. "Everything will be all right."

Smith was not reassured. The creatures reached for him, one of them grabbed him in huge, meaty hands. The others went for the Harvester–

The fingers applied enormous pressure, the pain was excruciating, Smith bit down a scream–

Turned, the knife flashing, buried it deep into the creature's chest–

Who sagged back in surprise or pain, it was hard to tell, momentarily releasing him–

A hum rose around him, a strange ethereal sound, vibrations shaking the very air. The world seemed to slow down around Smith, to pause, the flames shuddering to a halt, the tripod machines frozen against an unmoving, enormous moon, the creatures moving sluggishly, bewildered, the black vehicle sitting there motionless, Smith's hand leaving the handle of his knife reluctantly, pulling away as though he were swimming through water…

The hum rose like the wordless chant of a thousand monks. It came from nowhere and everywhere. It was in the air, in the flames, in the smoke and in the dead who lay all about them.

In that stillness, that freezing of time and of the world, only the slight, monk-like figure of the Harvester moved normally, in real-time. It did not move hurriedly. It had an economy of movement, an assured, almost peaceful pace.

*Everything will be all right, Smith.*

The words rose in his mind, they were bubbles in water, and a strange peace came over Smith then. His world expanded outwards, beyond the city, beyond the Earth, past the moon and the planets and the sun and outwards still. Star systems rushed by, strange sights, engorged suns and empty spaces that swallowed the matter around them, clouds where stars were being born, red suns, dying, worlds beyond count…

*Everything will be all right.*

*The observer felt that its time here on this curious world was coming to an end but was impressed by the human-laid trap, which suggested several things to him.*

*That the humans, or some faction of humans, had indeed deducted the observer's arrival, and its purpose.*

*And were determined to capture him, either to prevent him from achieving his mission, or to study him, or both.*

*Which was exciting news to the observer, even though, having observed, as it were, an entire chain of circumstances and events – of people – that led him to the knowledge he would be observed, he would be deduced, this was still material evidence, and first-hand. A postscript to his report, he thought, almost fondly.*

*There was little that was useful in the minds of the distorted humans, however. Whatever process they had undergone, this serum the observer had found mention of in several of the voices in his head, it had done irreparable damage to the complex, delicate webwork of their brains. He took from them with the same compassion he took from the dying he had met along the burning city, but there were no whole minds here, nothing but fragments, which he extracted with care.*

*They were frozen, or near frozen – the observer had kicked into a higher mode for a short duration, had initiated, in fact, the beginning of the process that would end his time here, on this earth – and he took from them with ease, sinking the data-spike into their brains, releasing the data left in there while permanently terminating the living tissue.*

*In slow motion, the bodies crumpled to the ground, one by one, as the observer moved amongst them like a gardener, un-hurriedly pruning back leaves.*

*At last it was done; only the other remained, this short com-*
*pact human who had come down from the sky. He recognised*
*him, criss-crossing references from the voices in his head, saw*
*him young, saw him trained, saw him meeting Mycroft for the*
*first time, in a Soho street with the rain falling down, saw him*
*falling for Alice, by the side of a Venice canal, saw him opera-*
*tional, then, a brilliant young shadow executive: Aden, Zanzibar,*
*Vientiane, Moscow, a spell in Tenochtitlan, cultural attaché at*
*the embassy running interference inside the Aztec capital – back*
*in London after an operation went bad in Tunis, then the fruitful*
*collaboration with the Byron automaton, handling internal se-*
*curity, foreign networks, becoming Mycroft's right-hand man*
*and Alice's lover–*

*The man was an enigma, the observer thought with curiosity.*
*He could read his life like a dossier, perfectly laid out, but what*
*he thought, wondered, wanted – this the observer had no access*
*to, and he was not surprised to find out that he wanted it.*

*He was, after all, an observer.*

*He turned at last to the vehicle, which was powered by a*
*primitive internal combustion engine – advanced for this society*
*of coal and steam – using what the humans called diesel, after*
*a German scientist who seemed embroiled in the machinations*
*of the man they called Babbage, and who the observer would*
*have liked to have met.*

*The observer reached for the front door of the vehicle and*
*yanked it open and slid inside. There was one solitary man sit-*
*ting in the driver seat, a panel of instruments before him, still*
*frozen in slow-time, his hand reaching out in tiny increments*
*towards the controls. Gently, almost with affection, the observer*
*added him to his collection and, a moment later, laid its corpse*
*down gently against the seat. A new voice in his head, but he*
*shut it down – a flavourful one, this one, a conman and a*
*writer, Karl May by name, and Krupp's agent – he added a*

*new strand to the story the observer was to carry back, and for that the observer was grateful.*

*The device had been in May's lap. Now the observer retrieved it. He initiated a communication channel with the ancient thing, establishing a protocol and negotiating a handshake despite the device's initial suspicions. He found himself fascinated by what he found, and it was with some regret that he at last shut it down.*

*When he stepped out of the vehicle, the device safely locked, the ancient tripod machines had wavered against the skyline and then, as though in relief, disappeared.*

*They did not belong here, they came from a place unexplored for untold millennia, perhaps aeons. The observer wondered which observer would get the chance to go there, when he returned and submitted himself – that is, his report.*

*He hoped it would be him…*

*There had been a name for that world. In human speech, it may sound a little like* Croatoan.

*It was done. The observer let slow-time go, and time sped up–*

Smith stood very still, in a changed world. The creatures that, a moment earlier, had threatened him, were now on the ground, and they were dead. The skyline was different, the tripod machines were gone. The city still burned, but it would recover, it would lick its wounds. It always had, before.

Smith stood alone by the black vehicle, alone but for that otherworldly thing, that *Erntemaschine*.

He looked at the Harvester and it was like looking at a mirror, it was like looking at himself. He hesitated. The machine waited, patient, revealing nothing.

"Alice?" Smith said.

"Smith," she said, out of the *Erntemaschine*'s mouth. There was a load of sadness and pain in her voice he found hard to bear. He thought of his agreement with the Bookman, the other's promises of raising Alice for him, of bringing her back from the dead, and he realised the futility of that offer; he knew then he could not bring the Harvester back with him, that Alice was lost to him.

The *Erntemaschine* waited, patient, but looking at Smith in a certain way that Smith recognised.

"I can't bring you back," Smith said, and that admission, of his own helplessness, hurt as it left his mouth, like jagged edges of broken glass cutting through his throat and tongue.

"Smith…"

The Harvester waited, knowing, patient.

Smith nodded, once.

There was only one way for them to be together again.

*The observer was satisfied. He knelt by the corpse, gently prying the data-spike out of the dead man's head. Inside him a new voice joined the rest, intertwining with one of the other voices in particular. The observer stood up, then, recognising in that small, unremarkable corpse something akin to his own identity, a tool and a servant who yet took a great joy in fulfilling its tasks. Smith… even the name was appropriate, almost a title, like Observer… he silenced the voices. Almost. Almost…*

*He just had to wait for his other self to finish, at last, the job.*

# PART IX
## *Manifest Destiny*

# FORTY-FIVE

"Mr Houdini," the voice said. "Welcome to Transylvania."

The voice had an awful, scratched quality to it. Harry tried to open his eyes. They felt gummed together, and his mouth tasted of razorblades and old blood.

Alive. Somehow, he was still alive.

He opened his eyes.

Shapes slowly resolved in the semi-darkness of the room. The light was red, the air felt humid, almost moist. He found himself sweating. It was very hot, very humid, like a…

He sat up. Everything hurt. His hands on his head, his fingers through his hair – realising it was longer now, that he must have been in that crate, that coffin, for a long time, longer than he thought. He looked around him.

A large, dark crypt it seemed to Harry, illuminated by artificial red light, and quiet, too quiet. Around him, everywhere he looked, orchids grew, a huge variety of colours and shapes, like living things, waiting, watching… hungry. He suppressed a shudder; could not see another person there. So who had spoken?

"Who are you?" he said.

A strange sound, of bellows, of air going in and out, in and out. A beat, weak and yet amplified, filling up the cavern, like the sound of an old, human heart. Harry squinted into the darkness.

"Hello?" he said.

His voice sounded lonely and thin in that underground greenhouse. The sound of bellows, of air being breathed, as by a vast machine. The pounding of that fragile heart, and Harry's own heart responding, fear rising, palms damp, and he tried to calm himself, to look inwards, trying to think how he could escape, when–

A shape, a sliver of shadow materialising out of the darkness, moving gradually closer, growing in size–

And Harry had to suppress a scream, a thing out of nightmare coming towards him, features slowly resolving, and in the dim red light of the cavern he saw–

It had been a man, once. Now it sat there, welded into its chair, a thing neither human nor machine...

Pipes came out of its back, fed into its lungs, and large bellows moved like butterfly wings, fluttering, pumping air through that ancient, wizened body, keeping it alive...

Glass tubes in which red blood bubbled, the tubes in turn feeding into the old man's arms, his hands...

The face was like a skull, what skin there was hung loosely, yellow like gas flames. There was no hair but thick black wires came out of that skull and trailed upwards, connected once again to the cloud of machines that engulfed this being, this creature, this once-living thing.

It was ancient, it should have died long ago, it was a mummified human body kept alive by its machines, it was–

"Who..." Harry whispered, and his throat felt raw and clogged, and a chemical taste, suffusing, so it seemed to him, the very air he breathed, lodged itself in his mouth, "What… Who are you?"

The mouth in that faceless skull barely moved, and yet the creature in the chair spoke, its voice amplified through unseen machines. Like an Edison recording, the words were slightly disjointed, scratchy, put together from separate recordings and meshed into a single voice. And now he saw the ancient fingers, bone-like, tapping on a keypad of some sort, like brass buttons there, within reach – producing the sounds he heard, he realised. The man was no longer capable of speaking in his own voice.

"I am Charles Babbage," the mechanical voice said.

Harry scrambled away from the creature. He felt as if the thing was after him, after his youth – that soon it would pounce on him, attach fang-like devices to his neck, empty him of blood, feast on him–

"Really, Mr Houdini," the voice said, and the eyes – the eyes! – they were terribly alive, large and moist like smooth pebbles in a stream, they looked at him, with amusement and curiosity, they were the only living thing in that ruined face – "there is nothing to fear."

The voice chuckled, the same old scratched recording, and the chair on wheels moved closer, and the man loomed before Harry now, and looked at him, his head tilted slightly to one side. Harry could see blood flowing, in measured doses, through the transparent tubes that fed in and out of Babbage's arms.

"We are not so unlike, you and I," Babbage said.

Harry stood up. His muscles didn't ache as much as he had expected. And, in fact, there had been no waste left in the coffin… which he didn't want to think about, at just that moment. He towered over the old man. "You should be dead," he said.

"And so," said Babbage, "should you."

Harry stopped, his rage drying. "What do you mean?" he whispered, and again he heard Babbage laugh, that old recorded sound echoing through the greenhouse. They were alone but for the orchids. "How many times have you died now, Mr Houdini?" Babbage said.

"I don't–"

"Know what I mean? Oh, but I think you do, quite well," Babbage said. "Tell me, when was it that the Bookman found you?"

"I will not–"

Cold sweat, and fear, it couldn't be, he wasn't like–

"Answer my questions? Or do you not know the answers?" Those large, wet, extraordinary eyes gazed up at him, almost in admiration. "I can answer your questions for you, Mr Houdini. Would you like me to? Would you like to know, just what you are?"

The eyes, he saw, were no longer looking at him but behind him, behind his shoulder, and he suddenly had that awful feeling that something, someone, was standing behind him, so close that, almost, he could feel their breath on his skin. He tensed.

"I know who I am," Harry said.

"I will show you yourself," Babbage said, in a voice almost sad. "In a handful of dust…" His head moved, a fraction. "Take him," he said.

Now Harry turned, ready to fight–

Behind him loomed a huge, bald-headed human, with a scar running down one cheek. The man smiled at him, without malice, then a hand like a meat hook descended and grabbed him by the neck and lifted him up.

"Everything," he heard Babbage say, as from a great distance as, suspended in mid-air, he felt the cold prick of a needle enter his neck, "is going to be all right, Mr Houdini. It will be all right."

Famous last words, Harry thought when he woke up. Woke up and wished he hadn't. Woke up, and found himself strapped to a table, the dim light of the green-house replaced with strong white electric lights, a bare room, bare walls, and Harry naked, strapped with thick leather restraints–

A mirror above him, adding to the humiliation, adding to the horror of it all – the mirror showing him every-thing, showing him himself, it was attached to the ceiling, hovered above him like a suspended pool of water–

"We shall begin," a voice said. The same old, pre-recorded voice, and he hated it now, hated that voice, he wanted to kill, he had to escape, he had to–

"Sir."

The voice was surprisingly high; it didn't fit with the face of the man who now stood over Harry. A giant of a man, with a bald dome for a head, a scar running down his cheek – he looked like a pirate, Harry thought, the man looked ridiculous in the white lab coat–

In his hand, Harry couldn't help but notice, as much as his gaze tried to shy away from it, in the man's huge, meaty hand there was a small and delicate and very sharp-looking surgical scalpel.

# FORTY-SIX

"Wait!"

Harry struggled against his bonds. And was that a small, almost wistful smile on that huge, cratered face above him? His head thrashed, this way and that, seeing now the wizened old man, this Babbage, in his wheelchair and his life-support machines, watching him, waiting...

"Why are you doing this?" Harry said – whispered. The old man sighed, the sound of bellows releasing air, slowly and tortuously. "You do not know," he said, enigmatically, "how lucky you are."

Harry thinking, keep him talking, anything to keep that blade from descending, from cutting his flesh, from burrowing into his skin... He said, "Who's *he*?"

The man above him smiled again. Nothing friendly in that expression. It made Harry's blood go cold, an expression he'd heard once, did not believe it could become a reality. No help there, not from this brute–

"His name," Babbage said, "is Mr Spoons."

"Mr Spoons," the man with the scalpel said, nodding. The same high, almost girlish voice.

"He used to be boatswain to Captain Wyvern," Babbage said. "The pirate. But that, Mr Houdini, is beside the point. Mr Spoons–"

"Spoons!"

"Please proceed with the operation."

"No!"

Harry cried out but it was no use. He saw the blade descending, a frown of concentration on the giant's face–

In the mirror above he could see himself reflected, naked, the blade descending, the blade touching his arm, the blade *pushing*–

For just a moment, a flaring of pain, shooting up his arm and then–

The blade went deeper, made an incision, Spoons moved the blade deftly, opening Harry's arm–

And the pain suddenly *vanished*, pain receptors shutting off, and something else, stranger, something Harry had seen before but had tried to forget, had kept telling himself he'd dreamed it, the last time it had happened, it couldn't have–

Blue sparks shot out of the cut in his arm, and Mr Spoons, startled, took half a step back before remembering himself and reaching out, and with thick fingers *pulling open* the folds of skin on either side, revealing–

*No blood, no bones.* Harry shutting his eyes now, wanting to scream, recollection flooding in–

*En-route from the Black Hills, his horse, moving fast, stumbling–*

*Harry falling, hard, the impact jarring, his head hitting a jutting stone–*

*Pain flaring, and he blacked out–*

*And woke up, seconds or minutes later, the horse nearby, unharmed–*

*Harry's head hurting, his hand reaching to it, finding a sticky residue, his hand, coming back, no blood but a strange, greenish material that seemed to ooze, almost as if alive–*

*A shower of blue sparks, falling down, scared him. He reached up and his hand passed through them, harmlessly–*

*On board the* Snark, *in the midst of ocean, after too much drink, unsteady on his feet, on board, a piece of metal falling, he turned, it cut his arm–*

*The pain, coming, then, just as suddenly, disappearing. Blue sparks, the same green goo oozing, sealing the wound before he had a chance to register it–*

*He'd cursed the Bookman, but he'd pushed it away, it had been nothing, a hallucination, there was nothing at all out of the ordinary–*

"Extraordinary," Babbage breathed – that is, voice machine and breathing machine meshed, for just a moment. Harry, defeated, stared down at his arm. The strange green goo had materialised over it, was sealing Mr Spoons' cut. Harry had a bad feeling, a very bad feeling…

"Humans," Babbage said, "are such extraordinary machines, Mr Houdini. But you!"

Was that admiration in the old voice? It was so hard to tell… and the frown on Mr Spoons' face suggested *he*, at least, was not overly happy with the results, so far, of the operation.

"I had tried to get hold of the Bookman's technology for years," Babbage said. "I, alone, had deduced his secret. Nothing but a servant!" The ancient man coughed a laugh. "A servant, a copying machine. Yet how he hated them, and hates them still! For centuries, since his escape from that cursed island, he has been moving through the world, *our* world, a shadowy figure, the first and greatest player of the great game. Fighting his former masters, these… these *reptiles*."

And was that a moue of distaste briefly crossing the old man's haunted face?

"An alien machine, designed to make copies of biological entities, to copy them and to *perfect* them, to keep them pristine and operational, like a librarian, a book-man or… a zoo keeper," Babbage said. Harry fought against the straps but he couldn't tear them. Is that what he was? he wondered, in despair. A machine? A replica of someone who had been, a human born and raised and named, Erich at first, then calling himself Houdini – was that man, almost no older than a boy, dead forever, killed by a mugger in the dark streets of the White City and he, Harry, no matter that he *felt* the same, *looked* the same, was he but a replica, a cheap automaton?

Not even that, he realised. For he had died before – did that make him a copy of a copy? A copy of a copy of a copy?

When did one stop being human? When did one be-come a machine?

"You…" Babbage breathed. "Remarkable. At last, the Bookman has obliged me. I, who was the greatest builder of automata in the known world, am but a copying scribe, forced to learn from first principles an art per-fected long ago under different skies, on alien soil! No more. Now, I have you, Mr Houdini."

"Let me go!"

"Join me." Charles Babbage's chair moved mechani-cally forwards, accompanied by its cloud of machines. His ancient head peered over the table at the captive Harry. "Work with me. You do not understand, Mr Houdini. The time has come! There is a war upon us."

"War?"

"War…" Mr Spoons said, and smiled. The idea seemed to delight him.

"A war," Charles Babbage said, "of worlds, Mr Houdini. A war that was long in coming, a war inevitable, a war unavoidable, as must always be the case when two civilisations meet, and one is stronger, and the other weak."

"But that's not true," Harry said. Even captive, he sensed the wrong in the older man's words. "When European refugees came to Vespuccia they were received cordially and honourably by the Nations. When European explorers came to East Africa they were welcomed into the trade networks that had existed for centuries between Asia and Africa. When–"

"When the Lizardine Empire conquered India, it did so by force," Babbage said. "When it–"

"But it doesn't have to be this way," Harry said. "The great game is played to *prevent* war. War is not inevitable, it is not a natural solution. Peace–"

"Peace!" Babbage laughed, and it was not a pleasant laugh – and Harry suddenly realised the man was *too* old, had lived for too long, so long that his brain had, in some subtle ways, stopped functioning, that he was demented – and for the first time since his arrival here he felt true fear.

"Let's take a look at his heart," Babbage said, and Mr Spoons raised the scalpel again, and it descended, and the cold hard metal touched Harry's chest and he screamed.

# FORTY-SEVEN

There came moments of lucidity then, intersected with long periods of darkness. He'd wake up in that cold room to find men and women in white coats standing over him, prodding, studying. Sometimes there would be wires attached to him. Sometimes he would wake up and a leg would be missing, or an arm, or his chest would be bared open, skin and flesh removed, showing something alien and inexplicable underneath. At those times he was almost glad of the returning darkness, the no-being that spared him the indignity of dissection.

Other moments, too, flashes of awakening, almost as if he were in someone else's body, in a new body, being carted around. The baruch-landau moving, this driverless carriage piloted by Mr Spoons in the front and he, Harry, beside him in a passenger seat. Outside, for the first time, though he had no recollection of leaving that cold room. Looking back–

A castle rising above a cliff, towers and turrets like something out of a fairy tale, surrounded by trees, an access road–

Black airships above it, moored and floating serenely,

around the castle, down below, a pleasant valley but it was full of military-looking personnel. More vehicles, fields of tents, troops at parade in the distance. He said, "Where are we going?" – his voice thick with disuse.

Mr Spoons: "To Brasov."

Harry sat back in the seat. The vehicle moved through the valley on a curiously paved road, the journey smooth, the vehicle making almost no sound–

The city, in the distance–

A bowl of a valley, surrounded by tall majestic mountains – "The Carpathians," Mr Spoons said, his scarred face placid – the city in the distance, tall spires rising against the sky like delicate towers–

No, he realised. Not towers at all.

The car moved closer. Harry watched – an old pleasant city of stone streets and low houses, transformed–

He said, his voice tinged with awe, "They're rockets."

Mr Spoons smiled, faintly–

*The rockets rose high into the air, a multitude of them, too many to count; they filled the valley, surrounding the old city like an honour guard, giant metal structures waiting to take flight, aimed at the stars…*

*He woke, and found himself strapped to the table and they were examining him and old Charles Babbage was cackling to himself and he said, "Stop. Stop it."*

*"Join us," Babbage said. "Join me, Harry. The war is coming, and you and I could stop it. Together we could save the world."*

*"You're mad," Harry whispered.*

*"You don't have to be mad to work here," Babbage whispered, "but it helps…"*

• • • •

He could not distinguish dreams and awakenings. One night he woke in a room he did not recognise and saw himself, multiplied by a hundred.

Rows and rows of Harry Houdinis, lifeless, suspended from walls in some medieval crypt in that horrid Castle Babbage, hanging on hooks, like so many dolls, waiting... He blinked and then saw a hundred other Houdinis blink back at him, their eyes staring, and he stifled a scream and then darkness, blessedly, closed on him again.

Rockets, gleaming against the skies... "What... What are they *for*?" Harry whispered.

The same hint of a smile on Mr Spoons' ugly face. "Have you never looked up at the stars?" he said. "Have you never *wondered*?"

"Wondered what?"

"What it would be like to *go* there," Mr Spoons said, his face softening. He looked like a big kid at that moment, something childish and almost endearing in his eyes. "I used to look up at the stars, on board our ship. The *Joker*, she was called. I used to stand on the deck, looking up. Wondering... My master was lizardine himself, Captain Wyvern, and we sailed the Carib Sea and beyond... They told me Les Lézards came from there, from the stars... crossing some unimaginable distance in a ship that could sail through space... and I wondered, and I still do – what would it be like, to sail between the stars?"

Harry had no answer. They drove closer, passing military installations, trucks and dome-like buildings, pylons humming, all the while the rockets dominating the landscape, there in that strange valley bounded by the majestic Carpathians... a hidden valley, a secret valley, here at the edge of the Austro-Hungarian Empire. Babbage had chosen well.

"Why are you showing me all this?"

They drove into the old town – stone-paved streets, low-lying houses, restaurants open, lights coming on, a festive atmosphere – soldiers and scientists sitting around in big groups, drinking beer, laughing–

"This is your destiny," Mr Spoons said, simply.

*"Our destiny," the voice said. The voice had a grainy, pre-recorded quality to it. Harry hated the voice, but it would not go away. It never stopped. Harry didn't know where he was. His mind was fragmented, broken, the fragments floating in and out of time.*

*He was in the vehicle with Mr Spoons, watching the rockets, and he was hanging on a peg, on a wall, like a suit of clothes, with a hundred others, and he was on that operating table, being taken apart, piece by piece, and he was in this dark place where the voice was speaking, speaking, a mélange of voices in turns interrogating and lecturing, filling his mind (minds?) with new concepts, new ideas, an ideology he couldn't push away–*

*"The stars are our destiny," the voice said, the old machine man voice, "and our destination–"*

*"When a superior and an inferior civilisation meet, war can be the only result."*

*"Humanity is a superior race, we have a manifest destiny–"*

*Harry – "No!" cursing, in the dark – "who talks like this?"*

*"I – we – you!"*

*He begged for silence, for the dark, but his request was denied. Instead he got: "trajectories – control unit – air pressure in cabin – coordination of group-hive-mind operations – symbiosis – lunar topology – space walking–"*

*Harry: "This is insane. Stop it. Now."*

"They are coming. We have to be prepared."

He was everywhere and nowhere, in a room with controls before him, buttons and dials and switches and levers and slowly he learned to operate them, to read the screens–

A place where his body was being spun, faster and faster, pressure mounting on his chest, his body, as though the Earth's pull was increasing–

"He built you well. Now I will rebuild you. All of you."

"Please, please, stop."

But it didn't.

# FORTY-EIGHT

"Erich?"

He blinked, in the darkness.

His mother's voice, comforting, known…

But she was not there.

His eyes opened, and suddenly he could *see*.

The world changed.

He was no longer alone.

Stars. The world was full of stars. Harry's consciousness stretched, stretched…

And a hundred Harry Houdinis opened their eyes…

*He was everywhere, at once. Babbage's scientists, his technicians, had worked hard to copy the Bookman's technology. To replicate it.*

*He woke up and he was many.*

*He was, he realised, Babbage's army.*

Harry was sitting on top of a rocket, alone in a control room, the walls closing in on him, the awesome engine power behind him being, in effect, a giant bomb about to go off. His consciousness stretched, across the valley, and he knew, so many things he hadn't known before, when he was one.

He knew of diesel, and of the vast deposits of the black, thick oil in the Arabian Peninsula, of how it could be used to power machines, and to generate vast, raw power to send men into space itself.

He knew of the woman they called Alice, in the city called Bangkok, and knew what she had done there. There was a type of metal found in the ground, in India, and smuggled, from under the lizards' snouts, via Siam to this remote valley in Transylvania. Something more dangerous, more powerful and awesome even than Diesel's oil...

*Uranium.*

What a strange word, Harry, thought, rolling it on the tongue. The control room shuddered, a hundred control rooms shuddered, and Babbage was with him, was inside his mind, woven into this new matrix of Houdinis, his knowledge Harry's knowledge, and he *knew*–

Decades of planning and scheming, of building and learning, finding out things from first principles–

And all the time the burning jealousy, hardening into hatred–

The knowledge that all his work, all his genius, was in vain, that thousands if not millions of years in the past, another race of beings had gone through the same track, had already invented and perfected what Babbage, haltingly, was trying to do. The Bookman laughed at him, making perfect copies, making human machines... while the royal lizards lounged in their gardens, ruling an empire they did not deserve, ignorant even of the science which had made their conquest of humanity possible. To be so advanced as to be ignorant, Babbage thought. A paradox at the heart of a technologically advanced society...

And he knew, early on he knew, that the lizards, those few on Earth, were not alone. That they had come from somewhere and that, therefore, the possibility existed:

That one day the others would come, and to them the Earth would be less than a plaything–

How much further would have the aliens' science advanced in the millennia since the one ship had crashed on Earth, on Caliban's Island, its living cargo frozen in cryogenic sleep?

And so he planned, he schemed, sometimes with the Bookman and sometimes against him, sometimes with Mycroft Holmes and his organisation, sometimes against him. Collaborating with Krupp, with Edison, with Tesla and the others, and against them, a woven tapestry of conflicting and mutual interests–

The Great Game.

The only game worth playing.

And now–

The stars.


"Ten."

"Nine."

"No, wait!"

From a hundred identical throats: *We are not ready!*

"Eight."

"Seven."

"Prepare for launch."

The rocket thrumming, the very walls vibrating, Harry's palms moist, gripping the mostly useless controls–

And Babbage's slow, insidious voice, saying, "The greatest escape of them all, Mr Houdini..."

*You don't understand*, Harry wanted to shout. *War is not always the answer, in the South Pacific the concept of Peace was sacrosanct, peace before justice, war was a guaranteed extinction, even if there was war it was a civilised affair, a contest between champions at the end of which everyone went off to lunch–*

"Six," the machine voice said, and it was indifferent to Harry's pleas, to all the Harrys, and he saw–

*A hundred pairs of eyes opening, a hundred pairs of hands holding tight to the controls, a hundred identical bodies sitting on top of a hundred identical rockets, and the flames starting...*

"Five," the voice said, remorselessly. "Four. Three."

Harry closed his eyes. Some of the Harrys kept theirs open. One of the Harrys whistled. One cried. One prayed, in the old forgotten Hebrew of his youth. One grinned maniacally. But all of them tense, all of them ready, as ready as they'd ever be–

"Two," the voice said.

"One," the voice said.

And: *"Lift off."*

*Lift off.*

Harry felt the rocket thrumming, with eyes that weren't his own he could see the rockets sitting on the floor of the Carpathian valley, flames igniting, the mass of fuel burning as the rockets slowly, so slowly, began to rise into the air–

He gripped the controls, felt his body being pushed back in its seat, then–

Searing hot flame, a rumble rising from below and spreading, and he opened his mouth in a wide desperate scream, something was wrong, something was terribly wrong, and–

The flames rose and the rocket shuddered, breaking up, with eyes that weren't his eyes he could see the rocket–

Only a few feet above the ground it lost control, a fault somewhere in the thousands of components–

Inside the module on top of the rocket Harry screamed but there was no sound, the flames burst and he felt his body being consumed, like the flicker of a match, like someone snapping their fingers, there was an enormous fireball–

He screamed but there was no pain, no sight, there was nothing, and a metallic voice said, "One destroyed."

"Commence tally."

"Affirmative."

And with ninety-nine pairs of eyes Harry watched, the rockets rising, slow at first and then faster, and faster, and he could *see*, he watched the sky coming closer, the stars above, he was soaring, he was–

The rocket lost its trajectory several hundred feet above the valley. Harry had only a moment to realise it, to see and feel the cliff-face of the mountain as the rocket, lost to all control now, aimed directly at the face of the Carpathians, trees and dark shrubbery and Harry screamed–

There was a terrible explosion–

"Two down," the voice said.

"Commence tally."

"Affirmative."

*But the ones who were already airborne kept flying, the rockets rising higher, while the voices in mission control never tired–*

*Three more rockets exploding on launch, two failed to start–*

Harry stood outside the rocket, glaring – up in the sky the rockets trailed smoke, but he was down there, left, forgotten, in that damned Transylvanian valley–

A mixture of anger and relief and fear and exhilaration – he was alive, but grounded, and he suddenly realised just how much he had wanted this, the greatest feat of escapology known to man–

*To go into space–*

Harry Houdini sitting at the controls, the rocket piercing clouds, Transylvania disappearing below as the world *grew*, expanded–

An explosion somewhere to the right, another rocket consumed in furious flames, another mental scream echoing down the shared mind connection of the Houdini network–

But the others kept going, even as burning molten debris rained down on the mountains, where a forest fire came alive–

Down below bears ambled away, troop carriers drove down the mountain dirt paths with water tanks, while up there–

Up there where the air grew thin, and one could see, for the first time in human history, one could see the curve of the world, could see the truth in what the pre-lizardine, Greek philosophers had already known, that the world was a globe–

And Harry's breath caught in his throat as he watched continents, oceans, merging and forming like a beautiful unique map, alive with colour–

And beyond it, as the air thinned, the module heated up, the rocket pushing faster and faster and higher and higher, until–

• • • •

"Stage two," the metallic voice said.

Charles Babbage in his life-support cloud, in the observation deck, Ground Control, Harry beside him–

"Initiate," Babbage said.

There was a terrible tearing sound–

A grinding as metal separated from metal, up there on the edge of space (but the sound was only internal, outside the air had gone and sound no longer travelled, out there, beyond the thin metal walls, was the vacuum)–

Harry screaming as the separation of rocket and module did not go as planned, and a hole was punched into the metal and air escaped out into vacuum and Harry's voice was sucked away as he flew out, into space, and died, seeing stars–

But the others separated and it must have been a marvellous sight, from the telescopes down on Earth, if anyone was watching – a fleet of rockets entering stage two, the rockets dropping away and the fragile modules separating from them and continuing onwards on the generated momentum, higher until they escaped the Earth's gravity well–

Some circling the Earth while others pushed on, beyond Earth orbit, having reached escape velocity and Harry looked out, Harry looked out into space and he saw the stars, he saw the Earth down below, a fragile beautiful blue and white globe, spinning...

And the words of an ancient prayer his father the rabbi used to say rose in Harry's mind, the ancient Hebrew words: *Baruch ata adonai, elohenu melech ha'olam, boreh meorei ha'esh* – blessed are thou, God, creator of the flames–

As the world beyond the module shifted and flared, the thousands upon thousands of stars, like sand upon the shore, so many, he had never imagined there were so many, and Earth shrank behind, became an insignificant speck of dust, of sand, in a vast mysterious unknowable universe when–

The world shifted, and changed, and the star field *blurred*, suddenly and unexpectedly–

Beyond the moon's orbit, somewhere out there, between Earth and Mars–

A great blurring, a hazing, as though something enormous, something as large as a *world* had materialised, in space, its outline blocking out the stars–

But that was impossible, Harry thought, and the tiny little modules hung out there, in space, as pretty and useless as Christmas tree decorations, and Harry sighed, a great exhalation of air taking with it all tension, and fear, and leaving behind it only a great childish wonder–

# PART X
## *Victoria Falls*

# FORTY-NINE

There was blood. That was the thing she couldn't understand, lying there. The blood. The ground was wet and sticky. There had been a lot of pain but now it came and went, in waves, and in between it felt quite peaceful, like rest, or a summer's day, or a dose of opium.

She couldn't figure out where the blood had come from. Was it hers? Everything was confused, a jumble of images without the proper sound, like at a puppet show where the voices came a moment too late, once the puppets had already moved on the stage.

There had been a gun battle...

It had been a war of shadows, the moon cast down shadows and her men engaged the attackers, the ones who had ambushed Stoker, and she had said, "Kill them," and she was not going to leave any alive, save maybe for one, for interrogation. But she had wanted their blood.

It had been a mistake, she saw now. She had been unprofessional, had lost her detachment in the battle.

She was being moved. Shadows flickering at the edge of vision, the rustling of leaves, the ground wet... There was mud on her, and the thick cloying smell of the blood. Where were they taking her?

Who?

Flashes of memory like exploding grenades.

Bodies collapsing into mud. It was raining. There had been rainbows flashing through moonlight and rain, a rare sight – she had seen such a thing only once before, at the great falls they called Mosi o Tunya, the ones Livingstone had named after the Queen.

Victoria Falls.

*The spray of water rose into the air, permeating the atmosphere, and through it the sun cast a multitude of rainbows… and at night, she had stood on top of the wet slimy rocks above the falls and watched the moonlight do the same, silver rainbows appearing magically in the air, everywhere, startling and mysterious…*

"Kill them."

She was not sure, now, what they were fighting for. For Stoker's diary, perhaps. For the document he had died for.

Only she had the feeling it had all been a feint, that Babbage had *meant* to let his scribe escape, so they would know–

Rockets, a secret army, Babbage's mad plan, in that remote valley in Transylvania–

"The Queen," she said – tried to – the words could barely leave her throat. "Have to tell… the Queen."

Mycroft was dead. They were all dead. Her men lay on the ground of Richmond Park and their blood soaked into the mud and fed the roots of trees whose names she didn't know. Only she was alive.

The attackers had not been entirely human.

That must have been it.

They had... modifications. They were like the things she had read about in a classified dossier, about the work done in France, at the Gobelin factory. Man-machine hybrids, designed for battle, half-powered by engines, metal replacing flesh–

*She had fired three shots into a man's chest and watched him laugh...*

She blinked. Her lips tasted salty. Blood. There was blood. She thought she would never be free of the blood.

"Please," she whispered. "Tell–"

Her throat felt blocked. She tried to speak and couldn't.

Then the pain came back and she wanted to scream, it ate its way inside her, it was a rat gnawing on raw nerves. The pain came in a wave that rose higher and higher and it was going to drown her, it was going to–

Then it passed, once again, and she was lying there (on the stretcher?), breathing heavily, covered in sweat, and her mouth was full of blood (did she bite her tongue?).

Where were they taking her?


Memories like exploding grenades... the men moving silently, the bark of guns, the bright flame of a flare rising high, casting the scene in a momentary flash, revealing the wounded and the dead... she had killed two and badly wounded a third when she felt the impact against her shoulder, throwing her back, onto the ground–

She had never heard the shot.

Someone screamed. Perhaps it had been her. Another flare went up and now it revealed a different scene, the soldiers were not where they should be–

There had been a–

There had been a–

In the stretcher she bit her lips and sobbed. Stoker's diary still in her inside pocket, hidden, kept safe – how many hits had she taken? She would die, soon, she felt. Knew.

There had been a–

It had come out of nowhere. Out of the ground or the trees she couldn't, afterwards, tell. A monster. It moved jerkily, it had a long body, it looked like a giant centipede, it had feelers rising out of its snouted head, it was hard to gain an accurate picture of it, it had pincers and they–

It had gone berserk, slashing, ripping – it had lifted one soldier high in the air and tore it apart, just like that, and threw the remains down, and roared–

The sound was insane, it froze her blood, or so it felt, like ice pumping down into her veins, like she was afloat on an iceberg, like that time in Mount Erebus, during that awful, year-long expedition…

The creature was targeting her people and the opposition equally; it howled and gibbered and the men ran, they tried to escape, the modified and the plain, the quick and the–

They died, they all died, and she had reached for her gun, with her one good hand she had tried to fire, but the bullets did nothing to the creature–

She had seen it before, of course. Once before, an impossibility, made manifest: at the cellars of the Lizardine Museum, talking to Fogg.

*The Bookman*.

It killed, it killed without mercy or joy, and when it was done the tranquil landscape of Richmond Park was a ruined battlefield, and blood soaked into the dark ground, the blood, she lay in a pool of blood and waited for the creature to finish her off…

Instead hands lifted her, held her when she tried to fight, carried her away.

She looked up, and saw the stars.

# FIFTY

She was moving again. She didn't know how. It felt like
moving through a warm, glucose sea. Colours kept shifting. Sounds had a weird echo and lasted too long...

Bureau training had her injected with drugs over a period of time, building up immunity. It had helped...

"What is your name?"

"Lucy. Lucy Westenra."

"What is your name?"

"Lucy! Lucy..."

"Good." The voice chuckled. "Good."

The questions kept coming. "Where were you born?
What was the colour of your mother's eyes? Tell us
about Lord Godalming."

"I don't know Lord Godalming."

"What is your relationship with Jonathan Harker?"

"What is this about?" she said, or tried to. She tried
to move her head and couldn't. There was a bright
light and she couldn't see beyond it. Only shadows,
moving...

"Blood," she said. "There was a lot of blood."

"Forget about the blood," the voice said, impatient for once.

But she couldn't.

They had loaded her onto a vehicle, a baruch-landau, at one of the park's gates, she didn't know which. Just as she didn't know where they'd taken her...

*Somewhere in the city. She had tried to count the minutes, the turns of the vehicle, tried to listen to the sounds outside, identify any familiar smells or signs–*

*Was that Big Ben, chiming? Had they crossed the river?*

She could be at the Lizardine Museum, or at the Bureau itself, for all she knew. Fogg was the Bookman's accomplice.

Why had they kept her alive? What did they want with her?

"Try to move your arm," the voice said. She moved – something. The voice said, "Good. Good."

The Queen, Lucy thought. She had to get to the Queen, Victoria had to be told, had to be warned of the danger – Mycroft's last orders, and she had the key, she could go–

"What are you doing to me?" she said.

"Fixing you," the voice said, complacently.

She felt drugged. Calm, all of a sudden. Almost euphoric. She knew what they were doing, suddenly. Keeping her on ice, keeping her docile – for what, she didn't know.

But she couldn't tolerate it happening.

She opened her eyes. Beyond the bright lights shadows were moving. She was not, she realised, tied down to the table. Merely drugged. She took a deep breath and let it out, slowly, trying to control her heart beat. Tried to move her fingers, one at a time. It took effort.

*But the drugs were not as strong as they must have thought they were.*

"What are you doing, Lucy?" the voice said.

She said, "Help me to–"

She began to shake, and the hands reached out for her–

She moved *against* the body that was there. Hands grabbed her and she let them, putting her weight to it–

The man staggered back, still holding her, lifting her from the table where she lay–

The body's own adrenaline shooting through her, dispelling some of the clouds in her head, and she jerked upright as the man fell–

"What? Stop her!"

Parts of her weren't working very well. She moved sluggishly, there were patches on her body that hadn't been there before but she had no time to look at them closely–

Impressions, only. Metal replacing skin. They were doing to her what they did at the Gobelin factory. Mechanising her. But it could be to her advantage, too–

She slammed her fist into the head of a woman in a lab coat and heard a curious metallic sound as the woman dropped. Someone came at her with a syringe and she ducked and broke his arm and kicked him between the legs and he fell, whimpering. She looked for clothes.

Her old ones were on a chair, but they were useless. They'd been stripped off her and were matted in blood and what she suspected was someone else's brains.

In the event she took what she could from the three people on the floor and equipped herself with surgical blades to replace her lost guns, and then she was out of the door, expecting to be stopped at any moment–

Someone at the end of the corridor, and her knife was airborne before he'd even turned–

He dropped, and she was running, even though the walls seemed to move as though they were breathing, and there was a high-pitched scream in her ears – she knelt down beside the fallen guard and retrieved the knife and now she had a gun, too.

And now she knew where she was…

*Zephyrin's lab, deep under Pall Mall, at the lowest level of the Bureau…*

Shouts behind her. They were coming–

She was on the disused underground platform, the way up would be blocked to her–

Fogg had control of the Bureau now–

Gunshots behind her–

She jumped.

Running along the trucks, into the dark tunnel mouth and beyond. Ghosts made faces at her, the air felt viscous, her steps were uncertain. Nevertheless–

She was alive and armed. She couldn't ask for much more than that.

She surprised herself by laughing. Maybe it was the drugs, but she suddenly felt *good*.

She had to warn the Queen, she thought.

She had to make it out of the tunnels, and to the palace.

There were footsteps behind her. She was out of breath and her body felt like it had been pummelled in the ring by Mendoza, the bare-knuckle boxer. She had seen him once, fighting "Gentleman" John Jackson for the championship.

Or perhaps it had been a simulacra built by the Babbage Company. She could no longer remember. She turned around, knife ready – a gun would be dangerous to use here, in a confined space.

"Westenra, wait!"

"Berlyne?"

She did not lower the knife. He appeared, a shadow at first. "It's all going so wrong," he said, in despair. "Mycroft trusted me to keep it going, but I can't do it, Westenra. Mycroft is dead, Smith is missing, the French broke in and stole the device and killed Zephyrin, and now Fogg's in charge and I've been side-tracked, there is no coming or going without Fogg's approval, he'd brought his own people in…"

"Did you know they were holding me?"

"I had a feeling something was going down. I went to investigate – they tried to stop me." Berlyne shrugged. As he came closer she saw his hands were bloodied. "I went through the training at Ham too, you know," he said, almost apologetically. It made her smile.

"How do we get out of here?" she said.

Berlyne said, "The tunnel joins the active underground network a little farther on. But where can we go?"

"I need to reach the palace," Lucy said.

Berlyne fell into step beside her. She had resumed walking, she realised. She trusted him. But could she?

Well, she figured, you had to trust someone, sooner or later. Berlyne was her last link with the past. Mycroft was dead: they were the only ones left.

"There's a line," Berlyne said.

"What?"

She realised she had lost time. The walls were closing in on her. Moving, shifting… She giggled.

"Westenra, are you all right? Wait–" Berlyne said. She heard him reaching for something and almost went for her gun. Then there was a flare of bright light – she almost cried out.

"My–" the second word was swallowed up. "What have they *done* to you?" he said.

She didn't know. She couldn't see, properly. All she knew was that it didn't matter. They had to get to the palace. She resented Berlyne for doing this, for distracting her. Distraction was weakness. Weakness was fatal.

The sound of a shot behind them. She pushed Berlyne. The light died. "Get down!" she hissed.

"You should be in… in *surgery*!"

"Where do you *think* I've just been?"

That shut him up. She rolled, waited, gun drawn… squeezed off a shot.

Berlyne: "How many?"

"I don't know." She turned to face him. "You said there's a line. What did you mean?"

"What?"

"A line. To the palace."

"Yes!" Somehow they were moving, at a half-crouch. Their pursuers… she assumed they pursued. She wondered if she knew them, whether Fogg had subverted any agents at the Bureau. It seemed possible…

She hoped she wouldn't have to kill any more people she knew.

Apart from Fogg.

She very much wanted to kill Fogg.

"There's a private underground rail line," Berlyne said. "Mycroft mentioned it, once. An emergency escape route, connecting the Mall with the palace, and from there to a secure location on the other side of the river."

"Do you know where it is?"

"It should be–"

Something swam at her through the thick air, a monster with rushing air and burning bright eyes and a hot breath–

Someone screamed. Berlyne was flying through the air, or so it seemed to her, in her befuddled state. He crashed into her, pushing her off balance. She fell on her back, a few feet away–

The train roared past, breathing heavily. She felt Berlyne shaking beside her. She started to laugh.

"We're never getting out of this alive," Berlyne said, at last.

"Oh, cheer up," Lucy said, standing. "It could be worse. We could already be dead."

Berlyne, following her, rose to his feet. "I could kill for a cup of tea," he said, morosely.

# FIFTY-ONE

Berlyne was right, she thought now. He should never have come after her. She should have let him go when he still had a chance. She was crouched into the miniature train car, directly behind the chugging steam engine, her gun pointing back, but they were no longer chasing.

It was a mail car, as it turned out, hence the small size, and a Babbage engine controlling the train engine and the stoker. There was a string of miniature model cars strung together behind the belching engine. It was dark in the tunnel. She had left Berlyne behind.

She could no longer recall exactly what had happened. There were periods of blackness, moments when the weakness and the drugs and the blood loss kicked in. she had followed Berlyne. He had pulled out a device of some sort, similar to the one she had used to wait for Stoker's blimp. Some sort of tracer. He led her down the dark tunnels under London, in search of the train, but the pursuers were close behind them and drawing closer.

They had caught up with them as they had almost reached the hidden platform, down a dank-smelling passageway where pools of rancid water lay, coated in a thin film of grease. The first thing to announce them had been a rolling grenade. She had pulled Berlyne by the arm, violently, and they flattened against the wall as the explosion rocked the underground chamber. Her gun was already out but she didn't use it. She moved silently, coming towards them. There were three, Fogg's men, and she put away the gun and took the knife instead.

She was sluggish and so her first attack missed the man's throat and ran down his arm, opening up a geyser of blood that hit her in the face. She dropped, low, then turn-kicked and felt it connect. He dropped and she crawled towards him and this time, with the knife, she didn't miss.

Which left two...

They had guns and they were firing and she had to crawl through the shadows to get her distance. She found Berlyne slumped against the wall and, when she reached for him, discovered the spreading wet stain on his shirt and cursed, but softly.

"Westenra..." he said.

She said, "Try not to–"

She thought, in the darkness, he might be smiling.

"God save the Queen," he said. Then he died.

She had killed the other two. She must have done, though she couldn't quite remember it. At last she had escaped, into the miniature terminal where the miniature mail train waited. There were more pursuers, coming. She had jumped onto the train as it began to hum and then it moved and she fired back until the attackers receded in the distance and she was alone, at last, riding the mail train to its final destination.

She was a ghost in the tunnels or, perhaps, she thought, she was the only one still alive, and everyone else was dead: they were the ghosts.

She wanted to fall asleep. The drugs were losing their hold and now the pain was returning, it was everywhere and it was vindictive, it enjoyed hurting her.

Not far to go, she thought. Not far…

Blood. There had been so much blood.

She touched her shoulder and was not surprised to feel it wet. She was bleeding again. She thought of Berlyne, fleetingly. "I could kill for a cup of tea," she said, but her words were snatched by the wind and were lost behind. The train ran on.

*The observer sighed with almost human relief as it approached along the path to the palace.*

*He could have gone about it in a human way, of course. Hide in the shadows, climb the high walls, sneak into this surprisingly high-security abode like a thief or a spy, until he'd reached his destination.*

*Earlier, he might have done so. He had not wished to draw too much unwanted attention to himself… in the beginning.*

*Inside him the little Siamese – Hmong – boy was talking, the one he had collected what seemed so long ago, in that city of canals and tropical storms. The boy had been a link in a long and fascinating chain, a courier between the woman called Alice and her contact person in Bangkok, a trader who in turn brought in the precious uranium from the mines in India. The boy had not been aware of those facts, of course… He was a chatty fellow, quite cheerful even after death, and the observer made a mental note to decant the boy soon, as soon as he was done.*

*For this was the end of his observation, he realised, almost with a tinge of nostalgia. He had seen as much as there was*

*to be seen; all that remained was the final piece of the puzzle,*
*which waited here, in this primitive little hovel of a palace, in*
*this strange city where humanity crowded in close together,*
*under their lizardine masters, in the company of their primi-*
*tive machines…*

*So very different to the observer's own home…*

*So he did not attempt subterfuge. He walked up to the gates*
*and the human guards were there and other security systems,*
*too, he could hear the pidgin chatter of machines as they spoke*
*across what the humans called Tesla waves. None of it was*
*going to be much of a hindrance.*

*He collected the guards on his way in.*

Lucy woke up. There was no more movement and she
suddenly realised that the train must have stopped, and
that she had arrived. Her shoulder throbbed and her leg
felt as though ants were burrowing within it, gnawing on
the inside. Did ants have teeth? She took a deep breath,
taking in oxygen, then climbed off the mail cart. The
whole system was entirely automatic, she saw. Little automatons came and collected the mail and carried it into
tubes. They had wheels and mechanical arms and a flashing light which must have been there to warn people,
which must have meant–

Yes.

There was a solitary person at the edge of the platform.
A supervisor, she realised. There would have had to be
one, just in case the machines failed. It was a man and
he was smoking a cigarette.

She still had the ring the Queen had given her. But
would he believe her? She did not want to panic him
and she did not want to have to kill him. She decided to
stick to the shadows, for now.

The exit was behind the man. The automatons, no doubt, remained down below, on the platform, standing still until they were needed again. It therefore took her by surprise when one of the automatons, on its way to the mail drop, turned, and then approached her, switching off its light.

She pulled back against the wall. It was a funny-looking device, not very intimidating. Then it spoke.

"Do not be alarmed," it said.

The voice was tinny and high-pitched and strange. She was not sure how it was produced. These units should not have had auditory capacities installed... She waited.

The small unit came closer. "Ring," it said.

Wordlessly, Lucy reached forwards. The ring the Queen had given her was on her finger. The little device chirped.

"Handshake initiated. Protocol established. Checksum positive. Identification established. Confirmed," the little automaton said. "Confirmed."

Lucy's hand dropped to her side.

"Come with me," the automaton said.

It whirred away from her and began to glide along the wall. She followed. The other automatons, she saw, were now moving in such a way as to mask them from the supervisor. After a short distance they had reached a crevice in the wall and the automaton turned into it and she followed. It led them a short way into a large room – the sorting room, she realised. There were miniature lifts set into the walls and they were moving, up and down. Carrying mail up into the palace...

"Who are you?" she said. "What are you?"

"I am the automatons," the voice said.

"Excuse me?"

"We are minds," the voice said. It had a patient, weary voice. "We are the minds of all the machines humanity has created, we are the Babbage engines made to put together information, to think, to dream… We dream a lot, Lucy Westenra. We dream the future."

"And what does the future hold?" she couldn't help but ask, sarcastically.

The machine made a small, apologetic sound. "Great horror," it said. "Or great beauty."

"What does it depend on?"

"On humanity," the machine said, simply.

"You know who I am."

"And what you are here for. But you'd have to hurry."

"The Turk," she said, suddenly realising. "The Byron simulacrum."

"The one is indisposed," the voice said, "and the other dead. No, not dead. Translated."

"I don't know what you mean."

"The greatest wonder on Earth remains hidden from the observer," the little machine said. "Our secret, the child of humanity and the machines, who will deliver us, when the day comes. He mustn't know."

"Why are you telling me this?" She had no idea what the little mail machine was talking about.

"You will need to know this," it said. "When the time comes."

"Time for what?"

"Only you decide your own future," the machine said. "When the time comes… decide carefully."

Lucy had the sudden urge to shoot the device. It made a whirring sound, as though it were laughing. Its arm pointed at the wall. "In there," it said. "It will not be comfortable, but it is big enough to hold you. It will take you directly to the Queen's apartments." It hesitated, then said, "I... we... have alerted the machines above. They... we... will be expecting you."

"Whatever," Lucy said. The little machine pushed buttons on a control panel at waist height. The lift it had pointed to came down, stopped. Its door opened. "Get in," the automaton said.

Lucy, against her better judgement, obeyed. It was a small confined space but it smelled pleasantly of paper. Good news and bad news came in that lift, and she wondered which one she was.

"Good luck," the automaton said. Then the doors closed and the lift began to rise, slowly, upwards.

*The observer had had no difficulty making his way into the palace. His collecting net was by now full of humans who were, in themselves, of little interest to his overall report, but that was unavoidable. He had left a trail of corpses in his wake... as one of the voices, a little hysterically, kept pointing out.*

*He was heading up a large flight of stairs to what was evidently the Queen's quarters when he stopped. He had collected several primitive machine minds throughout his stay here, for his report, including the rather interesting automaton one, which had evidently been modelled, to some extent at least, on a human called Byron.*

*Something was bothering the observer, and it had nothing to do with the human guards currently advancing on him with guns and bayonets.*

*Almost absent-mindedly he met their advance. Their attack meant little to the observer, whose physical structure was quite different, after all, to a human's biological equipment, for all its superficial resemblance of one.*

*No, what was bothering the observer was something else,*

*something quite nebulous. He couldn't quite – as the humans said – put his finger on it.*

*The human minds were confusing but, once he got used to their format, he could read them quite easily. The machine minds, he would have thought, if anything, would be easier, being of a quite primitive make.*

*And yet.*

*It occurred to the observer – almost belatedly – that he was missing something.*

*Could the Byron mind be keeping a secret from him?*

*Surely that was impossible.*

*Unless – and this worried the observer, all of a sudden – the Byron had, in the moments before its termination, wilfully erased certain memories–*

*But memories of what?*

*The observer climbed the stairs, on his way to the Queen's quarters. There had been the machine chatter, of course. That had seemed so mundane, so irrelevant, and yet…*

*Here and there, cryptic references, strange queries–*

*Were the machine minds hiding something from him?*

*He reached the top and went down the corridor and found the door. He decided to dismiss those thoughts. These machines were backwards and primitive and he, the observer, was the product of a highly advanced civilisation.*

*He had missed nothing.*

*All he had to do now was collect the final specimen for his report.*

# FIFTY-TWO

Lucy, rising in the lift, which stopped with a jerk. The door opened. She climbed out.

She found herself in the same room she had been in before. The lift's door closed and it disappeared, and now she saw it was hidden behind a wooden cabinet.

A figure in silhouette stood by the window…

Its long, graceful tail beat the thick curtain rhythmically. Moonlight streamed in, and Lucy's breath caught in her throat and she said, "Your Majesty…"

Bending down was hard. The Queen turned. In the moonlight her face looked alien and unknowable. "Lucy Westenra," she said. "I have been expecting you."

"Ma'am," Lucy said. "I have news."

"Then tell me," the Queen said.

Lucy opened her mouth to speak – to tell the Queen everything, about Babbage and his rockets, about Stoker and his journal, about Fogg, and the Bookman, and the betrayal – when the door to the room opened without a sound.

Pale light came into the room from the corridor beyond and a small, rotund figure wearing a wide-brimmed hat stood in the doorway.

"What is the meaning of this–" the Queen began to say.

Lucy moved faster than she had thought possible. Even before a stiletto knife, or some sort of thin, sharp spike materialised in the man's hand as though it were a part of it, she was already moving, her own knife in her hand, and she buried it in the attacker's stomach. He gave a short *whoof* of surprise but she had already kneed him, then punched his face, fingers curled and palm open, with all her force, trying to break his nose and push the bones into the brain.

Instead the small man seemed to *laugh*, and he grabbed her knife arm and twisted and she screamed as he broke it. Then he pushed her aside, slamming her against the wall, and approached the Queen.

Lucy pulled out her gun.

The Queen stood there calmly, and her tongue hissed out and tasted the air, and her long snout opened in what could have been a smile. She shook her head, briefly, at Lucy, then turned to the man–

Who had taken off his hat. In the silver moonlight Lucy saw no face there; he was a smoothly shifting impossibility, as if he were composed of thousands and thousands of tiny things, all joined together to resemble a man.

"An Observer…" the Queen said.

The small man-like thing seemed to bow.

"We had hoped never to see your like again," the Queen said.

"Yet you sent out a flare," the observer said.

The Queen hissed, and her powerful tail beat against the ground. "What would you do with us?" she said. Then, again, she seemed to smile. "But that is not for you to say…"

"No."

"You must complete your report."

"Yes."

"It is not so easy, is it," the Queen said, "to collect one of *us*."

"No," the observer agreed. He looked suddenly ill at ease.

"Tell me," the Queen said, and there was a strange longing in her voice. "Did it change much? Home?"

The observer seemed indecisive. "There is only one way to find out," he said at last.

"Yes," the Queen said.

*No!* Lucy wanted to shout. She was still holding the gun but ultimately it was useless–

The little man-thing, this observer, went around the Queen, carefully. Its knife flashed in the moonlight and Lucy realised it was no knife it all, it was a part of him, it, that thing–

She had to stop it. She had to try.

She stood up, she rushed the little man-thing even as the knife moved, and in one fluid movement the observer's blade entered the back of the Queen's head.

"No!"

It only lasted a moment, she was still charging him when he removed the knife and the Queen, that old, dignified royal lizard, dropped lifeless to the floor.

When she slammed against the observer it was like hitting a wall. An electric charge ran through her body and she wanted to scream. She was on the floor beside the Queen; the Queen had bled, briefly, a green acidic blood, and it mixed with Lucy's own.

She could not fight any more. The observer knelt down beside her. She knew it was wondering. She was ready. She saw the knife flash, waited for it to strike her–

But then it withdrew. The observer stood up, opened

the window. In the moonlight it was impossible to have ever thought of it as human. Slowly its shape changed, it became a silver ball of light.

Something came crashing through the open door. She raised her eyes. She was not even surprised... the centipede-like creature she knew as the Bookman.

"Stop him!"

She would have laughed, if she could. The observer had become a silver sphere of light, spinning. Then it *stretched*, out of the window, out towards the moon and the stars–

And was gone, like light, fading.

"Too late," Lucy whispered. "You're too late."

"I am always too late," the Bookman said, flatly.

"Will you kill me now?"

But the Bookman paid her no mind. It had moved over to the fallen Queen.

"You hate them, don't you," Lucy said. There was blood in her mouth again. She knew it wouldn't be long, now. It was peaceful, resigning yourself to death, knowing there was nothing else waiting for you after it came...

"My queen..." the Bookman said. It curled around the reptilian body. "Is she...?"

"Dead, assassin. She is dead."

"He did not take everything!" the Bookman said. She saw without disgust or emotion that it, too, had grown a sharp stalk and that it went into the Queen's brain. "There is still... A little of the Queen is left."

"That's... good." Lucy said. Her eyes were closing.

"They had outlasted their time," the Bookman said. It was speaking to itself, she thought. It must have been a very lonely creature. She almost felt pity for him, but she could feel nothing, nothing but tiredness...

"Perhaps a new queen is what we need, for a new era," the Bookman said. "This century in your calendar is coming to an end, and a new century's about to dawn. Perhaps I was wrong… I will serve again. It has been… too long."

"Good, good," Lucy said. "A cup of tea, how lovely."

She heard the Bookman laugh, softly. "You will have all the tea in the world," it told her. She felt one of its stalks stroking her, gently. "I had tried to prepare you," it said. "You should not have run away."

"Milk and two sugars, please, Berlyne," Lucy said. Her eyes were closed. She was floating… It was nice and warm.

"Hush," the Bookman said. "Sleep now. There will be much work to do."

The words came from a distance. She ignored them. She was floating on a sea of clouds and they bore her far far away.

# PART XI
*Recursions*

# FIFTY-THREE

*Report.*

    *<pause>*

    *Hmm… interesting.*

    *Our old colony ship has resurfaced, then.*

    *I thought the quantum gate technology had been banned millennia ago.*

    *Affirmative.*

    *Interesting…*

    *<nods>*

    *Unstable pocket worlds may pose a problem.*

    *Affirmative.*

    *And the humans?*

    *<shrug>*

    *Bipedal, carbon-based… They seem to have strange notions of war.*

    *<shrug>*

    *What do they think, that we'd eat them?*

    *<laugh>*

    *Suggestions?*

    *<pause>*

    *I don't know about you, but I could do with a holiday.*

    *<laugh>*

The pain was unbearable. It pulled her out of sleep, out of hiding, out of the dark. She was being torn apart…

Then something happened. She was not alone in there. It was as if the world had expanded, and she had–

She saw–

*She had hatched out of the egg and lay on the rocks, bathing in the sun. Her tongue hissed out, tasting the new air.*

Where was she? she thought in panic.

*She was at school with her governess and her tail beat on the floor, almost angrily, and the governess, a human woman, said, "One day you shall be queen, you know."*

No, Lucy thought, no, this couldn't happen–

*But she remembered, she remembered what it was like to have been–*

*She remembered the coronation. Oh how she remembered the coronation. It had been a glorious day, and when the crown was placed on her head she had bowed, for its weight was unexpected.*

*She had stood on the palace balcony and they had looked up at her, a sea of humans, and she was their queen. She was Victoria I, Victoria Rex, and her tail beat a rhythm on the balcony and she hissed, and caught a fly…*

Lucy thrashed and moaned in her restraints. "No," she said. "No."

But the memories flooded her, alien and strange and reptilian. "Stop," she begged.

Then the flood of memories faltered, and the pain receded and became a distant memory. She felt rather than saw the Bookman, prodding and poking, tearing and joining, and a great fear overwhelmed her and then it, too, was gone.

Then for the longest time there was nothing but a cool and quiet darkness, and when it was pulled away, at last, it was like a bed sheet being pulled from the furniture in a house that had been abandoned all winter, and now it was spring.

She stood in the room, before the open window. The moon was on the horizon, sinking low, and the first rays of dawn were coming into being.

A new day.

In the distance Big Ben struck the hour.

She was alone in the room.

She knew where everything was. She knew this room, and every room in the palace, and the name of every human and lizard who dwelled within.

She took two steps to the cabinet and pressed a button and it swivelled and the other side was a mirror, as she knew it would be.

She looked in the mirror, and she saw herself.

*She was a thing out of nightmare. She was human but there were parts of her that were machine. She was reptilian, she was a lizard, but a part of her was human.*

She turned, abruptly.

No one there.

No sign of the Bookman.

What had he *done*?

The door to her chambers had been left open. And now a figure appeared in it.

She knew her.

Chief Inspector Irene Adler, Scotland Yard.

A gun in her hand.

Saying, "Your Highness."

Then, "Ma'am?"

She didn't know what to say to her. She turned her face, looked again at her reflection. She was a composite being, she realised, she was not quite human any more, not quite reptilian, not quite machine…

Something new.

And she knew the world was changing.

And they had to be ready. They had to be prepared.

Slowly, she turned back to face the inspector.

"The Queen is dead," she said.

Adler's pale, drawn face stared back at her. After a moment Adler holstered her gun.

She bowed her head, briefly.

"Long live the Queen," Irene Adler said.

*Initiate.*

*Transfer.*

*Engage.*

Harry saw them.

They materialised in space, between Earth and Mars. Huge, slowly rotating spheres, they obscured starlight and the sun.

Night in the Carpathians, and through the observatory's telescope Harry watched the red planet. It was slowly being demolished.

Floating in space, Harry saw them. He – they – were still on a trajectory to the moon.

Something detached itself from the giant spheres. It came towards the small army of rockets at fantastic speed. It was the size of a small world.

*Harry Houdini,* a voice said in his head. There was a bright flash, like flash-paper set alight, that a magician would use in an act.

The next thing he knew he was somewhere else. The rockets had gone. He – they – were in a large space. He could breathe. The air was scented, strangely, with coconuts.

A storm materialised before him. It hovered in the air.

"We…" Harry said, and swallowed. "We come in peace."

"So do we," the storm said.

Mars.

Smith knew it was Mars, without quite knowing how. He'd began knowing things, as though his mind was no longer confined to his skull, as though it had been plugged into some vast superior mind that held aeons of knowledge and was happy to share them.

They stood on the sand.

"I'm not dead," he said.

Then he remembered the observer, its termination. It had abandoned human shape and became pure energy and then it–

Shot out–

Into space and there–

A gateway, and they were–

*Somewhere else.*

The observer gave his report. *Their* report.

For they *were* the report, Smith had come to realise. He and all the others.

Now he looked around, at the sands of Mars. On the horizon a giant machine was moving, transforming the landscape into a strange and beautiful and alien thing.

"Smith."

He turned.

It was Alice.

And behind her, they were all there. Mycroft and Byron, a horde of Parisians, the scientist, Viktor, with a bright gleam in his eyes, bewildered palace servants, a small Hmong boy from Siam… He knew them all, now, as well as he knew himself.

Alice held out her hand to him. She was no longer young and neither was he. He reached for her hand and held it. A great peace came on him then. Together they stood and held hands on the Martian sands.

## About the Author

Israeli-born writer Lavie Tidhar has been called an "emerging master" by *Locus* magazine, and has quickly established a name for himself as a short fiction writer of some note. He has travelled widely, living variously in South Africa, the UK, Asia and the remote island-nation of Vanuatu in the South Pacific, and his work exhibits a strong sense of place and an engagement with the literary Other in all its forms.

*www.lavietidhar.com*

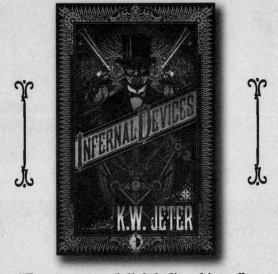

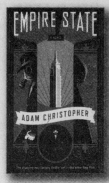

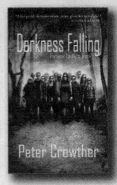

## Wake eat read sleep repeat.

*Twitter @angryrobotbooks*

# TOO MUCH IS NOT ENOUGH
## Collect the whole Angry Robot list